# My MacArthur

## A Novel

## Cindy Fazzi

My MacArthur: A Novel
Published by Sand Hill Review Press, LLC

www.sandhillreviewpress.com,
1 Baldwin Ave, #304, San Mateo, CA 94401

ISBN: 978-1-937818-96-8 paperback
ISBN: 978-1-937818-97-5 case laminate
ISBN: 978-1-937818-98-2 ebook
Library of Congress Control Number: 2018951952


Cover art direction by Tory Hartmann
Graphics by Backspace Ink
Photo of Isabel Cooper by Jose Reyes, 1940

*My MacArthur* is a work of fiction. All incidents and dialogue, and all characters with the exception of some well-known historical figures, are products of the author's imagination and are not to be construed as real. Where real-life historical figures appear, the situations, incidents, and dialogues concerning those persons are entirely fictional and are not intended to depict actual events or to change the entirely fictional nature of the work. In all other respects, any resemblance to actual persons, living or dead, events, or locales is entirely coincidental.

To my husband, Vincent Fazzi,
and our daughter, Nina Fazzi.
I live for both of you.

# My MacArthur

A Novel

Cindy Fazzi

# Part One: Philippines

# 1.

# April 1930

DOUGLAS MACARTHUR. Her pulse quickened as she read the name. His neat handwriting exuded confidence, but just the same, his note struck her as an anomaly, a mistake. The white man who acted as his messenger stood next to her at the bar.

Men of all ages filled the Olympic Boxing Club, waiting for the fight to begin. Filipinos, Americans, and Europeans caroused and mingled freely here, unlike the Elks or the Army and Navy Club, which banned Filipinos.

The foreigners sat at the tables, drank Cerveza San Miguel, and smoked cigars. The Filipinos stood at the cheap section of the club, jostled and bet among themselves.

"I'm Captain Ed Marsh, by the way." The messenger extended his hand.

An American officer in civilian clothes. It was Saturday night, after all.

"A pleasure to meet you, sir." She shook his hand, but withheld her name.

Isabel Rosario Cooper came to the club in search of her brother, or rather his car. She needed Ben to drive her to the Manila Carnival.

Women didn't come here because they didn't watch boxing, so when she stepped inside the club, she'd grabbed everyone's attention without trying. The men had erupted in whistles and cheers. The crowd had parted as she crossed the room. Just the way she liked it. She was born to part crowds—to turn heads. For an aspiring actress, every place was a stage.

Who knew MacArthur sat amid the boisterous horde? She read the note again. *I can't help but notice your gracious presence. I would love it if you can favor me with your company. Please join me for dinner at The Grand.*

This time, the words made sense. Not a blunder on his part or a misinterpretation on hers. The message hit her like a jackpot—bigger than the Carnival Queen title that her best friend, Nenita, aimed for. He was the most important man in the Philippine Islands. He could open doors for her and her family.

She stopped herself from blurting out a yes! She couldn't afford to give herself away. Nothing compelled a man to pursue a woman more than her lack of interest.

"Who's Douglas MacArthur?" She stood with the note in one hand and her silk purse in the other hand. Chin up and chest out, despite the sweat underneath her lace blouse. Her skirt squeezed her waist and constricted her breathing, but she'd worn it because it displayed her figure. The stifling humidity now made her regret her choice. Even the garter belt and stockings itched in such heat.

"You've never heard of Douglas MacArthur?" His eyes widened.

She shook her head. A saxophone wailed, distracting them both. They turned toward the elevated boxing ring—empty. Below it, a band warmed up.

Captain Marsh offered her a pack of Lucky Strike. "Care for a cigarette?"

"Why, thank you." She tucked her purse under her armpit and took one stick, which he lit with a lighter. They stood side by side, watching the band.

"Do you see the gentleman in the middle?" He pointed at a table not far from the band. "White suit. Gray-striped tie. Do you see him?"

"Yes."

"*That* is Douglas MacArthur."

The man stared at her while smoking a long-stemmed pipe, the bowl shaped like a corncob. He didn't smile. The band played a jazz-style rendition of a Filipino folk song. The audience, packed ten deep, hooted and screamed for the fight to begin, but MacArthur didn't even blink.

She glanced at his note again before inserting it in her purse. "This is nice. But I don't know him."

"It's unbelievable. You really don't know him?"

She shook her head and shifted her weight to one hip.

"He's the Big Cheese!"

She arched her eyebrow.

"Major General MacArthur is the most powerful American not just in the Philippines, but in Asia."

She took a drag on her cigarette. "I know what big cheese means, thank you."

MacArthur stood out in his expensive suit, slicked-back hair, and intimidating pipe, but he was as old as her father, if not older. His title was commander of the U.S. Army's Philippine Division, though everyone treated him like a king.

Rumor was, he had his eyes on the White House. He flaunted his kinglike authority using the Philippines as his stage, like William Howard Taft had done. His photographs graced the newspapers almost every day, stealing the spotlight from the American governor-general. He snubbed the American bureaucrats and saved his charm for the old money in Manila.

MacArthur, like his compatriots, didn't seem to mind the local fools around him. The Americans seemed content just to drink booze, something they couldn't do without getting in trouble back in their country because of Prohibition.

In this melting pot of drunken indulgences, the Filipinos behaved the worst. A man had propositioned her and several others had called her "sexy" and "beauty." Not a compliment, but a catcall. She'd cursed them under her breath, but she couldn't blame them. For once they felt entitled like the Americans, happy to be admitted to the Olympic at all. Here they could pretend to be equal to the white man and display their drunken braggadocio.

The music ended. The boxing match would start soon. She better find her brother or she might miss the coronation of the Carnival

Queen. She could have taken the streetcar, but she wanted to ride in the Chevrolet Tourer that her brother drove, one of the few in Manila. Ben had finagled to use the car this weekend, courtesy of their father's newest business venture, an outfit that imported American cars. He'd predicted that Papa's latest gamble wouldn't survive unless a rich American or European backed him. She and her brother wanted to use the car while they could.

She swept the club with a glance. No Ben.

"Are you looking for someone?" asked Captain Marsh.

"My brother. I thought he would be here." It was just as well. Ben would have chastised her for this brazen foray into his territory. He refused to accept she belonged in a man's domain. What was acting but acting *for* men? "You're not an actress. You're a child," he'd said. It had made her laugh, which irritated him. He was three years older than Isabel, short on prospects but long on impudence.

At last, Captain Marsh smoked. He thrust his chin at her cigarette. "You like it?"

"It's all right. It helps me keep my figure."

"You're worried about your figure?"

"Every girl worries about her figure."

"Not you." He appraised her from head to toe. "You've got nothing to worry about, except the trail of devastated men you leave behind."

He was right. She wasn't worried about her body, as much as the trail of men who had left *her* devastated—the men who owned theaters, presided over movie studios, and directed vaudeville shows and motion pictures.

In countless auditions and meetings, those men had crushed her spirit with a shake of their heads. How easy for them to dismiss her when dozens of pretty young things lined outside their doors.

*"Too short." "Too white." "Not white enough." "Not dark enough."* Their decisions had nothing to do with her ability to act or sing or dance. Men judged her for her looks alone. She ought to ignore their shallow criticisms, but instead, each objection assaulted her. Their rejections kept her awake at night, bled her dry of hope, left her dead inside for days and weeks at a time.

And when she recovered, it would be just in time for another audition. *"Sorry, but your breasts aren't big enough.""Your dimples are pretty, but they could be too distracting in a close-up shot." "Your facial mole is even more distracting than your dimples.*" And another round of rejections would begin.

Her heart pinched. Time could never heal the pain as much as an acceptance and a contract. So, what did this American know about her worries?

"Captain Marsh, I have to go." She tossed her cigarette butt in the trash can and inspected her purse to make sure she had enough coins for the streetcar. "I want to catch the coronation of the new Carnival Queen."

"*You* should be the Carnival Queen, if you ask me." He winked.

Wrong. She could never win the competition. Sure, she was the right age and the right size and shape. But contestants in this beauty pageant must have a "good reputation," which meant no previous experience in the theater or night clubs or moving pictures, all of which were fertile ground for immorality and bad reputation. She couldn't explain this to the American.

He brought the cigarette to his lips and sucked smoke with evident pleasure. "We're rooting for Gloria Luna."

"Who is 'we'?"

"Me and everyone at that table." He waved at a group of white men behind MacArthur, all of them wearing Army khakis.

"You're rooting for her sponsor, *Manila Times*. It's pro-American."

"I thought all newspapers in the Philippines are pro-American."

She gave him a closemouthed smile. "Do you speak Tagalog?"

He made a face.

"Ask your buddies if they know what *sipsip* means. That's what being pro-American means to Filipinos."

"Sip. Sip."

"Say it faster. As one word."

"Why don't you tell me what it means?"

*Sipsip* meant someone who kowtowed so low he might as well have been a doormat. No American wanted to hear *that*. "I have to go."

"I don't even know your name."

"Isabel Rosario Cooper."

"Cooper?"

"My father is American. My mother is Filipina."

"That explains your perfect English. Isabel—what a lovely name."

It wasn't her only name. She reserved "Isabel" for the authority type, like the tyrannical nuns at Colegio de Santa Maria Dolorosa, or nosy American officers for that matter. Family and friends called her "Belle." In the entertainment world, she was known as "Dimples" for the cursed dimples on both of her cheeks that had cost her movie roles.

"I think you're swell," he said.

Compliments from strange men were as common as a sneeze. They wouldn't bring her a job at a club or a movie role. She turned on her heel.

"Wait!"

She stopped.

"What about the Commander's invitation? What should I tell him?"

She glanced at MacArthur again. He continued to stare with a cool expression, pretending to be uninterested. The man was an actor. Perhaps they were not too different.

Her heart thrummed and her thoughts raced as she reconsidered. Part of her wanted to accept his invitation. She would look him in the eye and discover what he was made of.

She bit her lower lip when the final answer hit her. No favors for the *Big Cheese* tonight. She would take pleasure in knowing that she, too, had the power to rebuff people. Not just any man but Douglas MacArthur. *My MacArthur*. Whether he realized it or not, a man whose desire drove him to write it down and risk her rejection was a man she owned.

She walked away, the heat of MacArthur's stare burning her back. It reassured her as much as acting on stage, under the spotlight. She was MacArthur's Carnival Queen; he was her captive audience.

"Before you go—" The American officer had caught up with her. "—at least tell me one thing."

"What is it?"

"How old are you? The Commander wants to know."

"Not old enough for him."

He chortled and shook his head. "Come on now."

They reached the door. The burly men blocking it swung around and whistled. "Hey, doll!" said one of them. "Don't leave," said another. "You're going to miss a great fight."

She ignored them and faced the American. "I'm sixteen."

His jaw slackened, his grin vanished.

It was her turn to chuckle. Someone opened the door for her, while the others moved to the side. She clutched her purse tight and sashayed outside, feeling tall in her five-inch pumps.

# 2.

THE MANILA CARNIVAL'S entrance glowed in the distance—a series of arches, domes, and parapets blazing with electric lights. Revelers roamed the grounds, dashing from ride to ride, from one show to another. At a glance, dancers and acrobats waiting in the wings appeared as clusters of colors, like bundles of cloths in the marketplace, their costumes a riotous mix of purple, red, gold, and green. The exposition booths overflowed with produce that could have fed the entire city, an abundance of mangoes, jackfruits, guavas, and endless crates of overripe squash and purple yams.

Isabel was running late for the coronation. She struggled with her high heels, elbowing her way through the crowd of American women. They swarmed the City of Baguio Booth and admired a wooden carving of a Philippine eagle in the act of devouring a monkey.

How bizarre. But Americans loved anything from Baguio, the Asian Adirondacks, the tropical Berkshires. As Isabel's father liked to say, "Where else can you find an American resort town outside of America? Only in the Philippines."

Most Americans in Manila summered in Baguio because of its cool mountain climate, but Isabel was only half-American and her Papa had less than half the income of most Americans in Manila. Oh, how she resented all the Baguio-loving American women who blocked her way. "Excuse me, please," she yelled.

They were military wives, their shapeless gingham dresses giving them away. No rouge or lipstick or jewelry. Wives of American men who owned banks and insurance companies wore cloche hats, silk georgette dresses, and pearl necklaces. They plucked their eyebrows and wore crimson lipstick. In Manila, one could judge a book by its cover. When, at last, she broke through the knot of milling women, she ran as much as her high heels would allow.

As soon as she stepped inside the packed auditorium, the man on the stage proclaimed into the microphone: "Ladies and gentlemen, let's welcome the 1930 Carnival Queen!"

She pressed against the standing-room-only crowd to get a better view, gripping her little silk purse close to her chest. Music from the live orchestra burst. A teary Gloria Luna glided on stage.

Isabel sighed. Poor Nenita. Her *amiga* would be crushed. Of course, the Americans' favorite had won. The competition was part of the annual cultural rigmarole created by the colonial government to promote goodwill. Two weeks of festivities, firework shows, and entertainment. Newspapers and magazines sponsored the contestants and funded the Carnival to show the world how successful the Filipinos were under the Americans. And the Carnival Queen served as the beautiful mascot of an American-governed Philippines.

An ecstatic cheer for Gloria went up. Isabel shifted her weight on her tottering heels, the blisters on her feet raw. The beginnings of envy stirred inside her. She eyed Gloria's tiara with a longing she hadn't known before. *If only I could be Carnival Queen.* She'd shared Nenita's hopes, after all.

She glanced down at her heels, wishing she could take them off and leave them behind. She would peel off the stockings as well. She could conceivably go shoeless, but she couldn't bear to stand so flat, so short. If blisters could kill, then she would rather die than be ordinary, a nobody.

Gloria walked across the stage and waved like a queen. Sure, she was pretty. But, more than her beauty, the crown on her head and the sash she wore with *Carnival Queen* written on it set her apart.

Isabel smoothed down her skirt and left.

Backstage, she found Nenita weeping. She embraced her. "It's not the end of the world." She led her friend to a corner, amid discarded stage curtains and cloth backdrops stuck together in a sorry heap. They sat on wooden crates containing old lighting equipment.

*"Kung hindi ukol, hindi bubukol,"* said Nenita. If it's not meant to be, it will never happen. They spoke Tagalog. "I guess I'm not destined

to be Carnival Queen." She cast her gaze down on her ankle-length Filipino costume bedecked with silver and gold sequins, glimmering even in the shadowy backstage.

Isabel offered her handkerchief.

Nenita wiped her tears. "I lost because I refused to wear a bathing suit." She blew her nose before she continued. "You should have seen Gloria Luna at the pictorial. She had no qualms displaying her body in front of all those men. I dare say she enjoyed it!"

Isabel bit her tongue. There was nothing wrong with wearing a bathing suit in public, especially for someone competing in a beauty pageant. She had told Nenita this after one of the contest's judges invited Nenita to his home for a photo session. *Please wear a bathing suit*, the invitation had said. It had scandalized Nenita. And so, she was the only contestant who had declined. The other ladies had paraded before an all-male panel of judges and a crew of photographers. The event was not an official part of the pageant, but everyone knew the judges put a lot of stock in it. Isabel squeezed her friend's hand. "You're far more beautiful than Gloria Luna. Who cares about a beauty title?"

Nenita's face crumpled as her tears flowed again.

So, the title meant the world to her. "I'm sorry," Isabel crooned, rubbing the tight muscles in Nenita's back.

"The Carnival Queen is going to compete in an international beauty pageant in Texas," she sobbed. "That's where the idea of wearing bathing suits came from. Americans think nothing of their ladies practically naked in public. It's scandalous!"

"You're too good for this competition. You don't need to go to Texas and let Americans judge your beauty."

Nenita sniffled. "You're being so kind to me."

Isabel meant it. Although it pinched her pride, she acknowledged openly that her friend was more attractive than her. While she had the advantage of light skin, dimples on both cheeks, and a natural beauty mark on her left cheek, Nenita was taller.

Nenita didn't smoke because she didn't need to lose weight. Her waist-long hair and ankle-length dresses were old-fashioned, but she wore them like a virtue. She embodied the quintessential Filipina beauty—dainty in looks, feminine in manners, and yes, a virgin. Nenita was also younger than her, bound to stay pretty longer, but she let her friend believe they were the same age. Better to lie than to admit she'd been held back in school.

The envy she'd felt earlier now bore down on her. Girls like Gloria and Nenita were everything she wanted to be, but never could be.

"Speaking of Americans—" She opened the clasp of her purse. "I stopped by the Olympic to look for Ben. An American officer gave me this." Smiling a little, she pulled the note from the purse and showed it to Nenita. Although she would never qualify for Carnival Queen, she'd snagged the attention of an important man.

"Who's Douglas MacArthur?"

Isabel pursed her lips. How could she not know him? "He's the commander of the Philippine Division. His picture is always plastered on the newspapers."

"I don't care what he commands. This note is uncouth."

Isabel nodded. True, but it stung.

"A gentleman must court a lady properly. Not like this." Nenita crumpled the note and tossed it in the heap of discarded props.

Isabel flinched at the meanness of the gesture. Her heart ached.

Nenita rose, patting the sheen on her forehead with the handkerchief. "We should go. It's too hot in here. My family is waiting in the lobby. I shooed them away. I couldn't bear their pity."

"Are they very disappointed?"

"I'm sure my mother is. She thinks being the Carnival Queen is the surest way to the perfect gentleman's heart."

Isabel stood up as well. "You mean, the surest way to Fabian Elizalde's heart?"

Nenita shrugged. Fabian belonged to an illustrious family of Spanish descent that owned gold mines, timber companies, and factories. Nenita's mother, a dear friend of Isabel's mama, had gone to great lengths to get Nenita introduced to Fabian during a soiree, with the ultimate goal of marrying her daughter into the Elizalde family.

The girls went out the back door.

In the auditorium's lobby, the Lopezes waited, their smiles wan. Isabel greeted Nenita's mother with a light kiss on the cheek.

"*Hija,* I prefer old-fashioned courtesy." Mrs. Lopez presented her right hand. Isabel bowed and let her forehead touch the older woman's hand. It was called *mano*, the traditional way of greeting an elder.

Nenita's mother fastened her gaze on Isabel and her skirt, which fell just below her knees. "You look lovely. But don't let that hemline rise any higher. It's unbecoming, dear. And how's your mother? I haven't had a chance to see her in weeks."

"She's fine, *Tita.*" Isabel called her "aunt" because she was like one to her.

"Are you performing tomorrow?"

"Yes, indeed, at five o'clock."

"I hope it doesn't involve wearing clothes that are too tight or too short. Look at Nenita. She didn't succumb to pressure and didn't compromise her values." Her voice cracked. Her eyes were moist. "We're very proud of how you conducted yourself in this competition."

"Mama, please." Nenita touched her mother's shoulder.

Isabel forced a smile. It was one thing for Mrs. Lopez to praise her daughter and quite another to remind Isabel of Nenita's superiority. She let the comment pass, knowing that Mrs. Lopez was heartbroken over her daughter's loss. Thank goodness, Nenita's father intervened, inviting Isabel to join them for dinner at a restaurant on Avenida Rizal.

She declined. It was late and her parents expected her at home.

The Lopez boys clamored for food, prompting the family to move on. Nenita kissed Isabel's cheek. "Thank you for being such a good friend." She glanced at the handkerchief in her hand. "Oh, I've ruined this. I owe you a hanky. I'll embroider one for you."

Isabel reached out for her friend's hand.

"What is it?" whispered Nenita. "Is there something you want to tell me?"

"I already told you."

A glint of realization in Nenita's eyes. "Is it the American? Is it Douglas MacArthur?"

Isabel shrugged.

"If his intentions are honorable, then he must conduct himself like a gentleman."

"You're right."

"Surely you don't want another Eddie Palma in your life? You deserve someone better. If Douglas MacArthur is any better, then let him prove himself."

"I know." She let out a small sigh. Her friend's disapproval filled her with sadness.

"Isabel, you must ignore him."

"All right." And yet, her thought had solidified—it would be unwise to dismiss MacArthur's interest in her. Nenita, despite her good looks and distinguished family name, had lost the beauty pageant. Isabel possessed less than her friend's qualities and prospects. She couldn't afford to squander her opportunity and lose MacArthur.

A moment passed, the two girls still holding each other's hand, before they said goodbye.

# 3.

ANOTHER DAY, another visit to the same auditorium where Nenita had lost the Carnival Queen title. This time, Isabel herself was on stage for a dance rehearsal. As soon as it ended, she ran backstage and out the back door to smoke.

A couple of girls, bit players in a comedic skit, were already puffing away. She acknowledged them with a nod, then found a spot amid chairs and tables waiting to be carried inside. She smoked Ben's brand, Chesterfield. He bought only American cigarettes, and she smoked only when it was free, so Ben's brand was her brand. Her brother, plus Mama, Papa, and Nenita would watch her dance tonight. They'd all promised to come since it was her first Carnival performance.

She inhaled, savoring the tingling throughout her body, then exhaled the smoke through her mouth. Chesterfield was smoother than any Filipino brand. Thank goodness, her family could still afford the goods at Ike Beck's American Bazaar—little luxuries like Ivory soap, Borden's canned milk, and yes, Chesterfield. Perks the Cooper family and Americans enjoyed; the products at Ike Beck's were too expensive for most Filipinos.

These fringe benefits aside, her family stood in the periphery of the favored class in Manila and always looked from the outside. The Coopers lived in a nice neighborhood on Calle Herran, though it paled in comparison to the mansions where Americans lived. Papa was a white, American citizen, but not the kind his compatriots fully accepted. He was never invited to parties in Malacañang, the American governor-general's residence. He could get a small loan from an American-owned bank to fund his fledgling business, but he didn't have the clout to secure two thousand acres of land to plant rubber. Only the likes of Harvey Firestone enjoyed that kind of privilege. So, for Isabel, being a half-American sometimes meant good fortune and sometimes a misfortune. She might as well enjoy her Chesterfield.

She flicked the ash off her cigarette with a finger and glanced down at her feet. She was still barefoot. The stupid *tinikling* dance didn't give her the benefit of wearing shoes. She was supposed to be a farmer working in a rice paddy. No matter. She puffed on her cigarette.

It relaxed her a little, a poor substitute for a nap, but better than nothing. She couldn't sleep last night. Thoughts of Douglas MacArthur had kept her up. He wasn't the only man who had written her a love note, but he was the first to do so within the first few minutes of seeing her. He flattered her. With just a few scribbled lines, MacArthur had given her the power over him.

But, of course, Nenita had dampened everything. She didn't even know who he was, except he was American. Enough reason to disparage him. Nenita praised Europeans and looked down on Americans. She spoke Spanish and French, but abhorred English. She loved Madrid, Barcelona, and Paris. Spanish zarzuelas and French operas were superior. Hollywood motion pictures were lowbrow.

Nenita claimed she loved Isabel like a sister. Was it because she saw her half-American friend as a charitable cause? From the moment they'd met in a schoolroom, they'd been drawn to each other. The Coopers didn't speak Spanish at home and Isabel struggled with the language. She'd already been held back at another school because of it, something she concealed. But, on that first day in school, her new friend had guided her through the *eñe* and the *elle* and the *erre*. At the end of the day, Nenita had declared they were *hermanas para siempre*. Sisters forever.

*Dios mio*, why did Nenita have to mention Eddie Palma? For someone who had never been kissed, she was uncannily perceptive about men. One look at Eddie and she'd said, "He's nothing but an adventurer. He'll forget your name as soon as he finds another adventure."

No doubt MacArthur was superior to Eddie Palma, but Nenita had already lumped the two together. What if she was right?

She tossed what remained of her cigarette and ran back inside.

In the dressing room, she sat in front of a makeup table to put on rouge. The heat from the mirror's light bulbs increased the humidity. The girls who occupied the other tables chattered nonstop. Like Isabel, they would perform that afternoon, beginning at five o'clock. They were all "fillers"—dancers and singers who marked time before the real attraction for the night began, a concert by Katy de la Cruz, the biggest vaudeville star in the Philippines.

Isabel worshipped Katy. She saved the little money she earned to watch Katy's shows. She'd auditioned to be a chorus girl in Katy's concert, but the director preferred tall girls with long legs.

She sighed at the memory of how she'd crumbled into sobs in front of everybody. Every rejection stung, but that one hurt the most. It was the closest she'd ever gotten to performing on the same stage as her favorite songstress. The choreographer had recommended Isabel to the crew of the *tinikling* dance, out of pity. God bless her heart! She'd passed that audition. Just her luck to be chosen for the most physically demanding and graceless dance.

She got up and inspected her costume before a full-length mirror. She wore a white *kimona* blouse and an ankle-length wrap skirt in garish red and yellow stripes. How ugly! Well, she had to make the best of this job.

A knock on the door. The stage manager called out her name. She glanced at the wall clock—an hour before show time. So what did he want? She cracked the door open.

"Major General Douglas MacArthur is looking for you," said the man.

*I knew it, I knew it!* She stepped out and shut the door behind her. The shrieks of the other girls who were getting dressed could be heard from the outside. She looked down on her bare feet. *Dios mio*! She went back inside, put on her high heels, and felt taller instantly. She followed the stage manager to the far end of the backstage.

And there he was—taller and more dashing than she remembered. A spark of attraction, like a small electric shock, shot through her body.

He wore a cream suit with a navy blue tie. He took off his fedora hat at the sight of her. His slicked-back hair shone.

The stage manager walked away, the clicking of his shoes receding. She stood alone with MacArthur in the narrow hallway.

"I'm very pleased to make your acquaintance." He held out his hand.

She shook it, but couldn't spit out a word because her heart thumped like crazy. Up close, his eyes were a dazzling blue. She swallowed hard. "How did you find me here, sir?"

"I have my way. I know you're an actress, singer, and dancer. Your nickname is Belle. Your *nom de guerre* is Dimples. You've appeared in silent films and *bodabil*. At times, you sing at Tropical Nights. You're a student at Colegio de Santa Maria Dolorosa."

She smiled, impressed. He knew enough Tagalog to say *bodabil* instead of vaudeville. He'd pronounced her school's name without tripping. How on earth did this man know so much about her?

As if reading her mind, he said, "I'm in the military. Intelligence is part of my business."

"You're wrong about one thing."

"How so?"

"Sir, I'm no longer a student at the Colegio. I don't plan to return when school starts in two months." Mama would kill her when she found out. Isabel had been thinking about quitting school. And, she'd just decided out loud in front of this stranger.

"Please call me Douglas."

"Douglas."

"That's better. Are you sorry to quit school?"

She tossed her hair back, pushed her chest out. "No. I want to perform full-time."

"I'm here to watch you perform."

She curled her lips into a smile. "I thought you're here to invite me again."

His face bloomed. He didn't seem to know what to do with his hat or his hands. Just like those adolescent boys who ogled her on the sidewalk or in church. How amazing to see the same effect on a grown man, the American commander no less. Her heart swelled with newfound self-confidence. *Who's the Big Cheese now?*

He cleared his throat. "Ed and I waited for you last night at the Grand."

"Who?"

"Captain Marsh, my aide."

"Did you really expect me to show up just because your subordinate handed me a note?"

"I'm sorry about that. I should have introduced myself to you directly. But I'm here now. I'd consider it a great favor if you dine with me after the show."

A group of men carrying props arrived. MacArthur moved to let them pass. He seemed even more awkward, his eyes darting toward the entrance, perhaps wary of more interruptions.

She frowned. "Sir, as you can see—"

"Douglas. Please."

"Douglas. As you can see, I'm wearing this awful costume. In less than an hour, you'll see me hopping over bamboo poles like a crazy bird. It's called *tinikling.* Maybe you should wait until then before you invite me. You might just change your mind."

He smiled at last. "I've seen the dance before and I quite enjoyed it. The invitation stands. I'll wait for you after the show."

"Isabel!" a girl called out. "Time to warm up!"

She bid him goodbye, neither accepting nor rejecting his invitation. The look on his face told her he expected a yes. What would happen if she said no? She turned around without looking back.

Twenty minutes after five o'clock, the show commenced. The stage lights burned and the music blared. The auditorium was half-full.

Isabel's troupe hopped and skipped over bamboo poles at an increasing tempo. Her focus intensified as the dance became more menacing. Her goal: To avoid getting caught between the poles. *Dear God, please spare me from public humiliation!* When it was over, she rushed to the dressing room to get out of the cheap costume.

By the time she reached the auditorium's balcony, the place was packed. She had already missed the American musical. She caught the last minute of an Indian folk dance—men and women in colorful garb dancing in a circle.

The attendance surged. She didn't see her family or MacArthur in the crowd. At last, the night's highlight came. Katy de la Cruz sashayed onto the stage in a tight-fitting red gown. She burst into a powerful rendition of a Tagalog love song. The audience went wild. She sang a jazz song and then another, alternately thrilling the horde into frenzy and hypnotizing it into silence. Her final number received a standing ovation. Isabel was on her feet applauding. If only she could be like Katy de la Cruz.

When the show ended, everyone dashed outside to catch the songstress and ask for her autograph. As much as Isabel adored Katy, she didn't follow the crowd. She was a performer herself. She was as good, if not better, than Katy de la Cruz. And younger.

Mama liked to brag that Isabel had danced before she'd learned how to walk; she had sung before she'd learned how to speak. Her grandparents had paid for the intermittent ballet and piano lessons over the years. Truth was, she'd barreled her way into the entertainment world by sheer audacity. Her good looks compensated for her lack of connections. Her unbridled ambition kept her afloat. Whenever her voice proved too weak for a solo number, she would double her effort as a chorus girl. She wasn't good enough to play the piano in a concert hall, but she could charm audiences in a comic skit. She was born a performer. She'd do anything to stay in the spotlight.

Let everyone else have Katy's autograph. She would rather have Katy's pluck, luck, and success. She was no mere fan, but a rightful successor. *One of these days, I'll show everyone.*

In the auditorium's lobby, Isabel's parents were chatting with Nenita. Not far from them, Ben was talking to Eddie Palma. Her blood rose. How dare Eddie show up at her show. *Hijo de puta.*

She met Eddie at a movie set a year ago. He used to be known as Eduardo Palma, but after eighteen months in Los Angeles, he'd become Eddie Palma—exuberant and flamboyant like the Charleston, handsome and elegant like the Cadillac. He claimed he'd worked at Warner Bros. and had seen John Barrymore in the flesh. At the end of their first meeting, he'd told Isabel, "You ain't heard nothin' yet!" Later on, she'd learned he had referred to *The Jazz Singer*, which she hadn't seen.

It hadn't taken long for her to fall in love with Eddie. He'd advised her to use a catchy stage name. He'd christened her Dimples because people referred to her as "the girl with the dimples." The Coopers didn't mind her alias, but Nenita had been horrified. It was vulgar, she'd said.

Isabel approached her parents and Nenita. Everyone hugged and congratulated her. She gave her friend the look, prompting the girl to glance over her shoulder. She rolled her eyes upon seeing Eddie.

Nenita was right when she'd judged Eddie's Hollywood glitter as a sham. The closest he'd ever gotten to Warner Bros. was when he worked as a busboy in a restaurant near the studio. Nenita had also predicted Eddie's abrupt loss of interest in Isabel. He'd found his next adventure, a girl named Lovely. Yes, Eddie had given Lovely her stage name, too.

Isabel's parents praised her performance while she simmered, too hurt to acknowledge Eddie and too proud to walk away. This was her show, her night. She was not in the mood for kindness. Ben and Eddie continued chatting. What on earth could her brother be saying to the bastard?

In a moment of stalemate when neither Isabel nor Eddie made the first move of saying hello, Douglas MacArthur and Captain Marsh appeared.

MacArthur handed Isabel a bouquet of orchids. "I enjoyed your performance. Congratulations!"

She introduced him to everyone. Her father fawned over MacArthur, while her mother kept mum, shy as ever. Nenita maintained a polite façade.

As awkward as MacArthur had been with Isabel backstage, he appeared comfortable in front of Isabel's family and best friend—at ease before an audience. He extended his invitation for dinner not only to Isabel but to everyone in her entourage.

"I would introduce you to my brother, but he's talking to an acquaintance right now." Isabel's voice was loud enough for both Ben and Eddie to hear.

"Where is he?" asked MacArthur.

She walked over to her brother and pulled him by the hand, ignoring Eddie. "Ben, I want you to meet Major General Douglas MacArthur. He's inviting all of us to dine at The Grand."

The two men shook hands.

She sensed Eddie gazing at her. The pain in her heart hovered like a bee sting. Neither his Rudolph Valentino-like charm nor his haughty stare could move her. Not anymore. He loped away.

"Shall we all go to The Grand?" MacArthur said. "This way, please. My chauffeur is waiting."

She beamed at him, letting herself be led to the waiting car.

# 4.

MACARTHUR FREQUENTED the restaurant called The Grand because it was luxurious in a way the Army and Navy Club could never be. The owner, a California entrepreneur, had built it in the style of Spanish missions in his home state, with clay-tile roof, adobe walls, and a delightful courtyard.

Rich American and European businessmen, not military officers, patronized the restaurant. MacArthur was the exception. When he stepped inside, the American restaurant manager immediately closed off the entire second floor for the general's privacy.

MacArthur patted the man's shoulder as they exchanged niceties. The poor man stammered. At the end of the conversation, he scurried to the bar to pick the most expensive champagne and served it to the group, on the house.

After the first round of drinks had been served, Isabel's father asked, "From whereabouts in the States are you, General?"

"My family has lived everywhere, like a typical military family. But I consider Milwaukee my home. My father grew up there. My mother is from Norfolk."

Isabel's father flanked MacArthur on the right and Captain Marsh on the left. Isabel sat across from MacArthur. Even as he spoke to the others, he kept his eyes on her.

"Were you born in Milwaukee?" added Mr. Cooper.

Before MacArthur could answer, Captain Marsh turned to him and said, "May I tell them the story, sir?"

He smiled. "Sure."

Marsh made eye contact with everyone. "On the day the general was born, the newspaper in Norfolk published an announcement. It said although the MacArthurs lived in different places, Mrs. Pinky MacArthur always came home to Norfolk, Virginia, to give birth. Her first two sons had been born there, but her youngest was born at Arsenal Barracks in Little Rock, Arkansas." Marsh paused and turned to him again. "Sir, I'm forgetting the exact words...what was the headline of the news article?"

All eyes on MacArthur. He took a sip of his champagne before speaking. "Well, you see, Virginians are fiercely loyal. For them, Virginians will always be Virginians. They couldn't accept that my mother gave birth somewhere else. So the headline read, 'Douglas MacArthur was born on January 26th of 1880 while his parents were away.'"

The table erupted with laughter. A demure smile played around Isabel's lips. He couldn't peel his eyes from her.

"Is this your first time in Manila, sir?" asked Ben.

The women had not said more than two words. Let the men speak, let the ladies charm. This native custom suited MacArthur fine. And Isabel was more than charming. If she'd been any less beautiful, he wouldn't bother inviting the entire family. He had not only worn his heart on his sleeve for her people to see, but he'd also inadvertently begun a courtship with her family. Too late to back out.

He took another sip of champagne. "Oh, no, I've been here before. The first time was in 1903, after I graduated from West Point. I took a commission in the Corps of Engineers and I spent some time in Tacloban, Corregidor, and Bataan. I worked on surveys, fortification installations, harbor improvements—those kinds of things. But I was sent back home the following year because of malaria."

"Malaria? *Dios mio*! I'm sorry to hear that," said Isabel's mother.

"I recovered fully, Mrs. Cooper, and came back in 1922 until 1925. This is my third assignment here."

Glancing at Isabel, he continued, "I would like to think of the Philippines as my second country. You see, before I ever stepped foot in this land, my father came here. Back in 1898, he commanded a brigade during the Spanish-American War."

"The Commander is too modest." Captain Marsh refilled his boss's glass with champagne. "Lieutenant General Arthur MacArthur became the military governor-general in 1900. He stopped the rampant violence of Filipino insurgents."

"If I'm not mistaken, Arthur MacArthur succeeded General Otis as governor-general. Emilio Aguinaldo was caught under his watch." Ben spoke with eagerness, snapping his fingers for emphasis. "Aguinaldo's capture crippled the insurgency. It was the beginning of the end of the Filipino rebellion."

MacArthur nodded, pleased that Isabel's brother knew his history. Ben struck him as smart, but he had none of his sister's resoluteness. MacArthur gazed at her, who stared back at him with bright, piercing eyes. He could see her ambition plainly. It took someone cut from the same cloth to recognize it.

"Speaking of governors…Sir, I believe the Filipinos would rather see you as their governor-general," said Isabel's father. "I know I would."

MacArthur was used to compliments, both the earnest kind and the fawning sort. This was the latter. His spirits sank a little at the thought of enduring many more tedious occasions such as this, if he were to win the daughter's affection. "Well, Mr. Cooper, Governor-General Davis is a friend of mine. I would hate for him to hear that."

"Are you really friends with the governor-general?" The thrill in Isabel's father's voice was audible.

"Yes, indeed. I enjoy a tennis match with him every now and then. As you know, he's the founder of the Davis Cup tournament. Needless to say, he's a much better tennis player than I am."

"I take it that he's rather aloof?"

"Aloof? How so?" said MacArthur.

Mr. Cooper shot a conspiratorial glance at his wife, as if they'd talked about this beforehand. "What I mean is that he doesn't care for Americans without official positions. He never invites them to Malacañang. I, myself, have never been invited to his residence."

*Aha.* MacArthur knew where the conversation would go. He waved at a waiter and inquired about the food. His way of dismissing the father's comment. And just when he thought he'd gotten away with it, Isabel spoke out loud for the first time since they arrived at The Grand.

"Sir, have you ever been to Malacañang?"

The question took him aback. "Why, of course. Many times. I was just there for a luncheon three days ago."

"My father would love to visit Malacañang. Wouldn't you, Papa?"

Mr. Cooper nodded and related a long story about how he'd almost been invited to the New Year's gala, and how he'd waited forever for his invitation, only to discover that his name had been removed from the guest list because he had no official position other than as an aspiring businessman. The initial plan to invite him had been a mistake.

MacArthur ignored him. He locked eyes with the daughter. She held his gaze for so long he was forced to give up when all conversation at the table had stopped. Everyone was waiting for him to respond.

"Forgive me, Mr. Cooper…I'm sorry to hear the governor-general canceled your invitation. I tell you what—" MacArthur directed his glance back to Isabel. Everyone remained quiet. "The governor-general has invited me to a reception for a group of American businessmen. Am I right, Captain Marsh?"

"Yes, sir. On Wednesday, in Malacañang Palace. Cocktails at seven o'clock, followed by dinner."

MacArthur continued, "I would like to invite you and your daughter—your entire family—to this reception as my guests."

"*Dios mio*! Thank you!" Mrs. Cooper covered her mouth, embarrassed at such a display of excitement.

MacArthur smiled. "The governor-general is expecting none other than Henry Ford to lead the delegation."

Everyone gasped. Isabel's father clapped his hands and thanked him.

MacArthur directed his attention back to Isabel, who was whispering in Nenita's ear. When Isabel finally looked at him, she mouthed "thank you," her crimson lips puckering, reminding him of her youth. He had never fancied anyone as young before. He forced himself to look away as his stomach churned a little with guilt.

When he glanced at her again, she was taking a sip of champagne. Then she wet her lips with her tongue. The mole on her left cheek, near her nose, all but hypnotized him. The sight—her tongue, her lips, her mouth, the beauty mark—overwhelmed him with desire. He wanted her.

The food arrived. The centerpiece was steamed lapu-lapu, a fish native to the islands, wrapped in banana leaves. As the waiter uncovered it, the steaming aroma of ginger and coconut milk escaped, teasing MacArthur's palate. It was his favorite Filipino dish. More food and drinks arrived, enough to feed a platoon. He hated waste, but he wanted to impress Isabel.

In the middle of dinner, guitar music emanated from the courtyard.

"Is that a *harana*?" A serenade. Isabel got up and ran across the hall and onto the veranda for a full view of the courtyard below.

The mother apologized for her daughter's behavior.

True, it was girlish, but also charming. MacArthur dabbed his mouth with the starched napkin. "Mrs. Cooper, there's no need to apologize. It's natural for someone like your daughter who's artistically inclined to be moved by such beautiful music. Now, if you'd let me, I'll try to convince her to come back to the table."

Nobody dared to stop him.

At the veranda, the sumptuous breeze from Manila Bay greeted him. A scattering of stars lit the black sky. He stood behind Isabel.

"Hello, General. I mean…Douglas."

"That's better." He took a cigar from a little case in his jacket pocket and cut it with a folding knife he always carried. He lit it with a lighter, glancing at the cigar's glowing foot to make sure it burned evenly. He puffed on it.

They watched the musicians below: three guitarists playing a popular love song. Lanterns blazed. Several restaurant patrons came out, attracted by the music. When it was over, they both applauded.

She glanced over her shoulder. "Do you like *harana?*"

"I've never been the object of a serenade. But yes, I quite enjoy it. How about you?"

"Unlike you, I'm lucky to have been serenaded before. And I love it."

He chuckled. What a pleasure to be teased by a coquettish young woman who happened to be beautiful.

"I'm guessing there's a long line of young men wanting to serenade you every night."

"I find them boring."

"The young men who serenade you? Or young men in general?"

"Both."

"How so?"

She turned around to face him. Her delicate beauty reminded him of the love poems of his youth.

"They know nothing about life. They know nothing about me," she said.

"You have to give them a chance to get to know you and to experience life."

"A chance to grow up, you mean? I haven't got the time." Her voice was laced with youthful impatience. She faced the veranda again, both hands on the railing.

The guitarists struck up a new tune. MacArthur drew a dense puff of smoke into his mouth and then slowly blew smoke rings. He savored the tobacco, the music, but most of all, her nearness.

When she spoke, he stepped closer.

"My brother told me you came to Manila in 1922 with a Mrs. Douglas MacArthur. That's the reason he tried to stop me from riding with you in your car. He thinks you're married."

"He's wrong. There used to be a Mrs. Douglas MacArthur—her name is Louise Cromwell Brooks, daughter of a millionaire—but not anymore."

"Where is she now?"

"Back in the States. As it turned out, she didn't like my military career. She hated living here. She prefers Paris to New York and New York to Manila. We got divorced."

"When?"

"Two years and a lifetime ago. We don't even speak to each other anymore."

"How sad. I'm sorry."

"Don't be. She's happy in New York and I'm happy here. I like Manila. And I like listening to serenades with you." He moved closer, so close he could smell jasmine in her hair and feel the warmth radiating from her body. "It's too bad I don't know how to play the guitar. I can't compete with all the young men waiting outside your balcony to serenade you."

She faced him fully. Though he was a head taller and so much older, she seemed unfazed. Her self-confidence struck him. She was certain of her charm and even more assured of her claim on him.

"Like I said, I find young men boring." A coy smile blossomed from her lips.

Holding the cigar with his right hand, he raised his other hand to touch her face, but she pivoted toward the hall abruptly.

"Shall we go back in?" She didn't wait for his response.

His arm fell to his side. Poor timing.

She walked across the hall with a dancer's glide, all grace and elegance. In that instant he realized one thing. He must have her soon. He had no choice but to follow her.

# 5.

ALTHOUGH IT WAS almost midnight, the Cooper household was wide awake, energized by the family's encounter with General MacArthur earlier that night. Isabel lit the gas lamp in her bedroom. She kicked off her shoes, tied the mosquito net hanging from her four-poster bed to one side, and plopped on the bed.

She started writing in her diary. Occasionally she glanced at the bouquet of orchids from MacArthur, which she'd placed in a crystal vase. He'd chosen her favorite flower. Was it military intelligence or a lucky guess?

Her bedroom door was closed, but she could hear her family talking. They called him Commander because that was how Captain Marsh addressed him.

"The Commander said so…all of us to the dinner party…"

She caught bits and pieces of Ben's plea to attend the soiree in Malacañang Palace. Of course, he wanted to go. Her brother had studied to become a teacher but didn't actually teach. Sometimes he helped Papa sell cars during the day. Many nights, he drank and ate for free and flirted with girls at parties. He would kill to attend a reception at the governor-general's residence.

But Isabel already knew. Mama had told her even before they left The Grand that they should let her Papa "shine" on this occasion. She didn't want the rest of the family to go.

Outside, the conversation went on. "Let your father get a chance to meet …" Mama said. "Your Papa needs this…you're not needed there…"

Isabel adjusted the gas lamp's flame to make it brighter. She could barely see her handwriting. If only their house had electric lamps. Restaurants, hotels, government buildings, and many houses in Manila had electricity, but not the Coopers' home. They lived in her Lola's two-story house. Her maternal grandmother and her servant occupied the ground floor, while the Coopers lived upstairs. A lovely nineteenth century Spanish-style house without twentieth century amenities. The windows didn't even have screens to keep mosquitoes out.

MacArthur's home was probably well-lit, sans mosquitoes, while she was going blind from staring at her diary in the feeble light.

Ben burst into the room. "Mama said we can't go to the party in Malacañang."

"Yes, I know."

"Well? Are you going to just sit there? Why don't you help me change her mind?"

"She has already made up her mind. There's nothing I can do."

"Let me guess—" He shut the door and sat beside her on the bed. "Mama heard the Commander is married and she doesn't want him around you."

She smacked the side of his head. "He's not married! You're full of baloney."

He ducked and avoided the second slap. He stood up. "I thought he's married."

"He's not. He said he got divorced 'two years and a lifetime ago.'"

"The Catholic church doesn't recognize divorce. He might as well be married."

"Well, he's not!" Truth was, Isabel couldn't care less if MacArthur were married. She wasn't looking for a husband, but an influential friend.

He headed for the door, but then looked back. "Does that mean he's going to be your beau? Does Mama approve of him?"

"Mind your own business."

He grinned. "Eddie Palma was jealous, you know."

"Why the hell were you talking to him?"

"He approached me. I was just being nice."

"Get out of my room!"

Finally rid of her brother, she went back to writing in her diary. *Nom de guerre*. MacArthur had used the phrase. Not pseudonym or alias, but *nom de guerre*. What an old-fashioned word. Well, he was old—fifty, like Papa.

Still, MacArthur was the youngest fifty-year-old she'd ever met. In comparison, her father appeared ancient with his thinning hair and errant white hair sprouting in his bushy eyebrows. Unlike MacArthur, Papa was not a sharp dresser. The General wore impeccable clothes. Even the cigar made him look expensive. No wonder he'd married a millionaire's daughter.

Isabel had never been courted by anyone as old as MacArthur, but then again, she'd never met anyone like him before.

"The Commander is a very important man..." Papa's voice trailed.

MacArthur was so important nobody addressed him by his first name. She had to call him "sir," at least in front of other people. How strange to call one's admirer "sir." Nenita thought MacArthur was plain strange: an old man wooing a young lady.

*Dios mio*, how Nenita had tested Isabel's patience. Her friend had not uttered a word at The Grand, not even a "thank you" for the lavish dinner. She had sat there full of gloom, prompting MacArthur to whisper, "Is anything the matter with your *amiga?*"

"Nenita has trouble speaking English," she'd lied, but only to an extent. Nenita didn't speak the language because she hated it.

Thank God, MacArthur wasn't married. Not that it mattered to Nenita. When Isabel told her the Commander was divorced, Nenita had shaken her head in disgust. None of Isabel's admirers was good enough. But Nenita didn't even have a beau, so what did she know about men?

A divorced man was a step above the married men she'd encountered before. Like that director of a *zarzuela* she'd auditioned for. He'd been smoking a cigar, displaying his wedding band on his finger, when he told Isabel up-front he wanted a *querida*. He was a successful director who felt entitled to a mistress. The man was younger than MacArthur, but he was the shape of a barrel and bald. The nerve! Thanks, but no thanks. And so, she'd failed to get the part. Another door slammed in her face. Who cared if MacArthur was married or divorced? She just wanted that door opened.

She set her diary aside, sat before the dresser, and wiped the cosmetics off her face with a wad of cotton.

Her parents loved MacArthur. Papa was beside himself about the invitation to Malacañang. When Mama told Isabel the rest of the family was not needed at the party, Isabel had to bite her tongue. MacArthur had invited the family to be with her.

Of course, Mama knew. But she wanted Papa to succeed so badly she was willing to overlook the obvious. Neither Mama nor she wanted to admit the simple fact—they needed MacArthur.

This last thought gave her pause. Her breath shortened in her throat, her shoulders drooped. To be at the mercy of a man's benevolence brought with it a kind of desperation and sadness nobody would understand, least of all, Nenita.

She shook off the thought and brushed her hair briskly, a nightly ritual.

Mama once told her physical beauty was a gift—a stroke of incredible luck that could neither be understood nor explained. *Just look around you. There are more ugly people than beautiful. Even within the same family, do you ever wonder why you are so pretty while your cousin Esperanza is cross-eyed? How do you explain that? No man would ever want poor Espie! But men will do anything for you. You are blessed with such beauty. Use it wisely.*

Did Mama regret marrying Papa? She could have aimed higher. Her mother had been a fabled beauty in her day. Isabel loved her father, but he disappointed the family. Mama's resentment appeared the way sunlight seeped through thick curtains. It showed no matter how hard she tried to hide it.

When they shopped in Escolta, her mother gazed with longing at the diamond earrings Papa couldn't afford. She stared at the rich American women who didn't think twice about buying them. Time after time, with one failed investment after another, she'd told Papa, "Your time will come, dear. You just wait and see." She had always smiled when she said this, but one could almost taste the bitterness of her words.

By marrying an American citizen, Mama must have thought she had guaranteed a bright future for herself and her children. Wrong. She must have expected they would move to the United States. Wrong again. Papa's family had immigrated from Scotland to New York to better themselves, and when Isabel's father couldn't "catch a break," he'd traveled to Manila in search of fortune. He was still searching.

So, what was wrong about asking MacArthur for an invitation to Malacañang? She shouldn't feel bad about it. Her request had surprised him, but he must have realized she'd given him the opportunity to continue seeing her.

She dropped the hairbrush in a drawer, opened the lone window in her room, and then untied the mosquito net. She went underneath the netting and continued writing in her diary. So much to write about!

MacArthur had obviously wanted to kiss her at the veranda. He may be the most important man in this part of the world, but he wasn't any different from the other men she'd encountered in the past. He wanted the same thing. She was not about to give it to him. Unkind? Perhaps, but she couldn't help it. The party invitation was for Papa, and it wasn't enough.

She wanted MacArthur—his power and clout, his money, his social status. But especially his America. Oh, she wanted his undivided attention and undiluted ardor. She would make him go mad with desire. She shouldn't feel bad about that either.

And so, the Commander must wait.

# 6.

MACARTHUR HAD never been to Tropical Nights before. It was one step above vulgar, a mahjong den masquerading as a nightclub. It reeked of men, most of them sweaty Filipino-Chinese merchants. Their mahjong tables surrounded the small stage, where a jazz band played. Fake coconut trees sprang from each side of the stage. Strings of cheap colored lights hung from the ceiling.

MacArthur strode inside, followed by his two aides, Captain Marsh and First Lieutenant Elijah Wallace. They all wore their khaki uniforms for it was the middle of the week, and they'd come straight from work. The locals paused to take in MacArthur's presence. After a while, they went back to gambling.

MacArthur spotted Isabel's brother at the bar, talking to a couple of men. He chose a table a few feet from the band, and sent Captain Marsh to ask Ben Cooper to join them.

MacArthur pulled the chair next to him, an invitation for Ben to sit there.

"Sir, what a pleasure to see you." The young man shook MacArthur's hand. "My sister will be so delighted."

"I thought I was going to see you both last week." The music blasted. MacArthur waited until it stopped before repeating what he'd said.

"It was very generous of you, sir, to invite all of us," said Ben. "But our mother didn't want us to go. She said Papa should go alone."

MacArthur sighed. "Well, it was a bit of a disappointment."

A disaster was more like it. He'd arrived at the Cooper residence in his chauffeured limousine, expecting to see Isabel and the rest of the family, but found only the father waiting outside. He didn't even invite MacArthur to come inside because he'd been raring to go.

When they arrived at the governor-general's palace, Henry Ford had not been there. The American industrialist had canceled his trip at the last minute. Ford's absence had dampened the mood of the party. While it was understandable that the governor-general had been disappointed, MacArthur was flummoxed that someone like Isabel's father had taken offense. Cooper had talked everyone's ear off about how thoughtless it was of Henry Ford to cancel, what an insult it was to the entire Filipino nation. For Christ's sake, the man was an embarrassment. MacArthur had ditched him as soon as he could.

He waved at a waiter. "Is it possible to get any service in this joint?"

Ben got up to find the manager, who came to take MacArthur's order: whiskey for all four men.

MacArthur scraped his chair back and crossed his legs. "Ben, tell me what your sister is doing here."

"It's her decision, sir. She works very hard."

"No doubt about that. But Tropical Nights? This place is a mahjong den that happens to have live music."

Ben chuckled nervously.

MacArthur disapproved of the gambling in the Philippines, whether mahjong or cockfights. It was an egregious weakness of character. Unfortunately, it was beyond his purview. American civilian authority tolerated gambling as a harmless part of Filipino culture.

Captain Marsh passed around a small humidor. MacArthur chose a cigar, cut the tip with his folding knife, and lit it. "What do your parents say about this place?" He puffed on his cigar, then passed the knife to Ben.

"Our mother refuses to come here. Belle and Mama argue about this all the time. But my sister can't find work elsewhere, and so Papa agreed to let her sing here—for now."

MacArthur shook his head. Why should a sixteen-year-old girl have to work at all? Was the father such a lousy provider he had to rely on his daughter? He glanced at Ben, but thought better than to ask him. They smoked quietly.

Their drinks arrived with a platter of what the manager called *pulutan*. Finger food— the kind served with liquor.

The man offered it to MacArthur first, coaxing him to try it. The lights were dim; there was no telling what it was. The greasy smell clung to his nostrils. He was in no mood to experiment with native cuisine. He passed it to the other men. They ate everything.

"How was it?" said MacArthur.

His aides said "crispy" and "delicious."

To Ben, he asked, "What was it exactly?"

"Fried pig's intestines."

The Americans looked at each other. "Hell, I'd eat anybody's intestine if it tasted as good," said Wallace.

They all laughed. "Let's have another platter. Or two." Marsh stopped a waiter passing by and ordered.

The band resumed playing. Without any introduction, Isabel walked onto the stage, prompting wild applause. MacArthur stopped mid-drink, mesmerized by the sight of her in a black beaded dress and matching headdress.

While the band played a prelude, she posed as if someone was painting her, the small tilt of her nose in profile. Under the spotlight, her dress and headpiece shimmered.

Men emerged from a room, perhaps a private space for the affluent gamblers. They took up all the empty seats, and some had to stand on the sidelines.

She belted out a Sophie Tucker song called "The Man I Love." The dress covered her from neck to ankles, but the beaded fabric clung to her body like a second skin, displaying ample curves. While the outfit didn't display any skin, it seemed to tease the men, challenging them to imagine what was underneath.

On stage, Isabel was all woman. No one would have guessed her age. Her voice was not as powerful as Sophie Tucker's, but the actress in her pulled off the number with ease.

When she reached the chorus of "The Man I Love," she fixed her gaze on MacArthur. She didn't look surprised. "Someday he'll come along…the man I love…he'll be big and strong…the man I love," she crooned.

What a melancholic tune. There might have been tears in her eyes. She sang to him and spoke to him. He froze in his seat, enthralled.

When the song ended, the audience burst into a deafening applause. "Gentlemen, my name is Dimples," she said, breathing into the microphone. "Tonight, I'm your *querida*—" She paused for dramatic effect, prompting lusty whistles. "Yes, just for tonight I'm your mistress—of entertainment!" More whistles and cheers.

She segued into another Sophie Tucker song, "Red Hot Mama," a faster tune that had her dancing. A Tagalog love song followed. When the set was over, the crowd was on its feet. She blew a kiss to the audience, her eyes resting on MacArthur. His heart lurched. The air kiss was meant for him alone.

The spotlight faded, darkness swallowing her. The musicians stretched their arms and mingled with audience members. The loud conversations broke her spell on MacArthur and swept him back to the reality at hand. How could he spend time alone with her?

He scanned the room. Small-time Chinese mestizo businessmen discussed their inconsequential commercial concerns, or whatever it was they talked about, while they played mahjong. All around him gamblers drank cheap liquor and gorged on pig's intestines or God-knows-what.

He glanced at his pocket watch and estimated about twenty minutes of break before she would get back on stage. "Ben, would you take me to Belle's dressing room? I would like to congratulate her for the excellent first set."

The young man jumped up on his feet. "Of course, sir."

They weaved through the packed room and entered a narrow hallway. The dressing room sat next to an office, where the manager chatted with another man. He saluted to MacArthur, who nodded in return.

Ben rapped on the door. "Belle? It's me."

"Come in."

MacArthur expected Ben to stay as her chaperone, but he said, "Sir, I better go back and see what Captain Marsh and Lieutenant Wallace are up to."

"Thank you." MacArthur patted his shoulder. Of course, Ben understood.

He entered the room, the size of a shoebox, and shut the door behind him. She sat before a dressing table littered with cosmetics and costume jewelry. She glanced over her shoulder. “Hello, Commander.” Not a hint of surprise. It seemed she’d expected him all along.

“Hello, Belle. Excellent performance—congratulations.” At last, they were alone. It was what he wanted, but it offered neither pleasure nor consolation. The air stood stagnant, her perfume suffocating. He loosened his khaki tie.

“Thank you. I’ve been rehearsing Sophie Tucker songs forever. I love Sophie.” She removed her headpiece and shook her hair, big curls bouncing on her shoulders. “You’ve got no idea how hot it is under the spotlight. My poor hair is fried.” She tossed the headdress into a box. Then she began brushing her hair. “I’m so glad you’re here.”

“I doubt that very much.” He couldn’t hide his irritation at the bunker-like room and the humidity—the shoddy nightclub and its miserable clientele.

They stared at each other in the mirror, which reflected his long face and her quizzical expression.

She turned around to face him. “Is there anything I can do to improve your foul mood?”

He stuck his hands in his trouser pockets. “You can try explaining why you didn’t show up for the party in Malacañang last week.”

“Mama refused to let me and Ben go. She wanted Papa to *shine*. There was nothing I could do about it.”

“Was it her idea to lock you up at home that day? You couldn’t come out to say hello? I thought common courtesy was in order.”

“I’m sorry.”

He pulled a stool and dropped on it.

She faced the mirror again and resumed brushing her hair. “You don’t know how Papa gets when he’s excited. He was so thrilled about the party, and that’s why he was waiting for you outside. You couldn’t possibly expect me to stand there with him. Not when I wasn’t even going.”

She dabbed rouge on her cheeks.

He heaved a sigh. “What are you doing in this dump?”

She stopped, locking eyes with him in the mirror. “Katy de la Cruz started in this dump. Look where she is now.”

“And when was that? A decade ago? I doubt if she’d ever return here. I don’t understand how your father can let you work in this mahjong den for Chinks.”

"Do you want me to quit my job?"

Heat rushed to his face. Goddamn it! All he wanted was for this woman to keep her end of the bargain when she asked him to invite her father. Would it have killed her to accompany him? The explanation about her mother was a lousy excuse. And now he just wanted her company in a decent establishment, not a gambling den. He was Douglas MacArthur. Tropical Nights was beneath him. But if he hadn't come, the only alternative was to call on her at home. It would mean seeing her abominable father. The hell with this! He stood abruptly and faced the door.

"If you want me to quit this job, then why don't you just ask me?"

He turned around, flabbergasted. Was she playing games with him? Worse, was she mocking him? "Your father is foolish to let you sing here. You have a sap for a father. There's no one protecting your interests. And don't tell me your brother is here to take care of you because he's a boy, a mere child—" He stopped, his anger pulsing in his throat. His face burned. He shook his head. "Oh, Christ! This is none of my business."

"Douglas, I'm sorry about last week. I'm sorry you don't like this place. I'm sorry I disappoint you."

Her voice was small. In an instant, she looked like a girl again, someone playing dress-up, caught in a game for grown-ups. It wasn't her fault her father was a leech. She couldn't have guessed that the first thing he did at the party was to solicit financing for his car-import business from an American banker named Stanley McBride. It had been mortifying. The man was insufferable.

Manila overflowed with American leeches like Isabel's father who had come to the Philippines to suck the country dry. Of all the women in Manila, MacArthur had to fall for the daughter of one of those parasites.

He took a deep breath and pulled his gold cigarette case from his pocket. But there was no time to smoke. She would have to get back on stage soon. He stuck the case back in his pocket. "I was dismayed last week and I feel the same way now. But no—you don't disappoint me."

She inched toward him and then rested her head on his chest. His heart galloped. Surely she could hear it?

She looked up to him. "But it's true that you hate this place."

"That's correct."

"Then I'll quit as soon as I finish performing tonight."

She craned her neck, her lips brushing his. He cupped her face in his hands and inhaled the warmth of her breath. Their foreheads and noses touched.

His gratitude washed over him, silenced him.

She closed her eyes, her face serene in his hands. His anger had already melted. Finally, he kissed her on the mouth.

# 7.

"SOMEONE VERY important came to see Belle tonight," said Ben as soon as he and Isabel entered the living room. Their parents were waiting.

Gas lamps glowed. A mosquito coil smoldered in a ceramic holder near the piano, emitting an odor as powerful as incense.

"The Commander?" Their father sat in the old rocking chair with a glass of brandy.

"Yes, he came with two aides." Ben plopped on the couch beside Mama, who was embroidering.

"Two aides. How about that?" Papa rose, presenting his right cheek for Isabel to kiss. "The man is very keen on you. What did he say?"

She kissed her father, then her mother. Her muscles ached. She would have preferred to skip the talk, but there was no stopping her brother.

"He was quite upset," Ben blurted out.

"Oh, shut up." Isabel perched on the piano bench.

"What?" said Mama.

"It's true. He was put out because we didn't accompany Papa to Malacañang. I told you, Mama, he wanted all of us there."

Their mother held up her right hand. "*Mahal*, I want to hear it from your sister." She called him love, a nickname she reserved for her children.

Papa fell back in his rocking chair. He swirled his brandy.

“He was upset at first, but I explained everything. I told him I was sorry.” Isabel crossed her tired legs.

“Whatever did you apologize for?” said Mama.

“For not inviting him inside the house. It was rude. And for not going to the party. He invited all of us.”

Their parents traded glances.

“Tell them about Mr. McBride.” Ben stretched his legs on the coffee table, but his mother swatted his thigh. He put his feet down.

“Stanley McBride? Did the Commander say anything about Stanley McBride?” Papa’s eyes grew wide.

“Oh, you’ll love this, Papa—”

“Let your sister finish!” yelled Mama.

“Sorry.”

“The Commander wants to invite Papa and Mr. McBride for dinner. I’m assuming it’s to talk business,” said Isabel.

“I met Stanley McBride at the party. He owns the Philippine Commercial Bank. I told him all about my car-import business. If I can just convince him to extend me a loan, then I can get a bigger property and order more cars.”

“With the Commander vouching for you, I’m sure Mr. McBride will give you a loan.” Mama turned to Isabel with a big smile. “This is wonderful news! This is your Papa’s lucky break.”

“MacArthur, McBride, and me—we’ll make a good Scottish gang! We’ll get along famously.” Papa took a sip of brandy.

Isabel let out a quiet sigh. Poor Papa. If only he knew MacArthur thought so little of him. Did Mama really think this was a “lucky break”? *Dios mio,* they had no idea. When the Commander entered Isabel’s dressing room, she hadn’t expected a lover’s fight. Ben was supposed to have stayed. “You owe me big time,” Ben had said, like he’d done it out of the goodness of his heart. She was positive MacArthur’s foul mood had intimidated Ben.

She gave him a knowing glance, daring him to tell their parents she’d been alone with MacArthur. He smirked. Yes, her insolent brother was afraid of the Commander.

“Do you know when this dinner is going to be?” asked Papa.

“No,” replied Isabel. “But I’m sure the Commander will invite you soon enough.” After that kiss? Of course, MacArthur would invite her father sooner than later.

Ben slapped his forearm, killing a mosquito. "Got you, *hijo de puta!*"

"Watch your mouth," Mama admonished. "Your Lola has complained that you curse all the time."

"Not at *her.*"

"Don't cuss around your grandmother. Better yet, don't cuss at all!"

"Now, now, let's not ruin the mood." Their father drained his drink and stood up. "It's wonderful to have friends in high places. Let's celebrate!" He played Jelly Roll Morton's "Boogaboo" on the gramophone.

"Dance with me, sweetheart." He pulled his wife up and they started slow-dancing.

Ben poured a drink for himself. Isabel retreated to her room.

She locked the door so Ben wouldn't barge in. She lit the gas lamp, took off her high heels, and sat on the stool before the dresser. She removed her jewelry.

When she'd first walked on stage that night, she had no idea MacArthur would be in the audience. She'd assumed he would come to her at some point, but she hadn't known when or where. His presence was both surprising and inevitable. Like their first kiss.

The memory returned—the whiff of cigar on his breath, the sharp taste of liquor on his lips. All combined, the sensation was delicious, a welcome rush. She would have preferred to make him wait, but she'd enjoyed it. If they had not been in a dressing room, a few minutes before show time, they could have kissed forever. She'd tried to slide off his arms twice, but each time, he'd embraced her tighter and kissed her again. She had to shove him out the door playfully to get rid of him.

She got out of the beaded dress MacArthur had complimented and slipped on a nightgown. She lit a mosquito coil before opening the window. Then she sat on her bed to write in her diary.

Truth was, she almost lost MacArthur. He'd been so angry she thought he would walk out on her. For a moment, she'd been tempted to let him go. Who really wanted to be around an old killjoy? Why he'd been so irritated by the gambling at Tropical Nights was beyond her. He'd lived in Manila long enough to know Filipinos were hypocrites and they would never call a gambling den a *gambling den* but a "nightclub." Nobody would call himself a gambler. He was just unwinding in a nightclub. Never mind that he'd lost all of his earnings, plus the shirt off his back, while relaxing.

And a brothel was never a brothel but a "dance school." Never mind that the "teachers" were checked for venereal diseases every month. Bribes to government officials were called "commissions." The Commander would never know about that because he was at the top, where nobody dared to give him a commission.

She wrote in her diary and fast—MacArthur's words coming back all at once. Of course Tropical Nights was no Grand Opera House. What did he expect? The way he'd called it a "dump" and a "mahjong den for Chinks" hurt. He didn't know Isabel's mother was a Chinese mestiza. Mama's father was a Chinese immigrant who made his money selling gold jewelry in Chinatown, God bless his soul.

The Cooper family lived in a Chink-owned house and lived off Mama's Chink inheritance. They wouldn't survive without Mama's money. Isabel's meager earnings helped pay for her clothes, acting lessons, and other expenses Papa would have to shoulder otherwise.

Filipino prejudice against Chinese immigrants and mestizos was bad, but MacArthur's bias against them was worse. What would he do when he found out Isabel was the worst kind of half-breed—part American and part Filipino-Chinese? Would he still want to kiss her Chink lips?

A knob of pain nudged her heart. She had to pretend she didn't understand his insults, calling her Papa a "sap" and Ben a "mere child." He considered himself too good for the Coopers because he was the most decorated American soldier during the Great War. The newspapers never failed to mention it in every story about him. He was so powerful he could eat lunch with the governor-general in Malacañang any old day of the week. Not only that, Captain Marsh had said that back in the States, the Commander could go to the White House and talk to President Hoover in the flesh any time he wanted. How about that?

The Commander must consider himself such a prize because he'd married a rich white woman. Look how it had ended. *Why doesn't he find another white socialite? That's right, it's because no white socialite wants an old grouch.*

She shut her diary. She wanted to cry. Instead, she rested her head against the headboard and closed her eyes. Music drifted from the living room. It calmed her. Even the smell of mosquito coil soothed her. No reason to cry, really. Everything had gone well in the end.

True, she'd never met a man whose idea of courtship was to scold her and show her how inferior she was. Douglas MacArthur was so full of himself and so sure of his power that he'd skipped the romance and went right ahead to proprietorship. They'd seen each other just three times in three weeks, but he'd acted as if he owned her. How ironic. She'd thought of him as *My MacArthur*, but it was clear he owned her as much as she owned him. Fair enough.

She opened her eyes and went back to writing. She could never tell Nenita about MacArthur's insults or she'd explode. And rightly so.

She had given up Tropical Nights as a last resort, as a peace offering to MacArthur. She couldn't afford to let him walk out. After her last song, she'd gone straight to the manager to quit.

Then she'd joined the Commander at their table. *Darling, you won't regret your decision.* He'd whispered it in her ear, mindful of the other men at the table. He'd revealed his plan to invite Papa to dine with him and Stanley McBride. She'd pretended like she'd never heard of the name before. *I believe your father will be very pleased.* He'd squeezed her hand underneath the table.

In the end, her bet had paid off. She'd lost Tropical Nights and she'd let him kiss her sooner than she'd planned, but she'd gotten something big in return. The Commander would grant her father a favor soon, even though he hated Papa's guts.

She got up to brush her hair. The curls looked defeated, flattened by humidity.

MacArthur was used to bossing an entire division. He couldn't help his ways. He deserved the benefit of the doubt.

She puffed out her cheeks and exhaled a gust of air. There, she felt better. No reason to cry.

# 8.

# May 1930

MACARTHUR STOOD by the huge window in his office at Fort William McKinley, five miles south of Manila. He took in the calmness of the empty parade grounds to counter the frustration rising in him. Soon the Infantry, the Cavalry, and the Philippine Scouts would be in formation to prepare for the big maneuver in Lingayen Gulf tomorrow.

The verdant lawn glistened from the previous night's downpour. In two months, the typhoon season would begin in earnest. It was time to pave the camp's dirt roads, or the troops would be marching and driving on mush as they did the previous year. Alas, the radiogram from yesterday said the War Department wouldn't provide funds for road pavement, or improved housing for MacArthur's men, or materiel for the defense of Manila Bay under the War Plan Orange.

He picked up the radiogram from his desk and read it. For your information *Plan Orange revised. No funds for Philippine Div. Do the best you can. Latest report to follow.*

Do the best you can? Goddamn it! He dropped the paper on his desk and went back to the window, hands on his hips. He drew a deep breath, trying to contain his anger.

MacArthur's pitifully inadequate resources made preparedness critical. He had only eleven thousand American regulars and six thousand Philippine auxiliaries. With rumors of Germany beginning to re-arm and Japan building up her empire in Manchuria, the situation was ripe for conflict. The Philippine Islands could easily get caught in the middle of a power struggle. But what did Washington care?

"Good morning, General." Captain Marsh entered the room with a cup of coffee.

"Those goddamned armchair generals in Washington have no idea." MacArthur paced the room. "They want me to defend America's only colony, but they have no idea what it takes to defend it in the face of a Japanese attack."

"I'm sorry, General. Bad news from Washington?"

"My request for more money has been denied—again." He accepted the cup from Marsh and pointed his chin at the radiogram. Marsh read it, while MacArthur sipped his coffee.

He set the cup on his desk. "I don't know why I bothered mapping Bataan. I scaled mountains and hacked jungles and waded across flooded fields to map forty goddamn square miles of rough terrain just to show Washington how to defend Manila Bay. And we're talking only of Manila Bay—just one point of possible entry. What if the Japs enter somewhere else?"

"I'm sorry, sir. Do you think the governor-general can help you persuade Washington?"

"I doubt it. But I still need to let him know. And I need to respond to the radiogram."

"Should I get the latest Plan Orange report for you, sir?"

"What for? I already know what it says."

"All right, sir. I'll check the governor-general's schedule. When would you like to see him?"

"Today."

"Yes, sir."

"Where's Wallace?"

"Sir, I believe he'll go directly to Escolta this morning."

"Escolta?"

"Yes, sir. He's going shopping for a bouquet of orchids and a bottle of Cognac."

MacArthur sighed. For God's sake. Yes, he'd asked Wallace to get the flowers for Isabel and the brandy for Stanley McBride and to deliver the gifts in person. McBride had approved Cooper's loan. Hence, the Cognac as a thank-you gift. He had never given a thought where Wallace would get those things.

"Very well. Shut the door on your way out, will you?"

"Yes, sir."

He sat down and began to scribble his response to the radiogram. He could hear the troops getting into formation outside. He rose to watch the men, but his thoughts wandered.

In the course of checking Isabel's father's business background, MacArthur had discovered that Isabel's mother was a Chinese mestiza, the daughter of an immigrant who had owned a jewelry store in Manila's Chinatown. Cooper probably thought his marriage to a local woman was his ticket to this tropical paradise. The poor sap. Cooper should have known better. Americans frowned upon marriages between their compatriots and natives.

Granted that Cooper was crazy enough to marry a Filipina, he should have chosen someone of Spanish descent—the only acceptable way for a foreigner to become part of Manila society. Instead, he'd chosen a Chink half-breed. Many Chinese immigrants had adopted Spanish surnames and spent their lives working hard. They were a diligent lot with a knack for business. But on the whole, Filipinos looked down on them. Except for the very wealthy and those who had married into Filipino-Spanish families, they remained outside of Manila society. So, for American men who lived in the Philippines, they benefited more by *staying* American. Going native and marrying a local brought pure trouble. MacArthur had allowed two whole weeks to pass without seeing Isabel. He'd been too busy preparing for the maneuver and negotiating with Washington. *I must see her soon.*

A slight thrill rippled through him as his thoughts swept him back to the night he'd first seen her. What was it about Isabel that had compelled him to write a note? He'd never done that before. His courtship with Louise had been fast, but conventional. They'd been introduced in January 1922 at a party in West Point, where he was the superintendent at the time. Louise Cromwell Brooks was a divorcée with two children. Her father was a descendant of England's lord protector, Oliver Cromwell. She was one of America's richest heiresses.

MacArthur didn't care about her money. She wasn't nearly as beautiful as Isabel. But Louise was ebullient, sophisticated, exciting, and most of all, she adored MacArthur. Her devotion resembled an unexpected sunburst amid the gloom that was West Point. He'd been so lonely back then.

One month after they'd met, they'd gotten married in her family's Palm Beach estate. A newspaper account of their wedding carried this headline: *Marriage of Mars and Millions*. It annoyed MacArthur, but not as much as the fact that his mother didn't attend the wedding. Pinky MacArthur never liked Louise.

The marriage lasted only six years, reinforcing Pinky's opinion that Louise was the wrong woman for him. MacArthur had loved Louise, but their values clashed. He cherished duty, honor, and country. Louise wanted status quo; she preferred the glitz of Paris and New York over the staid military life in Manila.

Toward the end of their marriage, she'd pestered him about working for J.P. Morgan & Company, her stepfather's firm. It hurt that Louise didn't know him. She was blind to his staunch belief in destiny. He was born to be an extraordinary soldier, a great man. How on earth could he fulfill his destiny by working for J.P. Morgan?

He picked up his cup and brought it to the window. The men were marching. The coffee was lukewarm. He sipped it anyway.

At least, he had gotten over Louise with little pain. His reassignment to Manila helped. But getting over Louise wasn't enough. He wanted more, and Isabel offered something different—or rather, *Isabel was different.* What were the odds that he'd fall for someone who was not only thirty-four years his junior, but also happened to be part-American, part-Filipino, and part-Chinese? Why did she have to be so young? That she was Filipino also bothered him. He loved the Filipino people, but never expected to fall for any Filipina. He hadn't planned on getting entangled with Manila society. He'd been happily above it all. So what to do?

It was 1930. He was a divorced man. His mother wasn't around to criticize him. He lived in a colony far away from America. Hell, he might as well have been in another world! Isabel was worth taking a chance.

A knock on the door. "Come in," he said.

Captain Marsh walked in with the latest War Plan Orange report. "Sir, I went over this quickly, and you're right. It's all bad news for the Philippine defense. But I think you should at least skim this. You see, we need your response."

MacArthur set the cup down. He fell onto his chair, opened a drawer, and took out a corncob pipe. "My answer is going to be the same. I didn't get what I've asked for, so I'm going to ask again."

"I understand that, sir. But we have to change the wording of your letter. You know…address some of the new items in the report. For example, this part here is new, and I quote, 'A Philippine militia might be organized to bolster the diminished American garrison.' Sir, you have to say if you're in favor or against forming a militia, and why."

"For Christ's sake, Marsh! Leave it on my desk."

"Yes, sir." The captain headed for the door.

"Ed."

"Sir?"

MacArthur stuffed the corncob pipe with tobacco. "Do you think the orchids are enough? Should I get her something else?"

Captain Marsh's eyes darted upward, mulling over the question. "Sir, the orchids are great. She loves them, but a little something extra might be in order."

MacArthur lit the pipe, puffed on it until it smoked. "Like what?"

"Jewelry is always good, sir."

"What kind?"

"Since this is the Philippines…then maybe pearls? How about a pearl necklace?"

"Good idea. I want the best kind."

"Absolutely, sir."

"Do you know a good jewelry store?"

"There are several in Escolta. I can help you with that, sir."

MacArthur raised his feet and rested them on the table. "I appreciate it. With the maneuver coming up and Washington screwing me up, I just don't have the time."

"General, you have to make time. *Presents* can't replace your *presence,* sir."

Ed loved puns. He arched an eyebrow, but let it slide. "I've been thinking of taking her to Baguio."

His aide winced.

"What's the matter?"

"Sir, the whole family might come along."

"For God's sake."

"You know how Filipinos are."

Indeed he knew them well. Isabel lived with her extended family: her parents, her unemployed brother, and her grandmother. It was common among Filipinos—both men and women, but especially the women—to live with their elders throughout their lives, even after they get married. Yes, Marsh was right. MacArthur couldn't invite Isabel without also inviting her family.

"What good are the orchids and pearls if I can't be alone with her?" He put his feet down.

"We might need some kind of cover, sir. I'll think of something. I believe she's filming on location."

"She is? Where?"

"She has a small part in a comedy. I can't remember the title. Wallace has to catch her before she leaves with the cast and crew for Tarlac today. She might not be on location for long. I'm guessing just one or two days."

How did he miss this? At least his aides had been keeping tabs. They were reliable. He puffed on the pipe. "Tarlac is on the way to Baguio. I can take her there while she's on location."

"Affirmative, sir. It's the best cover. After tomorrow's big maneuver, I'll see to it that you'll have some time for *your* maneuver."

"You should be court-martialed for such bad puns."

Captain Marsh grinned.

"What time does the maneuver start tomorrow?"

"O-six-hundred, sir. I'll make sure your driver knows."

"Thank you."

After Marsh left, MacArthur riffled through the papers before him. A pile of correspondence needed his reply. Another heap awaited his signature. The rest he must peruse.

And, of course, the latest War Plan Orange file. He began reading it. A bolt of energy shot through him, his heart fluttering. It would take more than a bad report to dampen his newfound enthusiasm. Only twenty-four hours till the maneuver. After that, he would take Isabel to Baguio.

# 9.

A KISS ON THE FOREHEAD awakened Isabel. For a confused moment, she didn't know where she was. When she opened her eyes, MacArthur's face hovered over hers. He wore sunglasses and an Army cap, the sunset a brilliant orange on the horizon. "We're here, darling," he said.

She had slept through the last hour of the trip from Tarlac to Baguio. His limousine was parked in front of a white house with dark green trim. Pine trees and thick rose bushes surrounded it.

The chauffeur opened the car door. The chilly breeze jolted her, the sleeveless dress unsuitable for Baguio's mountain weather. She wrapped her arms around herself.

"Here, I think you need this." MacArthur removed his Army khaki jacket and draped it around her shoulders.

He got out of the car and she followed suit. He carried her leather valise with one hand and clutched her hand with his other hand. They sauntered down the paved path to the house. How touching that MacArthur had not only given up his jacket but also carried her luggage. How sweet—a far cry from the nasty old man with a foul mood at Tropical Nights.

A Filipino maid opened the front door and ushered them into the living room. MacArthur said hello to the other servants in the kitchen. He treated restaurant managers, waiters, drivers, and servants like he was running for mayor. She couldn't decide whether he was a politician or an actor at heart. Either way, the effect was the same. He charmed the masses without any effort.

She waited for him in the living room and stared at the portrait hanging above the fireplace. When MacArthur came back, she asked, "Who's this man?"

He took off his sunglasses and set them on the coffee table. "That's John Hay. This camp is named after him. He was secretary of state under President Teddy Roosevelt."

"Whose house is this?"

"Mine. That is, it was built for the American commanding general in the Philippines. Right now, that's me, and this house is my vacation home. Welcome to my home." He tilted her chin up, then kissed her lips. "You look tired."

"I've been working long hours for such a small part. I can't afford to turn it down." She stepped back and smoothed down the front of her dress. "This morning, we got up at the crack of dawn because the director wanted to catch the sunrise for a scene outside the church. The sunrise came and went, but we never left. I'd been on the set for nine hours straight when you arrived. It takes nine hours to prepare for a scene that will run for five minutes on screen. And you think acting is easy."

"No, I never said that." He sat on the couch, took off his cap. "Why don't you come here?" He patted his lap.

She sat beside him instead.

He sighed. "I know you work very hard, and that's why we're here. I want you to take a break."

"I'm going to miss a scene tomorrow morning."

"Another sunrise scene by the church?"

The Commander was in a teasing mood, which annoyed her all the more.

"I'll take you back to Tarlac tomorrow, if that's what you want."

"It will be too late. I have only one more scene, and it's first thing in the morning. If I'm not there, they'll find someone else. They won't wait for me."

"Don't you want to be with me?"

She pursed her lips into a frown. She wanted to be with him, but did it have to be always on his terms? The way he beamed at her meant yes. Douglas MacArthur expected everything to be according to his schedule. "Of course I want to be with you."

A servant knocked and asked the Commander what time he wanted dinner. He turned to Isabel, who shrugged.

"How about you prepare dinner now?" he told the servant. "After that, you can call it a day. Tell the others. You can take tonight and tomorrow off." To Isabel, he said, "Darling, you want a drink?"

She shook her head. "I'd like to freshen up first."

In the bathroom, she shut the door and leaned against it. She drew a deep breath.

MacArthur's unexpected visit had pleased her at first. How many girls ever got visited by the American commander? She'd been only too glad to introduce him around. She had expected him to stay in Tarlac for a day, while she worked. She'd snagged the role as one of the leading lady's sidekicks at the last minute, substituting for an actress who had fallen ill. It was a bit part, but an opportunity just the same.

But did the Commander care? No siree. He had his own plans. He wanted to take her *somewhere special*. Oh, that could only mean one thing. After Stanley McBride's approval of Papa's loan, she'd fully expected to return the favor. But why now?

A trip to Camp John Hay would have been a lovely treat at any other time. The Coopers had never been here before. It was an exclusive rest-and-recreation camp for American military personnel and their guests. There were non-military cottages and hotels in Baguio, but the Coopers couldn't afford them. In as much as she was thrilled to see the "tropical Berkshires," it was poor timing. Try explaining that to the Commander. She powdered her face and put on some lipstick. She had to make the most out of the trip. When Lieutenant Wallace brought her the orchids, he'd explained how important the military maneuver was. The entire Philippine garrison would be mobilized as though the Japanese were there to attack. She'd made the mistake of saying, "But it's only a pretend attack." Wallace had looked like she'd slapped him in the face. Oh, heavens.

But Wallace had made his point. The Commander was a busy man. Stealing away to Baguio was a luxury. He wanted to be with her, to pamper her with the beauty of Baguio and the comforts of a chauffeured car and a vacation home. And, of course, she mustn't forget about that huge favor to Papa.

Back in the living room, the electric lamps were on and the door to the balcony was open. MacArthur stood facing the manicured garden in the backyard. There were wicker chairs and a small table with a hurricane lamp behind him. He gazed upward, watching the bluish pall covering the sky. He looked sad. Was it because the sunset was gone, or because she'd been cold to him earlier?

She put on his huge Army jacket before stepping onto the balcony. It felt and looked like a blanket. No matter.

She stood beside him. "Do you come here often?"

He glanced sideways. "You mean, Baguio? No. Not anymore."

She placed her hands on the balcony railing. "When was the last time you were here?"

"Last year."

"I would come here every month if I were you."

"I'm too busy. It was Louise and the children who liked coming here."

"Children?"

"She has two children from a previous marriage."

"Oh." The mere mention of the former Mrs. MacArthur inflamed her. Was she the reason why he looked sad? Was he remembering a time spent with her on this balcony? Giving up a movie role to be with him was bad enough, being reminded that another woman once stood in her stead was worse.

She turned around abruptly.

"Where are you going?" he said.

"Inside. It's getting dark."

"Stay here a little longer." He lit the lamp on the table. He smiled with a sheepish expression. "Is that better?"

How handsome he looked in his uniform. And the way his eyes held her gaze—it was as if she, not the lamp, lit the balcony.

She nodded. "Yes, that's better. Thank you."

"Would you like a drink now?"

"Actually, I would like to make you a drink."

He looked puzzled.

"I've been irritable and you don't deserve it. I'll make you a drink. Brandy?"

"Sure."

"Do you like mango?"

"Love it."

In the dining room, she picked the ripest mango from a fruit bowl. She asked a servant to dice it and to bring some crushed ice. When the woman came back, Isabel mixed brandy with ice and mango. She brought the drinks to the balcony.

"What's this?" said MacArthur.

"My own concoction."

He took a sip. "Wow!"

"Do you like it?"

"I love it."

She took a sip as well, pleased.

"What's in it?" He tilted his glass, appraising the drink.

"Spanish brandy, crushed ice, and mango."

"What do you call it?"

She moved closer, looking up to him, searching his blue eyes. "I think I'll call it the Douglas."

He laughed. "Darling, you'll have a hard time convincing other people to drink anything called Douglas."

"Who cares about other people? I made this drink for you."

"For me?"

"For you alone."

He caressed her cheek, bringing his face close to hers. She held her breath in anticipation of a kiss. It didn't come.

*Dios mio*, was he saving it for later? She rested her head on his chest, hiding her disappointment. He put his arms around her, the glass still in his right hand.

She was like a lighthouse sending out signals, which his boat continuously missed. He wanted her on his lap when she was vexed, but now that she was ready for a kiss, he gave her a hug. Was it always going to be like this? Was it because he was old? Or because he was a foreigner? Maybe both.

They kept their embrace without speaking. She listened to the soft thud of his heart and the cawing of birds in the distance.

The tree branches clattered in the breeze. She inhaled the brisk mountain air and her dismay dwindled. She began to feel at home. She belonged right here in his arms, in this luxurious vacation home at the exclusive resort in picturesque Baguio, the ballyhooed Asian Adirondacks. If only she could stay in this moment forever.

A maid rapped on the door, breaking the tender moment. Dinner was ready.

After the helpers left, Isabel played mistress of the house. She served the steak dinner and made coffee. It was wonderful to walk around the big house, use the expensive china and silverware, and take whatever she wanted from the well-stocked kitchen without regard for cost. How grand! She could get used to this.

The night grew colder and the sound of the crickets louder. Unlike in Manila, there were no mosquitoes in Baguio. She prepared another round of the "Douglas," while he lit the kindling in the fireplace. A phonograph sat in the living room, but he only had classical music. How old-fashioned.

They spread a white-and-yellow quilt on the rug, by the fireplace. They were sitting there with their drinks when he gave her a present. She opened the box—the most exquisite pearl necklace she'd ever seen. He put it around her neck, kissing her nape.

"This is the first genuine pearl necklace I've ever owned." The first genuine *piece* of jewelry was more like it. She wore only costume baubles, a cruel joke considering her grandfather once owned a jewelry store. Both the store and her grandfather were long gone.

"I'm glad you like it."

This time, she needed no coaxing to sit on his lap. She pressed her lips on his, but as soon as he reciprocated, she got up. She moved backward, one step at a time, wanting him to follow her to the bedroom.

His eyes widened in apparent alarm. "What's the matter?"

She stopped. Oh, her little dance of seduction was lost on MacArthur. His boat had missed yet another signal. She recognized the expression, the sternness that camouflaged fear. Not too long ago, under different circumstances, she herself had asked Eddie Palma that question. Anyone afraid of being rejected probably looked that way.

"Nothing's the matter." The plan to lead him to the bedroom had failed, but she kept her frustration at bay.

She inched closer, sliding her fingers through the length of the pearl necklace. "Did you think I was going to run away?"

He rose. For the second time, she expected to be kissed. Again, he did not.

He played a record on the phonograph. "Chopin," he said. "The first Nocturne."

She stood beside him, riffling through the records. "Don't you have Al Jolson? I like Al Jolson."

"Louise liked him too. Sorry, I don't have any of his records."

*Louise again.* The fire hissed. Her cheeks grew hot. She held her breath and waited for his move.

Nothing happened. "Why did you bring me here?" she said.

He faced her, his blue eyes mesmerizing.

And just like that, he unbuttoned the front of her dress. It slid easily. The chemise and the underpants even more so. She stepped out of her high heels. When all she had left on was the pearl necklace, he fell back on the quilt, his weight resting on his elbows.

Her skin rippled in goose bumps. She was as vulnerable as butter melting in heat. She filled her chest with breath, imagining a stage. What was this but a performance? The music wasn't right for a dance, but she swayed her hips.

No hurry. She let him ogle her like a coveted prize in a display case. Drive him mad with desire—let him look without touching.

The opposite was true. Her heart raced in anticipation of the first touch. She grew damp between her legs. "Are you going to just stare all night?"

The corners of his lips turned up in a mischievous smile. "Why not? We have all the time in the world."

Her face bloomed with heat. She forced a smile. How could she be the Commander's coveted prize when it was she who craved his touch? It was she who wanted him with such urgency her heart might just explode.

He leaned forward and pulled her toward him. She fell into his arms. "You know, you were right," he said. "I was afraid you'd run away." He corralled her with his embrace, his breath warm on her face. "Now you can't."

# 10.

# June 1930

ISABEL WIPED the face of the antique Santo Niño statue with a cotton rag, gently, like a mother caring for her child. The wooden statue was a foot tall, the paint on its face so faded that the infant Jesus appeared to have only one eye and half a mouth. His right hand was long gone, but the left hand still carried the globe with a cross on top.

If she had anything better to do, she wouldn't be spending Thursday afternoon dusting off Lola's collection of Santo Niño statues. She couldn't find a job in motion pictures or the theater, not even a performance at a town fiesta or the circus. On top of that, she had quit school two weeks ago.

The thought of this "transgression," as her mother called it, deflated her spirits. Papa had been disappointed, and Ben had scoffed at her decision, but Mama had been furious. Since then she'd barely spoken to her. Isabel had been eating meals at the ground-floor home of her grandmother. In effect, she'd been banished. She only went upstairs at night to sleep in her room. She spent most of her time with Lola, who was more forgiving. Her grandmother was a self-taught woman who didn't care for formal education.

That afternoon, Lola and her long-time servant whom Isabel and Ben called Manang, meaning "big sister," were out shopping at the wet market in Quiapo. Isabel didn't go with them. She hated the stench of fish and slaughtered pigs, the endless haggling, the muddy ground.

After cleaning the statue's face, she removed his tiny gold crown and red velvet garments. She dusted off its naked body, feeling sorry for the missing hand. Lola had been a devotee of Santo Niño ever since her husband's jewelry store was spared from a terrible fire thirty years ago. An *insurrecto*, a remnant insurgent who once fought the Spaniards, had set fire to bazaars and restaurants in Chinatown. A message of discontent over American colonial rule. Entire blocks had been engulfed in flames, but the arsonist's fire had stopped outside Isabel's grandfather's store. Was it any coincidence the Santo Niño with the missing right hand had been inside the store? No, Lola didn't think so. She'd proclaimed it a miracle.

If there was anyone in dire need of a miracle, it was Isabel. She prayed quietly as she dressed the statue with a gold-and-silver robe that Lola had sewn.

*Santo Niño, forgive me for quitting school. You know I'm not a good student, so why bother? You gave me the talent to act, sing, and dance, so why not let me do that instead? Please, please help me get a job as soon as possible, or I'll lose my mind.*

The figurine's face shone, the gems on his garments sparkled. She hoped he would answer her prayer, and soon. Should she pray for the Commander too? At the thought of MacArthur, she fingered the pearl necklace underneath her blouse. She made sure it was tucked inside, or her grandmother might notice. She wore the necklace underneath her dress every day.

Without any job or prospects, it was the only thing that made her feel special. Someone important had chosen her. *Santo Niño, please bless the Commander for he's the only one who understands me. He cares about me. Maybe he even loves me.*

Maybe she should have waited until she got a new job before quitting the convent school, but she couldn't have endured another day, another hour spent memorizing Latin prayers she didn't understand, not another minute listening to a nun criticize her Spanish or her penmanship or her embroidery.

Isabel had spent her newfound freedom accompanying Lola to various errands and helping around the house. "Freedom" had quickly turned to boredom. By the second week of her idleness, she had run out of things to do. She'd wanted to see MacArthur. She hadn't seen him for a month, not since their trip to Baguio.

He had sent her two letters, more orchids, a box of American chocolates, and a lavender silk chiffon dress to make up for his absence. He had alternately sent Captain Marsh and Lieutenant Wallace to bring presents. The aides had explained what was keeping the Commander busy—something to do with the training of Filipino Scouts and meetings with visiting Navy General Board members or something or the other. Heavens, she no longer remembered half of it. She understood only that he was a busy, busy man.

MacArthur had always come to her, or sent his aides. He was the one who needed her, or so it seemed. She didn't even know how to get in touch with him. She knew where he worked and where he lived, but she'd never been to either place. She'd bribed Ben to deliver a note to the Commander. He'd taken it to one of MacArthur's aides at the Army and Navy Club, where most American officers spent their evenings.

The following day, MacArthur's limousine had picked her up during siesta when Lola and the servant napped. The chauffeur had dropped her off at a Spanish mansion on Calle Victoria in the walled section of Manila. The Commander had been waiting inside.

She told him she had quit school and expected him to scold her like the other adults. *I understand.* That was all he'd said before showing her the bedroom upstairs. The room was huge. She couldn't help but do a pirouette turn—her hair flying, her skirt blowing, and the Commander laughing. Next to the room, a veranda revealed the most spectacular view of Manila Bay. They'd held hands as they watched seagulls gliding along the water, hunting for fish.

He had taken her in his arms and onto his bed. The breeze had been deliciously cool. They could hear the waves splashing from a distance. It was as if no one and nothing could ever hurt her. Not the people who had rejected her in countless auditions, not the nuns who had deemed her unpromising, not even Mama and her wounding accusations. She wanted to be with him forever.

After an hour, he'd gone back to work, but she'd stayed. She'd traipsed through the place, the sight of a bathroom shower making her giddy. At home, there were many days when water barely trickled from the faucet. So, she'd stood naked underneath MacArthur's glorious shower for the longest time, letting the water crash on her face, pretending it was her very own waterfall. It was wonderful. Then the chauffeur had driven her back to Calle Herran.

A couple of days later, MacArthur and Isabel had done the same thing. Siesta was the only time he enjoyed privacy at home. In the evening, his aides came home with him. They were all bachelors and they shared the house. Other officers lived at Fort McKinley with the rest of the troops, so MacArthur didn't complain in spite of the lack of privacy. He'd changed the work hours of the servants and gardeners, so the house was empty during siesta. As for Isabel, her banishment to her grandmother's apartment was a blessing in disguise. She could sneak out without repercussions. She'd been to his mansion four times in one week.

She moved on to the next Santo Niño in the collection. It was smaller than the previous one, so dusting it off was trickier. Sighing, she begged the infant Jesus for a job, anything at all. MacArthur had promised to get her a part in a new vaudeville. She was dying to get back on stage.

The front door opened. Manang came in, carrying a basket loaded with fish and vegetables.

Lola followed suit with bundles of cloth and lace. "Look who's here to see you!"

Nenita entered. She wore a blue-and-white school uniform, a book satchel in her hand. "Hello, Belle."

"Oh, Nenita!" She jumped up and hugged her friend.

"We stopped by Quiapo Church to light a candle, and there she was—your dearest *amiga*—praying before the Nuestro Padre Jesus Nazareno." Lola's voice trailed off as she proceeded to the kitchen. The servant followed her.

She and Nenita sat on the sofa in the living room. "Sister Petra misses you," said Nenita.

Isabel made a face. "She's practically blind from old age."

"Blind or not, she still misses you. She wants you to come back. It's not too late. The nuns will take you back if you apologize."

"Only the blind nuns like me. I'm never going back there."

"I wish you'd reconsider. That's why I went to church today, you know."

"To pray for my soul?"

"To pray for your enlightenment."

"Shouldn't you be praying for Fabian Elizalde's enlightenment?"

Nenita smiled, her cheeks turning pink.

Isabel widened her eyes. "Has he called on you?"

Her friend nodded. "Last Sunday, he asked my parents if he could take me to the *baile* at Ateneo de Manila. I couldn't believe my ears!"

"He's in love with you."

"You think so?"

"Why else would he invite you to a dance at his university?"

A lock of stray hair fell over Nenita's left eye.

Isabel leaned forward to tuck it behind her ear, marveling at her friend's flawless face, her waist-long tresses, her good fortune. If only she could be as lucky. The Elizalde heir was going to show Nenita off at one of Manila's most exclusive social events. She was a girl whom men introduced to society, while Isabel was someone whom men kept a secret.

Why did she allow MacArthur to meet her during siesta? He wasn't married, so why was he being secretive? When she'd asked him this question, he'd said he wanted privacy. He didn't want the public to scrutinize his personal affairs. Like a dumbbell, she'd accepted his explanation. Like a harlot, she'd rushed in and out of his mansion according to his whims.

At the thought, Isabel groaned.

"What's wrong?" said Nenita.

Telling the truth wasn't an option. Instead she said, "I'm desperate to get a job. I don't know what to do with myself."

"Can General MacArthur help you? I don't care for him at all, but my father says MacArthur has the ears of Governor-General Davis and President Hoover." Nenita crossed her arms over her chest. "If he's *that* influential, I'm sure he can help you. Your Papa told my parents the general watched you perform at Tropical Nights. Has he called on you?"

"No, he hasn't."

MacArthur never called on her because she'd been too willing to meet him in secret. The image of the fireplace in Baguio flashed in her mind. There had been blood stains on the quilt. He'd concluded she was a virgin.

In fact, the blood was from the onset of her menstruation. She didn't have the courage to correct his misconception. So she let him believe it was her first time, that he was her first lover. And the drink she'd concocted for MacArthur? She'd called it the Douglas. Well, Eddie Palma used to make it for her. Guilt nudged her heart.

She pressed her lips together. What's the harm of a lie here and there? MacArthur was the type who needed to be pleased. Sometimes lies—not truth—were more pleasing.

"Maybe it's for the best that he hasn't called on you," continued Nenita. "I'm sure there's someone better for you."

"I agree. I want someone better, not an old man and divorced to boot."

Nenita slid closer, whispering, "He hasn't tried to kiss you, has he?"

"Heavens, no! Do you think I'd let him touch me?"

"No, I didn't think so. Besides, how could he try, if he hasn't even called on you. How silly of me." Nenita giggled.

Isabel gave her a wan smile. She couldn't tell her that after her first afternoon with the Commander, he no longer bothered taking her to bed. His bedroom on the second floor seemed too far away, the long staircase too much of an inconvenience. Just yesterday, they had managed to reach only the second step before they'd stripped their clothes. This morning, the delicate spot below her navel had twitched in pleasure at the memory of her straddling him on the stairs. Now, in front of Nenita, the thought disgusted her.

She had kept too many secrets from Nenita as it was. She wouldn't know how to begin to tell her everything about MacArthur. She trained her gaze on the Santo Niño with the missing right hand. The infant Jesus would never grant the prayers of a lascivious girl. If only she could find a job, then she wouldn't go to Calle Victoria anymore.

She turned to her friend. "I need a job. If I don't get a part soon, I'll kill myself."

Nenita swatted her hand. "Don't say that!"

Isabel's grandmother called out from the dining room. "*Hijas*, let's have some *merienda*. How about some rice cakes and a nice cup of cacao?"

"I'm not hungry," said Nenita. "Let's go to the garden and sit in the hammock."

"Lola might think we're conspiring."

"Well, we're not."

"I don't want to cross her, or she'll banish me too."

"Is that pearl necklace new?"

Isabel adjusted the collar of her blouse to cover it. "No. It's the same fake pearls I've been wearing."

"Don't hide it underneath your collar." Nenita leaned closer and lifted the strand to display it on Isabel's neck. "There. It's so beautiful. I would have never guessed it's fake."

"You never could tell genuine from fake."

Nenita pinched Isabel's thigh playfully. They chuckled.

"Don't you want to talk?" asked Nenita. "We can go outside."

"No, we better not."

"Are you sure?"

She nodded. She led her to the dining room. By all means, it was better to feed one's best friend with rice cakes than more lies.

# 11.

# July 1930

MACARTHUR and a bespectacled man, Colonel Thomas Rooney, sat on the veranda at the second floor of the Army and Navy club, overlooking Manila Bay. A partial moon appeared on the horizon. The light from a passing fishing boat flickered like a firefly.

"For your eyes only." Rooney handed him an envelope.

A letter from General Charles Pelot Summerall, the Army chief of staff. He read it—President Hoover wanted to appoint him as the new chief of engineers. The White House would announce the decision as soon as MacArthur accepted the offer. The president was waiting for his response.

He shook his head as he folded the letter.

"Doug, don't say no yet."

He waved the paper close to Rooney's face. "What's this supposed to mean?"

"It's a great opportunity."

"I didn't ask for this. I asked for a bigger budget—tanks, guns, trucks, and ammunition to defend these islands. Not this."

Rooney raised his index finger. "Philippine defense is a separate matter."

"Not to me."

"Doug—"

"I can't just leave this country and tell the Filipinos…by the way, you're on your own when the Japs attack. If Washington can't give me enough money for the defense of this country, then the War Plan Orange is a sham! We can't grant the Filipinos independence unless they're ready to defend themselves."

"Just hear me out, please." Rooney wiped his foggy spectacles with a handkerchief. "Jesus, how can you stand this humidity?" His khaki uniform was damp, his graying hair, slick from sweat.

Even with the sea breeze, the night remained sultry. MacArthur shrugged. "I quite like it. It feels salubrious."

Rooney knitted his eyebrows together.

"It's an acquired taste. You have to live here to appreciate it."

"I can't decide which is worse, you liking this horrid, sticky weather, or you using the word *salubrious.*"

"Don't forget frisson and recreant and equipoise. You liked those words, if I remember correctly."

"You're still the only man I know who uses those words."

MacArthur shook his head and smiled.

Rooney put his spectacles back on. "I'm sorry you didn't get the budget you asked for. There's no money for Philippine defense. Even if you stay here forever, there still won't be any money. It's nothing personal. It's not about you."

More men arrived—all American officers. The club was exclusive. A few of them slowed down when they saw MacArthur, out of deference or out of curiosity. He nodded in their general direction.

After the noise from the comings and goings subsided, Rooney continued, "However, this new appointment is about you. The president handpicked you. He wants to reorganize the Army Corps of Engineers. He needs an innovator to implement the Flood Control Act."

MacArthur smirked. "An innovator?"

"Someone who's not afraid of the establishment. He wants you to revamp the Corps just like you overhauled West Point. No one could have changed West Point the way you did. And besides, General Summerall thought this might be of sentimental value, considering you started with the Corps."

MacArthur turned his gaze toward the water, to the dots of light blinking from fishing boats, then back to Rooney. "When I was with the Corps, I killed two desperadoes. Not only that, I nearly died from malaria. Talk about sentimental value."

"It's precisely why you're the man for the job—you always come out on top!" Rooney chuckled.

A waiter brought whiskey. MacArthur took a sip, letting his friend order steaks for both of them. He didn't have the appetite, not after being reminded of that afternoon twenty-seven years ago on the Philippine island of Guimaras. The Corps had been constructing piers and docks. He'd taken a small detachment with him to cut timber in the jungle, known to be the hideout of brigands.

Neither outlaws nor the wilderness intimidated MacArthur. He grew up in military outposts on the Western frontier. One of his earliest memories was that of a march from Fort Wingate to Fort Selden in New Mexico, where his father's K Company guarded the fords of the Rio Grande against Geronimo's men. MacArthur had learned to ride and shoot before he could read or write. He grew up riding horses and tracking trails with the Apaches. No bandits could stop him. So, on that fateful afternoon more than two decades ago, when two armed Filipinos had ambushed him on a narrow jungle trail, he'd shot them dead. He was twenty-three.

He'd been hailed as a hero. The path for building his own reputation apart from the illustrious name he shared with his father had opened up.

While he enjoyed the attention, the experience had not felt heroic. He took pride in his skills as a marksman, but he'd been unprepared for the shock of witnessing two men go down from shots he'd fired. One moment he'd been exhilarated to see how powerful a pistol was. The next moment he'd thrown up from the burnt smell of gun powder, the sight of human blood spilling—the realization of his own stark power. Right or wrong, hero or not, he had killed two men. It devastated him. It was almost as if he'd willed the malaria that followed. He'd been glad to leave the Philippines.

"Lytle Brown is the man for the job." MacArthur tucked the letter in a pocket of his khaki uniform. "That's my recommendation. Tell General Summerall."

"Tell him yourself. While you're at it, you can tell the president, too."

"For Christ's sake."

Rooney looked him square in the eyes. "I'm here to convince you to take the job. Come back to the States."

"Stop acting like Summerall's courier, for God's sake." MacArthur gave him a dismissive wave of a hand. "Make this a vacation. There's plenty to see and do around here. Did you see the walls of Intramuros on the way here? Take a walking tour of old Manila. Drive up north to Baguio. It's beautiful up there."

"I just got off a ship. I traveled ten thousand miles for five weeks. I'm sweaty and wet as a mop. I have a headache as thick as the fucking walls of Intramuros. Stop kidding me." Rooney downed his whiskey.

MacArthur exhaled a sharp breath. He took out a metal tube from his pocket. It contained two cigars. He offered one to his friend. They took turns using MacArthur's folding knife to cut their cigars. They smoked without speaking, just watched the waiters who carried bunks to the veranda. The men pushed the beds against the wall.

"What are those for?" asked Rooney.

"For the idiots who are too drunk to go home. It's called the Officers' Row."

They both chuckled and reminisced about their own drunken misadventures.

After a while, Rooney said, "Is it the job of chief of engineers you don't like, or is it the idea of leaving Manila that's eating you up?"

MacArthur drew cigar smoke slowly into his mouth, letting it linger there before exhaling. "I don't know what you mean."

"Doug, I've heard stories."

"I still don't know what you mean."

"Here. Take it." Rooney handed MacArthur a brown paper bag. It contained a small bottle of Chanel perfume and an Al Jolson record called "Swanee."

"Much obliged, Tom. I was afraid my radiogram was too late."

"I got lucky with the French perfume. It just so happened my sister-in-law was back from Paris."

MacArthur set the paper bag on an empty chair beside him. "They're presents for Mrs. Quezon. I've gotten quite close to Manuel and his wife."

"Quezon is the slick politico, right?"

"He's the president of the Philippine Senate. He's a good man, but he has many detractors, so don't believe everything you hear about him. His wife, Aurora, is lovely. She makes the most sublime Spanish flan. She embroidered a *barong* Tagalog for me. The shirt is so beautiful I'm afraid to wear it. I want to give her something in return."

"I can understand the French perfume. But Mrs. Quezon listens to Al Jolson?"

MacArthur let the comment slide. "I should introduce you to the Quezons. You'll love them. They invite me for lunch almost every Sunday. You should come with me this Sunday."

Rooney puffed a small cloud of smoke. "How about you introduce me to Dimples instead?"

MacArthur took a sip of whiskey. "How are Rose and the kids?"

"Rose sends her love. The kids want pineapples."

"Pineapples?"

"Don't change the subject. Tell me about Dimples."

The waiter arrived with their food. MacArthur sliced his steak meticulously if only to delay the conversation. He had known Rooney since West Point. The two of them had survived the most horrific hazing as plebes, during which MacArthur had fainted, and later on, he'd testified before a special court about the incident. Rooney had also been with him for eighty-two days of combat on the Lorraine front in France during the Great War. Thomas Rooney had been his only friend at his wedding.

He set the steak knife aside. "Her name is Isabel. Dimples is just a *nom de guerre*. She's an actress, a performer."

"A very young one, from what I've heard." Rooney's voice dripped with sarcasm.

"For Christ's sake."

"Talk to me."

"What's there to talk about?"

"Why her?"

"Why not her?"

Rooney grabbed the salt and pepper shakers and sprinkled a copious amount of the condiments on his steak and potatoes. "I take it your mother doesn't know. I saw her two days before I left, and she didn't mention anything about Isabel."

"Well, what did she say?"

"Come back home. Also, she wanted to know if you've received a letter she sent in April, and why the hell haven't you responded?"

MacArthur rolled his eyes.

Rooney began eating, wiping grease from his lips with a table napkin. "Take the job in Washington and make your mother happy."

"You, of all people, know I deserve something better."

"You want a promotion, right? This is a huge promotion. This is very important to the president. That's why Summerall sent me here. Take the job."

"No."

"Your father would have wanted you to take this job."

MacArthur took a big bite of steak and chewed fiercely. "My father was a captain for twenty-three years before he got promoted to assistant adjutant general. Twenty-three years! He never became chief of staff, even though everyone knew he deserved it. I will not settle for less. My father would turn in his grave if I did that."

"Doug—"

"The answer is no." His nerves buzzed with resentment over his father's mistreatment.

"Talk about graves—you're digging your own professional grave. You'll be stuck here for ages. Or maybe that's what you want."

MacArthur drained his drink and held back a retort. Rooney wasn't the problem, after all. "You have to try Filipino beer. It's my favorite." He waved at a waiter, who scrambled to his side. "Two glasses of Cerveza San Miguel, please."

As soon as the man left, Rooney said, "Do you love her?"

"I don't know."

"The last time I asked you this question, you also didn't know. Then you got married a month later. We both remember how that ended."

"At least I'm happy."

"Tell me more about her."

MacArthur attacked a mound of mashed potatoes. Why did he have to answer to anyone about his affairs? It was bad enough he sneaked around like a recreant just to be with Isabel. *Recreant*. Yes, that was one of the words Rooney hated because he had to look it up in the dictionary.

MacArthur dreaded asking Rooney about the stories circulating in Washington. He'd stopped seeing Isabel, at least for now, because of all the goddamn talk. Manila was like a huge quilting bee that patched lies upon lies without end.

One day, rumor had it MacArthur was seeing a sixteen-year-old actress named Dimples. The following day, Dimples was neither sixteen nor an actress, but a twenty-year-old whore, according to gossip. Then it was said MacArthur got a loan for Dimples' father. After that, the story grew worse. Rumormongers alleged MacArthur paid the father ten thousand dollars to sleep with Dimples. Where did these stories come from?

Genuine quilting bees at least combined tittle-tattle with actual work. Manila's equivalent only sewed layers upon layers of exaggerated stories, creating a quilt of vicious fabrications that led to other people's ruination.

Was it any wonder Isabel had quit school? Of course, she'd intended to drop out, but the rumors hastened her decision. She was tough. The innuendos couldn't stop the girl from auditioning for the Diamond Theater's new vaudeville production. That MacArthur had prodded Manuel Quezon to recommend her to the show's director was beside the point. What mattered was she refused to let anyone stymie her ambition. MacArthur admired such quality in her. *The hell with the gossip.*

He gobbled up his food, astonished at how famished he'd been. He covered his mouth with a napkin and belched as quiet as could be. "My private life is nobody's business but mine." He glared at Rooney. "I'm divorced. I'm free to see anybody."

Rooney stopped mid-bite, his eyebrows raised. "She's not just anybody, she happens to be a juvenile. And Filipino. Yes, you're divorced, but you're *not* free. You're Douglas MacArthur, and that means you're *not* free to screw a native. You're *not* free to screw the United States Army and the government. Jesus, Doug!"

MacArthur's face burned. "What exactly do you want me to do?"

Rooney shoved the half-bitten piece of meat into his mouth. He spoke while chewing. "Forget the girl. Accept the president's offer and come back home."

"I can't do that."

A soused officer lurched toward a waiter who carried an armful of china. The plates crashed, stopping every conversation in the room. The officer and the waiter got up. Other waiters rushed to sweep the debris off the floor. Everyone went back to eating and talking.

"Listen," said Rooney. "If you turn down the president, the entire Washington establishment will never forgive you."

"So be it."

Their waiter arrived with two glasses of beer. MacArthur took a long drink, the beer gurgling as it went down his throat.

Rooney took a swig and winced. "What the fuck is this? It's bitter as hell."

"*Cerveza negra*."

"This is your favorite?"

"It's an acquired taste."

Rooney shook his head. "I'll never understand you."

"No, I don't suppose you will."

# 12.

MACARTHUR AND ROONEY left the Army and Navy Club an hour before midnight. They drove straight to MacArthur's mansion, where Rooney was going to stay for the duration of his visit. Captain Marsh greeted them at the door, all slicked up for a night out.

Rooney complained about his headache and went to bed. MacArthur stopped Marsh before he could step outside. "Ed, wait a minute."

"Sir?"

They stood in the foyer, beside a console table.

"I need you to find Ben Cooper. Ask him to bring his sister," said MacArthur.

"Bring Isabel *here,* sir?"

"Shh." MacArthur brought his right forefinger to his lips. He'd been reduced to whispering in his own home, for God's sake. "Not here. She can't come here while Rooney is with us."

He conducted his affair the same way he fought a battle. He must outwit and outmaneuver the enemy, or in this case, anyone who disapproved of his relationship.

He rubbed his forehead to collect himself. Nobody would ever understand the way she made him feel, the futility of trying to forget her. He couldn't get her off his mind. Plain and simple, but impossible to explain to others. She crept into his every fantasy, his every goddamn thought. Her face, her scent, the electric sensation of her mouth on his, the incredible combination of supple breasts and hard nipples, the irresistible warmth of her thighs—everything about her drove him mad.

Thoughts of her crowded his mind all the time. She had rendered him defenseless. But this was a fling and such intensity—hell, such insanity—was the nature of romance. And so, he would fight this battle to win back his good sense.

"Sir, how about Manila Hotel?" said Marsh.

The question brought MacArthur's attention back to the problem at hand. *Logistics.* Planning was paramount, but he had no plans. He couldn't anticipate when and how his maddening desire would overtake him. "No hotels. You know that."

"Sir, it's late. Manila Hotel is less conspicuous at this time. There will be fewer guests."

"Even with fewer guests, the staff and the help will be there. They'll recognize me no matter the time of day."

"Of course, you're right." Marsh raised his gaze upward, toward the second floor, where Rooney slept.

Hands on hips, MacArthur looked up as well, almost regretting his decision to invite Rooney. "Have you got any suggestion?"

"I'd let you use Margaret's little apartment, but we need it tonight, sir." Marsh flashed a naughty smile.

"Margaret is the teacher from New Jersey?"

Marsh nodded. "I've been seeing her for six months now."

"Good for you. Have a great time tonight. I'll ask Wallace to help me. Where is he?"

"Calle San Sebastian."

"Is that where the rich Filipino widow lives?"

"Actually, it's where the widow's daughter lives."

"Wallace is seeing both mother and daughter?"

Marsh grinned. "They don't know that, sir."

"For God's sake. Tell Wallace to stop playing games. Those women will skin him alive if they find out."

"He's very discreet, sir." Marsh flicked his fingers, as though remembering something. "There's a place that's very discreet. It's perfect, at least for tonight."

"Where is it?"

"It's the old clinic just outside Fort McKinley."

MacArthur gave him a quizzical look. "I ordered that place closed because it's run-down. The troops deserve better, that's why we built a hospital."

"Absolutely, sir. But once in a while, the clinic is used as an overflow facility. You know...for vaccination of the children in the neighborhood, that sort of thing."

Marsh opened the drawer of the console table and retrieved a bunch of keys. He riffled through them until he found what he was looking for. "Sir, this is the key to the clinic."

"Why do you have this key?"

"Like I said, sir, it's a discreet place. Sometimes, we just need a place that's not a hotel or a house. Wallace uses it, and I've used it as well."

"What I mean is, how did you get the key?"

Marsh looked befuddled. "I work for you, General, so I can get all the keys I need."

"You used my name to get this key? I'm the man who shut down the clinic after spending one-third of my budget building a new hospital. Stop throwing my name around, for Christ's sake!"

He strode to the living room and fell onto an armchair.

Marsh followed suit. "I'm sorry, sir." He stuck his hands in his trouser pockets, his eyes cast downward. "After tonight, we can shut down the clinic for good. Should I give the key to the driver?"

"I already let him go. It's very late."

"Do you still want me to find Ben Cooper?"

He let out a long sigh. He couldn't afford to give up the chance to see Isabel just because his order to close a derelict clinic had been disobeyed. His fastidiousness was getting the better of him. He pressed his temples, exhaustion beginning to creep. "Do you know where to find Ben at this time?"

"It's either the new place called Circle or his old haunt, Tropical Nights."

The mere mention of Tropical Nights brought back the memory of Isabel in a tight-fitting beaded dress, crooning to a bunch of Chinks. It had pained him to see her in such a dump.

"I haven't seen her in twenty-six days." He groped his trouser pocket to find his pocket watch and glanced at it. "No, make that twenty-seven days. It's already midnight. Tom Rooney wants me to forget her. He wants me to take a job in Washington."

Marsh kept his gaze down, as if the clinic, Tom Rooney, and MacArthur's inability to see Isabel had all been his fault. "Sir, I'll go find Ben Cooper right now. Should I drop you off at the clinic before I get him?"

The speed of Marsh's decision amazed him. He would have spent all night brooding and feeling embattled, but his aide had already resolved the issue! Of course, he must see her. Even Marsh knew it.

"No, I'll drive there myself." He held up his right palm. Marsh pressed the key into MacArthur's hand and left.

Almost two hours later, MacArthur parked outside the small building near Fort McKinley, several blocks from a schoolhouse and a road that led to a residential area. The U.S. Army had bought the clinic from Spanish nuns who had administered basic medical needs to the poor.

Captain Marsh was right. The place was discreet, far enough from the barracks and the residential area both. He glanced at his pocket watch—two o'clock in the morning. He brought with him the brown paper bag with the goods from the States, courtesy of Tom Rooney.

MacArthur unlocked the clinic's door. The hinges squeaked; the wooden floor creaked with his every step. The ceiling paint was peeling off, but at least the electric light in what had been the reception room worked. A desk and several chairs were still there. The narrow patient beds had been stripped of their mattresses.

MacArthur set the paper bag on the desk and opened a window to let fresh air into the stuffy room. Unfortunately, the mosquitoes flowed in, as well. Outside, there was nothing but darkness and the silhouette of trees in the distance. He'd taken the time to wash up, shave, and change into a cotton suit and silk tie. He took off his jacket and hung it on the back of a chair.

Where was Isabel? He'd driven as fast as he could to make sure he arrived first. He scanned his surroundings, wishing for a cup of coffee. From his jacket pocket, he took a leather pouch containing his corncob pipe and a small tin of tobacco. He packed the pipe with tobacco and lit it with a match. He drew small puffs and paced the room. What was keeping her so long? What if Marsh didn't find Ben? What if she refused to come?

Along with the thoughts of Isabel invading his head at all hours, the unending questions came uninvited as well. A torrent of "whys" and "what ifs" kept him distracted during the day and restless at night. He'd always been confident—in school, on the battlefield, in the halls of bureaucracy, at home or overseas—until he met Isabel, who had ignored his note that night at the Olympic in such a flagrant manner. Nobody had done that to him before.

The disadvantages of falling for a woman of a different race and different generation were numerous. Just thinking about them exhausted him. The unconventional nature of their relationship bred a singular insecurity he hadn't experienced before. This lack of confidence—he needed to get a grip, for God's sake—was the worst part of it all. He couldn't get used to it.

Automobile tires crunched on the dirt road. *Isabel.* His heart pounded. He opened the door. To his relief, she stepped inside: a flurry of long hair, fringed shawl, and pleated skirts. She didn't greet him.

He expected to see Ben Cooper, but Captain Marsh had driven her. Marsh remained in the doorway. "Sir, is there anything else you need?"

"No, nothing else. Thank you, Ed."

Poor Marsh. He was very late indeed for his own tryst. MacArthur shut the door and leaned against it, relieved. She wore a pale pink blouse and pleated skirt, a picture of femininity punctured by the scarlet high-heeled shoes.

She inspected the room, the bare floor creaking underfoot. "What is this place?"

"It used to be a clinic." Thank God, the building had not been razed yet.

She waved her hand over her head, warding off mosquitoes. She pivoted around. "What on earth is going on? Why are we here?"

"Well, hello to you too, darling."

He walked up to her, his pipe in his left hand. He looped his right arm around her waist, drawing her toward him. "I missed you."

He bent his head to kiss her, but she placed a hand on his mouth. "Stop it." She broke away.

How irritating. After all the trouble it took just to see her. "You know, I expected your brother to drive you here." Marsh must have paid Ben Cooper enough money on MacArthur's behalf for this favor.

"He wanted to, but Captain Marsh said this place is *confidential.* He didn't want my brother to drive me." She stood by the desk, peeking at the brown bag. "What's this?"

"Presents for you."

She removed the contents, examined the Al Jolson record, and sniffed the perfume. She murmured thank you like he'd given her a glass of water. The presents had traveled ten thousand miles, the perfume from Paris even more. They'd arrived wrapped in Tom Rooney's self-righteous indignation. Her insouciance grated on him, but it need not ruin the occasion.

She took off her shawl, pulled a chair, and plopped on it. "My brother dragged me out of my bed. I didn't get a chance to put on any powder or lipstick." She opened the silk purse she always carried around, and took out a little mirror to look at her face. "*Dios mio*, I look horrible."

He smiled. Without any cosmetics on, her face was like porcelain, her eyes wide and intense. The beauty mark on her left cheek stood out. When she made a face, the lovely dimples appeared. If only he could kiss those pouting lips.

She applied red lipstick, ignoring him. Her tantrums irked him, but they added to her allure.

"Is the lipstick for me?" He pulled a chair and sat across from her, drawing deep puffs on his pipe.

She stared at the mirror. "What do you think?"

"It's unnecessary. Isn't it more important that I'm here at two o'clock in the morning against all odds?"

She dropped the mirror inside her purse and looked into his face. "You didn't attend my opening night."

*Ah, the opening night.* The vaudeville at the Diamond Theater opened two nights ago. If he'd been there, every rumormonger in Manila would have confirmed what a big fool the American commander was. How could he explain it to a sixteen-year-old girl?

"You wanted a job, so I got you a job with a reputable theater company in a respectable establishment. When we were in Baguio, you wanted Al Jolson music, so I got you an Al Jolson record. Is there any way I can please you at all?"

She crossed her arms and looked away with a churlish expression.

He couldn't help but smile. When she was petulant, she exuded a kind of innocence he found sexual. Every pout, every sigh teased him without mercy.

He'd been so tantalized it took him a while to notice the corncob pipe's light had gone out. He set it aside on the desk.

"Darling, President Hoover is offering me a promotion. Don't you want to hear about it?"

That got her attention. She shifted her gaze back to him. "President Hoover?"

"He wants me to be the chief of engineers."

"Well, congratulations." In the same breath, she slapped her arm, trying to kill a bug. "The mosquitoes will eat us alive."

She got up to close the window. She lingered there, her back toward him.

"Don't you want to know if I'm going to accept the job?"

Silence. She just stood there in those bright-red high heels and stared out the window.

"I'm going to say no. I'm going to turn down the president's offer."

She spun around, her eyes on fire. "I don't care what you do! You pay my brother to drag me in the middle of the night like you own me. You bring a record and a little bottle of perfume and I'm supposed to jump up and down with joy. I'm not a whore!"

His eyes narrowed. He didn't see *that* coming. "This is the only way for me to see you. I can't watch you perform at the Diamond. Everybody's talking about us already."

"So what? We have nothing to hide."

"You're right." He kept his tone conciliatory. "But I can't have people talking about us. It's too much of a distraction, and my position is too important to accommodate such a distraction."

He pushed away from the desk and walked toward her. He clasped her tiny waist with both hands, pulling her toward him. How he wanted this girl.

She slapped him.

He touched his cheek, stunned. His anger frothed high. The tantrum had ceased to be charming. He was Douglas MacArthur. Who did she think she was?

He answered her arrogant contempt with a staggering whack across her face.

She hit the floor. She scowled at him, nursing her lips. Did he draw blood? No, it was the smeared crimson lipstick. She didn't cry. She wasn't the type to cry.

"I'm turning down the president because of you." His vision blurred with fury. "I refused to go back to the States because of you!"

He grabbed both of her arms and pulled her up, then shoved her against the desk, face down. The corncob pipe, the silk purse, and the brown bag all spilled. The Al Jolson record broke. He pinned down her arms on the desk, his body covering her back. She bucked against him, her buttocks protruding, her feet kicking. Her shrieks were muffled.

"You said you're not a whore. You know what you are? A first-class cockteaser! That's just as good as a whore, so I'll treat you like one!" He swept her skirt up and yanked down the stockings and underpants in a single violent motion. He unbuttoned his fly, pushed his pants and drawers down, and slammed his body against her, taking her from behind.

His heart banged against his chest. His sheer bulk and force could crush her. He had killed men in combat. How hard could it be to snap the life out of a dainty little thing? The last thought struck him. This was rape! He withdrew from her abruptly.

"Goddamn it!" Panting and sweating, he pulled his drawers and pants up.

She turned around—her hair wild, her eyes ablaze. "Why did you stop?"

"What?" The pulse of violence throbbed in his temples.

She wiped the smeared lipstick on her mouth with the back of her hand. Then she flashed her bedimpled smile, tossing her hair back. "You can't stop now."

"What?" He'd heard it all right, but it didn't make sense. He expected a rebuke, more sulking.

Instead she sat on the desk, her bare legs glaring, the red high heels dangling. She reclined, her skirt hiking up a tad, the palms of her hands flat on the desk, like she was bracing for something.

The gesture was unmistakable. What a radical transformation from wrathful lover to lustful kitten, all in a moment. The battle was *against* them and *between* them. He could overcome the struggle against his detractors and the rumormongers. Hell, he had withstood enemy raids and gas attacks and fought the Germans hand to hand in the Great War, and came out unscathed. But now, for the first time in his life, he accepted the certainty of defeat.

# 13.

ISABEL WOKE UP to loud rapping on her bedroom door. She glanced at the clock on her dresser—two o'clock. In the afternoon. She'd slept ten hours straight after her tryst with MacArthur in the godforsaken clinic near Fort McKinley.

She got up, struck by the soreness between her legs. She opened the door.

"I left your lunch at the *comedor* downstairs," said Manang, Isabel's grandmother's servant. "There's hardly any water coming out of the faucet, so I'm going to fetch water from the pump." She shuffled away.

Isabel changed from a nightgown into a silk chiffon dress, MacArthur's gift. Her breasts and thighs showed bruises. Well, he'd given her those too. She wore the pearl necklace for good measure, so his presents and his memory covered her.

She went to her grandmother's dining room downstairs. The house was empty. Lola was out visiting a sick friend. Mama helped Papa at the car showroom. He took care of prospective American car buyers, while she talked to the Chinese mestizo customers. Only God knew where Ben was. Sometimes he helped Papa, but most of the time, he worked on an idiotic business scheme with his friends.

She sat down at the table, the *empanadas* already cold. Manang had also left her a ripe mango, sliced into two halves, its seed tucked between the two sides. She wrinkled her nose at the smell of the greasy meat pastry. At least, the mango was ripe and golden.

She spooned the tender mango flesh into her mouth, licking its juices from her lips. How much did Ben get for the early morning "errand"? That was how her brother had called it.

He'd driven her to Tropical Nights, where she hopped into another car with Captain Marsh. She'd been determined to give MacArthur a hard time for getting her out of bed in the wee hours and for missing the opening night of her vaudeville performance. Boy, was the Commander furious when she'd slapped him.

The incident at the clinic played out in her mind like scenes in a movie. He'd turned down the president of the United States because of her. What a revelation! He cared about her after all. It had been more than enough. She'd been willing to forgive him, but his rage had already been unleashed. Everything had happened fast.

If her slap had surprised MacArthur, she'd been doubly shocked when he slammed his body against her backside. She hadn't known until then that a man could enter her that way. Eddie Palma had never done that. Her impulse had been to resist, to kick and scream.

Just as fast, something had changed. The impact, the friction, his bulk on her, the sheer force—all combined, it gave her raw pleasure: sharp and intense. She'd been manhandled. But, was it really manhandling when it felt that good? So, when he'd stopped, she almost slapped him again. How dare he leave her unsatisfied!

It had not been a simple tryst, but a discovery. She'd learned how to have sexual intercourse on a desk in a dilapidated room, without ever lying down. MacArthur's unpredictability—the unselfish act of declining a promotion, his capacity for brutal pleasure—had jolted her into a brand new desire. It was like finding a new lover altogether.

She licked the mango's sweetness and succulence off the spoon. She'd finished eating both halves. Still not sated, she peeled the skin of the seed and bit the flesh covering it. When there was no more flesh to be had, she sucked on the seed itself, sticky juice trickling down her chin. *I want more, more, more.*

Her heart stirred. Douglas MacArthur had left her plump with pleasure, swollen with insatiable desire. It weakened her inside, as vulnerable as an overripe mango. She didn't know whether to love or hate him.

She wiped her mouth with a napkin and went to the kitchen sink to wash her hands. She stood there, her fingers under the faucet, and watched the water drip. Why was it that the Commander always got the better of her? Every time she wanted to punish him, he always left her wanting. It had been so much easier with Eddie.

She turned off the faucet and dried her hands with a kitchen towel. She hadn't expected to work with Eddie again, but he'd been cast as a substitute dancer in the vaudeville at the Diamond Theater. MacArthur had not asked about Eddie. He appeared unaware of Isabel's former lover.

Eddie had flirted with her during dance rehearsals, showering her with compliments and sultry stares. When she'd declined his invitation to go out for drinks, he'd said, "Don't you think Douglas MacArthur is too old for you?" She had laughed, knowing that her laughter alone would drive him crazy with ardor.

After she'd turned down Eddie a few more times, he had changed his tune and began talking about his plans to return to Hollywood. She'd told him, "You want to go back to being a busboy in Hollywood?"

His face had turned red, like a lobster caught in a boiling pot of water. He'd claimed he worked as a busboy in between jobs at Warner Bros. Most actors in Los Angeles did the same. Well, perhaps. She kept her distance. Their one-sided breakup still stung. Also, she couldn't risk any gossip that might reach the Commander's ears.

Her thoughts veered to Manang—still out—which in turn reminded her of MacArthur. Their fight last night had prompted the wild sex and obliterated any precaution. A terrible combination that made her smile, until her secret fears emerged. She must ask Manang for advice. She applied lipstick in a hurry and stepped into a pair of pumps. She would rather die than live without cosmetics and high-heeled shoes.

She emerged from the house with a parasol to protect her skin from the sun. She walked the short distance to the community water pump near a small plaza. The sun glared, the air remained muggy. Another oppressive day.

Two old men played *sungka* on a bench under a tree. The cowry shells they dropped into the holes of a long wooden board clanked—loud and monotonous in the stillness of the plaza. It was siesta time.

Manang waited behind a boy drawing water. She wore traditional Filipino clothes, the black skirt falling to her ankles. It must be uncomfortable in this heat. At least, her white *kimona* blouse was lightweight.

"What's the matter?" asked the old woman. "Don't you have a show to perform?"

"I'm going to the theater in a little while." Isabel chewed the inside of her cheek as her fears started afresh. "I want to ask you something."

The boy lugged two buckets, water spilling with his every step. Manang placed a wooden bucket underneath the pump and started drawing water, pushing the handle down.

"I think I made a mistake in my calendar," said Isabel.

The servant stopped. "A mistake?" She was a few years younger than Lola, but time had not been kind to her face. She looked battered by the years, covered by wrinkles and spots. Her teeth were stained from chewing tobacco. "How can you make a mistake? Can't you count?"

She was the hardest working and the most loyal servant Lola had ever had, but not the most cheerful. It seemed like she'd been born old and cantankerous. She'd lived with Lola for so long, so the family treated her like a relative, not a helper. Manang's husband had been dead for decades and her five children had left her without any resources, forcing her to work even in her old age.

Isabel closed the parasol. "Of course I can count. What I mean is…I made a poor choice on a Bad Day in my calendar. It may be the worst day in my calendar."

Manang made the tsk-tsk-tsk sound Isabel hated. Like a house lizard, noisy but harmless, so she couldn't, in conscience, kill it. The servant resumed drawing water, the pump's handle squeaking as it went up and down.

The old woman had also made the same lizard-like noise when Isabel sought her advice the first time. She'd been intimate with Eddie a few times and the thought of pregnancy had terrified her. Nenita was useless when it came to matters of the heart or the body. Mama would kill her if she even dared to broach anything about carnal matters. And she didn't have the courage to ask Lola. Manang had been her only recourse.

She'd approached her in the kitchen back then. *Can you please explain how a girl can avoid getting pregnant?* The old woman had been frying fish. Amid the hissing of the lard in the hot pan, she'd said, "You mean, how *you* can avoid getting pregnant? Why don't you just say so?"

Boy, she was direct and to the point. *Oh, all right.* Only then did the servant explain the menstrual cycle. She'd grabbed the church calendar, which bore the image of the glowing sacred heart of Jesus, and showed Isabel how to calculate the most fertile days—the Bad Days, as she called them—during which Isabel must abstain from sex.

On the same calendar, Manang had marked the Bad Days with large Xs, the grease from her fingers leaving an indelible mark. Isabel had been grateful the servant had not given a sermon on chastity. She'd been as pragmatic and efficient in dispensing advice of sexual nature as in frying fish. That had been a year ago.

*"Sino ang salbahe?"* said Manang. Who's the bad man? When Isabel didn't respond, Manang stopped pumping and glowered at her. "Is it the Commander?"

Isabel frowned. "It's not anybody you know."

"I'm not stupid. You can lie to everyone, but don't lie to *me*."

"Whatever do you mean?"

"You've been sneaking out during siesta. I know where that pearl necklace came from. And I know the day you were born, so don't lie to me!"

"Oh, why do you have to say that?" Isabel pushed the pearls underneath her dress. "Let me help you with the water."

She set the parasol on the ground. With both hands, she pushed the pump's handle down. The helper clucked her tongue again.

When the bucket was full, Isabel offered to carry it. The old woman smacked her hand. "You'll trip in those ridiculous shoes."

She glanced at Manang's abaca slippers. She would rather be struck by lightning than wear those awful slippers. "Don't you like my shoes? They're brand new."

"I don't know how you can walk in them."

"It's not easy, but I manage. They're pretty. And they make me taller."

"Taller? *Hija,* you're not fooling anyone but yourself."

Manang's directness could be annoying, but also endearing. She would always tell the truth, no matter how ugly, because she cared about Isabel.

When the old woman motioned for her to go, Isabel gave her an appeasing smile. She opened the parasol and they walked side by side. “Manang, yesterday was a Bad Day for me, and I made a mistake. What should I do?”

“You mean today is a Bad Day for you.”

“What?”

“You left the house at half past one o'clock in the morning and returned shortly after the sun rose. Your Lola was sound asleep, but I was waiting for you. So today is a Bad Day for you.”

“All right. Yes, I admit. So you know all about it.”

“It's the Commander. He's your lover! Don't lie to me.”

Isabel nodded. No use lying. Besides, she'd kept Isabel's secret about Eddie Palma. She trusted her. “Don't you like the Commander?”

“How can I like the man when I've never even seen his face? He's the big *Americano* in a big, expensive car. That's all I know.”

“He cares about me.”

“Oh, is that so? Then how come he has never called on you?”

“He's a very important man. He wants to be discreet.”

“Does *discreet* mean he doesn't want to be seen with you? Does it mean he can pretend he doesn't know you? He may be the most important man in this country, but he doesn't care about you if he wants to be *discreet.*”

Isabel inclined her head. Only a few minutes ago, she'd been sure MacArthur loved her. After all, he'd refused to return to the States because of her. But she couldn't discount the truth in what Manang had said.

Her doubts returned, anxiety rolling up her throat. “What should I do?” She glanced sideward. “You know…about my Bad Day?”

“Pray that you're not pregnant.”

“Pray? Is that all?”

“One Bad Day doesn't mean you're finished. It only means the likelihood of pregnancy is a little bit more.”

“Are you sure?”

“There's no use worrying. You won't find out if you're pregnant until you actually become pregnant. Let's just hope for the best.”

“How can you be certain?”

Manang stopped on the side of the road, panting. She set the bucket down and wiped the sweat on her forehead with her sleeve. Isabel stood beside her.

A carabao-drawn cart passed by and created a small cloud of dust. It was loaded with coconuts. The animal reeked of dung, attracting flies. Isabel covered her nose with her hand.

"*Hija*, I've been pregnant seven times, bore five of them, and buried the other two. Of course, I'm sure," said Manang. "If, God forbid, that today really is your worst day—"

"What should I do?"

"I'll take you to the *manghihilot.*"

Manang knew all sorts of healers and quack doctors.

"So there's a remedy?" asked Isabel.

"It's the last resort, so don't ever make the same mistake." She picked up the bucket. Again, Isabel offered to carry it, but Manang kept on walking.

When they reached the back door of Lola's house, Manang placed the bucket on the ground and wiped her feet on a bulky doormat made of rope.

Isabel closed the parasol. "Thank you." She hugged her.

Manang broke free from the embrace. Pointing a finger for emphasis, she said, "Don't be stupid. Don't make any more mistakes. Mind your Bad Days."

Isabel picked up the bucket. "I promise it won't happen again."

A stern smile materialized on the servant's face. "And don't spill my water."

# 14.

# August 1930

MACARTHUR WALKED into the dance hall of the Officers' Club at Fort McKinley amid salutes followed by applause and congratulatory cheer. The military band launched a marching tune.

A banner that read *Congratulations General MacArthur, U.S. Army Chief of Staff*, was plastered across the wall. Below the banner, a table displayed a huge cake and a silver punch bowl. The U.S. Army logo depicting a star and the words *Good Luck General MacArthur* adorned the cake.

The dance hall had been turned into a dining room for the evening's celebration. MacArthur inched across the room, shaking hands with well-wishers, including his entire staff, Colonel Tom Rooney, and all Army officers in the Philippines. Except for the waiters, they were all Americans.

MacArthur, in his Army khakis and cap, greeted as many people as possible. When he got to Rooney, he said, "I told you I won't settle for less."

Rooney whispered in MacArthur's ear, "You son of a bitch, you always get what you want." They laughed and slapped each other on the back.

MacArthur sat at the head of a long table, with Rooney on his right and First Lieutenant Wallace on his left. He reserved the chair beside Wallace for Captain Marsh.

MacArthur took off his cap and glanced at his pocket watch—half past seven. "Marsh should be here by now," he told Wallace.

"Any moment now, General." Wallace craned his neck in the direction of the door.

An Army major took center stage just as the waiters served punch. One officer after another delivered speeches. They all congratulated MacArthur for his appointment as the U.S. Army's new chief of staff and the successor of General Summerall. The White House had announced the appointment a week ago.

Colonel Rooney took his turn at the podium. "Douglas MacArthur is the most extraordinary soldier I know. He continues to set new records in the U.S. Army. First, he was the youngest West Point superintendent and the youngest major general. Now he's about to become the youngest chief of staff and the youngest four-star general in the history of the U.S. Army."

MacArthur crossed his legs and brimmed with satisfaction. He'd been right to turn down President Hoover's previous offer of the chief of engineers' position. His detractors had criticized his big ego. And yet, within weeks, even before Tom Rooney could report back to Washington, the president had presented a second offer.

His new appointment represented the summit of his career. Every ambitious West Point graduate dreamed of becoming chief of staff. He'd won the job that had eluded his father. When he received the radiogram from the White House, he had known right away that he would accept the president's offer, but his mother had felt the need to send him a cable. *Your father would be ashamed of your timidity if you don't accept*. Pinky MacArthur always had the right words for the right occasion.

MacArthur took a sip of his punch, only half listening to Rooney's lavish praises. He didn't need Rooney or anybody to state the obvious—he would make the best Army chief of staff. His tremendous self-confidence was marred only by the timing of his new appointment. The country wallowed in the Great Depression. He had plenty of brilliant ideas for building a modern Army and strengthening America's national security. But, what good were his ideas without the money to implement them? He was about to become the most powerful man in the military, one of the most important decision makers in America. A stalwart leader deserved a budget befitting his power. He would have to see about that.

With his new appointment, MacArthur would join Washington's "armchair" generals whom he had belittled in the past. How would he fare? What kind of battles would he fight?

Rooney shifted his weight and gripped the podium with both hands. "When General MacArthur was assigned to command the Eighty-Fourth Brigade of the Rainbow Division, the staff presented him with a gold cigarette box that was inscribed, *The Bravest of the Brave*. Nothing could have described my friend better. We are lucky to have as our new Army chief of staff, the one and only, the bravest of the brave—Douglas MacArthur."

The hall exploded with applause. The audience rose. MacArthur waved and motioned to the audience to sit down. The clapping wouldn't die down, forcing him to get up and speak.

"Thank you, everyone!" He waited until the noise died down. "Special mention goes to my staff members for their loyalty and dedication. And, for putting up with me." The latter elicited smiles.

He fished a gold cigarette box from his trouser pocket and raised it for everyone to see. "Colonel Rooney told you about my cigarette box. I've always felt its inscription is too extravagant. Just the same, the sentiment is much appreciated."

He glanced at the gold box, collecting his thoughts. An unexpected calm came to him. Once he'd considered it odd to be comfortable in front of an audience of hundreds, even thousands. Now he accepted it as part of his nature.

He trained his gaze on the crowd. "I don't have a monopoly on courage. We can all be brave right here, right now. As you know, I'm leaving Manila in three weeks. So I'm asking all of you to continue your hard work, to pursue our commitment to the Filipino people with courage. Our government intends to grant the Filipinos their independence in the next decade. It's a daunting plan. It requires many men and munitions, sufficient training, and money to prepare them for independence. It's our duty to prepare them well."

The room stood still, the audience hanging on to his every word. A warmth and a clarity settled inside him. He made eye contact with the officers nearest to the podium. "My appointment as the Army chief of staff is very important to me, but my assignment here in Manila is very dear to my heart. I have said this before: I love the Philippines. I consider it my second country. I see my role here as a continuation of my father's work." He paused, sweeping the hall with a glance.

"Lieutenant General Arthur MacArthur wanted to see the Filipinos as a strong nation capable of defending itself. It's my duty—indeed it's my personal mission—to make sure the Filipinos are capable of protecting and defending themselves when the United States grants them their independence. It's my deepest wish to bring my father's work to successful completion. And I'm asking each of you to help me—to help the United States—prepare the Filipinos for the independence they've fought for and their ancestors have died for."

Everyone looked somber. His heart flared—he'd expressed his message and got the reaction he wanted. Time to lighten up the mood.

He raised the gold box again. "Folks, after all that has been said about this box, it's still a cigarette box, and I'd like to enjoy a smoke after dinner. So, my question is, where's the food? When are we going to eat that beautiful cake?"

The men chuckled.

"Thank you, everyone. May God bless America and all of you!"

The audience rose to its feet again. The band played a merry tune. The waiters brought out a dinner of pot roast, country ham, mashed potatoes, biscuits, and baked beans.

Captain Marsh arrived while a waiter served MacArthur his food. Wallace exchanged seats with Marsh, so the captain sat to MacArthur's immediate left.

"What took you so long?" said MacArthur.

"Sir, I had to stay so I can give you a first-hand report." Marsh downed a glass of punch.

MacArthur, Wallace, and Rooney leaned forward, bringing their heads closer to the captain.

"When I got to the studio, one of the actors told me they were about to shoot a kissing scene—the first ever to be recorded in a motion picture in this country. A historic moment in Philippine cinema. Guess who the recipient of the kiss was?"

MacArthur shook his head. "No, it can't be."

Captain Marsh nodded. "Yes, sir."

"Was it a kiss on the lips?" said Wallace.

Marsh swallowed hard. "Yes, lips to lips."

Rooney adjusted the spectacles on the bridge of his nose, glancing at MacArthur, then Wallace, and finally at Marsh. "What are you talking about? *Who* are we talking about?"

Captain Marsh turned his face to MacArthur, who looked away.

"Is anyone going to tell me what the hell is happening?" said Rooney.

"It's Isabel." MacArthur felt the heat running from his neck to his face. "She's filming in a studio. She's apparently decided to do a kissing scene."

"I was there. I saw everything." Marsh gulped another glass of punch, his Adam's apple rising and falling.

Rooney looked puzzled. "What were you doing in the studio?"

Marsh shot a glance at MacArthur, who said, "I sent him there to tell Isabel I'm leaving, to give her my letter."

The band struck up another tune. Everyone ate and listened to the music. MacArthur turned to his plate and began eating. His aides did the same.

"I hope it was a goodbye letter." Rooney was slicing his ham.

In fact, it *had* been a goodbye letter, without actually spelling it out. MacArthur had told Isabel that perhaps they would see each other again someday. Did she not want to go to Hollywood? Perhaps her father would move the family to Los Angeles, so Isabel could pursue an acting career. The letter sounded hopeful without promising anything. He wanted to end the affair in an amicable way.

But Isabel's stubborn nature didn't allow for anything to end in peace. Had she filmed the kissing scene to spite him? How dare she do this! Who did she think she was?

MacArthur bristled, stabbing a big piece of ham and shoving it into his mouth. He chewed furiously. He turned to Marsh. "You have the name of the film director? Who's bankrolling this goddamn movie?"

Marsh, Wallace, and Rooney exchanged looks. "Sir, I can get you that information tomorrow," said Marsh.

Rooney spread butter on his biscuit and took a bite. "Doug, you're leaving soon. What do you care about this movie?"

MacArthur wiped his mouth with a napkin. "I told her not to do the kissing scene. In fact, I told her not to do the movie. It's a lousy project. "

"Well, what are you going to do about it?" said Rooney.

"I could stop it."

"Stop the kissing scene? How? You heard Marsh. It's done."

"I could ask the studio to edit the scene."

"You can do that?"

"I can do anything I want."

Rooney sniggered. "Oh, I'm sure you can. But what for?"

Before he could respond, an officer butted in to shake hands with him, wishing him good luck. A couple of men joined them, all three standing by MacArthur's side.

After the exchange of pleasantries, MacArthur pushed his plate aside, irritated.

Rooney stood up. "Doug, may I have a word with you, please?"

He and Rooney excused themselves and went next door, to the Officers' Club restaurant. They sat at the bar—empty because everyone else was at the dinner.

Rooney ordered whiskey for both of them. After the bartender poured their drinks, he told MacArthur, "You've just been promoted to the job that you and your father both always wanted. Forget the girl. How many times do I have to tell you that?"

MacArthur held his drink and stared at it. The promotion meant he would leave Isabel behind and live with his mother in Washington, D.C. His heart sank at the thought. He was fifty years old—the youngest Army chief of staff in history, but much too old to be living with his mother. Too old to give up his happiness, his pleasures. He'd been willing to forego the position of chief of engineers for Isabel, but becoming the Army chief of staff was what he'd always dreamed of.

He took a sip of his whiskey, thinking back to his conversation with Isabel a week ago at his home. She had auditioned for a role in a romantic motion picture and got the part, her most important to date, without MacArthur pulling any strings. She had whirled on her toes like a ballerina, as she was inclined to do when she was happy. Round and round she'd twirled in the bedroom, with only her humming for accompaniment. *I'm going to be a star!* She was beautiful. He had watched her dance without any trace of lust, just a quiet appreciation for her person. He understood her hunger for success, as well as the euphoria of triumph.

Then, as casually as she'd stepped out of her high heels, she'd said there might be a kissing scene. Anticipating his reaction, she had aimed to disarm him first. She'd climbed on the bed, spreading herself before him luxuriously. But it had no effect on his grievous opposition. "I forbid you to do this movie. I especially forbid you to do the kissing scene," he'd said. He was already the talk of the town for their liaison, no matter how hard he'd concealed the affair. He was not going to be a laughing stock as well. Of course, she'd sulked. He hadn't budged, and he thought the matter was settled.

When he received the radiogram about his promotion, he'd felt elated. In a gesture of magnanimity, he'd relented and allowed her to accept the movie role—minus the kissing scene. They had agreed on that. But she had defied him.

He took another sip of his whiskey. "I'm going to stop the kissing scene. Hell, I'll shut down the movie, if I have to."

Rooney sighed. "I'm going to ask you again, what the fuck for?"

"This ridiculous kissing scene in a second-rate movie is an insult to me. I can't have it!"

Rooney shook his head and sipped his drink. They could hear the band playing lively music. Laughter and hoots from next door spilled out.

After a while, Rooney said, "If it satisfies you to kill the movie—go ahead and do it. That way you can have some closure before you leave. You'll start your job in Washington a new man." He raised his glass. "How about a toast?"

MacArthur ignored his friend's attempt to cheer him up. "I don't understand why I have to give her up just because I'm getting promoted."

Rooney's eyes widened, his jaws slackened. He set his glass down with a splash. "Are you insane? What are you trying to say?"

"I know what I want, and I'm going to get it."

"You want to shut down Isabel's movie, right? Yes, go ahead and do that."

"I don't mean that."

"Then what the hell do you mean?"

He looked Rooney in the eye, but kept mum. They had known each other for so long it was enough to convey his meaning.

Rooney looked exasperated. "What exactly do you intend to do?"

"I don't know."

"Sleep on it. You'll come to your senses by tomorrow morning."

He downed his drink, savoring the warmth traveling down his throat, rippling throughout his body. Snatches of Isabel's memory barged into his thoughts—her soft chiffon dress in his hands, his fingers on her breasts, her tongue thrusting between his lips. A hot rush of exhilaration descended upon him.

Rooney waved at the bartender and asked for more whiskey. After the man refilled their glasses, he said, "You're the reason I traveled here against my will. You owe me big time, my friend. Not only that, you owe your new job to me."

MacArthur smirked. "If I had listened to you, I'd be the chief of engineers, not the Army chief of staff."

"I advised you to take the chief of engineers position because I know you'd do the opposite. You always do! So you see, you owe me your new job."

He shook his head, smiling. "I'm really glad you're shipping off tomorrow. I will personally see you off at the pier."

Rooney laughed. "We'll have a swell time back in D.C." He raised his glass again. "Here's to you, Douglas MacArthur. Here's to the new Army chief of staff."

They clicked their glasses and drained their drinks. The band next door played "America the Beautiful."

Rooney clapped MacArthur's shoulder. "It's time to go back to your party."

He nodded. Good 'ol Tom Rooney was right—MacArthur always did the opposite of his friend's advice. He'd just made up his mind. *I'm going to take Isabel with me to Washington.*

# 15.

# September 1930

ISABEL WAS NO virtuoso, but she could play Beethoven's "Moonlight Sonata" from start to finish. On Sunday afternoon, three hours after siesta and two hours before evening prayers, she played the first movement like someone strolling in a park. Mama was helping Lola sew new curtains downstairs, while Papa and Ben were changing a flat tire in the driveway. Time wore on with endless persistence, so why hurry?

Without any movie or vaudeville job, she was back to being idle as Mama liked to remind her. Thanks to the Commander, she'd lost her part in a film. His wrath—how far he would go to punish her—shocked her.

Three days after Isabel had filmed the infamous kissing scene that had sent Manila's gossips into a tizzy, the producers shut down the movie set. The American bank funding the project had backed out of the deal. Neither the director nor the producer would speak to Isabel. Gossip had it that some powerful Filipino politicians had pressured the bank's president to cease financing the "morally bankrupt" motion picture because the shameless kissing scene in the movie insulted the Filipina's virtue.

Guess who had informed the politicians about the kissing scene? Yes siree, none other than the Commander himself. He'd told them if such a degenerate film were allowed, he would ask the governor-general to impose film censorship.

MacArthur's threat had sent the politicians marching into the bank. Overnight Isabel had lost her chance at stardom. She dropped her head on the piano, ending the sonata with an angry clang.

What on earth did he want from her? He was leaving Manila and moving upward in his career. Why should a film matter to him? True, she had reneged on their agreement, but he would be in America by the time the movie was released, so how could it hurt him?

She lifted her head up, sighing. His letter made it clear they were through. He was cutting out. It hurt, but her tears wouldn't change a thing. She'd always known he would return to the States one day. Thank God, she wasn't pregnant! Manang was right—one Bad Day wouldn't necessarily lead to pregnancy.

She flicked through the sheets on the piano's music rack and found Beethoven's "Für Elise." She could start the piece without trouble, but always stumbled in the middle section. She played it anyway.

What a blessing to be able to read music. It helped in her singing, in understanding harmony and melody. Thank God for Lola's generosity, for buying the piano and paying for music lessons.

Someone was galloping up the stairs. Ben burst into the living room. "The Commander is here! He's here!"

"What?"

"His limousine just arrived."

She glanced down at her slippers and her plain dress. *Dios mio*, she looked like a peasant. She dashed into her bedroom and picked a blue georgette dress and matching high heels. She changed in a hurry. Papa's exuberant greetings and nervous laughter dominated the conversation in the living room.

She applied rouge and crimson lipstick. She dabbed a drop of perfume—the very same one MacArthur had given her—behind her ears. Why on earth did she want to smell good for him? The man had ruined her acting career. With just one letter, he'd discarded her like a worn-out hat. And yet, she couldn't help but make herself look pretty for him.

She waited a few moments, listening to the voices outside her bedroom door. Mama and Lola had joined the men.

"I'm so glad to finally meet you..." MacArthur said.

Lola responded in Tagalog for the poor woman didn't speak a word of English. Ben translated for her, telling MacArthur what an honor it was to meet him. Papa offered the Commander a chair. She could almost see everyone's big smiles.

Isabel drew a deep breath to calm herself down and prepare for her entrance. It was an appearance, a role—make no doubt about it. She didn't know what the Commander wanted, but she would show him what he was going to miss.

She stepped outside her room. "Hello, General." Everyone turned around.

MacArthur rose. "Hello, Belle." He wore an ivory linen suit and a gold tie, his fedora hat in his hand. Although it was muggy, he appeared fresh and crisp. He didn't even remove his jacket.

She eased around the couch to sit beside Lola, who was strategically positioned between her daughter and granddaughter. Isabel had not talked to her mother without arguing in months.

MacArthur sat in the armchair across the sofa and placed his hat on the coffee table. Papa sat in his old rocking chair.

"General, congratulations on your promotion. It's all over the newspapers." Ben perched on the piano stool.

Papa and Mama both chimed in with more congratulations. For a while, all MacArthur said was "thank you."

Manang arrived with a silver tray of tall glasses of cool, freshly squeezed *calamansi*. She served it first to the Commander, then to the others. She reserved her scowl for Isabel. Oh, heavens. She'd told Manang her relationship with MacArthur was over. The servant's look could only mean one thing. She thought the affair continued and Isabel had lied to her.

"*Calamansi* is my favorite citrus drink." MacArthur set his empty glass on the coffee table. "I'm going to miss it, among other things."

Isabel smiled at his perfect pronunciation of *calamansi*, though he didn't speak Tagalog.

He glanced at her, then at her parents. "I'm leaving in two weeks, so I thought I should call on Isabel now. I hope I'm not intruding."

Mama pulled the fan tucked in her skirt waistband and began fanning. She generated weak breeze and nervous energy.

"Mr. and Mrs. Cooper, I have a proposition to make. I would like Isabel to come with me to the States."

Isabel gripped her juice glass with both hands, MacArthur's words ringing in her ears. Was he saying what she thought he was saying?

Her parents exchanged glances. Papa uttered what everyone in the family must have been thinking. "General, are you asking for my daughter's hand in marriage?"

MacArthur's face clouded with concern. "I'll be honest with you. I care about Isabel very much, but I can't marry her. I'm asking you to entrust your daughter to me."

"Let me get this clear—you want to take my daughter, but not marry her?"

MacArthur reared back in his chair, crossed his legs. "Mr. Cooper, as you know, we have anti-miscegenation laws in the United States. I'm guessing that's the reason why you live here in Manila instead of the States. When I become Army chief of staff, I will work in Washington, D.C., but I'm going to live in Fort Myer in Arlington, Virginia. The state prohibits marriage between persons of different races. I can't marry your daughter."

Isabel drew a choking breath. She'd never heard of the law before. Could it really be the reason her father had never taken the family to the States?

"No, I suppose you can't." Papa ran his fingers through his thinning hair.

Mama stopped fanning. She placed a hand on her mouth, as if trying to stop the words from spilling out of her. Lola covered Isabel's hand with hers. The Commander might as well have doused cold water on all of them.

MacArthur cleared his throat. "What I'm asking for is no trifle. I know that. But I believe it's for the best. Isabel will have better opportunities in the States. She can continue her education, or pursue an acting career. There's nothing here for your daughter, but small parts in morally questionable motion pictures and second-rate vaudeville acts. She deserves better."

When he trained his gaze on Isabel, his blue eyes turned steely, as if daring her to refute him. "I'm sure Belle would agree."

She set down her glass and returned his stare, as cool as could be, while her heart bled. It took everything in her to act nonchalant. So, this is what Douglas MacArthur is all about.

He had killed her acting career, so he could play hero and save her from Manila's immoral film industry. He had fooled around with her for five months without any guilt, and yet a harmless kissing scene in an insignificant film had offended him. He would take her to the Land of Milk and Honey and milk her for as much honey and pleasure he could get, without marrying her.

He had come in his spotless white suit and perfectly slicked back hair to present himself as her savior. He rode a horse so high he couldn't see the irony of his proposition.

Before she could say anything, Mama emitted a guttural sound that drew everyone's attention. She sobbed into her handkerchief—the gesture confirmed that her parents had wanted MacArthur to marry Isabel. They'd hoped the marriage would elevate their standing in society.

MacArthur uncrossed his legs and leaned forward. "Mrs. Cooper, I'll provide for your daughter the best way possible. I promise you I'll take good care of her."

Mama wiped her tears. "You don't know a thing about my daughter."

He looked unfazed. "I know she's not of age. But she's an intelligent girl—"

"Not of age?" Ben sneered.

Isabel flashed her eyes at her brother. *Shut up or else.*

MacArthur furrowed his eyebrows.

"General, what Mama is worried about is this: What happens if things don't work out between you and my sister? Would you return her to us through the post?"

Oh, her insolent brother and his big mouth! "I can make up my own mind, thank you very much," snapped Isabel. "Why is everyone talking as if I'm not in the room?"

MacArthur looked her in the eye. "I want you to come with me to the States."

How typical of him to command instead of ask. Another man incapable of offering marriage would have professed his love and begged her to elope with him. Not Douglas MacArthur. He told her what to do, the way he ordered his aides around. She shook her head in disbelief. The tears gathering in her eyes threatened to overflow.

Her reaction seemed to have emboldened Mama. "My daughter is not going with you, General."

MacArthur shot a glance at Isabel's father. "As long as we're having this family conversation, I'd like to know your opinion, Mr. Cooper."

All eyes on Papa. If beauty were a random blessing, then he was a picture of nature's random cruelty—a balding man with wild thickets for eyebrows. He rocked his chair in response, his gaze moving upward, resting on the ceiling. He rocked nonstop, the chair squeaking.

"Speak up. Say something," said Mama.

Papa stopped. "I can't pay the loan."

"What?" Mama looked stricken. "What are you talking about?"

"I'm broke. I haven't made any payments to the bank." Papa turned to the Commander, his eyes pleading. "Stanley McBride is threatening to sue me."

Nothing could stop Mama's tears now. She buried her face in Lola's lap.

"What's that got to do with anything?" Ben crossed his arms over his chest.

Papa knitted his thick eyebrows, sweat glistening on his forehead, but he had no answer. He rocked his chair again. His staggering failure as a family provider had never been as clear. Isabel's face burned with shame and fury. The creaking of the rocking chair grated on her nerves.

"*Dios mio*, stop it, Papa." She bolted to her feet, hands clenched.

Papa sneaked a sheepish glance. To her horror, he cried. She'd never seen him shed tears before. She eyed Ben, who sat slack-jawed.

"Belle, please sit down," said MacArthur. "I can assure all of you that everything will be all right. Please let me finish explaining my proposition."

She sank into the sofa. Papa blew his nose with his handkerchief.

The room grew stifling, the air ripe with resentments and regrets.

"Here's my proposition." MacArthur loosened his gold tie, still looking impeccable. Did the man ever sweat? He was born a winner. From head to toe, he looked victorious. "I will provide for Isabel, and Mr. Cooper, I will take care of your loan. Don't worry about Stanley

McBride. I will sort it out with him as soon as possible. Tonight, if necessary."

Papa heaved a sigh. "Thank you, General. I will never forget—"

"No need for that." MacArthur waved.

Isabel gnawed at her lower lip, meeting the Commander's eyes. *Douglas MacArthur, savior of the Cooper family.* Add *that* to his long list of accomplishments.

Someone knocked on the door. Ben opened it, ushering MacArthur's Filipino driver inside. "General, you left this in the car." He stepped forward, a brown paper bag in hand.

"Ah, yes! I completely forgot about it. Thank you, Mario."

The driver left.

MacArthur rose and handed the bag to Isabel. "I thought you might like this."

She peered inside. An Al Jolson record, a replacement for the broken one. She pulled it out, removed its cover, and let her fingers slide across its shiny surface.

Tears sprang to her eyes. Despite MacArthur's all-important promotion and his opposition to her kissing scene, he'd remembered. He'd retained the passing comment she had made in Baguio about how she liked Al Jolson. He'd secured the record, not once but twice. Something inside her melted. Moments like this, when MacArthur surprised her with little kindnesses, touched her most. Right then, he was neither a powerful commander nor the Cooper family's savior. The warmth of his affection washed over her and flowed through her like a sad song.

She filled her chest with breath. "I've made up my mind."

Everyone turned to her. She glanced at her family, before finding MacArthur's eyes. "General, I will go to America with you. That's my decision."

He nodded. No hint of surprise. He stared like a man who had always gotten what he wanted. Why should it be any different now?

"It's for the best." Papa's voice had been reduced to a murmur.

Isabel waited for the others to object, but no opposition ensued. Mama had lost her fire. She rested her head on Lola's shoulder. Ben scowled, his arrogance out of place.

In this atmosphere of defeat, the Commander's presence grew immense. He enveloped the living room with his assured silence. He had come with a proposition and won. The Coopers had lost.

And yet, Isabel's heart fluttered. She was going to America. At last! Where Papa had failed, the Commander would deliver.

She knuckled her tears away and managed a smile. "Thank you for everything."

His eyes seemed bluer, more striking. "You won't regret it. I'll do everything in my power to make you happy. I can promise you that."

There. She'd made the Commander promise. What was marriage but a promise to stay together? So what if his vow took another form? There was no turning back from this point—that was what mattered.

# Part Two: America

# 16.

# Virginia, October 1930

QUARTERS ONE, the official home of the chief of staff of the U.S. Army, stood on Fort Myer's ridge in Arlington, Virginia. A striking red-brick Victorian mansion with a stone foundation and a slate roof. MacArthur had moved into the house with his mother.

They enjoyed taking their breakfast and lunch in the sunroom, amid orange and yellow chrysanthemums in cedar planters and potted ficus trees and ferns. Warmth and sunlight inundated the room, a pleasant little corner in a cavernous house with twenty-one rooms.

On Saturday afternoon, two days before MacArthur's swearing-in, he entered the room and kissed his mother on the forehead. "I'm sorry to keep you waiting."

Mary Pinkney Hardy MacArthur—Pinky to friends and family—sat before a round table, pouring coffee into two cups. "Martha made chicken sandwiches and potato salad. I hope this is sufficient, especially because you didn't bother telling her or me what you wanted to eat for lunch."

Pinky's father had been a wealthy cotton merchant. She'd been raised in a mansion in Norfolk, Virginia, called Riveredge. When MacArthur broke the news that they would be living in Quarters One, she'd said, "It's about time." She had lived an itinerant life as an Army wife, enduring many years in remote military outposts. She was more than happy to return to living in a mansion.

MacArthur pulled a chair and sat opposite his mother, his eyes drawn to the plant stand behind her. A small clay pot of delicate white orchids in full bloom perched on it. *Isabel.*

"Where did the orchid come from?" he said.

"Isn't it precious? I saw it in a flower shop this morning and bought it for you." Pinky served him a cup and spooned potato salad onto his plate. "I thought it's a nice reminder of the Philippines. I know how fond you are of Manila."

She couldn't have chosen a worse gift. His heart ached just looking at the plant. It had been six weeks since he last saw Isabel. He missed her so acutely he would swim across the Pacific Ocean to see her again. He would drown trying to get back to her, but his death would be justified. It would end his infinite longing for a girl halfway around the world.

He sipped his coffee, his eyes still on the plant. "It's very beautiful. But how can it survive here? In the Philippines, orchids grow from tree barks, with their roots exposed to the air. That's how they grow."

Pinky turned around, appraising the plant. "You mean, like a parasite? I can't believe something as beautiful as that is a parasite."

"Not a parasite. It's a tropical plant. It's different." He would rather not discuss the very reminder of his lovesickness.

She got up to move the plant stand closer to a window, a shaft of light falling on the flowers. The orchid stood out in its whiteness. Its exotic beauty seemed a defiance of nature.

"It's so pretty, I just couldn't resist it," said Pinky. "The florist assured me it will survive."

MacArthur took a bite of his sandwich. "I hope the florist is right."

She returned to the table. He eyed her short hair, which had been colored a golden brown, covering the grays. She sported gentle waves that framed her longish face. Cosmetics helped cover the age spots, but not the wrinkles and eye bags.

Her newfound interest in grooming was probably brought on by her new role as mistress of the house at Quarters One. As a divorced man, MacArthur had no one but his seventy-eight-year-old mother to co-host official functions. They would have to throw parties on a regular basis as part of his job.

"Did you have a good ride with Rooney?" asked Pinky. "Were there new horses at the stables?" She picked at her potato salad.

She had lost weight. She was a tad less spirited, moved a little slower. Her health had not been the same since she'd suffered a heart attack seven years ago. The prospect of making her entertain guests on a regular basis displeased him.

"Yes, I rode one of the new horses. We had a great time," he said. "Tommy came along for some riding lessons."

"Thomas Junior?"

"Don't call him Junior. He goes by Tommy now."

"Heavens. How old is he now?"

"Twelve. A chip off the old block. He loves horseback riding. I told him I'll give him another lesson next Saturday. He's keen on playing polo eventually."

"Twelve, my goodness. How old is his sister?"

"Natalie just turned six. Rooney said she's not interested in riding. She's more into swimming."

"How time flies. They were babies the last time I saw them." She sighed, looking away from her half-eaten salad. The glass walls showed the garden outside, in full bloom under a perfect October sky.

"What's the matter?"

She waved her hand in a dismissive way, but MacArthur was attuned to the tiniest ripples in her moods. Her forlorn expression meant she was probably wishing for something impossible—wishing to be with people who were forever gone.

MacArthur's father had died of a massive stroke eighteen years ago. His two older brothers were both dead as well. Pinky's sorrow over losing Malcolm, her middle son, to measles at the age of five had grown exponentially upon the death of her oldest son, Arthur III. Arthur had been a decorated Navy officer when he'd died of appendicitis at the age of forty-seven.

He had lived with his mother or near her most of his life, with the exception of his years overseas and those spent with his former wife. Pinky was the kind of mother who wrote poems for her son. She corresponded with the bigwigs in the Army, most of whom she knew courtesy of her late husband. Douglas was the subject of her letters.

More than once, she had exhorted the military brass to promote her son.

MacArthur loved and cherished his mother, but to be known as a Mama's boy chagrined him no end. Was it any wonder that his time in Manila had been his happiest? Those years had been a most welcome respite from Pinky's smothering love. But now MacArthur was not only back in the States, but also back to living with her. The Mama's boy reputation would soon resurface.

"Mother, I can see plainly that something's wrong."

She shifted her gaze back to him. "Wouldn't it be nice to have your own Douglas Junior to ride horses with? Don't you wish you have someone pretty and lively to host your first dinner as the chief of staff instead of your old mother?"

"Please don't worry about the dinner on Monday night. Just stand beside me and say hello to everybody. Leave the preparations to Martha and the house staff. They know what to do. They've worked for my predecessors."

"Everything has been arranged already," she said. "That's not the problem."

He finished his sandwich. He began eating the potato salad; there was no telling what she would say next.

"I hope you're not still pining for Louise. It's time to move on."

"Believe me, I'm not pining for her."

"Then how come you haven't found anyone?"

So, it wasn't the dead she was thinking of, but far worse, his love life. "You asked me to come back—well, here I am. Why are we having this conversation? Aren't you happy I'm back?"

"Of course, I am. But I'd be happier if you have someone. You know what the problem is?"

He shook his head. No matter what, she would tell him anyway.

"You've spent too much time in Manila. How could you possibly find someone suitable?"

He smirked. "Do you mean to say there are no suitable women in all of Manila?"

"Well, are there?" Her voice had gone up a notch, dripping with sarcasm.

He opened his mouth, but words eluded him. He pursed his lips. How could he begin to explain the presence of Isabel in his life?

"How many eligible American women live in Manila?" she continued. "Name *one* suitable woman you've met in Manila."

When he failed to answer, she added, "You see? My point exactly!"

She poured more coffee for both of them.

He took a sip. During the long voyage back to the States, he'd contemplated the possibility of introducing Isabel to Pinky when Isabel arrived in December. While he might not be free to flaunt Isabel's company in Washington society, he could at least enjoy the peace of mind of not having to hide her from Pinky. He was divorced, for Christ's sake. And he hadn't wandered too far away from his own race. She was half-white after all. Would that make a difference to his mother?

Of course, there was also the issue of age. She would chastise him for choosing someone that young. Surely his mother would understand he was a healthy man with healthy desires. Pinky should understand *that.* He would be able to endure the gossip and the criticisms if he had even just a modicum of his mother's approval.

He shot a glance at her, then at the orchids. His heart plunged. Choosing Isabel made as much sense as growing orchids in Virginia. Pinky would never understand.

"Why don't you ask the Rooneys?"

Her voice cut across his thoughts. "What are you talking about?" He'd lost track of their conversation.

"Ask the Rooneys to introduce you to someone suitable." Her eyes glinted with excitement. "Rose belongs to the right social circle. She's an active member of both the Vassar College Alumni Association and the Arlington Ladies' Art Society. I'm sure she knows someone who knows someone."

He took a cigarette from his gold cigarette box and lit it with a lighter. "Tom Rooney has found me someone suitable all right—a suitable aide, that is. In addition to Marsh and Wallace, I'm going to have another aide. His name is Dwight Eisenhower. He's a young major currently working for Payne."

"Who's Payne?"

"Frederick Payne is the assistant secretary of war. Rooney thinks Eisenhower—they call him Ike—would jump at the opportunity to leave Payne and work for me instead."

"I can understand that. No one's ever heard of Payne. Not me certainly. Meanwhile, the newspapers are abuzz about your appointment. Everybody's excited about the new Army chief of staff."

He puffed on his cigarette, wondering what else Washington gossips had said about him. He waited for his mother to mention any rumor about his personal life in Manila.

"Would you like some dessert?" she said. "How about a slice of pound cake or apple pie?"

No, she hadn't heard anything about Isabel. "Sure. I'd like some apple pie."

"I'll go get it. Martha is out grocery shopping."

While his mother was in the kitchen, his thoughts raced. How would he hide Isabel from Pinky? He drew on his cigarette and exhaled slowly through his mouth. Although he lived at Fort Myer, he would work at the State, War, and Navy Building in Washington, D.C. He could find an apartment for Isabel near his office. But was Washington far enough or big enough to hide her?

Pinky came back with two dessert plates. "Here we are." She served him his pie.

He crushed the remains of his cigarette in an ash tray. They began eating. Every time he looked up from his plate, he saw the orchid. It was like a whisper in his head. *Isabel.*

He let out a sigh. For God's sake, he needed no further reminder of what was in his heart. She filled his head during the day and prowled his dreams at night. It was enough to drive any man insane. He had two months to figure out where she would live before she arrived, and how he would keep their relationship private in spite of his extremely visible career.

"About that orchid—" He pointed his chin at the plant. "It's not a parasite. It's an epiphyte."

"A what?" Pinky looked startled.

"Epiphyte."

Slowly she nodded. "Oh, really?"

"An orchid doesn't depend on a tree for nutrients, but only for support. It gets everything it needs from the air: sunlight, moisture, and nutrients. It's not a parasite."

"Well, look at you! You almost look offended. I'm sorry I called your beloved orchid a parasite." She chuckled.

He smiled, though his mind wandered far away—back to Manila and a question Tom Rooney had asked. *Do you love her?*

He had no answer back then. Love was an enigma best left unexamined and unexplained. Time and again, Rooney's question would come back to him. Still, he didn't know the answer. But now, in front of his mother, he knew.

# 17.

# New Jersey, December 1930

THE OCEAN LINER carried a thousand passengers. It traveled for thirty-eight grueling days from Manila to Hong Kong, to San Francisco, to Havana, to Jersey City.

Isabel was among 150 passengers fortunate enough to occupy first-class cabins with their own private bathrooms and toilets. The rest of the masses occupied rows and rows of bunks stacked three high in the vast steerage, also known as the Economy Section. In other words, the low-class section, a repository of seething squalor located in the middle and lower decks, where Filipino and Chinese travelers languished. Those poor souls. They slept, ate, and vomited there. When the sea was not too choppy, they also sang, gambled, and brawled.

MacArthur had instructed her to stay within the upper decks and to interact only with first-class passengers. Leave it to the Commander to write numerous pages of detailed instructions for her first sea voyage.

She stood before the mirror fastened to the cabin's wall, putting on her pearl necklace. At the thought of MacArthur's instructions, she frowned.

Since he left Manila, he'd written to her almost every week. Sometimes the letters and radiograms arrived all at once. They were full of "do this" and "do that," most of them pertaining to her legal documents and travel arrangements.

They included lines of impassioned pleas to never forget him and to join him as soon as possible. But the salutation of "My Darling" or "My Own Sweetheart" annoyed her, as though he'd already forgotten her name. Why couldn't he scrawl "My Darling *Isabel*"? He'd also been signing his letters "Daddy."

Of course, he was being cautious in case the letters fell into the wrong hands, but it irritated her just the same. Only God knew why he chose Daddy as an alias. Did he see himself as Isabel's "sugar daddy"? She'd never heard of the term until her brother informed her it was slang for an older man who spent lavishly on a young woman.

It was bad enough Ben called MacArthur a sugar daddy, but it was worse when Manang called her a "plaything." She'd been helping Isabel pack when the old woman said, "If you go to America, you will forever be a white man's plaything."

How dare Manang say such nasty things. Isabel should have been angry, but instead, she'd felt the hair on her nape rising. Manang's remark had sounded like a curse.

She sighed and let her shoulders droop. She'd left behind four broken hearts: Mama, Lola, Nenita, and Manang. They had begged her to stay. Nenita, who had been in the dark about the extent of Isabel's relationship with MacArthur, was hit the hardest.

Isabel had explained her place was not in Manila. For so long, she didn't know where she belonged. On that fateful night at the Olympic Boxing Club, she'd caught a glimpse of her destiny. It came in the form of a note, which Nenita had promptly thrown away. But a glimmering was enough. She had known then what she still believed now. MacArthur and America—they were her destiny.

At least, she'd placated the men in her family. Papa no longer owed any money to Stanley McBride's bank. MacArthur had taken care of that. Her loafer of a brother worked full time as the assistant manager at the Army and Navy Club, thanks to the Commander.

She picked up her little silk purse from the bed. The two leather suitcases containing her belongings stood near the door. Her luxurious fur coat, a birthday gift from the Commander, hung in the closet. Within an hour or two, the ship would dock in Jersey City. Her new life would begin.

A sudden calm filled her heart. She'd already expended her restless energy in the past thirty-eight days of excruciating journey. She had strolled along the promenade deck when the weather was fine and slept when the sea was rough. She had read all the ladies' dime novels in the ship's parlor. How many hours had she spent fantasizing about her new life in Washington with the Commander? Now she was ready.

She took another glance at herself in the mirror before leaving the cabin.

Even after weeks of this trip, the ship's jouncing nauseated her. She walked gingerly to keep her balance. She went downstairs to get to the salon deck. Along the way, her fellow first-class passengers said hello—the British father and son who had spent six months traveling in the Far East and the Canadian woman who had taught English in Hong Kong.

Inside the lounge room, a group of men played cards, a few women drank tea, and a family played a board game. Some people relaxed in the sofas, reading magazines or just talking and smoking.

She sat at the table of Mr. and Mrs. Wesley Grant, an American couple older than her parents. She had dined with them before. They were tourists from New York who had boarded the ship in Havana.

"Are you excited?" Mr. Grant offered Isabel a cigarette. He and his wife were both smoking. They'd also been drinking coffee, judging by the empty cups on the table.

"Yes, I can't wait to get off this ship. I'm tired of feeling nauseated." Isabel accepted the cigarette, which he lit with a match.

"You look beautiful, dear." Mrs. Grant touched the sleeve of Isabel's lavender silk chiffon dress. "Those pearls look gorgeous."

MacArthur's gifts swathed her. *Sugar daddy*. Oh, how she despised Ben and his merciless slang.

"You're going to need a coat. It's cold where we're going," said Mr. Grant.

She'd told them it was going to be her first time in America, though her Papa was American. She glanced at their attires: knitted sweaters and tweeds. They both had solid build, with the same ruddy cheeks and hearty smiles.

"I have a new fur coat." Isabel puffed on her cigarette, holding the smoke in her mouth for a few seconds before exhaling. "I can't wait to wear it."

The coat had been shipped from Washington to Manila on the occasion of her birthday the previous month. The Commander had instructed her not to bring too many clothes because they would be inappropriate for Washington's weather. He had promised to take her shopping for a new wardrobe when she arrived.

"Who's going to pick you up at the pier? If you need a ride, you can come with us. My brother is going to pick us up," said Mrs. Grant.

"Thank you, but my uh…daddy…will pick me up." Isabel felt a blush spread across her face. Why on earth did she say that?

"That's wonderful. Your father is in New Jersey? I thought your family is in Manila."

"Daddy left Manila in September. He lives outside Washington, D.C. He's making the trip to New Jersey just to pick me up. My mother and my brother are in Manila, but they'll join us next year." *Dios mio*. Once she started lying, she couldn't stop.

"I'm glad to hear that, dear. It must be so hard to have your family living in different continents." Mrs. Grant waved the hand holding the cigarette when she said "different continents," the ashes flicking. She brushed them off her sweater.

"As for us, we're moving to California soon," she continued. "Our son and his wife live in Los Angeles, and we want to be close to them. They're expecting their first child."

"Los Angeles?" Isabel widened her eyes. "Is that where Hollywood is?"

"Yes, that's right." Mr. Grant seemed to ponder the ash-tipped end of his cigarette. "Our son lives in Bunker Hill. He works for the Pacific Electric Railway." He tapped the cigarette on the edge of the ashtray and the ash fell in it.

"I wish I could go to Hollywood."

"You mean, to pursue an acting career?" asked Mrs. Grant. "You said you were in the theater in Manila?"

Isabel nodded. "Theater and motion pictures."

"Motion pictures!" Mrs. Grant's eyes bugged out with excitement. "You're the first movie actress I've met."

Small film roles, but nobody needed to know that. She smiled, wondering whether the Grants thought she was white. She didn't tell them her mother was Filipino and the couple didn't ask about her heritage. Could she pass as white?

"Would your father allow you to go to Hollywood?" said Mrs. Grant. "You're so young."

"I haven't talked to him about it."

"If you're going to L.A. anytime after February, be sure to come and see us." Mr. Grant took a last drag on his cigarette before depositing the butt in the ash tray. "We'll be there by the first of March. We don't have a new address yet, but we can give you our son's address."

"His name is George and his wife is Lucy," added Mrs. Grant.

"Let me write it down for you." He took out a pen from his jacket pocket and scribbled on a paper napkin.

"Honey, you should write down our address in New York, too." The wife turned to Isabel. "We live in Brooklyn. If you and your dad will be in the area for a while, maybe you'll come and see us?"

Isabel forced an eager smile. "Well, you never know."

Mr. Grant gave her the napkin. "It's fortunate my company recently opened a facility in Los Angeles. I'm going to work there as soon as we've moved."

She doubted the Grants would have been as willing to invite her to their home if they had known she was only half white. The thought nagged her.

She thanked Mr. Grant and said, "What do you do for a living?"

"I work for Peerless Electric Manufacturing Company. We make fuses and cube taps."

"Oh." No idea what those were. She folded the paper napkin and put it in her purse.

"What about your father, what does he do?" said Mr. Grant.

"He's in the Army." *Oh, heavens.* Soon she would blurt out that he was the new Army chief of staff. She took a whiff of her cigarette. Why on earth was she lying? She could have told them she was going to America to join her beau. MacArthur was divorced—nothing to hide. In Manila, they had sneaked around to avoid any talk because

Filipinos were provincial. But America was a hundred times more modern. Americans would be more sophisticated and more tolerant.

MacArthur always said he wanted privacy, but she suspected he was waiting to see if their relationship would last. Well, it had endured long enough to warrant her move to America. Even so, his use of "Daddy" and "My Darling" to conceal their identities in his letters told her their relationship would remain a secret. *That* was the reason Isabel was lying to the Grants. Her heart dipped.

"No wonder your family is in Manila. I heard we have thousands of troops in the Philippines." Mrs. Grant beamed at Isabel.

"Yes, that's right."

The husband eyed Isabel's pearls. "Is your father an officer?"

"Yes, he is."

The conversation flagged. The Grants were waiting for her to continue, but the more she lied, the greater the likelihood she would slip. "Enough about me." She smiled. "Tell me about Brooklyn and Los Angeles."

Mr. Grant described their neighborhood. His wife interjected with her observations about L.A.

Isabel continued smoking. Thank God, she'd steered the conversation away from the Commander. When she set foot in America, she would no longer hide her relationship with MacArthur. If he couldn't marry her, then he should, at least, not hide her.

Mr. Grant ordered coffee for the three of them. They were sipping coffee when a horn blared. The ship was approaching the pier. They abandoned their cups and ran up to the promenade deck at the top of the ocean liner.

They emerged from the stairs breathless. The deck, enclosed by a railing, provided a continuous open walkway from the ship's bow to its stern. A blast of cold wind greeted them. Only four o'clock in the afternoon and already the sky had darkened. Eager passengers stood along the railing, chatting and pointing at the horizon.

Isabel shivered. Mr. Grant offered his tweed jacket, which she put on. They found a spot near the bow, with a clear view of the New York harbor. Barges, ferries, and ships of all sizes swarmed the area. Horns were blowing and bells were ringing. Tall buildings loomed over the skyline. The air reeked of smoke rising from ship smokestacks.

"Oh, look!" Isabel pointed at the Statue of Liberty in the distance.

The waves churned. Her nausea came back. She inhaled deeply, willing herself not to vomit. She tucked her little purse into the jacket's pocket and gripped the railing with both hands as she took in the image of the colossal statue, the world's most famous symbol of freedom and democracy. Lady Liberty—her right arm aloft with a torch—seemed to be welcoming her.

She couldn't believe it. *I'm finally here!* This was the land of Sophie Tucker and Jelly Roll Morton and Al Jolson, the Promised Land for entertainers. The realization hit her at once, filling her heart with joy. Her eyes brimmed up.

She hugged Mrs. Grant.

"Oh, my dear child." Isabel's sudden display of emotion had startled her into an awkward embrace.

The wind tousled Isabel's hair and strands were stuck on her face. Mrs. Grant lifted her chin, then peeled off the straying hair. "You have your whole life ahead of you. Welcome to America!"

She flashed a smile. "Thank you."

The couple pointed at the horizon, showing Isabel which part was New York and which was New Jersey.

Light snow tumbled. Dusk descended. The lights on the promenade deck came to life. It was the first time Isabel had seen snow. She would love to watch it fall all day!

"We better go inside and get ready to disembark," said Mr. Grant.

He walked toward the stairway, the ladies following suit. The ship's horn blared once again. Isabel stopped to take another glance at Lady Liberty. Then she looked up at the dreary sky, her eyelashes catching snowflakes. She blinked hard. She was in this country only because of the Commander. *This is MacArthur's America.*

Just as fast, she reminded herself it was Papa's America, too. She belonged here as much as the Grants and anyone on the ship. She would prove Manang wrong. She wasn't anybody's plaything. She resumed walking and hurried to catch up with the old couple.

# 18.

ISABEL CAME DOWN the gangplank in Jersey City at eleven o' clock at night, the ground slick from the light snow earlier. Her breath curled into the freezing air.

Although it was late, business continued. Passengers embarked and disembarked, stevedores moved cargo with forklifts, and workers loaded and unloaded crates. The night bustled with the din of boat whistles, ship horns, hollering workers, and honking cars.

Isabel, bundled up in a fur coat and gloves, put down her luggage and scanned the faces in the crowd. A man in a dark trench coat and hat waved at her. Fighting nausea, she picked up her suitcases and pushed past the crowd. She wanted only one thing: Douglas MacArthur.

He tilted his hat, revealing his face. Not MacArthur but Captain Marsh. "How are you? How was your trip?" He took the suitcases from her hands.

Her heart slumped. She'd just endured thirty-eight days of sea journey and six hours of disembarkation procedure. Her stomach churned as if she were still on a moving ship. In response, all she could do was nod. Then she staggered past him and threw up.

Captain Marsh rushed to her side. "Are you all right?" He offered her a handkerchief.

She wiped her mouth with it. "I feel seasick." Setting foot in America wasn't as magical as she'd imagined it to be.

"It's normal. I was nauseated for three whole days after I arrived from Manila."

After she regained her bearings, Captain Marsh led her to a taxicab. He opened the door for her. "You'll see the Commander at home."

She ducked inside the cab, sank into the seat, and closed her eyes. The driver stowed the suitcases in the trunk.

She sensed Marsh sliding beside her and the car pulling away. The cab smelled of stale cigarette smoke, but it was warm.

Did Captain Marsh say the Commander was at home? Where was "home"? Why didn't MacArthur pick her up? Before she could voice those thoughts, she fell asleep.

The next time she opened her eyes, MacArthur's face hovered over hers. "Hello, Belle." He kissed her forehead and helped her get out of the cab, which was stopped on the side of a street.

While MacArthur spoke to Captain Marsh, she appraised her surroundings. A landscape of skyscrapers and electric signs. The Christmas wreaths hanging from the lamp posts and the lights adorning the buildings reminded her it was December. Slow-moving cars, buses, and cabs clogged the streets in spite of the late hour.

Pedestrians—whites and blacks, not a single brown face—were getting ready to cross the street when a police car zipped by, its siren blaring, its tires splashing wet snow. They all jumped back. "Damn it!" yelled a man whose coat got spattered.

The towering buildings and car noises induced her dizziness anew. Everyone was taller and bigger. Or maybe the coats, boots, and hats—she'd never seen people in winter wear before—gave the illusion of bulk. She was a half-American girl, who had interacted with Americans all her life, but still unprepared for this country's foreignness. The word "uprooted" came to mind. She had been severed from her roots. Manila was very far indeed.

Captain Marsh bid her goodnight. He got back inside the cab. MacArthur and Isabel watched the car leave.

She stuck her hands in her coat pockets. Even with the gloves, her fingers felt numb. The tips of her ears and nose stung from the cold. Goodbye balmy Manila, goodbye perennial summer. Her heart faltered. "Where are we?" she asked.

"West Fifty-first Street and Seventh Avenue." He pointed his chin at the building before them, and they both gazed upward, scaling the building's height with their eyes. "That's the Prentice Building—thirty stories high. It's your new home. Welcome to New York City."

He smiled, picked up the suitcases. "This way, darling."

At the building's entrance, the doorman offered to carry the luggage, but MacArthur declined. Another man greeted them at the elevator, opening its door and then the gate.

Both men wore white uniforms with gold buttons. Both nodded at the Commander with deference and eyed Isabel with a glint of suspicion. Did they know who MacArthur was?

She and MacArthur stepped inside the wood-paneled elevator cab. He set the suitcases down. "Tenth floor, please."

The man hopped inside the elevator and shut the gate with a loud clang. He began operating the levers. The elevator lurched before it moved upward, heightening Isabel's nausea. She'd never ridden in an elevator before. How many times did the elevator man go up and down the building? Did he get dizzy?

"I'm sorry to hear you got sick," said MacArthur. "How do you feel?"

"Woozy."

He took her right hand. They stood side by side. She fought the urge to get inside his arms. The Philippines was a world away, but home was inside his arms. He held her hand until they reached their floor.

"Watch your step, Miss." The elevator man picked up her luggage. "After you, General."

So, the man knew who MacArthur was.

MacArthur ushered her inside the apartment, and then went back outside to tip the man.

The apartment reminded her of rich cream and butter. Everything—the walls, the upholstered sofa and chairs, the lamp shades—was in the shade of milk white, or pale yellow, or luminous taupe. The rugs displayed intricate patterns in deep blue and bold saffron. She walked around the living room, letting her fingers slide across the smooth mahogany sideboard. She stopped before the marble fireplace and admired the silver clock on the mantel. It bore a *Tiffany & Co.* logo. Never heard of the name before. She put it back carefully.

"Do you like the place?" MacArthur shut the door.

She nodded, intending to praise the apartment. But her foggy, travel-weary mind would not cooperate. Instead, she blurted out, "I expected to see you, not your aide, at the pier."

"I barely arrived here myself. I took the train from Washington." He removed his overcoat. He wore a dark gray suit and blue tie. She hadn't seen him in three months. He appeared taller, more handsome, more strapping than she remembered. Her chest pounded.

"I sent Marsh ahead of time in case I'm late. I couldn't get away from meetings with congressmen and senators…all about next year's military budget, which is not looking good."

"How far away is Washington?"

"Oh, about 240 miles. That's about 400 kilometers. The trip took almost five hours."

"What about Captain Marsh, did you send him back to Washington?"

"He's staying in a hotel tonight. He's going back tomorrow."

He hung his overcoat on a coat tree by the door, then he helped her get out of the fur coat. "This coat fits you perfectly." He stood behind her. "When I bought it, I was afraid it might be too long."

She got a whiff of him: citrusy soap and musky cologne, with a trace of cigar. It comforted her.

"I hired an interior decorator to furnish this place." He swept his arm. "I didn't want you to arrive to an empty apartment."

Exhaustion seeped into her bones. She sat on the sofa or she might collapse on the rug. She'd traveled so far to be with him, and her thoughts spilled out of her. "You said 'this is your new home.' Does it mean you're not going to live with me?"

"I can't." He didn't look at her.

She followed his adroit movement with her eyes, hanging her coat on the coat tree, then picking up the suitcases, and going into the bedroom. When he came back to the living room, he'd already taken off his suit jacket, but not his tie.

He removed his cuff links and rolled his sleeves up. "Are you hungry?"

She shook her head.

"I got you a sandwich from Penn Station. It's in the kitchen." He pointed to his left. "This apartment came with an icebox, but we need a refrigerator. And a telephone."

He knelt down before the fireplace, arranging the kindling and the logs. Then he lit the tinder with a long match. The logs burned and circulated warm air.

The Commander was efficiency itself, getting everything in order and thinking of refrigerators and telephones. But they didn't matter as much as his reassurance.

She gazed at his back, aching to touch him. It was Friday night. He would probably stay only for the weekend. She couldn't overcome the feeling she would always have to fight for his time. "I thought we were going to live together in Washington. Isn't that what you said in your letters?" Her voice gave away her resentment.

He glanced over his shoulder with a surprised expression, as though he'd forgotten all about those letters. He stood up. "No, I didn't say I was going to live with you. I simply can't. However, I *did* say I was going to find you an apartment in Washington. But I changed my mind."

He fished a handkerchief from his trouser pocket and wiped his hands. "Darling, you don't look well. Let me get you some water." He strode to the kitchen.

She rose, immediately overcome by vertigo. She would have followed him, but she got only as far as the sideboard. She gripped it with both hands.

He returned with a glass of water. She declined, shaking her head. "In Manila, we sneaked around during siesta, stealing an hour or two whenever we could. Here you'd spend a few days, instead of a few hours, with me, but disappear. I thought you wanted to be with me."

He set down the glass on the sideboard. Then he took her face in his hands, bringing his face so close to hers she might as well swim in his blue eyes. "Of course I want to be with you."

"But you don't want to live with me."

He let go. His hands fell on his sides, his back stiff as a flag pole. He towered before her—immovable and formidable like the Prentice Building, thirty stories high, but without the benefit of an elevator.

"It's complicated." He released a big sigh. "As the Army chief of staff, I have to live in an official residence at Fort Myer, and my mother is there. She has moved in with me."

"Your mother?" He'd mentioned her but once before. She was a long-time Washington resident. Of course, it made sense for her to move in with her son. But why had he not said anything about her in his letters? He'd hidden his mother from Isabel and vice versa.

"She's seventy-eight and not in the best of health. I have to take care of her."

"And she doesn't know that I exist. That's why you chose this apartment far away from Washington."

"Darling, don't let us quarrel." He embraced her. "I missed you terribly."

She rested her head on his chest and took solace in the soft thud of his heart. After the Grants, she'd promised herself no more lies about her relationship. If he couldn't marry her, then he should, at least, not hide her. Especially not from his mother. It was only the first hour of their reunion, but he'd already shattered her expectation.

She pushed away from him and moved toward the windows. The venetian blinds deprived her of a view. She had seen those blinds in banks and offices in Manila before, but never inside a home. How strange they looked. Wide wooden slats suspended helplessly, dependent on cords to hold them together. Sure, they were modern, but they had neither the softness nor the grace of even the plainest curtains.

She fingered the slats and tugged at the lift cord.

"You have to pull it harder." She could sense him walk toward the sofa.

She pulled the lift cord hard and gasped at the exhilarating view of lights that stretched as far as her eyes could see. Illuminated buildings and bright neon signs. Coca-Cola, Mitchell's Restaurant, Emerald Hotel, Singer Sewing Machines.

New York City. How dazzling, how unfamiliar. When she left Manila, she'd wanted MacArthur's America: a fresh start, the opportunities, and the good life. At the sight of the Statue of Liberty, she had harbored the same desire.

All that had changed. Her gaze dropped, the moving cars below making her lightheaded. She grew weak with loneliness. She needed his reassurance that he would stay with her—that she wouldn't be alone in this strange country. It wasn't America she wanted after all, but MacArthur.

She pivoted around. "I want to be with you."

His eyes narrowed. "Darling, you look awfully pale."

"You're not listening to me!"

She took a step forward, but her surroundings spun. Her breathing became fast and shallow, the air too dense. She placed a hand on her clammy forehead. He leapt to her side and swooped her up with both arms, lifting her up.

He had caught her seconds before everything turned black.

# 19.

MACARTHUR'S ARM brushed against something supple, like a bundle of satin, when he surfaced from sleep. The cast-iron radiator rattled. It was hot, though he'd gone to bed only in his underpants.

Before he could open his eyes, she came to him as in a dream. Her breath was warm on his face. Their noses bumped, her soft lips on his mouth, and her tongue played with his. Isabel had slid into his bed in the middle of the night.

Since her fainting spell late Friday, she'd slept in another bedroom, getting up twice but only briefly. The first time was on Saturday morning. She'd eaten a piece of toast and taken a shower. In the evening, she'd eaten the potato soup he'd bought from the deli. The rest of the time, she'd slept.

MacArthur supposed she'd fainted due to dehydration and exhaustion. A common ailment among young soldiers during the Great War. The antidote was rest.

While she'd slept, he had gone food shopping, something he hadn't done in years. He was accustomed to having aides, servants, and chauffeurs. He'd stopped at a sidewalk stand with the sign, *Buy an Apple a Day and Eat the Depression Away.*

Similar signs greeted him everywhere. He'd obliged, buying fruits and vegetables from every stand he'd passed by, and enjoying small talk with vendors and grocers. He savored his anonymity in Manhattan. In Washington, his uniform alone screamed his presence. He couldn't step out in public without being recognized by a bureaucrat or a serviceman or a newspaperman.

After food shopping, MacArthur had tackled the papers he'd brought from the office. He'd spent the rest of the day signing letters, reading reports, and going over his proposed Army budget. He'd examined the funding cuts Congress had recommended. He wanted to bridge gaps and reconcile differences.

By the time he hit the hay, he'd felt worn out by work and anxiety over Isabel's arrival. The apartment had two bedrooms and he'd slept in the guest room so as not to disturb her. He'd left his door ajar in case she woke up sick in the wee hours. His foresight had served him well.

He peeled off her satin nightgown—slippery and luxurious in his hands. She wore no undergarments. He felt keenly alive, as if it were zero hour in a battle.

But, in fact, this was friendly territory. He explored her body with the vehemence of someone who was lost—his hands, mouth, and tongue finding all the possible paths toward deliverance. It was deeply gratifying for a man of fifty to find a beautiful young woman flushed with desire for him. Their bodies twisted together in the waxy heat as they pursued each other's pleasure in a dogged manner. When they stopped, he felt whole and empty at the same time. Satiated but spent.

They didn't speak. No mention of whatever grievances she had earlier.

She fell asleep with her face curled to his neck, his arms and legs enclosing her. How snugly she fit inside the cocoon of his limbs. After a while, he loosened his hold so he could look at her. He tucked a wisp of hair behind her ear and kissed her forehead. In the aftermath of sex, her skin smelled a rich, sharp scent.

The day brightened outside, seeping into the slats of the venetian blinds. He should get some sleep. Instead, he marveled at her nakedness, the opalescence of her young skin, the tautness of a sixteen-year-old body—no, seventeen. He'd sent her the fur coat as a birthday present last month.

He closed his eyes. *Seventeen*. At that age, he'd taken the competitive West Point exam and received the highest mark. Compare that with Isabel—a high school dropout sleeping with a fifty-year-old divorced man who couldn't marry her.

He drew a big sigh. If he hadn't been born white, male, and American, would he have fared any better than her? He doubted it. His heart twitched at the randomness of luck, the cruel nature of fate.

He opened his eyes and turned to her, once again struck by her youth, her luminous beauty. *She's mine.* An overpowering male instinct to own and protect came over him.

The sight of her filled him with tenderness, with enormous satisfaction. He felt justified for bringing her to America. She was worth every penny he'd spent on her. Not to mention the trouble of dealing with immigration bureaucrats to hasten the processing of her travel documents and the sheer inconvenience of hiding her from his mother. He didn't know how to live two lives, one in Washington and another in New York. He would take things one day at a time.

He shifted his gaze upward, tucking one hand underneath his head, his thoughts drifting to the political situation. He'd chosen a ship route for Isabel that began in Manila and ended in New Jersey instead of Manila to San Francisco for a good reason. He couldn't risk the growing anti-Filipino sentiment in California, where a Filipino had been killed during a recent race riot against Asian workers.

Lobbyists in Washington had stepped up their demands to block Philippine imports. Labor unions had called for curbs on the flow of Filipino immigrants into the country.

American resentment over new immigrants was bound to grow. It targeted Filipinos because their status as colonial subjects was seen as a "special treatment," and the Depression magnified the ill effects of favoritism. Well, too bad. He was Douglas MacArthur. He always got what he wanted.

He sat up. No point in trying to get back to sleep. He could hear the city coming to life: car engines starting, a bus rumbling by.

She moved, grinding her teeth and moaning in her sleep. He covered her with the blanket and kissed her bare shoulder before slinking into the bathroom to shower.

He would make breakfast and then take her clothes shopping. The poor darling owned only chiffon and cotton dresses, woefully inadequate for the freezing New York winter. He would also buy her another birthday gift, something she herself would pick out.

But like any general worth his salt, MacArthur knew when to forge ahead with a plan and when to abandon it. His second zero hour began at seven o'clock plus five minutes, right after he'd finished making coffee and scrambled eggs.

The alluring enemy clad in the same nightgown he'd cast off earlier ambushed him. She jumped into his arms, pushing him backward, so he fell on a chair. She yanked his trousers and underpants down, lifted her nightgown up, and straddled him, right onto his erection. He scooped his hands under her buttocks and guided her movement up and down.

The breakfast grew cold and the shopping excursion postponed. He relegated all other plans for the day to the wayside. They made love without regard for time or comfort. They ravished each other standing up or sitting down or sprawled out, despite the glare of sunlight bursting through the blinds in the kitchen or in the bathroom. And when it grew dark, they groped each other under the soft light of a candle or in pitch-dark, in the living room or in the bedroom.

They were making up for lost time, doing what they'd always wanted to do, but couldn't in the past eight months they'd known each other. He'd planned to return to Washington on Sunday evening, but did not. He was on his honeymoon. He'd be damned if he let anything interrupt it. He stayed on for the next three days and showered her with extravagant affection. He'd never spent as much time with her before.

He enlisted the help of his aides—Captain Marsh, Lieutenant Wallace, and Ike Eisenhower—to cover for his absence at work. With reluctance, he telephoned Tom Rooney to cover for him at home.

Rooney, who hadn't known until then about MacArthur's continuing relationship with Isabel, was shocked. In the end, he did what a good friend would do. He lied on behalf of MacArthur and made up an elaborate story for Pinky about her son's unexpected trip to West Point.

On Wednesday afternoon, MacArthur and Isabel had just returned from Saks Fifth Avenue, where they'd bought the "midget cathedral" radio she'd wanted as an extra birthday gift.

He installed the one-foot-high radio on the sideboard. It ran on electricity and required no antennas. He made sure it worked before he returned to Washington or she wouldn't be able to use it while he was away.

"It's beautiful." She touched the radio's shiny wooden cabinet in the shape of a gothic arch. A fancy floral grille covered the opening for the speaker. "It sure looks like a little cathedral."

He showed her how it worked. "This is the power switch. And this is the volume control. The farther away the station you're listening to, the fainter the sound."

They stood side by side, her arms wrapped around his waist, her head resting on his shoulder.

"This knob is for tone control. Click to the left for more treble and click to the right for more bass." He kissed the top of her head. They listened to orchestra music. When it ended, the radio announcer read the weather forecast.

"I have to get ready, or I'll be late for my train." He disentangled himself from her arms.

He went to the master bedroom and collected the reports scattered about. He picked up his shaving kit from the bureau, but changed his mind. "I'm going to leave my toiletries, shaving kit, and dirty clothes. Tomorrow Margaret's cousin, Patty, will pick up the laundry. Just tell her how often you want her to do the laundry." He turned around and hollered, "Belle, did you hear what I said?"

He shoved the folders and papers inside the suitcase, shut it, and carried it to the living room.

She stood by the window, looking outside.

He turned off the radio. "Darling, did you hear what I said?"

She turned around. "Yes, about Margaret's cousin. What's her name again?"

"Patty. She works two days a week in a dress factory on Thirty-fourth Street. The rest of the week, she's available to help you—clean the apartment, do your laundry, buy groceries. Tell her what you need."

"So Captain Marsh and Margaret are engaged to be married?"

"Yes."

"When are they getting married?"

"Next year."

"That's fast. They met at the same time we met."

"No, they met several months earlier."

He detected a trace of envy in her voice. Both MacArthur and his aide had wanted their women to follow them. Marsh could easily marry Margaret, an American teacher whom Marsh had met in Manila. They were both single, white, American, and of legal age. MacArthur and Isabel's situation was, unfortunately, far from easy.

"Margaret must be so excited. How lucky she is." She plopped on the sofa.

Time to change the subject matter. He went to the kitchen and found a pen and a notepad. He started scribbling. "I'm writing down my telephone numbers at home and at the office. My home number should be your last resort." He said it loud enough for Isabel to hear. "I'm also writing down the phone numbers for Marsh and Wallace. If you can't reach me, call one of them."

He went back to the living room with the paper. "I'll leave this beside the radio. You can use the telephone in the supervisor's office downstairs. There's always someone there, either Oscar, the building supervisor, or one of his employees. If you need to use the phone, or if you need anything at all, you can go there. When I come back, I'll talk to Oscar about getting our own phone."

"When are you coming back?"

"In nine days."

"And Christmas?"

"I'll try to be here."

"Try?"

"Most likely I'll be here. I'm working on it."

She looked dour. She kicked off her high heels in a careless way, clearly to get his attention. Or rather, more of it.

He slid beside her, draping an arm across her shoulders. "I'll be back before you know it. We'll catch a musical on Broadway when I get back, the one with Ginger Rogers."

She leaned on his shoulder. "Are we going to attend Captain Marsh and Margaret's wedding?"

Boy, she wouldn't let go of the topic. And he thought she was still thinking about Christmas. "They haven't even picked a date yet. Also, usually you get an invitation. Until then, you can't make any plans to attend the wedding."

"I've always dreamed of a wedding, even just a simple one."

There was no avoiding the elephant in the room. His heart contracted. "I better get going." He squeezed her shoulder and kissed the side of her head.

A sigh escaped from her.

He rose to put on his suit jacket, then his overcoat, without glancing at her. He threw a scarf around his neck. He picked up his suitcase and put on his hat. Only then did he look at her. She remained seated on the couch, facing the windows.

"Why don't you walk me to the subway station?" he said.

When she turned to him, her eyes were moist.

"Belle, darling." He put the suitcase down, removed his hat, and set it atop the suitcase. He inched forward, but stopped at a safe distance, tucking his hands inside his coat pockets. If he got any closer, he might never leave. "You have to stop thinking about Marsh and Margaret. Our situation is nothing like theirs. And besides, you're seventeen years old. You have your whole life ahead of you."

She put both feet up and hugged her knees. "That's what Mrs. Grant said—you have your *whole* life ahead of you."

He knitted his brows together, trying to remember who she was talking about. "Ah. Well, Mrs. Grant was right."

"If I were older…if I were as old as Margaret…would you marry me?"

"There are laws in this country prohibiting mixed marriages. We talked about this in front of your family."

"What if there were no such laws, would you marry me?"

"Belle." He took another step forward, but resisted sitting down beside her. He glanced at his pocket watch. "I really have to go."

She rose, petulant. He opened his arms.

She walked toward him, meek as a puppy, and buried her face in his chest. So unlike her. A tantrum would have been normal, and perhaps more welcome because he was used to it.

He locked her inside his arms. A rush of guilt—the instinct to own and protect—surfaced again. She was his girl. And she dreamed of a wedding. Nothing wrong with that.

He kissed her forehead and buried his nose in her hair. For the first time in his life, he felt incompetent. He couldn't do what was necessary. He was more than incompetent. He was an ass, a goddamned jerk! He could give her an expensive love nest and a state-of-the-art radio and bring her to America amid the Great Depression, but he couldn't give her what she deserved.

"I'm sorry—" He hugged her tighter.

But the words were stuck in his throat. Why was he sorry? There were too many reasons. His emotions sprawled like a whole new, undiscovered country. He couldn't begin to traverse it without getting lost. He might never find his way out.

She tilted her head away from him. "You don't have to apologize. It's all right. Come on, I'll walk you to the subway station."

"You will?" He smiled.

"Of course." The dimples appeared when she frowned, making her look like a child who had succumbed to doing a chore.

"Attagirl!" He gave her a smack on the lips. *A reprieve.* He drew a long sigh of gratitude.

# 20.

# New York, January 1931

ON THE MORNING of MacArthur's fifty-first birthday, Isabel woke up early to make breakfast. It was Monday. He should have been at work in Washington, but she'd succeeded in making him feel guilty about not spending New Year's Eve with her. And so, he'd relented and stayed in New York.

She wore an apron over her silk blouse and wool tweed skirt. Her hair was tied in a neat pony tail, her face powdered. She'd slipped on high heels to complement her outfit, but skipped the stockings. Frankly, there was no need to dress up just to cook, but an actress should never look frumpy, unless a role called for it. Although she hadn't performed since she'd left Manila, she was, and always would be, an actress and an entertainer.

She fried some chorizos, the pan sizzling. While waiting for the sausages to brown, she made coffee with the electric percolator. In Manila, she used to help Manang boil the ground beans at just the right temperature and then strain the brew to get rid of the grounds. Goodbye to all that.

Two months had rushed by like a hurtling train, her homesickness a blur in its wake. New York City offered so many new sights and smells, everyday a sea of eager faces and purposeful strides on the streets and the sidewalks. She embraced and absorbed its massive energy and endless possibilities. How could she stay homesick?

She lived in the theater district, a stone's throw away from Broadway theaters and fabulous restaurants and clubs. The comforts of her apartment and the leisurely pace of her new life almost made up for MacArthur's absence. His official life away from her created friction between them, but she tried to understand.

For the first time, she owned a bank account, courtesy of the Commander. She had her own help, though she considered Patty a friend, too. She possessed a refrigerator and a telephone! Mama would kill to have these things.

Isabel's apartment was equipped with the miraculous amenities of shower and indoor plumbing. A far cry from her childhood home in Manila, which had an outhouse and a bathroom with just a faucet and a bucket for bathing. And don't forget her radio, phonograph, and yes, a brand new piano. He'd bought the piano as a Christmas gift.

All she got for him was a necktie from Macy's. She spent his money with care. Besides, what could anyone buy for Douglas MacArthur? She'd compensated for her meager Christmas present by giving him other gifts, or "perks" as Patty called them—all the pleasures a girl could provide a man under the covers.

Patty, twenty-eight and desperate to get married, performed house chores and ran errands for Isabel twice a week. They talked a lot, especially about their lovers. Patty was "dating" an Italian immigrant named Alessandro, who couldn't find a job and had resorted to bootlegging.

Isabel had never heard of dating before. In the Philippines, gentlemen called on ladies to court them. Patty lived in a tiny apartment with her family of six and no space for Alessandro to "call." Instead they went to coffee shops, movie theaters, and the back of a car for some "privacy." Alessandro didn't own a car, so they had to borrow a friend's jalopy if they wanted "privacy"—Patty's special term for sexual intercourse. She and Patty shared a common gripe. Their lovers had no plans of marrying them.

When Isabel fretted about getting a Christmas present for MacArthur, Patty had said, "You already give the general enough 'perks.' You're always here for his pleasure." They'd joked about it then. But it irked Isabel now. Manang's words ricocheted in her head. *If you go to America, you will forever be a white man's plaything.*

She admitted, if only to herself, she'd softened up in America. Back in Manila, she'd been quick to throw tantrums or to withhold a kiss, but now her life revolved around pleasing the Commander. Sadness rippled through her and she let out a sigh. The perks had to be worthy of the bank account, the Manhattan apartment, and everything inside it. They had to deserve the long train ride he must endure to see her every other week. They had to be special for him to spend Christmas with her. Only God knew how he got away from his mother.

And so, America was changing Isabel into a sweeter, kinder, more subservient girl. How ironic was that? She'd pushed aside her own demands, subverting her natural inclination to take and take. She'd become the incomparable perks giver. Now might be the right time for something huge in return.

But first, MacArthur's birthday. She didn't know what to give him. She'd picked a coffee mug with an image of coffee beans and *I taste so good!* written on it. How meager indeed. The occasion called for a unique perk. She could only hope what she had in mind was extra special. She could never ask him about it.

MacArthur fit the mold of an old-fashioned gentleman. The rough sex in the abandoned military clinic never happened again. He didn't talk about what he wanted in bed, or what he'd done with other women.

She removed the chorizos from the pan and made fried rice, Filipino style, with lots of chopped garlic. The percolator gurgled, sounding giddy. In no time, she had everything ready: a plate of chorizos with fried rice, sliced tomatoes on the side, a small pot of coffee, a table napkin, and silverware.

She took off her apron and entered the master bedroom with a breakfast tray. She set the coffee pot on the dresser. It was only half past six in the morning, but the Commander had begun work, though he was still in his silk pajamas. He sat on his side of the bed and read a thick folder. "Good morning, darling."

She frowned. "Why are you up so early? I wanted to wake you up myself."

He shut the folder. "Sorry. It's a habit. I'm usually up at this time reading reports, before I even get dressed for work."

"Not today—no reports today. I made you an authentic Filipino breakfast." She set the tray on his lap. "Happy birthday!"

"This is wonderful. What a treat. But you're forgetting something." Of course, he wanted a kiss.

Not yet. She perched on the edge of the bed facing him and sliced the sausages. She fed him a piece.

After a bite, he said, "Where did you get Filipino chorizo?"

"Patty found it for me."

Patty was resourceful. She even found out that the state of New York had no law preventing interracial marriage. MacArthur couldn't marry Isabel in Virginia, where he lived, but he could in New York. She had thought long and hard about it. In Manila, marriage never crossed her mind. And when he'd told her family he wanted to live with her sans marriage, she'd taken it in stride. It had been sufficient. But on the night she'd set foot in America, something had changed. Perhaps *everything* had changed.

"Darling, how can I drink my coffee without a cup?"

She snapped back to the present, moving her gaze from the sausage to his smiling face. His docile demeanor could have fooled her into thinking that he'd give her anything. She fed him a piece of tomato. Did she have the power to tame the Big Cheese?

She rose to pick up a wrapped box from her closet. "Happy birthday." She handed it to him.

He said thank you, pausing—waiting for a kiss. She sat back on the bed facing him, but still, she withheld her kiss.

He unwrapped the box. "I taste so good!" He chuckled. He put the mug on the tray, then leaned sideways to set it on the floor.

Her pulse sped up at the sight of the bulge in his pajama trousers.

He grinned as he reached inside her skirt, caressing her bare thigh. "You know what tastes so good?" His blue eyes shone with mischief.

She shook her head, feeling warm where he stroked her. Her heart raced. She fixed her eyes on his and didn't reciprocate his touch.

Heavens, he looked so good even though he was unshaven. His temples showed some gray, but otherwise his rumpled hair was dark. With his stubble, he exuded a roguish charm. She pressed her lips and planted her palms on the bed, fighting the urge to jump him.

He fondled her crotch without hurry. “You,” he continued. “You taste so good.”

“That’s not what the mug is all about.” And yet, she couldn’t help but open her legs a little to accommodate him. She caught herself and closed her legs before his fingers could meander inside her undergarment. She made a face. “It’s not a pun.”

“It’s not?” He traced her mound with his fingers, teasing her.

Her skin prickled. “No. *Delicious* refers to the coffee.”

“It does?”

“I don’t think you even like my gift.”

“I do. I really do.”

“Well then, I want you to use it.” Good heavens, she’d grown damp between her legs. She peeled his hand off her and got up. Such unusual restraint only intensified her lust. But she’d planned something different altogether.

He heaved an extravagant sigh and swung his legs off the bed. His bare feet landed a few inches away from the tray.

*The tray with the cup.* Still on the floor, offering an opportunity. She got up and took the coffee pot from the dresser. She knelt down before him and poured coffee into the mug. “Coffee?” She handed it to him.

“Sure.” He took a sip. “Thank you.”

As casual as could be, she rested her face on his thigh. His manhood grew stiff. Her body tingled in response. She looked up to him.

He’d stopped mid-drink with the cup in his hand. He didn’t move.

The radiator clanked as the heat came up, the air charged with desire. She lowered her face and kissed his groin tentatively, the silk pajama cool and smooth against her lips.

When she lifted her face again, he appeared to be holding his breath. She gave him her bedimpled smile. “I’m curious, that’s all.”

His face glowed—permission granted. He was allowing her to satisfy her curiosity. She wasn’t wanton.

She snatched the mug from his hand and set it down on the floor. Then she pulled down his pajama bottoms. She pressed her mouth on his navel, moving lower until her lips brushed his erection. She fumbled a little, like she didn't know what she was doing. He gasped at her feigned clumsiness.

"You have to show me how," she said.

He pulled her face toward him, his cock nudging her lips. She secreted him fully into her mouth. *Happy birthday indeed.*

Once she'd started, she couldn't stop. What was wrong with her? She always planned to drive him mad with lust, but the opposite always happened.

Her body grew feverish with greed. She'd never been as rapacious. He groaned *no,* but too late. The warm liquid squirted into her throat, making her almost gag. With calmness, she swallowed. *That* was something she'd never done before. She sucked and swallowed again. Her heart swelled with inconceivable joy—he was hers. It was the only way she could claim the whole of him.

"I love you," she murmured.

His eyes were closed; he was panting. He said nothing, just stroked the top of her head.

They spent the entire day in bed with the blinds shut. The ringing telephone woke them up. It had been installed only a week before.

He put on his trousers and padded to the living room. After a few minutes, he returned to the darkened bedroom. He flicked the light switch on.

"Who was it?" She sat up, pulling the blanket to cover her body.

"Marsh." He sat on the bed. They were face to face.

"What did he want?"

"It's about work. And he wished me a happy birthday. Should we go to Waldorf-Astoria for dinner?" He caressed her cheek with the back of his hand. "I didn't make a reservation, but if I tell them my name, I'm sure we can get a table."

"You better call now."

He squeezed her nose affectionately before going back to the living room.

True, his name alone opened doors. When he wanted his identity known, everyone considered his presence a grace wherever they went.

She, of course, got the curious stares. *Who is she?* That was the expression on people's faces when they walked into a room. Then the attention would revert to him. People cared only about Douglas MacArthur. They fawned over him. It was both a relief and a pain. A relief to be waited on promptly and a pain to know she was invisible beside him.

Most of the time, he preferred anonymity. They would go to obscure restaurants and clubs. In those places, he charmed managers and waiters. They gave him preferential treatment without knowing his name. His effect on people, whether they knew who he was or not, was the same. His presence loomed so large it reduced her to a shadow.

When he came back to the room, he said, "The manager will save a table for us. We can go anytime."

"Anytime? At the Waldorf-Astoria?"

He nodded. "How about we plan on getting there at seven-thirty? Will that give you enough time to get ready?"

The alarm clock on the nightstand showed it was five o'clock. "More than enough time." She fell right back in bed. Her bare leg peeked from the tangled blanket.

He patted her ankle playfully, but he didn't sit down. "You know… Marsh mentioned something about your documents."

"Is there a problem?" Captain Marsh handled Isabel's immigration papers.

"No. He just thought there was a mistake. Your documents listed 1910 as your birth year, not 1913."

*Damn it.* Lieutenant Wallace hadn't noticed it back in Manila, but Captain Marsh was too damn attentive. Before she could say anything, MacArthur had slinked to the adjacent bathroom.

She rose and slipped on a chemise. She could hear rustling in the bathroom and then running water. She should set her hair in pin curls, but her mind roamed. It was the Commander's birthday. Was it the best time, or the worst time, for her to tell him the truth? What would she tell him? How much?

She rummaged through her closet, trying to pick a dress, but couldn't decide. She paced the room, eyeing the bathroom door.

It opened, revealing MacArthur in a white robe. The cloud of vapor dissipated. As was his habit, he shaved after a shower.

She watched him from the bedroom, her anxiety bubbling up. He filled the sink with water and soaked the shaving brush in it. Then he wiped the fog off the mirror before him. At last, he noticed her. "Darling, what's the matter?"

She shook her head. She glanced at her fingernails, painted bright red. A hangnail on her right thumb protruded.

He removed the brush from the water, shook it, and dipped it in a tub of shaving cream. He brushed his cheeks and neck with the white lather in an up-and-down movement, like someone painting a wall.

She walked toward him, stopping in the bathroom doorway. "About what Captain Marsh said—"

"Hmm?" He set the brush down, picked up his razor, and began shaving his face.

"About my birth year—"

He looked at her in the mirror. "I told Marsh it better be a mistake because if you're twenty years old, then you're just too old." He glanced at her sideways, smiling. "That was a joke."

"What if there's no mistake?" She fidgeted with the hangnail. "I *am* twenty years old."

He stopped to face her, the razor still in his hand. "You lied about your age?"

"Is twenty too old for you?"

"No, it's not. Twenty—like seventeen—is too young for me. I'm well aware of that. But that's beside the point, which is, why did you lie about your age?"

"Actresses lie all the time."

"Why did you lie to *me?*"

"I'm sorry." She bit the hangnail.

"For God's sake, stop doing that."

He finished shaving and set the razor down. He rinsed his face and wiped it with a towel. "Is there anything else you lied about? Because now is a good time to let me know."

She continued nibbling her thumb. Finally she pulled the hangnail, drawing blood. It hurt like hell. She sucked it. Her plan to broach marriage in New York had evaporated.

"This morning...what you did this morning... were you acting?" His jaw was rigid, his voice clipped. "Was that Dimples the actress making love to me?"

She shook her head. Her thumb remained in her mouth, her blood tasting like metal. She'd lied about her age, about not knowing how to suck his cock, and pretended to be a virgin, but she hadn't lied about one thing. She loved him. She'd fallen for him like a glass toppling and shattering on the floor. Unplanned, unwelcome, and irreversible. *That* was the radical change she'd felt on her first night in America.

She couldn't voice those thoughts. Instead she said, "I was held back in school and I was the oldest in my class. So I lied about my age." Her eyes rested on her hands. She pressed her thumb to stop it from bleeding. "In the entertainment business, the younger a woman, the more desirable she is. That's why I lied."

"Isabel, stop that, please." He opened the medicine cabinet, riffling through it.

Her stomach roiled with fear. When was the last time he called her *Isabel?* It was always darling or Belle. He was going to leave her. The thought rose from her gut to her throat like bile.

He found a Band-Aid and removed its covering. "Let me see your finger." He wrapped the adhesive around her wounded thumb with tenderness, like he was afraid of hurting her. He kissed the thumb, then her hand.

Her tears welled up. *Unworthy* came to mind. If he'd cursed or slapped her, or kicked her out of the apartment, she would have understood. His gentleness filled her with guilt.

He cupped her face with both hands and bent his forehead to touch hers.

"I'm sorry," she said. In those earnest blue eyes lay her salvation. They could lift her up, heart and soul.

"No more lies," he replied. "From now on, no more lies."

# 21.

# Virginia, May 1931

IN THE GARDEN of Quarters One, the Victorian mansion where MacArthur lived, he and his mother welcomed the new Dutch ambassador and a delegation of government officials from the Kingdom of the Netherlands. It was an official reception for the Dutch ambassador.

"Congratulations on your new post." MacArthur shook the ambassador's hand. "It's a great honor to meet you."

"The honor is all mine, General."

Ever since MacArthur went to Amsterdam as the head of the U.S. delegation at the 1928 Olympic Games, he had maintained friendly ties with the Dutch government. Queen Wilhelmina and the prince consort, Prince Henry of Mecklenburg-Schwerin, were very fond of MacArthur and vice versa.

For the party that evening, the queen had sent a roomful of red roses, which adorned the tables. They were MacArthur roses, named by the famous horticulturist, Luther Burbank, for Douglas's father, Arthur MacArthur.

In addition to the Dutch delegation, MacArthur had invited U.S. Army and War Department officials and their spouses.

A brisk wind, pleasant and comfortable for a garden cocktail hour, stirred the tree branches. Pink azaleas and purple rhododendrons bloomed. Even the apple trees displayed profuse white blossoms. An Army band played lively music, a new style called swing.

Due to Prohibition, the waiters served only non-alcoholic cocktails. But the Dutch delegation brought several cases of French champagne as a present to the MacArthurs. Everyone oohed when a waiter popped open a bottle.

"I took the liberty of bringing champagne. I hope you don't mind," the Dutch ambassador told MacArthur.

"No, not at all. Call it diplomatic privilege." MacArthur squared his shoulders, his dress uniform stiff. In Washington, nobody wanted to be accused of being rude for turning down a gift of wine from Europeans, whose alcohol consumption was ingrained in their culture.

"You have a beautiful home," said the ambassador's wife. "I've heard that you can see the Washington Monument from your house."

A white-coated waiter offered champagne.

"Yes, that's true. You can see it from the second floor." MacArthur pointed at the mansion. "Later, I'll give both of you a personal tour and you'll see the spectacular view."

"Please extend our thanks to Queen Wilhelmina for the lovely roses." Pinky MacArthur beamed at her guests. "I can't tell you how deeply touched I am by her thoughtfulness."

The ambassador regaled Pinky with anecdotes about the queen's travels. MacArthur circulated, making sure he talked to every Dutch guest. He finished his champagne and handed the empty glass to a waiter.

He stopped at the table where his three aides and their women sat. Only Ike Eisenhower was married. Captain Marsh sat beside Margaret, resplendent in a yellow dress, a diamond ring on her finger. Isabel would have been twice as envious at the sight of the engagement ring.

Wallace, on the other hand, had yet another new sweetheart. MacArthur slapped his back with fondness. Whether in Manila or in the States, the man juggled his amorous pursuits, incorrigible.

MacArthur pulled Marsh aside and draped an arm across the young man's shoulders. The band had taken a respite, so he whispered in Marsh's ear for privacy. "Did you talk to Belle?"

"Yes, sir. She wanted to know if you can still catch a train tonight."

He pulled his eyebrows together. "How can I do that?"

"We can tell Mrs. MacArthur you need to visit the Watervliet Arsenal. It's next on your list of 'surprise' visits."

To see Isabel in New York every other weekend, MacArthur had told his mother that as the new chief of staff, he needed to make random visits to various facilities. It provided an excellent cover.

He crossed his arms over his chest. "It's not my mother. It's the Dutch ambassador and all of these people. I can't go AWOL at my own party."

Captain Marsh nodded.

"How did she sound on the phone?" said MacArthur.

"Unhappy, sir. She said she misses you."

He felt a blush bloom across his face. Although Marsh and Wallace were privy to his love life, moments like this embarrassed him. Eisenhower knew about Isabel, but he hadn't met her, and so MacArthur relied on Marsh and Wallace when it came to matters pertaining to Isabel.

"Call her again. The phone is in my study. Tell her I won't be able to see her until next Friday. Tell her I'm sorry."

Marsh grimaced.

"Okay, tell her I'll call tomorrow."

"Sir, you should probably call tonight, after the party."

"You think so?"

Marsh nodded. "I highly recommend it, sir."

"Very well. I'll call later…but it might be quite late."

"I'm sure she won't mind."

MacArthur patted Marsh on the back. "You better make that call now."

"Yes, sir."

Marsh whispered something to Margaret before going inside the house. MacArthur sighed, wishing Isabel were by his side. He stayed at his aides' table and listened to Wallace and his girl talk about how they'd met at a dance, while the Eisenhowers reminisced about their first date.

His heart pinched. His aides were having a great time with their loved ones. Why couldn't he enjoy the same thing?

He moved on to the next table, greeting some War Department top brass and their wives. The band started playing again, so MacArthur and the bigwigs stopped talking. They listened to the music. It suited him just fine, allowing him to return to his private thoughts.

If not for the party, he would be en route to New York. He was killing himself traveling every other week to be with the woman he loved. Yes, he loved her. He couldn't deny it.

Loving Isabel was like going through a never-ending obstacle course. Crawling in the mud, sliding down hills, and climbing ropes were easy compared with what he had to do to capture a few hours with her. It wasn't just the inconvenience of hiding her from Pinky and the general public and the considerable distance between Washington and New York. Isabel herself proved to be his most formidable challenge, the source of his biggest pain—and his greatest joy and pleasure. *My beloved obstacle.*

He would have chosen one month in the worst boot camp on earth over one painful moment with her. Such as her dreadful revelation she'd lied about her age. He wouldn't normally tolerate such rank dishonesty, but because it was Isabel, his anger had melted before it could solidify.

Back in Manila, when MacArthur had called on her, Ben had smirked when her age was brought up. MacArthur had been puzzled back then, but now he understood. That she'd lied about something so fundamental made him question her integrity, her loyalty, the very reason she accepted him.

What else was she capable of lying about? She could have spared him the needless remorse. The pleasure of sleeping with a young woman would always be tinged with guilt, but twenty, past the age of consent, was certainly better than seventeen!

He wasn't bothered Isabel's family had milked him for cash and influence—a small price to pay. But he always believed she cared about him. Whenever she professed her love, he never questioned it. He didn't want to start doubting now.

The band finished a number, drawing applause. Tom Rooney waved at him. He'd just arrived with his wife, Rose, and another woman, the daughter of a brigadier general.

MacArthur excused himself from the War Department top brass. He walked toward the Rooneys and hugged Rose first and then Tom.

"Do you remember Agnes Pearce?" Rose said.

"Yes, I do." MacArthur shook Agnes's hand. "How are you?"

"I'm fine, thank you." Agnes tilted her black hat, the curls of her short blond hair peeking. "We met ten years ago, at a party celebrating my dad's promotion."

"Yes, that's right. It was at your house."

She stood almost eye to eye with MacArthur. She wore a prudish long-sleeved dress that reached her ankles. Her shoes were flat.

"Where's your dad? He better not stand me up," teased MacArthur. "He lives a block away, so he has no reason to be late."

"I'm afraid he has a very good reason to be late—my mom." Agnes laughed. She wore no cosmetics; when she blushed, her freckles grew more prominent. She slouched like she was uncomfortable being tall. She joked about how long it took her mother to get dressed, how it drove her father crazy.

Three waiters came. One carried drinks, another had a tray of deviled eggs, and the third offered shrimp cocktail. Everyone but MacArthur ate appetizers and sipped drinks.

Ten years ago, Ernie Pearce and Douglas MacArthur were promoted brigadier general within months of each other. Douglas went on to become major general and now a four-star general and the Army chief of staff. Ernie, at least ten years older than MacArthur, remained a brigadier general. He and a few other generals resented MacArthur.

All his life he had to deal with other men's envy. Even as a West Point cadet, his last name alone caused jealousy among boys whose fathers were not the subject of newspaper headlines. Did Agnes know her dad begrudged MacArthur's success?

From the corner of his eye, he saw Pinky approaching them, hopping in excitement. He turned his head toward her and wished she would slow down. He'd asked for an elevator at Quarters One so she could go up and down the mansion with ease. It cost over five thousand dollars. The expense, amid the Great Depression, had caused more than a few raised eyebrows.

He didn't care. The government wanted him to live in an official residence, so it should meet his requirements. What vexed him were the two words that likely followed the raising of eyebrows: Mama's boy.

Pinky hugged the Rooneys and then Agnes, telling her, "I'm so pleased to see you, my dear! I've been trying to invite you over, but Rose said you're very busy."

The comment surprised MacArthur. Why did his mother want to invite Agnes?

"I'm sorry, Mrs. MacArthur." Agnes clasped her hands behind her back, like a timid school girl. "It's true, I work long hours, but I'm glad to be here today."

"Doug, do you know Agnes is a nurse at Walter Reed Hospital?"

"No, I didn't."

"Isn't it wonderful she takes care of our veterans?" Pinky turned to Agnes. "Your parents must be so proud of you. Where are they? I hope they're coming."

Agnes repeated the explanation for her parents' tardiness.

MacArthur sidled up to Tom Rooney, and whispered, "What's going on?"

Rooney pushed his eyeglasses on the bridge of his nose. "Your mother wants to play matchmaker."

"Why didn't you warn me?"

"I had no idea until an hour ago, when Rose told me we had to pick up Agnes from her apartment."

MacArthur shook his head.

"I have nothing to do with this," Rooney insisted.

MacArthur rejoined the conversation. "Miss Pearce, I hope you can tell me more about your work at Walter Reed at another time. First-hand observations will help me tremendously in evaluating the needs of our veterans. Right now…if you'll excuse me…I have to go. I have to give the Dutch ambassador and his wife a tour of the house before dinner starts."

He walked away.

"Doug, just a moment." Pinky had caught up with him.

He stopped.

Her face opened into a big smile. "How about I invite Agnes for dinner next Friday or maybe Saturday? Which day would you prefer?"

He held Pinky's elbow and guided her toward an apple tree. They stood a safe distance from the Rooneys and Agnes Pearce.

Dusk had descended, dark as a bruise. Waiters scurried to place lighted lanterns on the tables. Someone turned on the lights strung in trees.

"Mother, please stop playing matchmaker. I'm not interested."

"Why not? She's very sweet." Pinky tossed a glance at Agnes. "She admires you. That's what she told Rose. Can't you see how you make her blush?"

"You're putting me on the spot. Ernie Pearce is my subordinate. And he hates my guts."

"Nonsense!" Her arm arched in the air. "Ernie speaks very highly of you."

"Please leave my personal affairs alone."

"If I do that you'll never find a suitable woman. You're too busy. At least let me invite her over next weekend."

"No. I won't be here next weekend."

"Where are you going? Surely you can postpone your trip to whichever fort you need to visit." She flashed a conspiratorial grin. "Listen, Agnes is thirty-seven and she's been working as a nurse for many years. She's more than ripe for marriage. She's waiting for the right man, so she can call it quits and have a baby or two."

She nudged him with her elbow. "It's not too late for both of you. You have to move fast, if you know what I mean."

"For God's sake. This is not the same as asking for an elevator."

"Well, of course, it isn't." She pinched her lips. "One dinner with her is all I'm asking. I know you're going to change your mind if you give her half a chance."

Hands on hips, he glanced at Agnes. Too tall, too blond, too freckled, and too plain. The dress, the hat, the shoes—everything about her was wrong. She was *not* Isabel. He'd ceased to notice other women. He'd been blind to anyone but Isabel. Agnes Pearce was just one of those women he didn't bother giving a second glimpse anymore.

"Oh, Ernie and Amanda Pearce are here!" Pinky pointed behind MacArthur. "Let's go and say hello to them."

He glanced over his shoulder and saw the couple. He turned his face back toward his mother. "If you think I'm going to court Agnes Pearce next Friday, marry her by Saturday, and procreate with her on the same day, you are very much mistaken."

"What a terrible thing to say!"

He touched her arm for emphasis. "I'm not interested in Agnes."

"Oh, Doug—"

"Please stop setting me up with Agnes or any other woman."

"Doug—"

"I'm in love with someone else."

Pinky's eyes grew wide. "What?"

"You heard me. I plan to be with her next weekend."

Her expression turned from bewilderment to steeliness as she put two and two together. He could almost read her mind. She was recalling his weekend trips, his absence last Christmas, and the late telephone calls.

He took out his pocket watch and checked the time. "Mother, please do me a favor and greet Ernie and Amanda Pearce. I'm going to take the Dutch ambassador and his wife inside the house for a tour."

"Why didn't you tell me before?" She glared.

"I don't think you'll understand."

"Who is she?"

"You don't want to know."

"I *do* want to know. I have the right to know."

*Mama's boy.* He was the most powerful man in the military of one of the world's mightiest nations—but it didn't matter to people who thought he was tied to his mother's apron strings. If he didn't assert his right to be with Isabel, then he deserved the label.

He looked her square in the eyes. "I'm sorry, but I won't introduce her to you because you're not going to approve of her. I haven't asked you for anything in a long time. Tonight I'm asking you this—please respect my choice. You can pretend she doesn't exist, but please leave me be."

He strode away.

# 22.

# New York, May 1931

MACARTHUR LEFT his office in Washington at noon so he could be with Isabel in New York by dusk. There was no need to lie to Pinky anymore. He could come and go as he pleased. She hadn't asked him again about the mystery woman in his life. He didn't care whether it was out of her pride, or respect for him. The peace between them, though superficial, mattered more.

MacArthur had endured five hours of train ride to see Isabel. The last thing he wanted was to socialize with Samuel Morgan Prentice, the millionaire who owned the building where she lived.

And yet, he found himself standing with Isabel outside Sam Prentice's door. The man lived in a two-story apartment at the top of the Prentice Building. A butler ushered them inside and up the marble stairs, Isabel ahead of MacArthur.

She wore a black silk dress with a plunging V-shaped back. An immense bow sat at the top of her derrière.

He ogled her ass—the ribbon bouncing—and the smooth canvas of her bare back. She sashayed in her high heels, the shapely legs covered with sheer hosiery. Agnes Pearce, who had slouched in her spinster's outfit and flat shoes, paled in comparison.

For the first time, he appreciated the effect of pumps on a woman's gait and posture, the beauty of a well-fitted dress that clung to her body like a second skin. Of course, it didn't hurt to have Isabel's figure. His libido came alive just watching her climb the stairs.

Inside the living room, they paused to take in the fifteen-foot-high Palladian windows and the twenty-foot-high ceiling. New York City's neon-lit streets and buildings flickered outside the windows. The massive crystal chandelier elicited awe. The drapes and floor rugs were opulent. Everything was in the shade of gold with splashes of cream and red.

Sam Prentice greeted MacArthur and Isabel. He was perhaps the same age as MacArthur, but his excessive wealth showed in the size of his girth. He wore a black tailcoat with white tie. MacArthur glanced down at his pinstripe double-breasted suit, feeling underdressed. *So be it.*

Prentice eyed Isabel like a man who hadn't eaten in months. "Hello, doll." He embraced her with too much enthusiasm.

"Her name is Isabel," said MacArthur.

"Isabel, of course."

MacArthur had told Prentice her name beforehand, but the bastard was too busy leering to remember. His hand slid down her backside.

"Hey, how are you, Sam?" MacArthur clapped his shoulder. It worked. Prentice withdrew his hand.

"I'm great! How are you, General?"

"I'm fine, thank you." They shook hands.

"I read something about you in the *New York Times* this morning... about the dangers of pacifism and complacency...about the menace of the 'peace cranks.' Did you really call those liberals peace cranks?"

"Yes, I did. It was meant to be a confidential report to the secretary of war."

"You mean, someone had leaked it to the press?"

"It seems like it."

"Do you think there are spies in the War Department?"

"No, not spies. Just overzealous newspapermen who bribe civil servants to steal a copy of my report."

"Those goddamn Communists in the *Times* called you a warmonger."

"I'm routinely slandered in the press. It's part of the job."

MacArthur already regretted this dinner, but he'd come because of Isabel. Prentice was producing a show on Broadway and she wanted to audition. When Prentice happened to invite them over, she was eager to go.

"How do you like your apartment?" Prentice asked Isabel. "Do you have a good view from the tenth floor? If not, I can arrange for you to move to the twenty-fifth floor. You'll have an excellent view there."

"We love our view. Thank you for asking." She glanced at MacArthur as though seeking confirmation.

"Now, don't be shy with me, doll. Just say the word, and you can have the apartment on the twenty-fifth floor."

"Sam, I picked the tenth floor for a good reason." MacArthur stuck his hands in his jacket pockets, modulating the irritation in his voice. "It's not that I don't trust your elevators, but if anything happens to them, I can't imagine Isabel or myself climbing twenty-five floors of stairs."

"Always strategic, always pragmatic! That's why you're a general and I'm not." Prentice's guffaw matched his size.

There were at least a hundred reasons why he was a general and Prentice wasn't, but he bit his tongue. He tossed a glance at the grandfather clock—half past eight. He could withstand only one hour, tops, of this agonizing conversation. He took a deep breath.

Prentice opened the French doors and showed them the terrace, revealing the marvelous view of the skyline and the balcony furnished with an outdoor sofa, chairs, and tables. Potted trees, hyacinths, and ferns thrived. The man blabbered about his properties, a dozen apartment buildings and hotels in the city, and those he wanted to buy. He pointed at buildings in the horizon while he spoke.

MacArthur's former wife, Louise, had introduced him to Prentice. She hobnobbed with New York's crème de la crème. She had dragged MacArthur to Prentice's soirees a few times. In spite of his success as a businessman, Prentice was too decadent and corpulent to earn MacArthur's respect. He never thought he would one day come knocking on Prentice's gilded door. But when he needed a discreet apartment for Isabel, he'd called Prentice.

The millionaire understood the sensitivities involved in MacArthur's love life. Prentice himself had a complicated situation. He consorted with beautiful young women, and yet he managed to stay married to the same woman and keep the peace with their children.

Indeed Prentice had promised MacArthur utmost privacy. His people would never talk to newspapermen or gossip columnists. They knew how to protect the couple from the scrutiny of other tenants in the building.

"Gracie Lynn, honey, our guests are here!" hollered Prentice, interrupting MacArthur's train of thought.

A young blonde emerged from one of the rooms, prompting Prentice, MacArthur, and Isabel to go back inside. Prentice gave Gracie Lynn a smack on the lips and introduced her.

Prentice's paramour wore a silver dress with a low neckline, a poor choice for a flat-chested woman like her. She resembled a stick in a fancy dress.

MacArthur gazed at Isabel with admiration and latched on to her hand—a proprietary gesture Prentice apparently appreciated because he acknowledged MacArthur with a nod and a smile.

A waiter served them whiskey sour. In spite of Prohibition, they raised their glasses as Prentice offered a toast. "General, forgive me for my lawlessness, but my physician prescribed whiskey for my nerves." Prentice winked.

"I'm sure your physician knows what's best for you." MacArthur smiled. "Here's to your doctor." They all chuckled.

Prentice and Gracie Lynn sat on the sofa, while MacArthur and Isabel perched on the loveseat opposite them. The waiter served a plate of toasted brioche topped with sour cream and black caviar. Only the men ate. The ladies glanced at each other.

"Isabel—may I call you Isabel?" said Prentice.

"My stage name is Dimples, but please call me Belle, Mr. Prentice."

"And please call me Sam. So, I heard you're an actress in Manila. Were you in the theater or the movies?"

"Both. I started making movies three years ago. I've been performing with vaudeville troupes since I was thirteen."

"Dimples! I love it. What an appropriate name." Gracie Lynn spoke in a theatrical voice, suppressing her Southern accent. "You have such lovely dimples."

"Honey, tell them about your revue," said Prentice, covering Gracie Lynn's hand with his. "Belle would like to audition in your show."

Gracie Lynn turned to Prentice. "I should have a stage name too. It will help my career."

"I thought helping your career is my job. Didn't I plunk a hundred grand for a revue by some unknown playwright just so you can act?"

"Oh, baby, you make it sound like it's such a huge sacrifice."

"In case you haven't noticed, the Great Depression is going on. So yes, it's a huge sacrifice to invest in something that will generate diddly-squat in ROI."

Isabel glanced at MacArthur sideways. He held her hand. Prentice and his mistress bantered, while they watched.

At last, the butler summoned them for dinner. Three waiters appeared. The lavish food rivaled the Waldorf-Astoria's menu: clear green turtle soup, lobster, and slices of guinea hen breast with roasted potatoes. For dessert, they ate cherries jubilee and sipped demitasse.

The conversation went back and forth from the revue Prentice produced, called *Lovesick*, to MacArthur's recent speech at a veterans' gathering, in which he'd called for a bigger and stronger Army. Gracie Lynn talked about her role in *Lovesick*, while Isabel described her last vaudeville performance in Manila.

After dinner, the ladies riffled through Prentice's record collection, while the men smoked cigars on the balcony.

"Have you seen Louise lately?" Prentice lounged on the outdoor sofa, surrounded by fluffy throw pillows.

"No." MacArthur was standing, puffing on his cigar.

The French doors were wide open. They both faced the living room and they could see the ladies choosing records.

"I saw Louise at a party in Paris last month," continued Prentice.

"How is she?"

"She's gotten fat. You should thank your lucky stars you got rid of her." Prentice gave out a drunken laugh. "I'm very fond of Louise, but boy, she's gotten fat!"

How could the man be oblivious to the irony of his comment? MacArthur said nothing. He glanced at his pocket watch, wondering when best to cut out.

Isabel put a record on the phonograph— "The Charleston." Gracie Lynn crossed to the balcony, and asked Prentice, "Baby, wanna dance?"

"No, no…why don't you and Belle dance instead? The general and I could use some entertainment." Prentice turned to MacArthur with a wink.

Gracie Lynn frowned and left. She pulled Isabel's hand and led her toward the center of the living room. They both glanced at the men.

Prentice waved. "Go on, girls. Let's see you dance!"

They stood close to each other, face to face. Gracie Lynn, who was taller, took the lead, playing the role of a male dancer. They danced the Charleston. Lots of short kicks, hops, and vigorous swaying of the hips.

"How old is Belle?" said Prentice.

"Twenty." MacArthur sat on a chair next to Prentice.

"Twenty?" Prentice whistled lustily. "How about that. And I thought Gracie Lynn was too young. She's pushing twenty-six. Why, she's old."

MacArthur's face and ears grew hot. "Isabel happens to be twenty. I didn't go out looking for a twenty-year-old."

"I understand." Prentice's eyes were fixed on the ladies. He puffed away, blowing dense smoke rings. "I thought Filipinos are dark-skinned. I mean, darker than Belle."

"She's a mestiza."

"What's that?"

"She's part white, part Filipino, and part Chinese."

"Well, whatever she is—she's gorgeous. If there are a few more like her in Manila, maybe I should go there myself." He turned to MacArthur, grinning. "Maybe I should look at possible 'investments' there."

MacArthur drew cigar smoke into his mouth and exhaled slowly. Prentice was a dirty old man, but wasn't he in the same boat as Prentice? His chest shrunk with dismay. "If you mean investing in a commercial enterprise—I would advise against it. Congress wants to block Philippine imports, and the farmers' lobby is demanding a tariff on Filipino coconut oil."

"Yeah, I've read about it. Who cares? Just look at her! If I can afford to waste my money on a Broadway revue, then I can certainly afford to waste it on some other venture in Manila."

A slower music was now playing on the phonograph. Gracie Lynn still assumed the male role, the palm of her hand sliding up and down Isabel's bare back as they slow-danced. She whispered something to her. It almost looked like she was kissing Isabel's ear.

He glanced at Prentice. A wolfish smile lingered on his face.

MacArthur's eyes darted from Prentice to Isabel. Then it hit him—she wore no undergarments! No chemise, no brassiere, no underpants. It was impossible to wear anything underneath the goddamn dress without a back. The same thought must be running through Prentice's lewd mind. *Goddamn it!*

MacArthur stood up and deposited what was left of his cigar in an ashtray.

"Leaving already?" Prentice rose, too.

"It's been a long day for me. I hope you don't mind."

The girls stopped dancing, a questioning look on their faces. MacArthur motioned for Isabel to come out. She and Gracie Lynn stepped out onto the balcony, where they all said goodbye on the spot. Prentice asked Gracie Lynn to write down the information Isabel needed to audition for *Lovesick.*

Within ten minutes, MacArthur and Isabel were back in their apartment. He removed his jacket and flung it to the sofa. He missed. It landed on the floor. When she bent down to pick it up, he was reminded of what got him all worked up.

"Don't wear that dress again," he said.

"I thought you'd like it." She hung his jacket on the coat tree.

"You're not wearing any underwear!" He plopped on the sofa.

"Of course not. Anything I wear underneath will show." The corners of her lips turned up in a smile, seductive as hell. "Don't you like it?"

"No, I don't."

She sashayed toward him. "You sound like Papa."

"I'm sure your father was right."

"Is that why you signed your letters 'Daddy'?"

"That's a different matter entirely."

She perched on the coffee table, facing him. She leaned forward to remove his necktie, her face a few inches from his. She radiated tempestuous heat, making him swell. He refrained from touching her.

"Should I make coffee?" She put the tie on the table.

He shook his head.

"Should I get your corncob pipe?"

Again he shook his head.

She rose and sat in the armchair, crossing her legs, her feet not quite reaching the floor. "I can't wait to audition on Monday. Gracie Lynn said all the major parts have been cast, but they still need dancers."

He pressed his fingers together, his blood frothing. "Why did you let Prentice call you Belle?"

"What do you mean?"

He gave her a stern look. "*I* call you Belle. Your family and Nenita call you Belle. You just met Prentice today, and he gets to call you Belle?"

"He's your friend."

"He's an acquaintance at best."

"I thought he's your friend."

"He's definitely *not* my friend!"

"All right, if you say so."

All of a sudden, her dark eyes lit up, as though an idea had dawned on her. "*Dios mio*, you're jealous!" She chuckled. "I should have known it. You're jealous of Sam Prentice."

MacArthur burned with embarrassment. At that moment, he wished he could put her inside a cage and lock it, if only to prevent the Prentices of the world from ever getting their hands on her. He'd never felt this way before.

"Poor Daddy's jealous."

"Don't call me that."

"I'm sorry."

She got up and strutted to the kitchen. She returned with an ice bucket, a spoon, and lemon slices in a crystal bowl. She stopped in front of the silver-plate cart that served as a mini-bar.

MacArthur followed her every movement.

"Patty got me a bottle of gin. It's Alessandro's bootleg, so there's no guarantee it's any good." She set the bowl and ice bucket down on the tray.

He faced her back, the goddamn bow calling attention to the ample mound of her ass. The very thought of gliding his palms on her exposed skin took his breath away. The sight could make any man murderous.

He rose and stomped forward. He towered behind her, breathing in the flowery perfume from her hair.

She hummed "The Charleston" as she picked up the gin.

His gaze fell to her backside—he slapped it.

"Aw!" She turned her face around. "Why did you do that?"

"With a dress like that, you're asking for it."

She stared at him with dubious eyes, lips curled, dimples showing. The mole on her left cheek gave her the mien of a seductress, but the dimples looked innocent. She faced the cart again and uncapped the bottle.

His heart banged. He expected a tantrum. Any minute now she would complain about his order to never wear the slutty dress again. When that happened, by God, he would spank her.

He unbuckled his belt and gripped it with his right hand. If she even dared to make a peep, he would whip her. May God help him.

She sniffed the gin. Not a word.

"Goddamn it." He tossed the belt over his shoulder. It fell with a soft thud. She didn't seem to notice it.

"Goddamn it," he said again, sighing. Then he shoved his right hand inside the lascivious V-shaped opening that led straight to her bare ass. He bent down his torso and his head to match her height. His lips grazed her delicate nape, not quite a kiss.

She mixed the gin and lemons in the bowl, like nothing was happening.

Yes, the girl could act. She could pretend she didn't feel his right hand stroking the hollow at the base of her spine.

He inserted his left hand inside her dress, ripping the fabric. His money had paid for the goddamn dress and he would do with it as he pleased. Even with both of his hands groping her ass, she continued to feign indifference. She stirred the cocktail, the spoon clanging against the glass bowl.

He encircled her hips with his arms, his hands reaching around so he could stick two fingers inside her. She moved a tad to accommodate him. But still she pretended to be unaffected. She added ice cubes to the bowl and stirred.

He buried his face in her neck as he thrust his fingers in and out, until at last, she moaned—the acknowledgement he'd been waiting for.

He scooped her up with both arms and carried her to bed.

# 23.

# November 1931

ON THE DAY Isabel turned twenty-one, she'd been rejected in an audition for a revue starring the brother-sister team of Fred and Adele Astaire. Isabel had auditioned only as an understudy of a minor character, but still she'd been turned down. She didn't even get to read a line. The director had given her one look and she'd been dismissed.

By noon, she was back at home, unlocking her apartment door. She got in and slammed the door shut.

"Jeepers creepers!" Patty jumped to her feet. "I thought someone just broke in."

"Sorry." Isabel had forgotten she'd asked Patty to come. She took off her fur coat and pumps. Her feet ached after walking several blocks to and from the theater in Times Square. She sat on the sofa.

"How was your audition?" Patty turned the radio off. She'd been listening to big band music. She trudged toward the ironing board, which she'd set up in the living room. She wore a new belted dress, though it looked like a sack on her. Poor Patty just didn't have the right curves with her mannish build—big arms and feet, muscular legs. She was taller than her beau.

"Can't you tell I was rejected?"

"What happened?" Patty plugged the electric iron and worked on a wrinkly dress.

"The director said I'm too swarthy." Isabel leaned back in the sofa and put her stocking feet up on the coffee table. "I don't know why I thought I could be in the same show as the Astaire siblings."

"What's swarthy?"

Patty wasn't schooled, but she was street smart. She might not know what "swarthy" meant, but she could at least tell Isabel the truth.

"Do I look like an Oriental girl or a white girl?" said Isabel.

"You're the prettiest Oriental girl I've ever seen in my life! And I've seen plenty. I see Chinese girls every day on the Bowery."

"Not white, but Oriental?"

Patty nodded. Well, that explained Isabel's failed auditions in the past six months. What an idiot she was trying to pass as a white girl. Mr. and Mrs. Wesley Grant on the ship had mistaken her for white, but it didn't mean she could go on pretending.

Since the day Isabel met Sam Prentice and Gracie Lynn, she'd auditioned twenty-five times for different roles. She'd been rejected in all but one. The closest she'd ever gotten to performing on Broadway was when she became Gracie Lynn's understudy in *Lovesick.*

That didn't count. The director accepted her only out of respect for Sam Prentice. She'd rehearsed the part for a month, but Gracie Lynn never missed a show, so Isabel never performed.

*Lovesick* had received a barrage of negative reviews, forcing Sam Prentice to shut it down after two weeks. Then he and Gracie Lynn had broken up not long after that.

For a while, Gracie Lynn and Isabel had practiced dancing at a studio downtown. They attended acting workshops and auditioned together until the Commander had put a stop to all that. He'd said Gracie Lynn was a bad influence because she changed beaus as fast as she got rejected in auditions. Sometimes, he acted like Papa. Did he think she would catch Gracie Lynn's promiscuity like a disease? He didn't care that Gracie Lynn had been her only friend in America, excluding Patty.

She lowered her feet to the floor with a thud. "No more auditions for me. I'm sick of being rejected." *Forget Broadway.* Although she was as good as any novice actress in New York, she would never make it because she wasn't white or tall or pretty enough. She was only half-American.

She let out a wistful sigh. How she loved to act. She could perform anywhere, anytime. She didn't differentiate between a makeshift stage in a town fiesta or a motion-picture camera. Performing was her second nature. Sometimes her desires as an actress and as a woman mixed together in a tangled mess. Was it any wonder she considered Douglas MacArthur her biggest acting coup so far?

A little knot of pain surfaced in her chest. The problem was she'd fallen in love with him. When he'd said he couldn't marry her, she'd pretended to be nonchalant, a hard act to sustain.

"Why do you need to work anyway?" said Patty, yanking Isabel from her thoughts. "The general gives you everything you need."

"Not everything." She glanced at the telephone sitting on a mahogany stand with a matching stool. The morning had come and gone, but still he hadn't called. Only God knew if he remembered her birthday. It was the middle of the week and he came to New York on weekends. How could he wish her a happy birthday in person?

"I almost forgot—happy birthday!" Patty dashed into the spare bedroom. When she returned, she handed her a gift. "Me and Alessandro made this especially for you."

A bottle of "bathtub" gin. She rose and hugged Patty, who said, "I wish I could give you something more. You're very good to me."

"There is something you can do for me."

Patty's eyes flared wide. "Like what?"

"Take me to the Bowery. My father's only brother lives there."

"Of course! I'll give you a grand tour of my neighborhood." Patty unplugged the electric iron and scrambled to put everything away. They took the subway.

Soon they were walking on Bowery Street in Lower Manhattan. Gusts swirled the garbage off the street. A group of men smoked and laughed, as relaxed as could be, though they stood next to an abandoned car with a burnt façade, a broken windshield, and missing tires.

"What's that?" Isabel gripped her purse with both hands.

"Some idiots stole the tires and set it on fire." Patty pulled her hand, drawing her closer. "Don't be scared. It's just trash."

The wind rose from the East River, stinging cold. Despite Isabel's fur coat, a hat, and a pair of gloves, the chill penetrated her bones.

"I thought maybe you wanted to go slumming." Patty wore a threadbare coat, no bonnet, and no gloves. And yet the piercing temperature didn't seem to bother her.

"What do you mean?" Isabel strode faster to keep up with Patty.

"A lot of rich Uptown folks come here for sightseeing…you know, to see how poor people like us live."

"I'm not rich."

"Douglas MacArthur is."

She couldn't tell Patty she wanted to find her uncle because MacArthur might dump her. Yes, he'd brought her to America and got her an apartment and bought her many expensive things, but he'd never said "I love you." Not once. Not even while he made torrid love to her.

He'd called her "love of my life" in his letters, but they didn't count. He'd signed those letters Daddy, and now it embarrassed him. If Sam Prentice could discard Gracie Lynn after investing a hundred grand in her career, then what would stop MacArthur from leaving her?

The Commander had become more possessive. He stopped her from wearing certain clothes even though she picked those for his pleasure. He prohibited her from speaking with Sam Prentice or other men. Befriending anyone was forbidden.

The supervisor in her apartment building, the doorman, and the elevator man probably kept tabs on her and reported her comings and goings to the Commander. Either that or MacArthur was clairvoyant. He seemed to know when Isabel and Patty went out for walks, or when Isabel shopped. "Where are you going Miss Isabel?" MacArthur's spies would ask. When she got back home, they would say, "Why, you've been gone for four hours." She suspected they jotted down everything.

So, why did she love him? He took care of her, for starters. Patty said such was the nature of "mature" men. Well, if it meant taking responsibility, keeping her safe, and providing for her, then she wanted an old man.

He remained young in other ways, blanketing her with passion and keeping her satisfied. Again, Patty attributed it to his experience. Maybe so, or perhaps he tried harder to compensate for his age. She couldn't explain her body's reaction to his, why she melted just staring at those blue eyes or why she surrendered to his touch, no fail.

His little thoughtful acts—making her scrambled eggs for breakfast or rubbing her back before they went to bed—contradicted his staggering power as the Army chief of staff. The contrast fueled her attraction as well.

She was unhappy not because he was possessive and demanding, but because in spite of her love and obedience, he wouldn't marry her.

"That's the most popular speakeasy hereabouts." Patty pointed at a run-down building whose battered sign read *Restaurant*. Time and weather had erased its name.

"That's a speakeasy?" Isabel pinched her nose as she hopped over a gooey substance that looked a lot like feces.

"It sure is. Don't be fooled by the ramshackle appearance. People line up every night just to get in." Patty chuckled. "The general will kill me if he finds out I brought you here." She pointed at the illicit joints where Alessandro sold his moonshine and other Bowery "landmarks"—brothels and opium dens Uptown folks patronized when they came slumming.

Indeed New York was not all about top hats, tailcoats, and the Waldorf-Astoria. For every Samuel Prentice who lived in the city, there were thousands and thousands who starved. From East Houston to Delancey to Grand, the signs of poverty manifested everywhere. Tramps scoured dumpsters for food. Women sat on stoops, their babies on their laps. "Their apartments are too cramped for them to stay indoors," Patty explained.

A gang of ragamuffins followed them, asking for coins. "Scram, you little hoodlums!" Patty hurled a stone at them for good measure.

"In Manila, I always gave alms to beggars," said Isabel.

"Those children are not beggars—they're thieves." Patty clucked her tongue. "This ain't Manila, but Bowery. No almsgiving here."

At last, they located the address for Papa's brother, Eugene Cooper, and his wife Eileen, and their three boys. Papa was the oldest, followed by two girls, and Eugene was the youngest. Isabel's father had lost contact with his siblings after living in Manila for so long.

To Isabel's dismay, the address turned out to be a tenement building. There were no Mr. and Mrs. Eugene Cooper living there.

After another hour of walking and futile searching, she gave up. She let Patty take the rest of the day off, while she went back home.

By seven o'clock, Isabel had taken a bath and slipped into a nightgown, eaten a ham sandwich for supper, and played the piano. Still, the Commander hadn't called.

Two letters had arrived this afternoon. She listened to Al Jolson and sipped Patty's gin, while she read Mama's letter. Ben had a sweetheart and he was planning to propose to her! He wanted to marry the only daughter of a prosperous landowner from Nueva Ecija. Her brother had found his meal ticket for life.

The other letter came as a surprise—from Eddie Palma. He'd gotten Isabel's address from Ben. Eddie had returned to Hollywood to resume his alleged acting career. Well, how about that? She answered Mama's letter first, using MacArthur's fine stationery.

*My dearest Mama. Today I turned twenty-one. I wish I were at home with you, eating Manang's rice cake and Lola's leche flan. Ben would sing "Happy Birthday to You" and Papa would join him and they would end up singing "For He's a Jolly Good Fellow" like they always do. We ladies would get a kick out of their off-key voices…*

Her chest had tightened and she put the pen down. If only she could admit her homesickness and how scared she was of being abandoned by MacArthur. Coming to America might have been a mistake, after all.

A knock on the door. *It's him!* She shoved the letters inside her nightstand drawer and ran to open the door.

"Happy birthday, Belle," said Captain Marsh. "The Commander's waiting for you in Highland Falls."

Her heart tumbled. "Where?" She opened the door wider, an invitation for him to step inside, but he didn't.

"Highland Falls—it's upstate. He's hosting a two-day summit of the Joint Army and Navy Board and the War Department. The top brass will be at West Point beginning tomorrow. He can't come here." He brushed the snowflakes off his overcoat and gave her a tired smile. "So, how about we leave in five minutes?"

For heaven's sake. She wished the Commander hadn't bothered remembering her birthday. It was Manila all over again. MacArthur would send someone to pick her up without any warning. She had to be ready at all times and go anywhere. Everything was always according to his schedule—even her birthday.

She blinked at Captain Marsh, emotions clogging her throat. "Five minutes, yes." What else could she do?

During the drive, Marsh entertained her with stories about the Commander. Now that MacArthur was the chief of staff, only Marsh, Wallace, and Isabel called him Commander anymore.

Did Isabel know the connection between MacArthur's ancestors and the heroic lore of King Arthur and the Knights of the Round Table? The general's ancestors—warriors called the MacArtairs—belonged to the Clan Campbell of Scotland. The clan's tartan was green, black, and gold. Its badge was wild myrtle.

"The Commander's family is so old there's even a famous Scottish adage about them. It goes like this…there's nothing older, except the hills, MacArtair, and the devil." Marsh smiled.

She nodded at his attempt to cheer her up, then stared outside the window. The car traveled on dark roads, faint snow drifting in the air. Captain Marsh whistled "Oh My Darling Clementine" as he drove.

MacArthur, in spite of who he was, had no right to drag her around like this. The captain "delivered" her like a package to a cottage tucked away in a maze of trees and foliage. Inside, the Commander sat in an armchair before the fireplace, smoking his corncob pipe. He was still in his uniform. He rose to meet her at the door. "Happy birthday, darling." He embraced her, kissing the top of her head.

He helped her take off her coat and led her to the dining table. A bottle of champagne from the black market, two crystal flutes, and a round birthday cake awaited her. The sight moved her in spite of herself.

He lit the big candle on the cake. "Be sure to make a wish before you blow it out."

She closed her eyes for a moment before blowing out the flame.

He opened the champagne, easing the cork out until it came off with a sigh. "Happy birthday, darling, and many happy returns!" He kissed her on the lips and they clicked their glasses in a toast.

They sat across each other at the table and began eating the cake. "I rented this cottage for the week," said MacArthur. "You can stay here while I attend the meeting. I'll come home every night. After the meeting ends on Friday, we can relax here until it's time for me to return to Washington on Sunday."

"I prefer to go back to the city, if you don't mind," she said.

He nodded, though his lips curled in apparent displeasure.

"This morning I auditioned in Fred and Adele Astaire's revue, but I was rejected." She picked at her cake.

"I'm sorry. Better luck next time." He sipped his champagne.

"Then I asked Patty to take me to the Bowery to look for Papa's brother."

"Bowery?"

She nodded.

"I don't want you to go there."

"It's too late now. Anyway, my Uncle Eugene doesn't live there anymore."

"The Bowery, for Christ's sake! I'm going to talk to Patty about this. Next time, don't go anywhere without telling me first."

She inclined her head. He'd just created a new rule for her, on her birthday. She pushed her plate to the side.

He moved, scraping his chair back as he stretched his legs underneath the table. "More champagne?"

She shook her head, avoiding his eyes.

"Darling, I'm sorry you didn't get the part in the revue."

She doubted he was sorry. He allowed her to audition only because he knew her chances of succeeding were nil. If she'd gotten the part, it would have meant working with men. He would have found a way to stop that from happening, just like he'd killed her movie with the kissing scene.

He fished a small box from his trouser pocket. "I hope you like my present." He leaned forward and set the box down before her.

*Dios mio*, a ring! The one thing that could wipe out all of her resentments. Her eyes grew moist. She opened the box, and indeed it was a ring—a large jade flanked by two small diamonds.

She put it on her finger. She rose. MacArthur stood up as well. She walked to his side of the table and flung her arms around his neck, her head tucked under his chin.

When she looked up at him, he smiled. "Do you like it?"

"I love it!" She craned her neck to kiss his lips. "Is this what I think it is? My birthday wish came true."

His smile disappeared. "I'm sorry for my faux pas." He took a ragged breath, the expression on his face grave. "I saw the ring and I thought it was very pretty. So I bought it for you."

Her heart nosedived. Heat rushed across her face. "But it's not an engagement ring? Of course not." She released him from her embrace and took a step back.

He ran both of his hands through his hair.

"You told me you can't marry me because the law in Virginia won't allow it. There's no such law here in New York. I'm twenty-one now. You can marry me here, if you want to."

He placed his hands on his hips, the way he did when giving Marsh or Wallace an order. "I don't want to talk about this." Then he strode to the living room.

She could do nothing but stare at her birthday cake. What now? She raised her left hand to appraise the ring, the diamonds shimmering under the ceiling light.

Lovely, but it meant nothing. Just a trifle MacArthur had bought, that was all. Just like her. She was pretty and he'd bought her with Papa's loan, Ben's job, the Manhattan apartment, and the bank account. What was she but a whore? She'd been whoring herself to Douglas MacArthur in the hope that he would love her back. She was less than a harlot, but a plaything. MacArthur's toy. Manang had been right.

She took off the ring and left it on the table. She crossed to the living room, put on her fur coat, and walked out the door.

"Isabel!" yelled MacArthur. "Where do you think you're going? Come back here."

Outside, the elements assaulted her—biting cold wind, steady snow, harrowing darkness. There was nobody and nothing out there. She trudged on the snow. She would rather freeze to death than stay in the same house as MacArthur.

She pressed on, her pumps sinking into the powdery snow. One shoe got stuck. She squatted down to pick it up.

He caught up with her. "Belle, please come back. Let's talk about this."

She raised her gaze. *So this is how everything ends.* They would talk so he could cut her out, the sooner the better.

He extended his hands and pulled her up. He looked her full in the face. “I’m sorry I can’t marry you. I just can’t. I’m fifty-one years old, and I’ve worked so hard to get to where I am today. Marrying you will jeopardize my career. The fact is, I’m a public figure, and the public will never approve of our marriage and never forgive me for it.”

She blinked away the snowflakes and tucked her freezing hands inside her pockets. She held her breath, waiting for him to dump her.

He took her face in his hands. “I can’t marry you. But I love you, and I want you to come to Washington with me—please.”

“Oh.” That knocked the wind out of her.

She’d expected to see the end, but he’d offered her a new beginning. At last, he’d declared his love! She would live with him in Washington! Her eyes blurred with tears. It was the coldest, most unpredictable, and happiest night in all of her twenty-one years.

She leaned against him, shivering. No need to “act” happy because she simply was.

He hugged her, then took her hand and led her back to the cottage.

# 24.

# Washington, D.C., July 1932

ISABEL LIVED in Chastleton Hotel, a mile away from MacArthur's office at the State, War, and Navy Building in Washington, D.C. He continued living at Fort Myer with his mother in the name of duty, but he spent his lunch hour almost every day with Isabel. Ever since the Bonus March crisis began in May, he had been working long hours. Many nights, he'd ended up staying in Chastleton.

The elegant apartment-cum-hotel was located in the affluent neighborhood of DuPont Circle, home to "official" Washingtonians: congressmen, senators, top-ranking federal bureaucrats, and diplomats. Nineteenth century mansions and Queen Anne row houses lined the neighborhood streets.

DuPont Circle offered privacy. Its residents were too well-off and too preoccupied with their own lives to bother with other people's love affairs. It suited Isabel just fine.

On a stifling Thursday morning when Washington police were said to be preparing to evict seventeen thousand Bonus Marchers, she ran errands downtown.

Police cars whizzed by, sirens blaring. Pedestrians stopped to watch. She overheard shopkeepers saying the police were en route to raze "Hooverville," the shantytown built by the Bonus March veterans along the Anacostia River. They speculated there would be riots. She hurried back to the safety of her apartment on the seventh floor of the Chastleton.

She found the Commander at home, though it wasn't even noon. He stood before a wall of windows, staring at the courtyard below and puffing on his corncob pipe.

"You're early," she said.

He glanced over his shoulder. "Where have you been? I tried calling you."

It wasn't the first time MacArthur had come home after failing to reach her by telephone. Was he trying to catch her off guard, in case she was cheating on him? Even though they lived in the same town now, he remained possessive. It didn't matter that she had no one and nothing else in Washington. Douglas MacArthur was her whole life.

She put the bag of groceries on the coffee table. She smoothed down the front of her peach-colored shift dress and patted the sweat on her forehead with her sleeve. "I picked up a few things at the grocery store."

She embraced him from behind, wrapping her arms around his chest, letting her head rest on his back. The familiar scent of his starched uniform and cologne, mixed with tobacco smoke, reassured her. "Should I make lunch?"

"I'm not hungry."

"There were a lot of police cars on the streets. Is it true the cops are going to evict the Bonus Marchers?"

"Yes. That's why I was trying to call you." He turned around to kiss her, a peck on the lips. "Don't go out anymore today. It's bound to get ugly. I just received my orders from Secretary Hurley. If the police fail to evict those men, then I'm going to send in the troops."

"Army troops?"

"I'll send in the Twelfth Infantry Regiment. I'm going to command it myself. I'll ask General Perry to lead the Third Cavalry Regiment. Those veterans have been infiltrated by radicals. This isn't about men who want their bonuses. This is a Communist conspiracy to undermine the federal government, and I won't have it."

He broke off, walked toward the sofa, and slumped in it.

Better to say nothing given his bad mood. She parted the curtains wider. All the windows were open, but there was no breeze.

He'd been cranky since groups of jobless Army veterans started arriving in Washington and marching in protest. That was in May. The Commander had tried to persuade them to go home and assured them they would receive their bonuses for their services in the Great War.

MacArthur thought it was less than patriotic to demand a bonus. Like President Hoover, he believed the answer to the Depression was hard work, not handouts. The Commander assumed every soldier was like him, serving out of duty and loyalty. It never occurred to him that most soldiers needed the money.

He'd gone out of his way to meet with the group's leader, whom he described as a "Communist agitator." He called anyone with a different, more liberal point of view a Communist. The veterans' leader had promised MacArthur they would leave peacefully when the Army was called in.

She glanced at him. He looked worried, smoking with a faraway expression. He'd said bloodshed between Army troops and veterans—soldiers against fellow soldiers—was possible.

She looked out the window, at the empty courtyard where she'd spent many pleasant afternoons since she moved to Chastleton at the beginning of the year. She liked to sip coffee and read a book or a magazine there. She allowed herself an afternoon break after doing chores. Unlike in New York, she didn't have Patty to help her. It was just as well because she had nothing to do otherwise.

Her days of futile auditions were behind her. The Commander had taken her to Washington on two conditions: give up performing and go back to school. Thank heavens the latter was on the back burner, while he wrestled with the Bonus March crisis. She dreaded going back to school.

She turned around and crossed to the sofa. He'd stopped smoking. His eyes were shut. She picked up the pipe with her left hand and the bag of groceries with her other hand. She went to the kitchen to put the groceries away; she would clean the pipe later.

When she returned to the living room, he stayed slumped in the sofa, but his eyes were open. "Duncan called while you were away."

"What did he say?" She perched on the settee opposite him.

"He wanted to remind you about your lesson tomorrow afternoon."

Duncan taught Isabel tennis. He was a high school teacher, but he gave tennis lessons in the summer. She only took up tennis because MacArthur liked to play sometimes and she needed to do something besides house work. MacArthur's friend, Colonel Tom Rooney, had recommended Duncan, who also gave Rooney's children tennis lessons.

"Did Duncan really need to remind you?" MacArthur gave her a forbidding look. "Does he call often?"

The teacher was neither handsome nor rich, but he was a bachelor and only thirty years old. That was enough to threaten the Commander.

"He's never called before."

"You know what? I think your tennis is good enough. Stop the lessons. You can practice with me instead."

She could barely hit the tennis ball, and the Commander didn't have the time or the patience to practice hitting balls with her. She pressed her lips to stop herself from arguing. "All right. Tomorrow's lesson is going to be my last."

She rose, eased around the coffee table, and stood before him. "If you're going to command troops this afternoon, you should eat. I made *embutido* last night. I'll heat it up in the oven for you."

MacArthur loved her Filipino meat loaf, but he said, "It can wait." He grabbed her hand and pulled her toward him.

She fell on his lap. He kissed her on the mouth. When he reached inside her dress, she jumped. "Today is a Bad Day for me."

"Oh, for Christ's sake. Saturday and Sunday were also Bad Days."

"Next week is safer." She flapped her hand to fan herself. Even with her lightweight georgette dress, it was still too hot.

The Commander had tremendous pressures at work, and her job was to ease those pressures. Her company, especially under the covers, comforted him. She did her part out of love, but she couldn't afford to get pregnant, not when he had no intention of marrying her.

He sighed, looking exasperated. "What am I supposed to do until then?"

Of course, he knew what to do. On her Bad Days, he could touch as much as he wanted. They could even have oral sex. They could even have intercourse, as long as he pulled out before he came.

He had numerous rules for her, from the clothes he deemed appropriate to the places she was allowed to visit. Well, this was her only rule, and the Commander must abide.

"Just take off your drawers." He sounded frustrated.

She shook her head. "Not a good idea."

The trouble with letting him finger her during a Bad Day was that they always ended up having sex and he had a difficult time withdrawing just before climax. They'd had too many near-misses already. MacArthur wanted servicemen to use condoms and the Army had a policy encouraging it, and yet she couldn't convince him to use one.

"Come here." His blue eyes shone with impatience.

She inched forward and knelt at his feet. She opened his fly, sliding her hand inside his trousers. Their eyes were locked together, as in a staring contest. When he leaned forward to reach for her backside, she removed her hand from his pants.

She stood up. "If you don't behave yourself, I won't do it."

His face turned red. Was he angry?

He slouched lower and pulled down his pants and drawers. "Go on," came the command.

She knelt down again. This time she took him in her mouth. The air grew thicker. Her dress clung to her damp back. She savored the delicious sensation of being wet between her legs. He grabbed her hair lightly, pulling her face away from him. He didn't want to come inside her mouth.

"Show me your dimples." No, he didn't mean the pretty dimples in her cheeks when she smiled, but the two little indentations on the surface of her lower back.

She shook her head.

"Show me now." It was an order, a perilous one. Why was it so hard to resist him? Right, they'd done this before and it drove them both wild.

She turned her back against him and bent forward, so her ass was on his face. She rested her hands on the coffee table for support.

He lifted her dress up and pulled her drawers down, but left the thigh-high stockings and garters on. She shut her eyes, loving his warm breath on her skin as he licked her other dimples.

Soon he knelt down and lapped the flesh between her legs from behind. Oh, it was hopeless! He knew how to make her surrender.

When he sat back in the sofa, he grabbed her by the waist and lowered her onto his erection. She gasped. He wrapped his arms tight around her waist, burying his face in her moist back. She bounced up and down on his lap until they both crumbled like a heap of dry leaves on fire. He came inside her after all. It was a very Bad Day indeed.

He took a quick shower and they ate lunch. Then he changed into a new uniform. Inside the master bedroom, he stood before the mirror. He wore a jacket and he was putting on a wide belt over it, where his holster and gun would normally hang. But it was peace time and he would face hungry veterans, not armed enemies, so there was no need for a weapon. "Darling, I need my boots."

She opened a closet and found them—knee-high leather boots, the kind officers wore when they rode horses. She took a piece of rag, perched on the bed, and began wiping one boot at a time. Her thoughts raced. "I'm worried."

"About what?" He stared at her in the mirror.

"I told you today's a Bad Day for me."

"It's too late to talk about this." He sat beside her on the bed. "I need my boots."

She knelt before him, putting the right shoe on his stocking foot. "What if I get pregnant?"

He appraised her, as if seeing her in a different light. "Maybe I want to get you pregnant."

"This isn't a joke."

"Who says I'm joking?" He took the left shoe from her hand and put it on himself.

"Why would you want to get me pregnant?" Her voice wobbled.

"I want you to be more responsible. You're too restless."

"But I *am* responsible. I take care of this apartment. I don't squander your money." She rose. "What do you mean by restless?"

"Taking tennis lessons with Duncan tells me you're restless."

Duncan! He was punishing her because Duncan had called her and he'd felt threatened! He would impregnate her to possess her, as if he didn't own her already. He wanted to knock her up just to prove a point. She was dumbfounded.

MacArthur got up and pulled a riding crop from a top shelf in the closet.

She sat heavily on the bed, her gaze on her lap as her emotions spun. No point in protesting against the unfairness of his opinion. She should have known better than to let his torrent carry her away on a Bad Day. It was her fault. Her biggest mistake was to love him.

He swaggered toward her and showed her the riding crop—a short leather whip.

"In France, I led my men to the battlefield not from the rear like officers are taught to do, but from the front. I didn't wear an iron helmet or carry a gas mask, and I was unarmed. All I had was this. It's my *anting-anting*." He fingered the length of the crop. "I was very lucky. Many men from both sides were killed, but I survived."

She looked up into his face. *Anting-anting* meant talisman in Tagalog. Yes, some magical power protected the Commander. He was favored by the heavens, destined to be great, always a winner.

He held the crop with his left hand and put on his general's cap with the other hand. "How do I look?"

"You look great." Her shock bordered paralysis, but he didn't even notice.

Colorful strips of ribbons representing his awards and accomplishments covered the left side of his chest. His cap, complete with insignias, might as well have been a crown.

She couldn't deny how smart, how handsome he looked in his uniform, especially with the tall boots and the riding crop. He was Douglas MacArthur, the U.S. Army chief of staff, the Big Cheese, the Top Dog, the Bravest of the Brave. The uniform made sure that everyone—especially Isabel—recognized that.

He brushed her cheek with his hand. "I have to go. You should listen to the radio. If things turn out badly, don't wait up for me. It means I'll be at Fort Myer."

After he left, she submerged herself in warm, soapy water in the bathtub. If she got pregnant, she would grow fat and ugly, and MacArthur would discard her. If the Bonus March veterans resisted the police, the Commander and his troops would evict them by force. It would be messy. He would become the most hated general in history. He would grow unhappy and he would leave her. No matter how she assessed her situation, she reached the same conclusion. He would soon get rid of her.

She couldn't shake off the image of him in his full dress uniform. She'd heard about the riding crop before. It was part of the MacArthur legend.

According to Captain Marsh, MacArthur had broken the rules by leading from the front and unarmed. The military had investigated him for his reckless behavior. When John Pershing, the general famous for routing Pancho Villa, read the investigation report, he'd said, "What nonsense! MacArthur is the greatest leader of troops we have." Instead of punishing MacArthur, Pershing had promoted him from commander of a brigade to commander of the entire Forty-second Division.

Given MacArthur's history of arrogant defiance, was it any wonder he'd violated Isabel's one and only rule? It was vintage MacArthur. He did as he pleased. Let everything and everyone be damned.

She sank in the bathtub, the water covering her ears, nose, and eyes. She jerked to the surface and gulped air. Soapy water and her tears stung her eyes.

The evening lay before her endless and steamy. She wore nothing but a silk kimono. She opened all the windows in the living room and stood gazing at the dark courtyard.

The radio was on. The police had shot two Bonus March veterans and a riot had erupted downtown. Thousands of civil servants had lined the streets to watch the riot, throwing rocks at the cops. The Army had been called in.

She poured herself a glass of black-market red wine. The radio announcer said, "Ladies and gentlemen, we've just received this special news bulletin. General Douglas MacArthur's troops have crossed the Eleventh Street Bridge leading to the Anacostia River. They are pursuing thousands of veterans who have fled the downtown area."

She pulled a chair next to the radio, which sat atop a mahogany table. She sat down to listen. Did the troops have to go after the veterans who were already fleeing? Knowing the Commander, he probably wanted to teach those Communists a lesson.

"Several eyewitnesses have called our station to report that the troops have advanced to the veterans' camp. They're tossing gas grenades without regard for the women and children who stayed at the camp to support their menfolk. One eyewitness called it the 'Bonus March War.' Another said the camp is burning down and hundreds of veterans have been arrested."

Isabel cranked up the volume. "I repeat—the Bonus March camp across the Anacostia River is burning and hundreds of veterans have been arrested! General MacArthur is waging a war against the Bonus Marchers! Ladies and gentlemen, this is all the report we have. Before we resume our original program, here's a short announcement from our sponsor, General Motors."

After the commercial, a drama aired. She moved to the sofa and sipped wine. Those poor veterans didn't know who they were up against. They didn't have a chance against the Commander. She imagined the stampeding women and children in their burning shantytown and felt kinship with them. Like them, she stood at the mercy of MacArthur.

An hour passed. The radio drama ended. Orchestra music played, interspersed with commercials for cigarettes, coffee, and soap. She got up and poured more wine. He wouldn't be sharing her bed tonight. The fearless general would be going home to his mother instead.

The radio announcer came back on the air. "Ladies and gentlemen, we interrupt this program to bring you a special bulletin from the Associated Press. The White House has just issued this statement. President Hoover said, and I quote, "Tonight, a challenge to the authority of the United States government has been met swiftly and firmly. I thank General Douglas MacArthur and our troops for maintaining law and order on behalf of the government of the District of Columbia."

She turned off the radio, seething. MacArthur had just trampled upon thousands of veterans whose primary crime was to be unemployed and hungry—and Hoover thanked him for it? MacArthur was so ruthless he didn't spare women and children, but the president praised him! No matter what he did, he always won. Call it destiny or genius or sheer luck. Maybe it was his stupid magic riding crop.

She gulped her wine and hurled the glass against the wall. It shattered.

Damn MacArthur! If she got pregnant, she would demand a wedding. She would insist that he make her *Mrs.* Douglas MacArthur, complete with a damn ring on her finger. If not, she would march around Washington, D.C., like the Bonus Marchers. Instead of carrying a placard, she would display his bastard.

# 25.

# November 1932

IT WAS SATURDAY. MacArthur and Isabel had left the Chastleton Hotel at dawn. Usually he had a chauffeur, but today he drove his black Packard. He liked his cars big and fast, and his women, small and feminine. He gave her a sidelong glance. Yes, he liked them precious as an orchid, every dainty limb proportionate, every curve neat.

She dabbed face powder on her nose, looking at her face in the little mirror she carried around in her purse. She wore a silk floral dress in a demure shade of yellow, looking soft and sumptuous.

"Darling, did you bring a coat? It might get cold," he said.

She applied crimson lipstick. "I packed it in my valise. I'm not cold."

Indeed the incandescent morning brought on mild air. It would take three hours to get to Williamsburg, where he'd rented a cottage for the weekend. He looked forward to showing her the Colonial District and teaching her a little history. They would eat traditional Southern food. A stroll through the historic village of Yorktown and a picnic along the York River would be nice.

This little vacation was long overdue. Ever since the Communist veterans took to the streets in May, he'd been so busy. He'd spent the summer trying to resolve the Bonus March crisis, culminating in the unfortunate incident in July, which the whole world liked to call the "Bonus March War."

The press vilified MacArthur almost every day. Newspaper photos and newsreels showed him leading Army troops in the attack against fellow Americans, causing outrage throughout the country. It didn't matter that his men had not fired a single shot. They'd answered the veterans' sticks, clubs, and stones only with tear gas. MacArthur had meant the cavalry charge, the battle tanks, and his very presence as a show of force—to intimidate the Reds. The arrests and the injuries couldn't be avoided. An infant who had been in the camp when it was tear-gassed had died. The death wasn't caused by tear gas, but just the same, he was blamed for it.

He sighed and kept his eyes on the empty road. "Darling, can you take a look at the *Washington Post*? It's in the backseat. Take a glance at the headlines for me, please."

She turned toward the backseat, but she couldn't reach the paper. She clambered around, her derrière protruding, to grab the newspaper.

He stroked her ass. "Atta girl."

She sat back up and flipped through the paper.

"Anything about me?" said MacArthur.

"There's an opinion piece about you…about the Bonus March War."

"The people who call it 'Bonus March War' have never fought a war. They know nothing about wars."

"The article says President Hoover lost to Franklin D. Roosevelt because of you. Your ruthlessness has cost the Republicans the election."

"They're calling me ruthless? Of course they conveniently skip the fact that I gave those veterans tents and camp equipment. I provided them with rolling kitchens or they would have starved. How easily these newspapers forget that it was Congress that stopped me from giving the veterans food and shelter."

She spread the paper on her lap, her index finger tracing a column. "It says here you disobeyed civilian authority…that Secretary Hurley sent two orders from the president, telling you *not* to cross the bridge."

He shook his head. Christ, he craved a cigar, but it was too much trouble.

"Is it true?" She folded the newspaper.

"Is what true?"

"That you ignored President Hoover's order?"

"Absolutely not! I received word to stop the operation while we were crossing the bridge. And I did. But, at that moment, those goddamned Reds had set fire to their own camp. It was too late."

"All right, I was just wondering." She stroked his arm like she was comforting a child.

He rolled down his window and inhaled the crisp air. The day after the riot, he'd made a statement to the waiting vultures, otherwise known as newspapermen. He'd told them what he believed. The Bonus March had not been about bonuses, but an attack against the government.

"I prevented a goddamn Communist uprising," he blurted out.

"All right, Daddy. That's enough. We're on vacation."

*Daddy* gave him a pause. He stole a glance at her. Her lips pursed in a mischievous smile, dimples appearing.

He accelerated the car. Signing his letters "Daddy" was meant to be a cover. He regretted it now. How she tortured him when she said the word with an inviting smile. And now, with just one word, he'd grown stiff.

"Oh, Daddy…give me your hand." She extended her left palm.

"I'm driving." For God's sake, could she see his bulge? No, it was impossible.

"Please?"

He relented.

She guided his right hand inside her dress. He pulled it away. "You're wearing stockings. It's too much trouble."

"Daddy's so irritable. What am I going to do with you?"

From the periphery of his vision, he could see her taking off her high heels, then her garters and stockings, and to his surprise, her underpants. He waited. Nothing happened. Meanwhile, he had a full erection. "Are you hungry? We could stop somewhere."

"No, I'm fine."

He focused on the road, though he sensed her balling her underthings into a wad and tossing it in the backseat.

She raised her bare feet up on the dashboard, her dress hiking up. Her toenails were painted a glossy red.

Damn, she was too distracting. They were only halfway to their destination. "Belle, don't do that." He didn't look at her. "Please put your feet down."

"Daddy's so grumpy this morning."

Daddy again. She was killing him. At least she'd lowered her feet down.

Isabel had grown and changed. They'd been together for over two years, from Manila to New York to Washington. She was turning twenty-two in another week. She was less likely to throw tantrums and more willing to obey him. At times, she surprised him with her submissive affection, just like when he'd stopped the tennis lessons with Duncan. Not a peep out of her. She'd even given up her ambition to perform, according to his wish. When he asked her why she'd agreed, she'd said without hesitation, *I love you*. His heart flared with gratitude at the memory.

He glanced at her. "Are you sure you don't want to stop at a diner?"

She nodded, her gaze on her lap.

This time, he took a double glance. Was her hand inside her dress? Between her legs? She closed her eyes, her hand moving underneath the silk dress, pushing the hem up. A flash of her thigh, smooth and pale, untouched by the sun. She moaned.

Goddamn it, his erection had grown heavy. "Belle?"

She released a satisfied sigh.

His gaze darted back and forth between the road and Isabel. Truth was, he liked watching her. "Darling?"

Finally she opened her eyes. She wiped her hand on the front of her dress. She turned to him. "Yes, Daddy?"

"Don't call me that."

"No? Well…one of these days someone will call you Daddy. I think you'll make a great father."

He narrowed his eyes. What the hell was she talking about?

"I'm very late, you know."

"I don't know what you mean."

"I haven't had my period since the Bonus March War."

"It wasn't a war, goddamn it!"

"Fine, it wasn't a war. But it doesn't change the fact that I'm pregnant."

"What?"

No response. Hell, she'd just derailed his composure, sent his thoughts tumbling down. All of a sudden, more cars appeared on the highway—a truck before him, a car behind, and another beside him. Jesus, where did all these vehicles come from? He weaved through the lanes to pass them, speeding the whole time.

She was pregnant! He tried to get his head around it. Of course, the idea had crossed his mind on that Bad Day, which happened to be the same day as the so-called Bonus March War. At the precise moment of coitus, he'd meant to knock her up. The very thought of it had excited the hell out of him.

And now this. He needed to talk to Tom Rooney and his mother. He knew what both of them would say. Tom continued to beg him to forget Isabel. His mother, on the other hand, acted as if Isabel didn't exist. As long as Pinky ignored her, he pretended everything was all right at home.

"I want a wedding," Isabel said.

*That* snapped his attention back into place. He glanced sideways. Her cheeks glowed, her hair tousled. Otherwise, she wore no expression at all.

"Just a small, quiet wedding," she added.

"Small and quiet?" He snorted. "You have no idea what you're asking for." He couldn't begin to imagine the scandal. The rapacious press would eat him alive. The Bonus March would pale in comparison.

She tossed back her hair. "You don't want to have a bastard, do you? I certainly don't. We have to get married before the word gets out."

Was she threatening him? As if reading his mind, she touched his right knee, letting her hand rest there, reassuring him.

True. If he didn't marry her, the disgrace would be worse. He would forever be known as the general who impregnated a poor Filipino girl. The scandal would annihilate him. A voice in his head said, "Damned if you do, damned if you don't."

He stared at the road ahead. He'd left a trail of cars and trucks behind. The sky hung low, a lazy blue. The sun struggled against a veneer of clouds. As he relaxed his grip on the steering wheel, a familiar smell filled his nostrils. He drew a deep breath. He loved the pungent animal scent of her sex. He was almost sure she'd climaxed earlier.

His eyes darted sideways. She was looking out the window, her right palm sliding up and down her thigh. Without hurry, up and down. Underneath the silk dress, she wore nothing. His heart thrummed faster. He'd grown hot and clammy despite the open window.

He'd never knowingly made love to a pregnant woman before, never had sex inside a car. He was too disciplined, old-fashioned, and perhaps a tad afraid to do those things. But that was before Isabel, before he'd discovered the many pleasures she alone could give him.

He breathed in the smell of sex. Was it stronger, richer, and more maddening because she was pregnant with his child? Or was it because he craved every inch of her body? Was it because he realized just then that he couldn't live without her?

He veered the car to his right, taking the nearest exit.

"Where are we?" said Isabel.

"I don't know. It doesn't matter."

They passed by a gas station, a scattering of houses, and a small church with a sorry-looking paint job. The barns sat far apart. Then they found themselves in the middle of nowhere.

He turned right where no road existed. He drove on, deeper into the woods, until he was sure they would be hidden by foliage. He would fuck her right there, in the backseat of the Packard. He'd be damned if he waited a moment longer.

And when the New Year came, he would marry her—just a small and quiet wedding like she wanted.

# 26.

# Washington, D.C., January 1933

ONE WEEK AFTER the New Year, Isabel discovered she wasn't pregnant. She'd missed her menstrual period for five months, but her belly didn't grow and she'd thrown up just once, not quite the morning sickness she'd expected. She'd seen spots of blood on her underpants. She couldn't tell the Commander about it, not when he planned to marry her at the end of the month.

He'd kept their wedding plan a secret just as he'd kept *her* a secret. So when his best friend, Colonel Tom Rooney, and his wife, Rose, invited MacArthur and Isabel over for lunch one Sunday, Isabel felt vindicated. It was the first step toward her introduction to Douglas MacArthur's official life. Slowly he was allowing her to come out in public.

The Rooneys lived in a one-hundred-year-old brick row house in the tony neighborhood of Georgetown in Washington, D.C., along the Potomac River.

"Finally, we get to meet you." Tom Rooney gave Isabel a hug and a peck on her cheek. "I've been asking Douglas for this chance to meet you since Manila. It took only three years, golly!"

"So lovely to meet you." Mrs. Rooney shook hands with Isabel, looking her up and down.

Isabel wore a burgundy velvet dress, with long sleeves and a hemline that fell four inches below the knees. She'd swept up her hair into a chignon. MacArthur's gifts—the pearl necklace and the jade ring—were the only jewelry she wore. Her outfit passed muster with the Commander.

She'd always been confident of her beauty, but Rose eyed her like she was missing an earlobe or a hand. It didn't help that Isabel wore a cumbersome Kotex sanitary napkin for the first time. She had seen it advertised in the *Ladies Home Journal* and she'd bought it for its novelty. The pad felt too huge for such a small blood stain, just a red dot really.

She shrank before the imperious Rose Rooney: tall, blonde, and rich. But old, perhaps in her forties. In that regard, Isabel had the upper hand.

A golden-haired girl burst into the parlor, jumping into the Commander's arms. He lifted her up above his head, making her dissolve into giggles. When he set her down, he handed her a paper bag. The girl pulled out a twelve-inch teddy bear from it and thanked him with a kiss on his cheek.

"Natalie, this is Miss Isabel Cooper." MacArthur turned to Isabel. "Belle, this is Natalie Rooney, my favorite girl in the whole wide world. She's nine years old."

"Hello, Natalie." Isabel shook the girl's hand.

"Hello, Miss Cooper. You're beautiful! You look like my china doll. Uncle Douglas gave it to me."

MacArthur nodded. "I got her a doll when I was in Shanghai."

When he left the Philippines almost three years ago, his ship had traveled from Manila to Shanghai to Honolulu to San Francisco. In Shanghai, he'd written a letter to Isabel, which he'd signed Daddy, the first of several letters with his alias.

Isabel had always wondered about that. Was the Commander thinking of the little Rooney girl and saw himself as a father back then? Was his desire for fatherhood the reason he'd agreed to marry Isabel? She'd assumed it was to avoid a scandal, but she hadn't seen his fatherly side before. Her heart warmed toward his uncharacteristic tenderness.

How would it feel to have a child like Natalie? A strange, perhaps maternal, longing flickered inside her. When she'd consulted with a family doctor a few months ago, even the doctor couldn't tell if she was pregnant. He'd said the new pregnancy tests were unreliable and hard to get. So until her belly started growing, he wouldn't be able to tell. The doctor had broached the possibility of a delayed menstrual period.

"Don't ask your husband to build a crib yet," the doctor had joked. Of course, she had to pretend she was married, introducing herself as Mrs. Isabel Cooper. Oh, how she wished she hadn't told MacArthur she was pregnant. She dreaded telling him that she'd been mistaken. Would he still marry her?

"My china doll's name is Fannie. Do you want to see her?" Natalie grabbed Isabel's hand.

"Miss Cooper and Uncle Douglas just got here, sweetness," said Tom Rooney.

The girl dropped Isabel's hand and ran back to the Commander, who enveloped her and her teddy bear with both arms.

"Natalie, where's your brother?" said Mrs. Rooney. "Go get him, please."

The girl freed herself from MacArthur and ran upstairs.

"I'm sorry about that." Rooney sighed. "Douglas spoils her."

MacArthur rolled his eyes.

Natalie returned to the living room with her brother, Tommy, a somber-looking fifteen-year-old, who wore spectacles like his father. The girl had a little basket carrying her china doll. The boy seemed too shy, avoiding Isabel's glance. She imagined having a son herself, with the Commander's blue eyes and her dark hair. He'd grow up to be a fine officer like his daddy. She'd bought an adorable blue romper with a matching pair of booties.

Two uniformed maids served a lunch of steamed blue crab fresh from Maryland, chicken stew, baked sweet potatoes, and cheese biscuits.

"So, you're an actress?" Rose gave off a hostile air.

"I was—in Manila." She felt a gush of blood. Thank goodness she wore a Kotex pad. A menstrual rag would have been inadequate for such a heavy flow.

"In the theater? Were you formally trained?"

*Dios mio*, Rose's tone resembled that of an inquisitor. "The theater and motion pictures. I've taken some lessons, but I learned more from experience. I learned the ropes from vaudeville veterans." Everyone stared at her. She took a sip of the iced tea and almost gagged, too sweet for her taste.

"Belle and I have agreed she should stop performing," said MacArthur.

It was his sole decision, but Isabel considered it the price of loving him.

"A prudent choice, I'm sure," said Rose.

He squeezed Isabel's hand before turning to the Rooneys. "I hope both of you can come to New York on January thirty-first. We could use a couple of witnesses at City Hall."

"Of course, we'll be there." Tom Rooney's eyes darted between Isabel and MacArthur. "We'll celebrate your wedding *and* Doug's birthday."

"I'm too old for a birthday celebration," MacArthur protested.

Rose munched on a biscuit. "I wish you'd get married here in D.C."

MacArthur shook his head.

"Is it Pinky?" Rose wiped the crumbs off the corner of her mouth.

"Among other things, yes."

"Doug's afraid FDR might show up at his wedding." Rooney poured more tea into his glass, then took a sip. "He and I can't get over the fact that soon we'll be saluting a commander-in-chief who was once an assistant secretary of the Navy. I can't decide which is worse, that he was a two-bit bureaucrat, or that he was a two-bit bureaucrat *in the Navy*. He could at least have chosen the Army. Tell me again, how did Walter Lippman describe FDR?"

MacArthur was spreading butter on a biscuit. "Lippman wrote in his column that Franklin Roosevelt is—and I quote—'a pleasant man without any important qualifications who would very much like to be president.'"

He and Rooney laughed. They joked about the president-elect whom they despised because of his liberal New Deal plan. They speculated that as soon as FDR took office, he would be doling out cash to every bum and go on a deficit-spending spree in the name of economic recovery. They didn't respect him because he didn't fight in the Great War, plus he was a cripple.

The conversation veered from FDR to Tommy Rooney's desire to attend West Point someday. Isabel felt left out. Worse, her abdomen cramped, her menses so heavy she might as well be pissing.

She wanted to go home, but she was too embarrassed to tell anyone she was bleeding. The prospect of telling MacArthur she wasn't pregnant filled her with anxiety. She breathed a sigh of relief when Natalie asked her mother, "Can I show my china doll to Miss Isabel?"

Rose exchanged glances with her husband and MacArthur before saying yes. Natalie clutched Isabel's hand and led her to the living room where not one but two fireplaces roared.

Isabel's sanitary napkin was thoroughly soaked and she hesitated to sit on the cream-colored sofa. Well, she had no choice.

"Doesn't Fannie look like you?" asked Natalie. The doll had a porcelain face and a body made of cloth. Like Isabel, its black hair was arranged in a chignon and her dark eyes were wide.

"Fannie is a lot prettier," said Isabel.

"Will you help me change her dress?" The girl took out three dresses from her little basket and displayed them on the coffee table. After a moment, she got up and moved closer to one of the fireplaces, plopping on the rug. "Come here, Miss Isabel. It's nice and warm."

She joined the girl near the fireplace, kneeling uncomfortably. But she didn't bring the doll's clothes. So Natalie rose to pick them up. She shrieked. "Is that blood?"

Isabel turned around, aghast. Part of the sofa was covered with her menstrual flow. She stood up, the pressure in her abdomen worsening. She pressed her stomach with both hands.

"Heelp! Miss Isabel is sick!" screamed Natalie.

The Rooneys and MacArthur dashed into the living room. They saw the blood-stained sofa. Isabel touched the back of her dress—damp.

"Darling, are you all right?" MacArthur put an arm across her shoulders. "I think we should go."

One of the maids came with a bath towel and wiped the blood from Isabel's hand and the back of her dress. Isabel wrapped the towel around her hips. The other maid scrubbed the sofa with a wet rag, but it was useless. The cream sofa was ruined.

Isabel apologized. MacArthur said he owed Rose new furniture.

Rooney made light of the situation. "Forget about the sofa. Just promote me to general." His wife glared at Isabel.

They all said goodbye in a hurry.

"Come back when you're not sick." Natalie kissed Isabel's cheek.

MacArthur led Isabel to the car, his face wrinkled with worry.

He drove in silence, not even glancing at her. Then it hit her. He wasn't worried, but simmering with fury. He gripped the steering wheel with both hands like he was strangling it. When the car stopped at a red light, he turned to her, his face warped with emotion. "You're not pregnant. You lied to me!"

"I missed my period for five months. I thought I was pregnant. Even the doctor thought so. I'm hurting so much. I think I'm having a miscarriage."

"Bullshit! You were never pregnant."

The light turned green. MacArthur accelerated, the car lurching forward. She pressed her palms on the seat. "I'm sorry I lost our baby." Her throat tightened, her eyes welled up.

"That's enough. I won't listen to another lie. My mother suspected you were scheming, and by God, she was right."

She turned her face to the window and brushed away a tear with her knuckle.

"Against my best judgment, I was going to marry you. You almost fooled me."

Then he clammed up. When they reached the Chastleton Hotel, he pulled over. "I'm going home to Fort Myer. I want you to go somewhere. Take a trip."

"Where would I go?"

"Go visit some friends."

She bit her lower lip. She had no friends in America. He wouldn't allow it because he kept their relationship a secret. The fewer people she knew, the better.

"You've been writing the Grants," he said. "Go visit them in Los Angeles."

How did he know? She'd written the couple because they'd been nice to her and she was lonely. She wrote letters to everyone she knew because she had nothing else to do. MacArthur was apparently privy to that.

Just like in New York, he'd been spying on her. He probably paid someone at the Chastleton front desk to check Isabel's mail, those she sent out and those she received. How dare he spy on her! But she was too heartbroken to fight him.

"I'm sorry I lost our baby," she repeated. She felt the miscarriage in her bones, not to mention the proof he ignored: the cramping and the sudden, heavy bleeding after five months of no menstruation. "Can we please talk about this inside?"

His blue eyes burned. "No, I don't want to. In fact, I don't want to see you. I'll ask Marsh to arrange a trip for you."

The Chastleton Hotel's doorman opened the Packard's passenger door. Isabel got out of the car. It pulled out in haste, making a screeching noise.

Chin up, she mustered enough dignity as she entered the building, the stained towel wrapped around her hips.

# 27.

# September 1933

IN THE MONTHS following the disastrous lunch at the Rooney home, Isabel's relationship with MacArthur was like a perilous voyage on turbulent waters. She believed she'd miscarried, but she couldn't prove it. He was convinced she'd lied about her pregnancy just like she'd lied about her age.

Isabel had gone back to the family doctor who had seen her in November 1932. He'd asked many questions. Did Isabel's sudden menstrual flow come with heavy cramps? Did she pass huge clots of blood? Did she experience weakness and abdominal pain? Yes, yes, and yes. "Then it's likely you had a miscarriage," he'd said.

She'd assumed that on the fifth month of pregnancy, the fetus would have been developed, so how could she have miscarried? "But you *don't* actually know you were five months pregnant," the doctor had said. "What you *do* know is you haven't had your period in five months. Perhaps your menstrual period was late and then you got pregnant. In all likelihood, you were only two or three months pregnant."

What was the point of arguing whether she'd been five months or three months pregnant? Without a dead fetus to show the Commander, he wouldn't believe her.

He'd grown distant, spending less time with her. She'd spent many nights waiting for him in vain, with only Al Jolson music and letters from old friends like Nenita and Eddie Palma keeping her company. Nenita was engaged to the Elizalde heir, while Eddie sought a change of scenery and planned to visit Washington, D.C.

Once in a while, she would take out the baby romper and booties and press her cheek against the soft fabric. *This is how hope feels.* Her tears would pour out in a torrent, but it also reminded her she needed to be strong to keep something as delicate as hope in her heart. As the Commander worked longer hours and grew grumpier after Franklin Roosevelt became president, she doubled her determination to please him. When MacArthur ordered her to take a trip and enroll in a school, she knew he'd meant to keep her at a distance. Still, she'd accepted his plan with grace.

She'd asked Mr. and Mrs. Wesley Grant if she could visit them in Los Angeles, to see Hollywood. The couple had countered with an offer. Isabel could join them for two weeks of rest and recreation in Havana. She'd been only too glad to do it. She'd traveled with the Grants, but she hadn't told them the truth. Not entirely. She continued lying to them about her daddy, though she'd finally revealed she was only half-white.

Upon Isabel's return to Washington, she enrolled in a beauty school. She was too old to attend high school, but the new field of cosmetology was perfect for her. In lieu of tennis, she took Hawaiian dance lessons.

Although MacArthur preferred Isabel finish high school, he hadn't been disappointed. He benefitted from her educational pursuits. Studying cosmetology meant she was always well-groomed and pretty, not that she'd ever slacked off in that department. And learning how to dance the hula meant she practiced in front of him. When he came home weary, she would serve him the "Douglas" drink and dance for him. She would wear a skimpy top and a provocative hula skirt and shake her hips for his pleasure.

Sex was the one thing that remained constant in their relationship. He might not want to see her for days and weeks at a time, but he always came back to her bed eventually. He might remind her of how disgusted he'd been about her lies, but his hunger for her remained steep. And so, she'd learned to ride the ups and downs of his moods.

Sex was her vessel, keeping her afloat in the tumultuous sea of MacArthur's love. The more difficult he was, the more she craved him. MacArthur's love had grown so elusive that fornication, not marriage, became the prize.

Obscene thoughts filled her mind, even as she pretended to listen to Miss Harper talk about the new technology of electric curling tools and hair dryers. Isabel and twenty other young women, most of them immigrants who could barely speak English, sat inside the classroom. Miss Harper, a well-dressed spinster, had to repeat herself at least twice before the class would nod, signaling comprehension. Isabel helped explain things for Miss Harper, but not at the moment.

She could think of nothing and no one else but MacArthur. She hadn't seen him for a month. He'd been traveling in France, meeting with political and military leaders. A postcard he'd sent from Paris said, *I feel miserable, really ill, without you. I must have you.* Of course, he hadn't signed his name on it. Still, it made her smile and caused her heart to flutter. She missed the Commander—all of him—even his numerous demands and unpredictable moods. It was Friday and he was supposed to have returned to Washington yesterday. She expected to see him tonight.

Miss Harper had moved on to the art of curling women's hair. She displayed huge photographs of Myrna Loy and Jean Harlow, comparing their curls. Isabel propped her elbows on her desk, sighing. She once dreamed of becoming a star like Myrna Loy and Jean Harlow. It seemed like a lifetime ago. She no longer aspired to see herself on the silver screen if it meant losing MacArthur. She just wanted to be the star of his life.

She glanced around her and wondered if her classmates were as crazy in love as she was. While Miss Harper showed more photos of pretty ladies with intricate-looking hairdos, Isabel's mind wandered farther away and deeper into her desires. A memory came back to her—his body on top of hers. She'd raised her right leg, letting it rest on his shoulder as he plunged inside her. They both had come hard and fast. She'd never experienced a more acute pleasure of using her body until then. How could she ever get him out of her mind?

The bell rang. She snapped out of her lewd reverie.

"Next week, I'll demonstrate how to use an electric hair dryer," said Miss Harper. "Be sure to come on time, ladies."

Isabel picked up her satchel and made her way out of the classroom. She waited at the packed lobby. The beauty school occupied two floors of a commercial building that also housed offices for lawyers, realtors, and dentists. People came and went all the time.

She scanned the room. No chauffeur. MacArthur had three drivers at his beck and call. Day after day, she never knew which one she would get. She would ask the chauffeur if the Commander was back in town. At the thought of seeing him, she found herself holding her breath, her impatience growing. She craned her neck toward the door.

A man in a gray suit and fedora stared at her. Was something the matter with her appearance? She glanced down at her green dress and white gloves. She straightened her hat.

He approached her. "Miss, I didn't mean to stare—I'm sorry. I'm a photographer." He carried a camera, which looked too heavy for his slight build. "I'd love to take your picture. Are you a model or an actress?"

She felt her cheeks flush. "That's very kind of you to say, but I'm neither."

"All the better. I'll have the pleasure of discovering you." He lifted his camera and pointed it at her.

"Please stop. I don't want my photograph taken."

The man's face fell. "At least tell me your name. I'm Howard."

The Commander had forbidden her from talking to strange men, but she didn't want to be rude. She didn't want to reveal her name either. "I'm Dimples. I'm sorry, I have to go." Dimples was a remnant of an ambition now dead, so it was all right to throw it around.

She waited in front of the building, one hand holding on to her hat and the other hand carrying the satchel. A pleasant September breeze swayed the canvas awnings of storefronts. Goodness, MacArthur's driver was late. She went back inside. Thank God, the photographer was gone.

She paced up and down the lobby. Lieutenant Wallace entered the building and waved at her. "Hello, Belle. Let me carry that for you." He took the bag from her hand. "The Commander's waiting in the car. He's taking you to Williamsburg for the weekend. He didn't want to walk into a place as public as this, so here I am instead."

"Williamsburg? But I didn't pack any clothes," she said. MacArthur had not taken her back to Williamsburg since November, when she'd told him she was pregnant and his response had astounded her.

"Don't worry about it." Wallace led her to the door, touching her elbow. "He bought you clothes from Paris."

"Oh."

"He wants to get to Williamsburg before dark."

Wallace opened the glass door for her. MacArthur's car was parked across the street. The Commander sat in the driver's seat. He wore a khaki uniform and sunglasses.

She and Wallace waited to cross the street, watching cars zip by. "I'm taking a cab and going back to the office," Wallace said. "The Commander brought piles of reports from Paris. I have to read them tonight."

She nodded. Poor Wallace. MacArthur did what he wanted, while everyone else tried to please him. Wasn't that always the case?

They crossed the street. Howard the photographer jumped in front of her and aimed his camera. A tremendous light flashed. She covered her face with her arm.

MacArthur opened the passenger door. "Get in!"

Wallace pushed her inside. A blinding flash went off again. Wallace slammed the door shut and the car peeled out. She looked back, just as the lieutenant shoved the photographer.

"Goddamn it," muttered MacArthur.

"What was that all about?" said Isabel.

"That was the goddamn press snapping a picture of you…trying to take a picture of us. I don't think he followed me from my office. Has he been following you?" She couldn't see his eyes through the sunglasses, but she sensed his anger. "Did that man talk to you?"

"No. I've never seen him before." She hated lying to him, but he would scold her for talking to the photographer. So the man didn't really admire her looks. He was only trying to confirm her identity before taking her photo. He wanted to use her and put MacArthur in a compromising position.

Cars jammed the streets. Everyone seemed to be getting out of Washington for an early start to the weekend. MacArthur, visibly irked, drove in silence.

Once they were outside Washington, the traffic eased up. He loosened his grip on the steering wheel.

She took off her hat and tossed it and the satchel in the backseat. "Are we going to Williamsburg?"

He nodded. "I could use a break."

And she could use a change of clothes. "Lieutenant Wallace said you bought me clothes from Paris? Otherwise, I don't have anything to wear when we get there."

"Clothes?" He tossed a sidelong glance. "*Clothes* might be an overstatement." He reached for her thigh, stroking it. "I bought you a silk robe and lace underthings."

She pouted, but her heart knocked. How handsome he looked. His presence warmed her veins like wine.

She scooted sideways to move closer to him, then turned her body toward him and put her arms around his neck. She kissed his cheek, his ear, his neck.

"I'm driving," he protested with a grin.

She buried her nose into the side of his neck, inhaling him. Sweet woodsy smell of his cologne mixed with tobacco.

"How was school?"

"Fine. I missed you."

"Be a good girl and go back to your seat."

She acquiesced. After a few minutes, he placed his hand on her knee, perhaps as a reward for her obedience. She unbuttoned the front of her dress and guided his hand to her bosom.

Her heart zinged with joy. What a hopeless case! She was in Douglas MacArthur's power completely—a dupe, a slave to sensation. "I love you." She let his fingers slip inside her brassiere.

# 28.

# Washington, D.C., May 1934

MACARTHUR WORKED in his office, thumbing through Army appropriation documents. He glanced at the wall clock—twenty-one hundred hours. The worst day of his life.

He had succeeded in adding forty-eight million dollars to the proposed Army budget, increasing the original amount allotted by the Bureau of the Budget from 196 million dollars to 244 million dollars. But his victory had been at the expense of his relationship with President Roosevelt. He'd won a fight with FDR—and also killed his Army career.

He took out a corncob pipe from the top drawer of his desk, stuffed it with tobacco, and lit it with a match. His wood-paneled office was spare, but well-lit. In addition to the ceiling lights, a lamp on his desk burned. He kept the hefty mahogany desk unadorned by necessity. Neat piles of folders, papers, and letters covered it.

He reared back in his swivel chair and puffed on his pipe until it smoked. What a nightmare the day had been.

This morning, he and Secretary of War George Dern had met with President Roosevelt to protest the fifty-one percent cut in the

Army appropriation. MacArthur had explained to FDR that the world had become too dangerous to allow such a budget cut. Germany and Italy were arming, while Japan continued its conquests in Manchuria. Cutting the Army appropriation by half could prove fatal.

FDR had scolded Dern and MacArthur like a couple of schoolboys. Dern had crumbled. Well, MacArthur had been fighting for a decent military funding since he became Army chief of staff four years ago and he wasn't about to back down. Most of all, he was Douglas MacArthur and he refused to let a cripple—president or not— berate him.

"Mr. President, when we lose the next war, I want it to be on your conscience, not mine."

"You must not talk that way to the president!" FDR had bellowed.

MacArthur had been furious, but he'd been out of line. Roosevelt was right. Worse, they were through. "Mr. President, I apologize for my impudence. You have my resignation as chief of staff." He'd headed for the door, but FDR had yelled at him. "Don't be foolish, Douglas! You must work on the budget."

FDR had rejected his resignation. He'd also agreed to a bigger budget. MacArthur got what he wanted.

Afterward, he'd fled the Oval Office, an elated Dern trotting behind him. "You just saved the Army," Dern had said. MacArthur had felt sick to his stomach and shambled outside the White House to vomit. It brought back the horrible memory when he was twenty-three years old—devastated after having killed two Filipino bandits. He'd also puked then.

He puffed on his corncob pipe and focused back on the revised budget sent to him two hours ago. The president hated his guts, but he was a savvy politician who needed MacArthur. Also, FDR believed in keeping his adversaries close.

A knock at the door. He expected Captain Marsh with bad news. The incident at the White House was Round One, and now Round Two would begin. As if the nightmarish meeting with FDR wasn't bad enough, MacArthur had been greeted today with yet another libelous Washington *Merry-Go-Round* column written by Drew Pearson and Robert Allen. They'd published many egregious lies about him before, even accusing him of being a dictator. Now they claimed he'd led a drive to oust Assistant Secretary of War Harry Woodring. This was the last straw. He would stop the slander.

"Come in, Ed. Let's hear it."

Marsh entered the room with a manila envelope in his hand. "Sir, I just spoke to Lieutenant Colonel Murphy on the phone. He said Pearson and Allen refused to publish an apology. Not only that, they threatened to publish more garbage about you. So, per your instruction, tomorrow the judge advocate general's office will send us the papers for the lawsuit against Pearson, Allen, and the United Features Syndicate. They will be charged with libel. Damages will be set at one-point-seventy-five million dollars."

"Good," said MacArthur. "Those bastards will never write a falsehood again."

He puffed on his pipe, his mind lurching back to the 1928 Olympics in Amsterdam. He'd headed the American delegation. He'd rebuked the boxing coach who had proposed to withdraw from the competition because of an unfair decision against an American boxer. "Americans never quit," MacArthur had said. His words had reverberated throughout the room and across the globe. Newspapers had accused him of treating the Olympics as a "war without weapons." Well, the hell with it. The United States—and MacArthur—had won the Olympics, receiving the most medals.

The memory boosted his self-confidence, but also twisted his chest. "Do you think I treat every situation like a war?"

Marsh stroked his chin, appearing to be unsure. MacArthur motioned to him to sit down.

The captain pulled a chair and perched on it. "Sir, are we talking about Pearson and Allen?"

"About them, yes, but also about the Olympics, the press, everything."

"Yes, sir, I do. And that's how you win."

MacArthur puffed on his pipe, nodding. He always fought to win. In everything he did, he expected nothing less than victory. Now he braced himself for Round Three. Earlier today, he'd found out that Isabel had met with Eddie Palma, her former lover, who was visiting Washington.

He raised his feet up, resting them on the desk. "Tell me what the private eye reported about Isabel."

"She had lunch with Eddie again today. That makes it two days in a row." Marsh handed him the envelope.

He set aside his corncob pipe and pulled out a picture from the envelope—Isabel and Eddie sat opposite each other at a table in a restaurant. His insides roiled.

The camera had caught Eddie leaning forward, as if whispering something, and she seemed very pleased. They both smiled. Were they about to fuck or did they already fuck?

In the four years of their relationship, his jealousy had come in waves, some bigger than others, but they'd come regularly. Now it threatened to capsize him.

He'd heard about Eddie in Manila, but never asked Isabel about him. Eddie was a boy, a struggling actor, a nobody. He wasn't a worthy rival. But when Eddie started writing letters from Los Angeles, MacArthur had felt threatened. Did he follow her all the way to America? Overnight Eddie had become an opponent worth investigating. The photograph validated his suspicions about Isabel all these years. He hadn't been paranoid.

He pulled out a one-page report from the envelope and read it. The private eye had no proof Isabel had slept with Eddie. It didn't mean she hadn't, or wouldn't in the future.

"I have to put a stop to this." He shoved the paper and the picture inside the envelope.

"Sir, the evidence is inconclusive," said Marsh.

"Let me be the judge of that." He covered his face with his hand. The ceiling light just about blinded him all of a sudden. Or maybe his heart sought the comfort of a darkened room somewhere far—a cave, a dungeon, anywhere but here.

"General, it's late. Let me drive you home to Fort Myer."

He put his hand down. "I'll drive myself tonight. Thanks, Ed."

"All right, General. Tomorrow you have a briefing at o-eight-hundred about your trip to Poland. Your trip is in three days."

"For God's sake, Marsh. Just go home."

"Yes, sir."

After Marsh left, he picked up his pipe, but the light had gone out. He couldn't dillydally anymore. He grabbed the manila envelope. Time to have a talk with Isabel.

When he entered his apartment at the Chastleton Hotel, she flung her arms around his neck. She was barefoot and stood on tiptoes to kiss him on the lips. "I wasn't sure if you'd come." A scarf tied her hair in a loose ponytail.

"We have to talk." He extricated himself from her embrace. He sat on the sofa, pushing the throw pillows to one side. He set down the manila envelope and his car keys beside him. An Al Jolson record was playing on the phonograph.

Although cold outside, the room stayed warm, the fireplace ablaze. He loosened his khaki tie and glanced down at his uniform. He sighed. He'd been in these clothes for more than twelve hours.

She knelt down to take off his shoes.

"Don't. I'm not staying."

She questioned him with a look, then got up. "I'll get you a drink. Whiskey?"

He nodded. The veins in his temples throbbed with agitation. He followed her movement as she prepared his drink. Prohibition was over, and the mini bar was well-stocked.

She wore a white cotton chemise, something she'd brought from Manila. Her hardened nipples showed through the flimsy fabric. In the past, this would have driven him mad. Not tonight. He steeled himself for Round Three of a long and excruciating day.

She served him a glass of whiskey, ice cubes clinking. Most nights, he drank his whiskey neat, but once in a while, he liked it over ice. How did she know he wanted whiskey on the rocks? Was he that transparent? She knew his moods so well. It unnerved him.

"How's work?" she said. "Did you go to the White House today?"

He took a sip of his drink, ignoring her question. Al Jolson was finished and the phonograph crackled. She turned it off. Afterward she lounged on the settee opposite him. When she moved, the straps of her chemise slid off and revealed voluptuous breasts, the color of honey.

The sight of her luxuriating on the settee reminded him that somewhere out there was a gossip columnist or a newspaperman who would kill to expose her. The man who had snapped her picture six months ago had neither surfaced nor published the photo.

But one day he might. MacArthur could almost see Isabel's picture splashed in newspapers across the country. His fear fluttered inside him like a little creature.

"I'm going to sue Drew Pearson and Robert Allen for libel," he said. "They're going to dig all the dirt they can find about me."

"Or maybe they'll stop writing rumors." She slouched lower, her gaze on her pink fingernails. "I read their column today…about a rumor that you want to change the rules so you'll be entitled to a nineteen-gun salute even after your tour as the chief of staff is over. It's ridiculous."

He took another sip of whiskey. His panic had sprouted wings and flapped inside him. "Suing Pearson and Allen means I'm waging a war against the press."

"It serves them right."

He drained his drink. The terror had grown full-blown, beating hard and fast. "The press will use *you* to smear my reputation."

"What are you talking about?" She narrowed her eyes, tossed her head back.

"I can't go on with this, Isabel."

She sat up, her dark eyes wide—the slow dawn of recognition that something was awry. But the girl could act. She rose, lifted her head high, and sashayed toward him. She was Dimples the vixen once again, radiating tempestuous heat.

She knelt at his feet, took the empty glass away, and guided his hand to her cheek, nudging her face against his hand. "Poor Daddy. Tough day at work, huh?"

Her sweet scent filled up his senses. The smell of a flower in the Philippines, whose name he couldn't dredge up. Was it her soap or her perfume?

"I want you." She kissed his fingers and licked his forefinger.

He thrust his finger into her mouth and she sucked on it. Instead of feeling aroused, he seethed. What a blatant manipulation! She used the word *daddy* like a weapon. She could devour him alive with that one word alone.

He snatched his hand away. He picked up the manila envelope and waved it. "I know about Eddie Palma."

He got up, tossed the envelope at her. Then he crossed the room and stood before the wall of windows. The curtains had been drawn back. The courtyard was dark. He could hear the rustling of the envelope as she looked at its contents.

"How dare you spy on me!"

He swung around just as she lunged at him, trying to claw at his face, but he intercepted her arms in mid-swing. By God, he wanted to hit her! But when he'd struck her back in Manila, they'd ended up having rough sex and she had enjoyed it too much. He wouldn't give her that satisfaction.

He released her arms and seized her shoulders instead. "I was right to spy on you. You're a goddamn liar and you'll never change. You lied about your age and about the pregnancy that never was. You pretended to be a virgin, even though Eddie Palma had fucked you long before I did!"

She aimed her saucer eyes at him. "Yes, Eddie was my lover, but not anymore. I want you—not him! I didn't lie about being a virgin. I never said I was, but you wanted to believe it."

He squeezed her shoulders hard. "Bullshit! There are outright lies and there are lies by omission. You're guilty of both. Eddie has been writing you letters ever since New York. Yet you've never mentioned him. You've been lying by omission all along."

"He's my friend, that's all! He's visiting Washington for a few days, and we had lunch together, that's all. I couldn't tell you about him because you're so possessive. You were jealous of Sam Prentice and even of poor Duncan. You're jealous of every man who looks at me."

"Everyone said you're just an itch I had to scratch. And one day I'd come to my senses. Guess what? That day is today. I've finally come to my senses. I want out!"

He let go of her abruptly, making her stagger backward. The scarf tying her hair came loose and fell on the floor.

He panted as his heart slammed in his chest. He expected her to fight back, try to hit him again. To his astonishment, tears had sprung from her eyes. She'd never cried in front of him before. It gave him pause.

She picked up the scarf and wiped her tears with it. Then she straightened herself. "I lied about some things, but I *never* lied when I said I love you."

"Maybe so. The point is, I can't trust you."

"You said you love me."

It sounded like an accusation. He felt a rush of blood across his face. "Not anymore!"

She blinked, looking dazed. He'd just slammed the door in her face, something he should have done a long time ago.

A flash of panic in her eyes. "I'll never speak to Eddie again. I'll do better, I promise. Tell me what you want, and I'll do whatever you want."

"It's over." He yanked his tie off and threw it on the floor. He was suffocating with fury and exhaustion.

"Douglas, I'm sorry. Please give me a chance."

He shook his head, swept the room with a glance. Little flames flickered in the fireplace as the fire dwindled. Perhaps it was just a habit, but his first instinct was to fix it for her. He crossed the room and knelt before it. He picked up the fire poker, pried the embers with it, then added firewood.

"I'm leaving for Warsaw in three days." He didn't look at her. "I'll be away for several weeks. I want you out of here by the time I get back."

"Where would I go?" Her voice cracked. "I have nowhere to go."

"Go back to Manila. Marsh will make the arrangements for you."

"Douglas, I gave you my everything!"

He rose and faced her squarely. "And I risked *everything* for you—everything that I've worked for!" He put his hands on his hips and drew a deep breath. "We both knew this day would come. It's over."

She inclined her head, trying to hide her tears. She turned around, her back toward him, and sobbed into her scarf. Her shoulders rocked back and forth as her sobs turned into a wail.

He didn't regret having loved her. He regretted only that he'd loved her this long, when he could have ended the affair in Manila. Now it was crushing her. But he was Douglas MacArthur. He'd never apologize for it.

He turned away, his glance falling on the floor, at the trail of her deception: the picture, the private eye's report, the manila envelope. He picked them up and fed them to the fire.

When he turned around, their eyes met. She'd been watching him burn the envelope and its contents. She blew her nose into the scarf. Then she pulled the neckline of her chemise to wipe her wet cheeks with it, a gesture he found aching with innocence. She was twenty-three years old—the same age MacArthur was when he'd killed a human being for the first time, not one but two men.

Was it a cruel coincidence that he'd killed those bandits in the Philippines, where she happened to come from? MacArthur, Isabel, and the Philippines. Their fates were intertwined, sharing a common sorrow. He'd survived the killing and had gone on to succeed. She would survive, too, but would she thrive?

She picked up the empty glass and brought it to the kitchen. When she came back to the living room, she wiped the wet ring on the coffee table with a rag. Then she rearranged the throw pillows on the sofa and put the rag away like nothing was amiss, like she was just fine.

He picked up the car keys. "I have to go."

She stood only a few feet away. She'd never looked so lovely, as if he'd seen her only in the dim shadows in the past four years, and now he was seeing her under the full light for the first time. Yes, she was beautiful. Yes, he had loved her. And yes, he was ready to move on.

He turned on his heel and headed for the door. He stopped—he remembered the name of the flower, the source of her sweet scent. *Sampaguita*. But still he didn't know whether it was her soap or perfume, maybe oil. Too late to find out.

He turned around. "Goodbye, Isabel."

She responded with a sad smile and a nod, but not a word—not goodbye, not his name, not even "I hate you."

Her forbearance, more than anything, broke his heart.

# 29.

# Los Angeles, August 1934

THREE MONTHS after MacArthur had removed Isabel from his life with the precision of a military mission, she worked as a hula dancer at a small nightclub in downtown Los Angeles. On a sweltering Friday night, dozens of men squeezed themselves at the tables or stood on the sidelines. They drank, smoked, and laughed in spite of the choking heat.

There was no stage. Isabel and four other Filipino ladies clad in grass skirts and tiny floral tops performed in the middle of the dance floor to live ukulele music. Isabel could hardly breathe, much more smile and pretend to enjoy shaking her hips before a soused audience.

The men rose from their tables to get a better view. Soon they closed in. She almost gagged from inhaling their ripe, boozy smell. The nightclub bouncers pushed the men back. At the end of the number, she and the other ladies fled the dance floor.

They took refuge at the back of the club, near a dumpster, where they passed around a bottle of rum. She didn't like drinking while performing, but in this case, it was the only way she could endure. After several minutes, three of the women went inside to freshen up. They were due back on the dance floor soon. After their number, Isabel and the other Filipina, Amalia, would perform. In the meantime, they stayed outside and took turns swigging rum.

The liquor flooded Isabel's veins with tingling warmth and her head with bad memories. The night the Commander had broken up with her proved to be the cataclysm of her life. Overnight, she'd plunged from the summit to the abyss, from being Douglas MacArthur's object of desire to being his castoff. Within weeks, she'd moved from the posh Chastleton Hotel to a ramshackle lodging house in a hardscrabble neighborhood in Los Angeles. She was like an old Army uniform he'd thrown away.

"Do you sometimes feel like a discarded uniform?" she asked Amalia.

"Not a uniform, but *discarded*. Period." Amalia's long, unruly tresses gave her a wild look. The club owner had asked her to lose twenty pounds, but many men liked her substantial hips and ass, not to mention her breasts, which always threatened to pop out of her top. "Night after night of dancing for drunks or dancing *with* drunks makes me feel discarded."

Isabel worked with Amalia two nights a week at the nightclub and three nights at a taxi dance hall, where men bought tickets and lined up to dance with young women like them. In both joints, their clientele consisted of drunks, mostly foreigners. European immigrants patronized the nightclub, while Asian men frequented the taxi dance hall.

"Why, who discarded you?" said Amalia.

"The person who paid for my hula lessons." Isabel placed her palms on her cheeks. The initial warm sensation from the rum had turned hot. Her face and breasts had grown clammy. Her heart raced.

"You took lessons? Who the hell paid for it?"

"It's not anyone you know."

None of her friends in Los Angeles knew about Douglas MacArthur, a testament to her loyalty. She kept him to herself, and Eddie Palma would never talk to anyone about MacArthur out of pride.

"So you're a trained hula dancer. How about that?" Amalia nudged Isabel with the elbow. "I learned it in a hurry on my own back home." She meant Honolulu, where Amalia and her family had immigrated to work in the pineapple and coffee plantations, like thousands of other Filipinos. She got tired of manual labor, so she wanted to try her luck in Los Angeles.

"And look what you got out of your hula lessons…a prime spot dancing for cheapskate drunks!" Amalia laughed, followed by a coughing fit.

"You better stop drinking, or you'll have an asthma attack," warned Isabel.

"It's the cigarette smoke inside that's killing me. And this stupid job."

Isabel couldn't refute her. The thought that she'd gone from dancing privately for one of America's most powerful men—the man she loved—to dancing in front of filthy slobs pierced her heart. Why did she come to Los Angeles? Should she have gone back to Manila?

She'd informed her family she was no longer with MacArthur, but she couldn't go back home. She would forever be known as MacArthur's reject. No respectable man in Manila would marry her. Meanwhile, Nenita had married Fabian Elizalde. Even Ben was married, with two children. She would always be compared to them. She would be the perpetual cause of heartache for Mama and Lola.

She took another swig of the rum. After the Commander had dumped her, Captain Marsh had come to the Chastleton with a one-way passage on a Manila-bound ship and a few hundred dollars of pocket money. She'd accepted them, but she didn't return to Manila. She'd cashed in the ticket and taken a bus to L.A. instead. She'd stayed with the Grants for a month, and spent her money on sightseeing and shopping, while still pretending to have a rich daddy in Washington. After she'd worn out her welcome and depleted her funds, she'd sought Eddie Palma.

Isabel and Eddie lived in Little Manila, not far from Hollywood. Amalia lived in the same building, right next to them.

Eddie spent most of his time auditioning. Newspapers listed casting calls and desperate actors like him showed up at the gates of the studios. He sometimes found work as an extra pretending to be a marauding Indian or a murderous Mexican bandit in Western movies.

Isabel had accompanied Eddie at casting calls a few times. It often meant waiting all day long for an audition that never happened. She'd felt like a cow at the rear of a huge herd. So she'd gone job hunting with Amalia, hoping to work at a salon, but they'd ended up as dancers.

She hated their clientele, but it beat cleaning houses. At least, dancing offered a steady paycheck in the city. Eddie, on the other hand, worked outside Los Angeles to supplement his acting jobs. This week, he harvested wine grapes in Napa Valley. He'd joined dozens of Filipinos from Little Manila who worked seasonal jobs in other parts of California.

One of the Filipino dancers came out and yelled, "It's show time, ladies!"

For the next forty minutes, Isabel and Amalia danced as a duo, then as part of the group. After that, they socialized for another hour as part of their job. The slimy customers bought them drinks and food.

Amalia ordered a hamburger, so she wouldn't have to pay for her own dinner. Isabel should have done the same thing, but food was the last thing on her mind. She couldn't shake off MacArthur's memories and the feeling she was expendable. Liquor might help drown her sorrow, so she ordered a whiskey sour. They left when Amalia started coughing nonstop.

Inside the tiny room she shared with Eddie, she turned on the electric lamp and found two letters on the floor. The landlord must have slid them under the door while she was away. One was for Eddie and the other was for her. She put them aside, while she changed into a house dress. She opened the window and took off her jewelry.

Afterward, she went to the common bathroom in the hall, which reeked of insecticide. The lodging house had been plagued by flies, ants, and bedbugs at different times, so the building always smelled of poison.

At least there was no line outside the bathroom. Half of the lodgers were men like Eddie who worked seasonal jobs elsewhere, so the two-story boarding house was almost empty.

An infant's cry rose, shrill and loud as a siren. It should have annoyed her, but no, it clutched at her heart. How sweet it would have been to awaken to her baby's cries. She would have sung a lullaby while feeding him and then nestled up with him in a cozy bed.

A young couple with a baby lived downstairs. Unlike Isabel and Eddie, they were married. The other Filipinos tolerated them living together out of wedlock because they assumed it was a question of money. They could neither afford to get married nor rent separate rooms. That was only part true. Eddie had proposed to Isabel, but she'd rejected him. How could she marry him when she pined for MacArthur?

Los Angeles resembled Manila in many ways—hot and humid and aswarm with Filipinos—but she didn't feel at home. Her countrymen had welcomed her with open arms to their Little Manila Civic Association, a close-knit group of immigrants helping one another. They shared their food and money, babysat each other's children, and cared for each other in times of illness. She couldn't have asked for a more supportive community, but she didn't belong here. Perhaps it was because she was only fifty percent Filipino and her heart was one hundred percent elsewhere.

She longed for her old life. She missed the Chastleton and all its modern conveniences. She missed the Commander, his little quirks, his fastidiousness. He was so particular he wanted everything custom-made—his clothes, shoes, corncob pipes, and even his Packard.

After their breakup, she began to see him in a different light. She was like an amputee who, in mourning the loss of her leg, refused to acknowledge the gangrene the amputation had stopped from spreading. She dismissed the Commander's faults and flaws. His jealousy and his rules used to oppress her, but now she called them his "protectiveness." She'd thought of him as unfair when he'd stopped her from performing and prohibited her from making friends, but now she considered it his prerogative.

People said Douglas MacArthur had a huge ego, but she saw only his formidable presence. MacArthur was a fortress. His power rested not in his position as the chief of staff or his rank as a four-star general, but in his ability to make her feel safe when he entered the room. Too late now, but living in MacArthur's shadow had been enough. She would crawl from Los Angeles to Washington—back into the bastion of his love—if he asked her. If only he would take her back.

She returned to her room and perched on the narrow bed she'd been sharing with Eddie. Her stomach hurt from too much alcohol and no food. Her head throbbed. She ought to go to bed, but lately she'd had trouble sleeping. Working nights was taking its toll, wreaking havoc on her spirits. She would come home from work well after midnight dead tired, but unable to sleep. Most nights, she would cry until daybreak, thinking of MacArthur, while Eddie snored beside her.

Without a dresser, she just massaged her face with Pond's vanishing cream and then wiped it off with a wad of cotton, all without the benefit of a mirror.

Would her life have remained the same had Eddie not shown up in Washington? How could she have known eating lunch with Eddie would unravel her life? How she regretted that day.

Glancing down at the bed was enough to remind her of the sex she missed. MacArthur had been as generous in bed as with material things. By comparison, Eddie Palma was poor in every sense.

She'd assumed she would continue to enjoy sex even after MacArthur. Eddie was close to her age, with a young man's body and appetites. But Eddie lacked imagination. He knew nothing of seduction or foreplay. His idea of lovemaking was to thrust in and out for a few minutes before rolling over to one side of the bed.

She could no longer remember why she'd chosen to lose her virginity to Eddie. It was poor timing. He happened to come along before MacArthur. Otherwise, she would have saved herself for the Commander.

Sighing, she got up to open the window wider. The weather remained stifling despite the late hour. She picked up her letter, plopping on the bed to read it. Mama's beautiful handwriting brought a pang of homesickness.

Halfway through the letter, her heart dropped, tears stinging her eyes. Manang was dead. Lola's faithful servant, whom Isabel loved like her own grandmother, had died in her sleep.

She flung herself on the bed. *No, no, no*. She wept like someone had cut her heart open. Manang had cared for her and Ben while they were growing up. Servants had come and gone, but she'd stayed, as reliable as the tropical sun. She would never see the old woman again. If Manang could die so suddenly, then Lola could, too. Then Mama and Papa. They could all die while she was thousands of miles away. She would never see them again.

She cried until her eyes and nose hurt. She sat up bathed in her sweat. Her mouth was parched, but it was too much trouble to go downstairs to the common kitchen for a glass of water.

She swung her legs over the edge of the bed, her feet touching the wooden floor. She pulled out the tin can containing her most cherished mementos from underneath the bed. The mere sight of the Commander's letters brought on her tears again. The baby's booties, gentle to the touch, flayed her heart. The urge to speak with MacArthur gripped her. If only she could hear his voice, she would be all right.

She put on her slippers and padded down the hall, where a shared telephone was fastened to the wall. She picked up the receiver and asked the operator to connect her to Quarters One at Fort Myer.

It was almost three o'clock in the morning on the East Coast, but he would pick up the phone in the middle of the night because of his job. He wouldn't risk missing an emergency call from the White House or the secretary of war.

After a couple of tries, the call went through. As soon as she heard someone pick up the phone, she said, "Douglas, it's me, Belle. Manang is dead…I can't take it. I need you. " Tears streamed down her face.

The other end of the line crackled.

She wiped her face with the sleeve of her dress. "Douglas, I need you—"

"Who is this?" said a woman. "Do you have *any* idea what time it is?"

Her jaw slackened. In the background, a man's voice.

"Mother, let me handle it." It was MacArthur. "Hello? Hello?"

Isabel had forgotten that MacArthur's phone was in the study and his mother could just as easily pick it up. She'd already lost heart. After a moment, he hung up.

She put the receiver down and rested her forehead on the wall. She'd lost Manang forever—and she'd just lost MacArthur. She'd squandered her chance to reconnect with him. She'd heard his voice, and she felt worse.

She cried, unable to control her hiccupping noise. The overpowering odor of insecticide permeated her lungs. It gave her an idea.

She trundled to the broom closet, next to the bathroom. She opened it and found what she was looking for: a bottle of insecticide and brushes for its application. The landlord bought poison mixed by a druggist and left it in the closet for boarders to use when insects invaded their bedrooms.

She carried the bottle back to her room. The boarding house slept on. She heard only her own footsteps and the heavy beating of her heart.

Inside her room, she set the poison down on the floor. She sat next to it, her back against the bed. Thoughts of Manang returned. She'd opposed Isabel's trip to America, warned her about being a white man's plaything. And she'd been right.

She stretched her legs on the floor and shut her eyes. The throbbing in her head had exploded into a full-blown headache. Grief drenched her. How tired she was. Alcohol, fatigue, sleeplessness, and heartache sapped her will to live.

Next door, Amalia coughed. A harsh sound like a dog's bark. Then silence.

Isabel opened her eyes. She unscrewed the bottle's top and took a sip. She winced. It tasted as foul as its odor. She hesitated for a second, and then drank it.

As she drained the bottle, a voice in her head taunted, *discarded plaything discarded plaything discarded plaything.*

# 30.

# Washington, D.C., December 1934

ISABEL DIDN'T DIE of poison ingestion, thanks to Amalia. Her friend had been awake because of a coughing fit and heard Isabel's animal-like noises next door as she threw up. How could Isabel have known that her body would protect itself from toxin? The more insecticide she'd drunk, the more violent her body expelled it. She couldn't stop vomiting.

After two days in a hospital, she'd recovered from the poison, but not from humiliation. What a loser she was. She'd failed as an actress and had lost MacArthur's love. And, finally, she'd botched her suicide. She'd done it on impulse, a misbegotten idea she now regretted. After the incident, everyone in Little Manila had treated her like a fragile little thing. Some of the lodgers had blamed Eddie for not taking care of his sweetheart. He could have taken her with him to Napa Valley, they'd said behind his back.

But Eddie knew MacArthur caused Isabel's heartache. He refused to believe she would kill herself over Manang, a mere servant. Their relationship had gone from tepid to frosty. She couldn't stand Little Manila. So she'd pawned a set of gold earrings and bracelet, from the

Commander. Then she'd bought a one-way bus ticket to Washington. That was three months ago.

On a nippy Sunday morning, when most people were coming out of church, she sat on a bench on the east side of the Washington Monument. She wore MacArthur's fur coat and a velvet cloche hat pulled low to cover her ears. A pale December sun rose, but it failed to make her feel warm. Why on earth did she choose the Washington Monument as a meeting place? Would the Commander show up? Or rather, would he send one of his aides to pick her up? She longed to see him. Just one more time.

Ever since her return, she'd been trying to see him. But he wouldn't take her calls, much less extend any help. The one time he'd responded to her letter, he had mocked her by sending a clipping of a *Help Wanted* ad from a newspaper.

If not for Miss Harper, her former instructor, she'd be living on the streets. Miss Harper, who had neither a beau nor a relative in Washington, lived by herself in a small apartment in the Foggy Bottom section of D.C. She was happy to let Isabel sleep on her couch and grateful for her company. "You must call me Betty," she'd insisted, though Isabel found it hard to call *any* teacher by her first name, especially a lady close to Mama's age. They talked shop in the evenings and practiced curling techniques on weekends, doing finger waves and brush curls on each other's hair.

Through Betty's connections, Isabel had secured a job as a "cosmetologist" at Coiffure Salon in their neighborhood. She wore a white uniform that made her look like a nurse. She washed, cut, and styled ladies' hair. Sometimes she gave facial massages. "You're a beauty nurse," Betty had told her. Although she didn't earn enough to move out of Betty's apartment, she contributed to the rent. They'd become confidantes, the best of friends.

Betty fueled Isabel's fantasy of getting back together with MacArthur with her romantic scenarios straight out of the ladies' dime novels she read. What if Isabel just happened to be in a restaurant he frequented? She could be in the audience when the Commander spoke at a fundraising event for the Historical Society. "All you need is a small window of opportunity for reconciliation," Betty had said.

Such opportunity came when a man who looked awfully familiar had shown up at the salon. He'd said, "Remember me? I took your photograph last year. General MacArthur was waiting for you in his car, and I took your picture." Howard the photographer!

Over coffee, he'd asked if Isabel would like to meet a couple of important gentlemen of the press—Drew Pearson and Robert Allen. The "yellow journalists" who had maligned the Commander, the very men whom he'd sued for libel. She'd headed for the door, but Howard had begged her to listen.

She had relented and found out that Pearson and Allen had paid for her photo. They never published it because it was worthless, with only a blurred image of a man who might be Douglas MacArthur. But it was a good photograph of Isabel and they'd been using it to locate her. Howard had traced his steps back to the beauty academy and got hold of Betty, who had directed him to the salon.

"What could Pearson and Allen possibly want from me?" Isabel had scoffed.

"They'd like you to persuade the general to drop the lawsuit," said Howard.

"How on earth would I do that? We're no longer together."

"Exactly!"

She'd been confused. Howard had explained that Pearson and Allen would use her as a bargaining chip. They would threaten the general to produce her as a witness who had first-hand knowledge of MacArthur's thoughts and feelings. In other words, she would be used to blackmail him. Thanks, but no thanks.

At home, Howard's offer had sparked Betty's imagination and tinged her face with excitement. "Once you talk to the general, once he sees you again…who knows what will happen? If you miss him, you can bet that he misses you, too." She'd hovered and buzzed like a honeybee. "Oh, Belle, this is your second chance at love!"

Indeed she'd dreamed and wished and prayed for a chance to see him again. And so, she'd followed Betty's advice.

She got up and walked toward the Washington Monument. More people had arrived—tourists strolling along the tree-lined expanse that extended from the monument all the way to the Capitol.

When she reached the base of the monument, she gazed up, shielding her eyes from the sunlight with her hand. The white obelisk rose to the sky.

She'd chosen this as a meeting place for its open space. It would show MacArthur she had no intention of seducing him. She just wanted to talk.

She gaped at the structure and couldn't help but compare MacArthur to the Washington Monument—towering in her life, occupying her heart. Sorrow soaked through her like water, making her tear up. She would always love him.

She walked around the base. In the winter, the park looked inhospitable, a swath of barren land with bare trees. By spring, the grounds would teem with grass but also with tourists. Today it stood peaceful, the crowds manageable.

She strolled back to her bench and perched on it. She prayed in her head. *Please, God, let me see him one more time.* But, the more she thought about her letter begging him to meet her, the more discouraged she became. How pathetic she was.

She should have known better than to listen to the advice of a spinster over matters of the heart. For better or for worse, she'd agreed to become part of Pearson and Allen's case, as a potential witness against the Commander. Not only that, she'd shown the lawyer MacArthur's letters, postcards, and radiograms to prove their relationship. She'd answered the lawyer's meddlesome questions.

What did the general think of President Roosevelt? *He called him "that cripple in the White House."* What did he think of the secretary of war? *He thought George Dern was a sleepy old fool.*

When the man had referred to her as "MacArthur's mistress," she'd bristled. "He's not married, so how can I be his mistress?"

"Yes, he's not married, but he kept you hidden from the public," the attorney had said, as disinterested as could be. "I take it he never introduced you to his mother?"

She'd shaken her head.

"That's what I mean. To all intents and purposes, you're MacArthur's mistress—*former mistress.*"

So that was how she was described in legal documents. It broke her heart.

The past four weeks had been filled with meetings. The attorney had asked the general to drop his lawsuit against his clients or he would make Isabel testify against MacArthur.

The general had been outraged. The lawyers negotiated hard before he'd agreed to end the case. He'd made one condition. He wanted his love letters back. Pearson and Allen would go scot-free, but Isabel would get nothing, plus she would have to give up MacArthur's letters. She'd allowed herself to be dragged into the case—earning the Commander's wrath—for nothing. Not even a chance to get a glimpse of him.

At this point, the lawyer had advised her to return the letters in exchange for cash. But she just wanted to talk to him. She'd been told a cash demand would make the general take her seriously, *and then* maybe he would talk to her. She cringed at the thought that Betty's idea of "opportunity" had turned into extortion.

"Belle, you have to listen to your lawyer. He knows how to deal with powerful men," Betty had assured her. "Trust me, no payment will be made and there will be no extortion because MacArthur will come back to you before then. He loves you. You've got to have faith, sweetheart."

She grew desperate. The more she resisted the attorney's advice, the darker her moods became. The bouts of hopelessness and sleeplessness always ended in tears and the inevitable question: Where would she find a druggist who would sell her insecticide?

So she'd succumbed to the lawyer to silence the voice of despair inside her, before she found the way to the druggist. She'd asked for fifteen thousand dollars, though the attorney had advised fifty thousand. She'd insisted on the smaller amount because surely it would never come to that? As Betty had supposed, the Commander would realize Isabel didn't want his money, just a chance to see him again.

As soon as the cash demand had been formalized, she'd written to MacArthur. If he would meet her at the Washington Monument, she would drop her request. One meeting and then she'd leave him alone forever.

The meeting was today. She'd been waiting for about thirty minutes. She removed her suede leather gloves to put on some lipstick.

A man walked up to her. "Miss Cooper? Isabel Cooper?"

"Yes."

"I'm Major Eisenhower." He extended his right hand. "Call me Ike."

She stood up to shake his hand. “Hello, Ike.”

Eisenhower was one of the Commander’s aides; MacArthur had praised him for his excellent reports.

“I’m sorry I’m late. I went straight to the monument, but I didn’t see anyone who matched your description.” He smiled.

“I expected Captain Marsh or Lieutenant Wallace,” she said. Eisenhower didn’t know her at all, so why did the Commander send him?

He took off his hat. “I’m sorry to disappoint you.”

His thinning hair surprised her. The man was a lot younger than MacArthur.

“The general said you have a beauty mark on your left cheek. And I know that your stage name is Dimples, so I was looking for a beautiful bedimpled lady.”

“That’s very kind of you to say.”

“General MacArthur called me just this morning. He actually wanted to come—”

“He did?” Her voice went up a notch.

“Yes, he did.” His blue-gray eyes blazed with warmth. “But his attorney advised him against it. You see, President Roosevelt is extending General MacArthur’s term as the chief of staff. The White House will announce it tomorrow. It’s not a good idea for a photographer or newspaperman to see him here.”

“Oh.” She looked away, her tears threatening. Of course his appointment would be extended. He always got what he wanted. Why would he risk being seen with her?

“The general can’t come here today, so he doesn’t expect you to drop your cash demand.”

“I don’t want his money.” All of a sudden, she felt damp warmth on her cheeks, her tears rolling down. She wiped her face with her gloves.

“Miss Cooper—”

“You can call me Belle.”

“Belle. The general wants you to have the money.”

“I just want to talk to him.”

“I see.”

“I thought that my demand, as ridiculous as it was, would make him talk to me.”

"I understand." He put on his hat.

There was nothing else to say. "Well, thank you." She shook his hand again. She strode off.

"Belle!"

She stopped and turned around. The sun had blossomed, making her squint.

Eisenhower inched forward. "General MacArthur didn't want Marsh or Wallace to come here because you know them so well, and he thought seeing them might be painful for you. He didn't want to hurt you."

She nodded. How ironic was that? He didn't want to hurt her feelings, after he'd already carved up her heart into a thousand pieces. She'd tried to kill herself over him, and yet he didn't have the foggiest idea of what he meant to her.

She forced a smile. "Thank you for telling me that. I appreciate it." Betty's scheme had failed. Once MacArthur decided, he never changed his mind. She should have known that.

She walked away.

The following day, MacArthur's libel case against Drew Pearson and Robert Allen was settled out of court. Isabel attended the settlement meeting, still nurturing a flicker of hope to see the Commander. He was a no-show, not even a second-hand message for her from his attorney.

She drew a choking breath. She would never see him again.

The business at hand commenced. Pearson and Allen paid one dollar—as a symbol—for the general to drop his libel suit. MacArthur paid Isabel fifteen thousand dollars in exchange for his letters. Affidavits were signed.

Her heart seized up as she signed a document saying she would never ask for money from MacArthur again. The ultimate proof that she'd extorted, that she'd become the lowest of the low. Pearson, Allen, and Isabel agreed they would never use or quote the general's letters in any way.

In less than an hour, everything had been signed, checks and letters exchanged.

Pearson and Allen's lawyer congratulated her. "You deserve more, if you ask me. The general treated you badly."

She nodded. A sharp pain hit her core, like someone had plunged a knife deep into her gut. She was worth fifteen thousand dollars—and none of MacArthur's respect. Was there anything more exquisite than this wound? If only she could dissolve and evaporate like the morning mist. No one would miss her.

Within seven days of the settlement, she was ready to leave Washington. She waited for her bus with Betty. A Christmas tree at the center of the bus depot emitted the sweet fragrance of fresh blue spruce. Red and gold ribbons dangled from the branches.

Isabel glanced at the wall clock—seven o'clock, a few hours before Betty's class at the beauty academy would begin. She sat with her on a wooden bench.

"Thank you for being such a good friend to me," she said. She wore the same fur coat and hat she'd worn at the Washington Monument.

"I'm going to miss you very much. Who's going to do my hair now?" Betty patted her hair, which Isabel had bleached à la Jean Harlow.

"The girls at Coiffure will take care of you. Stay blond. It suits you."

"You think so?" Betty blushed. "Will you write me as soon as you arrive in Los Angeles?"

"Of course."

When a clerk yelled that the L.A. bus had arrived, Isabel picked up a suitcase, while Betty picked up another. They were the same luggage Isabel had brought with her from Manila. They passed through a door and stood before Isabel's bus.

Several buses pulled into their spots at the same time. They bore signs of destinations Isabel had only heard of: Cleveland, St. Louis, Miami. It seemed like the world was at her feet, if only for a moment.

They let the other passengers board first.

"You know, you can always come back here." Betty put her hand on Isabel's shoulder.

"Sure." She smiled, trying to stifle her tears. "Or you can come and see me in California."

"Yes, I'd like that. After you get settled and all."

They hugged each other. Isabel handed her suitcases to the driver and she climbed into the bus. She sat by the window, watching her friend wave goodbye before leaving.

She stared at her reflection in the window. She was twenty-four years old—a kept woman no more. No longer a source of embarrassment for Douglas MacArthur.

Freedom, at last. And yet her heart resembled a violin playing a high-pitched note, screeching higher and tighter, until a string snapped. She was broken.

In her purse, she had the check for fifteen thousand dollars, the largest sum she'd ever received in her life. She had his money, but not his good graces. She couldn't stay in Washington. Despite what she'd told Betty, she would never return out of respect for the Commander.

She would always love him, but he would never know it. She would go back to Los Angeles, but not to Little Manila or to Eddie Palma. Was this the end or the beginning of the road for her? For the second time since she'd first glimpsed the Statue of Liberty from the ship, she would try to belong here and make this country *her* America.

The bus departed as scheduled. It rolled onto the street, the odor of exhaust fumes filling her lungs.

She glanced at the empty seat beside her, then out the window. *Bahala na*. Come what may.

# 31.

# Colorado, May 1937

ON THE LAST DAY of May, when the air carried more dust than God had intended the human lungs to absorb, Isabel woke up to the pouncing winds at dawn. She'd barely gotten a couple of hours of rest. Her sleeplessness, on top of her lingering unhappiness, had plagued her from Washington to California to Colorado.

She slinked out of bed, leaving the dark form of her sleeping husband, to change from her nightgown into a dress. God bless his heart. Even when she cried at night, he never stirred, as though sleep transported him to another planet. She'd even taken out the tin can and spread her mementos on the floor. She'd returned the Commander's love letters to him, but she still had the baby romper and booties. The woodsy smell of the cedar moth balls tucked with the delicate fabric pricked her heart. She'd clamped her hand over her mouth as she wept, while her husband's snore filled the room.

She traipsed downstairs, which she and Bruce had turned into a barber shop and salon. A fine layer of dust had settled overnight on the wooden floor, though all the windows were shut. She sighed. When she married Bruce Robert Conrad two years ago, she had no inkling she was headed for a semi-arid Colorado town, where dust storms were common.

"You're now the wife of a man with three first names." Amalia had poked fun at her during her wedding celebration in a Chinese restaurant. They both had chuckled. The civil ceremony had been nondescript, presided over by a judge. Amalia and Bruce's buddy, Bill, had been their only witnesses and guests.

Isabel stepped outside to grab the newspaper from the mailbox. She unrolled it. The photograph and headline on the lower part of the *Denver Post's* front page grabbed her attention. *General MacArthur Marries Second Wife.*

Her breath hitched. She gripped the paper against the dusty wind and scurried inside. Underneath the photo of a petite brunette and the Commander was a caption: *Read story on page 10.* She laid the paper on the shop counter, her heart pounding. She found the article on the *Life and Culture* section. Another picture of the couple accompanied the news that MacArthur had married Jean Marie Faircloth in New York City. Mrs. MacArthur looked up to her husband with an adoring smile, her arm linked with his, while he faced the camera, his lips turned up in an austere smile. She wore a hat and a fur-collar coat; he was in a dark suit. He towered over her, straight as a ramrod, as imperious as ever.

Of course, he would marry sooner or later. The realization stung, reawakening the raw yearning and enormous loss she'd felt only a few hours ago. She sobbed, gasping for air. *Oh, God.*

The old cuckoo clock chimed. Six in the morning on Memorial Day. Was it worth opening the shop? Would anyone care to get a haircut or a shave today?

She set the paper aside and pulled a shaving towel from Bruce's barber closet. She wiped her tears and blew her nose into it. What now? Yet another long stretch of a day without any possibilities.

She dropped the towel on the counter and walked toward the window. The pall of dawn had parted. The high wind hissed as it pounded the trees. Their neighbor Milton's red truck rumbled by, perhaps on his way to visit the cemetery. Bruce would want to do the same, to clean the graves of his great-great uncles who had fought in the Civil War.

Bruce had been a barber to her cosmetologist in Los Angeles. They'd worked in adjacent shops in Chinatown, always bumping into each other. He was the token white man in his establishment, his employer's attempt to attract Caucasian clients. He'd been attentive and she'd been lonely.

One Sunday afternoon, while they strolled along the Santa Monica Pier, he'd told her, "If you don't mind me for a husband, I'll be honored to make you my wife." The earnestness of his proposal had taken her breath away. She'd said yes. They seemed perfect together.

After their wedding, he'd convinced her to use MacArthur's settlement money to start a shop in his hometown. They would be surrounded by his family and childhood friends. Having been uprooted from across the world, she'd longed to become part of his family. But how would a half-breed fare in a town so tiny it didn't appear on the map? There were no Filipinos, but plenty of Mexican immigrants in his home state, where counties were called Baca, Las Animas, Otero, and Pueblo. He'd assured her she would feel at home.

She'd packed her bags with a brand new optimism, moving to a part of Colorado without the majestic mountains and breathtaking scenery she'd imagined. Now they lived and worked in a squat building on Main Street. Although Springfield was over five thousand feet above sea level, it stretched flat as far as the eye could see.

Their business had yet to turn a profit. The forbidding weather of late hadn't helped. The "dusters" had intensified in the past ten months, the Dust Bowl states suffering from lingering drought and annihilating winds.

She climbed upstairs to make coffee in the kitchen, which also served as the dining room. They'd turned the second floor into an apartment, with a bedroom so small it didn't have a door. A red-and-white gingham curtain partitioned it from the living room, which had a mismatched sofa and a wing chair. She was back to using an outhouse like in the Philippines, with a shower stall next to it. They never invited anyone to their home. There was no money to buy decent furniture or room to entertain.

She poured a cup of coffee and paused outside the bedroom, ready to rouse Bruce. On second thought, she would let him sleep longer. The poor man had worked past suppertime yesterday, repairing fences at Mary's ranch. She was a cousin of his, a spinster who needed male relatives to do manual labor around her property.

Isabel tiptoed back to the shop, the stairs creaking underneath her shoes.

She picked up the *Denver Post* and sat before a desk, setting down her cup. Then she spread the newspaper before her.

*The happy couple entered matrimony at the New York City Municipal Building on April 30, 1937. When reporters asked General MacArthur for a comment, his only reply was, "This job is going to last forever."*

She read the rest of the article again. MacArthur was fifty-seven, while Jean was thirty-eight, the daughter of a wealthy banker and businessman. She belonged to an illustrious family from Murfreesboro, Tennessee. Her grandfather had been a Civil War officer of the state's Confederate Infantry Regiment.

The couple had met in 1935 aboard *SS President Hoover*, while MacArthur was en route to Manila for a two-year tour of duty as the field marshal responsible for establishing a Filipino army. She'd been traveling in Asia for leisure. They would return to the Philippines to finish his assignment.

Isabel looked away. Dust motes swam in the beam of faint sunlight streaming from the window. A chorus of birds flitted from a tree all at once. The sign atop the building rattled as the wind pummeled it. She'd christened their shop Modern Barber Shop & Beauty Salon.

The name seemed suitable two years ago. Now it sounded ridiculous, considering what was inside. On the left, an old barber's chair. On the right, a hairstyling chair with an adjustable electric hair dryer the size and shape of a bucket. There were two sinks, one for Bruce and one for her. They'd hung mirrors everywhere so customers could see themselves from all angles. No one would have guessed such a modest establishment cost so much. Out of her fifteen thousand dollars, only five hundred remained.

She turned her face back to the paper. The Commander had chosen a Southern belle like his mother, a white, well-traveled socialite. He'd married a small woman like Isabel in the very city where he'd once planned to marry her. They'd met on the way to Manila, where they were now headed to live as husband and wife.

Was it a coincidence that he'd picked a wife on the way to Isabel's country? It could have been and *should* have been her. Amalia would probably joke about the coincidence, but Isabel wouldn't laugh. What a heartless hoax of life. Just like her marriage.

Bruce's footsteps came light and quick. "Hon?" His voice, too nasal for a man, preceded his presence.

"In here."

"Morning, hon." He stopped in the doorway, yawning. He'd brought his own coffee. "Any good news?"

She scanned the rest of the page, focusing on an advertisement. *Perfectly Suited*, said the heading. It showed a model in a Jantzen bathing suit, a polka-dot bra and overskirt. "I'm just looking at this pretty bathing suit."

He plodded toward the window. "Looks like another duster today."

"Should we open the shop? I don't think anyone will come."

He nodded, his back toward her. "You're probably right. There won't be any customers, and there won't be any parade either…the first Memorial Day without any fanfare."

"No parade? I don't understand why we can't have one." She couldn't stop staring at the photo of the MacArthurs.

"Haven't you heard? The Warren kids are sick. Asthma, eye infection, measles…you name it."

"Charlie is sick?" He was the youngest, born the day after the New Year, now a sixteen-pound ball of giggles and gurgles. The child she longed to have. She babysat him every chance she got, which was a lot, because his mother was harried from taking care of four other children ages three to eight.

"The boy's got pinkeye. Maybe Eunice will ask you to help with the other kids."

"I'd take Charlie anytime. I don't know about the rest. But what's that got to do with the parade?"

He swung around, his right hand holding the mug. He had MacArthur's height, but not the general's good looks. He inserted his left hand inside the pocket of his overalls. "Rose, honey, don't you know?"

*Rose*. It sounded strange even after two years. He'd Americanized her middle name, introducing her to his family and friends as *Isabel*

*Rose Cooper*. A pet name, he'd said, instead of admitting *Rosario* was too foreign. Everyone in this town called her by the wrong name.

"All this dust can make little kids very ill," he continued. "Dr. Griffin says they should stay indoors. The council voted on his advice. They got enough people who favored skipping the parade. Besides, nobody's got jack to pay for the floats."

He dragged a stool toward the desk and sat across from her. "Let me have a look at the *Post*."

She handed him the paper.

He slurped his coffee. "So your ex, what's his face…General Big Shot got married. She ain't a Sheba, but she's rich. They look good together, don't you think?"

Her heart ached as if squeezed in a fist. Bruce had never been attuned to her emotions. Taking care of things, not people, was his *métier*. That was a word MacArthur used. Bruce replaced the motor oil in his old truck, patched the holes in their shingle roof, and washed the shop windows every other Sunday without fail. But he said the wrong things at the wrong time. He squirmed when she vented her frustration at the lack of Oriental ingredients common in California and New York but not in Colorado.

She drank the last of her coffee, now lukewarm, in one gulp.

"They got married on April thirtieth?" His eyes were still on the paper. "It took one whole month for the news to travel to Baca County."

Indeed everything took longer, moved slower in this part of the world. The ten hours she spent every day, six days a week, in the salon dragged on, interminable and unhurried.

"Bruce, I've been thinking…" Fatigue seeped in every grain of her body, the sleeplessness and despair taking their toll. She couldn't bear another day like this—empty like her life.

He brought the paper closer to his face. "Looks like there's no honeymoon for the newlyweds."

"Bruce."

"It says right here, they have to go back to Manila because of his work. She can't be happy about that."

"Are you listening to me?"

He dropped the paper, his gray eyes wide. "What is it?"

"I want to go back to Los Angeles." Her stomach tilted, her pulse skittered. She'd rehearsed this moment in her mind over and over and postponed it twice. Now it was time.

"Come again?"

"I'm going back to California." Her sorrow surged in her chest. She swallowed back her emotion or she might come apart.

He scratched his head, rumpling his straw-colored hair. "Is this about the baby? We've talked about this before. You're twenty-seven and I'm thirty. We can try again. We've got plenty of time."

She turned her face toward the window to keep her tears at bay. The wind swirled a low cloud of dust along the ground. More dirt in the air. She'd gotten pregnant a month after arriving in Springfield. They'd both been ecstatic. They would name the baby after one of her favorite singers. Al if it was a boy, after Al Jolson, and Katy if it was a girl, for Katy de la Cruz.

The euphoria lasted three months and then she'd bled and cramped, just like before. Dr. Griffin could do nothing about it. Since the miscarriage, Bruce had made love to her with the determination of a mountain climber and the urgency of a runner. *We can try again.* There had been little passion to begin with. Now there was none. It died with the fetus and their hope of starting a family.

She shifted her gaze back to him. "Nobody deserves to have her heart broken exactly the same way twice. I can't try again. I won't be able to survive a third miscarriage." This time, tears leaked from her eyes. Her heart was wilting.

"You're saying that now, but you might feel different next year. Like I said, we've got plenty of time."

She shook her head and scrubbed her tears away with a knuckle. "I'm sorry, but I'm going back to L.A."

He swept the place with a quick glance. "We've got something going here. It's a little slow right now, but business will pick up. Springfield folks are staying. They don't give up easy like the others." He pushed his mug aside. "Be reasonable. You know I can't just leave everything behind."

"I'm not asking you to come with me." A terrible pity washed over her. If Bruce had even a whiff of malice in him, this ending would have been easier.

"What? What are you saying, hon?" He gaped.

They'd never had a serious fight before, nothing they couldn't fix before bedtime. Now his expression asked whether this was going to be their first. He didn't hold her gaze for long—he never could—so he cast it down on the newspaper. With Bruce, the subject at hand was irrelevant. Whether it was moving to Colorado or buying a new tire, his demeanor was, *fine if you do, fine if you don't.*

He always let her win an argument. He didn't mind waiting things out. He was a lamb she didn't want to hurt, a tender heart she'd tried to protect. In all the time they'd been together, he'd gotten everything he wanted because of that. Not today, not at the expense of the rest of her life.

"I'm getting a divorce. I'm so sorry." Pain clogged her throat. Her breath grew shaky as she suppressed a sob.

He looked her in the eye. His mouth formed a grim line, his thin lips pressed together. "Wait a minute, honey…just hang on for a minute. You're being rash." He got up and knelt before her like a supplicant. His eyes moistened. "Please don't make a decision just yet. Now, Rose—"

"I'm not *Rose.* I never liked that name, but I didn't have the heart to tell you. You're a good man. I don't want to hurt you, but I can't go on living like this."

"What about this shop? We built it together. I thought you were happy." His tears fell, his head hung. "Please don't leave me, honey. Give me another chance." He buried his face on her lap.

She stroked his hair. The Jantzen ad came back to her. *Perfectly Suited.* Her life made as much sense as wearing a bathing suit in a town with neither a beach nor a swimming pool. In the past two years, she'd coped, but never thrived. She'd accepted his person, but never loved him. He wasn't a lover or a husband, but a companion. "Bruce, it's not your fault that I don't belong here. If you care about me, please let me go. You have to let me find my real home. I'm sorry."

He raised his head and looked up to her. "No, *I'm* sorry. I got it all wrong." He clasped her hand with both of his. "I want to do right by you. Tell me what I should do and you got it." She steered the conversation to practical matters. That much they could handle; their relationship was as functional as the chair she sat on.

"I'd like you to keep the business and the apartment. You deserve it. Try to find a buyer in Denver for the hair dryer and my other tools.

They should be worth something. It's probably better if I leave now, so people won't get a chance to ask." She wiped his tears with her fingers and palmed his cheek. "You're the kindest man I've ever known. I'll always be your friend."

He blinked in a deliberate way, like baby Charlie sometimes did right before a crying bout when nothing could console him. "What are you going to do in L.A.? Where are you gonna live? What about money?"

"I have five hundred left over. I'll stay with Amalia until I get a job."

"I'll pay you back."

"You don't have to." MacArthur's money couldn't have served a better purpose than to help this kind soul.

"I want to. This shop is ours, not just mine. I'll send you the cash, I promise."

"All right, if you can. Thank you." She let go of his hand. "I should pack up."

"Do you mean to say you're leaving right this minute?"

The look on his face begged no, but he wasn't one to resist. He wasn't a fighting man. His resilience resembled Springfield in the face of this devastating dust and wind.

She blew out a long breath. "I'm sorry," she whispered. "It's for the best."

He nodded, the tears pooling around his eyes again.

The shaking on the roof startled them both. The whooshing of the wind against the trees intensified. There was nothing more she could do. She pushed away from the desk and got up.

He clambered to his feet. "Let me drive you to Denver, at least."

"Yes, I'd like that. Thank you. I'll catch the bus there."

"Mary would want to say goodbye. She'd never forgive me for letting you go."

"I wouldn't leave without seeing her. We can stop by her ranch and the cemetery on the way out."

"You'll do that? Go to the cemetery with me?"

"Of course."

He enclosed her in a tight embrace. His sniffling told her he was crying again. "Write me when you can, Rose—" He clucked his tongue. "I mean, Belle…so you prefer Belle?"

She broke away from his hug. "Yes, I've always been Belle."

"I'll try to remember from now on."

She smiled at the innocence of his remark. He was the male friend she'd always wanted. How did she ever confuse their friendship with romantic love?

She glanced at the clock, then outside. Billowing dust had covered the weak sun, darkening the skies. Yet her heart felt lighter, her mind open to possibilities. It was half past seven in the morning and maybe her life was about to start anew.

# 32.

# Los Angeles, December 1941

"NEWS FLASH from Washington! The White House announced that the Japanese attacked Pearl Harbor from the air at seven fifty-five this morning, Honolulu time. Stay tuned for more details."

The radio broadcast was scratchy, but it was enough to make everyone in the drugstore pause. Isabel exchanged a questioning look with another woman before she picked up a bottle of aspirin and a jar of shaving cream. They both approached the checkout counter. Harry, the store owner, stood behind it, next to a cash register and a portable radio. The other customers gathered to listen.

"...President Roosevelt said in a statement that the bombing had caused widespread damage and death in all navy and military facilities on the island of Oahu..."

"Where's Oahu?" said a young man, chewing gum while speaking. "Is it near us?"

"...The Japanese also bombed Clark Field airbase on the island of Luzon in the Philippines, under the command of General Douglas MacArthur. The president is going to ask Congress to vote on a formal declaration of war against Japan..."

Isabel's heart quickened. Her family lived far from the military base, but was MacArthur all right?

"What does that mean?" said a woman, as she balanced her toddler on her right hip. "Are we going to war?"

"We already are, as far as I'm concerned," said a man at the back of the crowd. "The Japs started it."

"Ssh!" Harry raised an arm and cranked up the volume.

By then the news bulletin had ended. The announcer had moved on to a proposed ten-cent increase in streetcar fares.

"This sounds like another *War of the Worlds* prank." An older man waved his hand dismissively. "Ha! I ain't buying it this time."

"However, if it's true…Lord help the Japanese! They picked the wrong enemy," said another man. The others snickered. They all scattered in different aisles.

Isabel stepped forward. "How much for these, Harry?"

"Thirty-nine cents for the Squibb aspirin and twenty-five cents for the Gillette." He dropped them in a paper bag.

She handed him a dollar bill.

"An airbase in the Philippines got hit, did you hear?" He pressed some buttons on the cash register, which rang. "You still have family there?"

"They're all in Manila."

He gave her the change. "Now, don't you worry. General MacArthur will whip the enemy in no time."

It had been seven years since she'd laid eyes on the Commander, but the very mention of his name clipped her breath. "Thank you, Harry."

Outside, the afternoon sun glared. She walked two blocks to their apartment. Claro should be home from school soon. There must be at least one radio at the college, but would the teachers let students listen to the news? Would the school let them out early?

Claro Bautista, her husband of two years, studied at Southern California Junior College. He was seven years younger, lacking in practical experience and full of suffering sweetness. He was a fellow Filipino, the only son in a family with three girls. They'd immigrated to California twenty years ago.

His name meant "clear" in Tagalog, an inside joke between them. "I'm *clearly* in love with you," he'd told her the first time he'd taken her to a dance. When he'd tried to kiss her, she'd stopped him and said, "I need to *clear* my head and my heart first." She'd been divorced less than a year at the time. MacArthur, of course, always loomed in the byways of her mind.

Claro had persisted. After she'd relented, he'd introduced her to his parents, who'd told her his name had nothing to do with clarity. It was a tribute to a famous Filipino statesman, Claro M. Recto, who hailed from their hometown.

Recto was a friend of MacArthur's in Manila, one of the politicians he used to dine with. Recto had visited the Commander in Washington to seek advice about government affairs. "I met one of your *kababayan* today," MacArthur had said, tripping on the word, which meant compatriot. "Senator Recto came by my office. We talked for a good hour and a half." Isabel had corrected MacArthur's pronunciation and rewarded him with a kiss after he'd finally gotten it. No matter where she turned, she found a connection, like a skein of yarn unrolling, leading back to MacArthur.

A policeman blew his whistle, then signaled for cars to go and pedestrians to wait. Isabel stopped, glancing around.

A fruit-stand vendor shared his opinions with shoppers about last night's football game between the Trojans and the Bruins. Men emerging from the California Savings and Loan office talked about the three-and-a-half-percent savings rate, whatever that meant. Did they know Hawaii had been bombarded?

A pickup truck pulled over and let out two newsboys.

"News extra! War extra!" They each waved the *Los Angeles Times.* The truck driver dropped a pile of copies beside them. "The Japs attacked Pearl Harbor!"

That caught the attention of bystanders who snatched up the papers. Isabel bought one as well. The headline screamed, *War! Japan Bombs U.S. Bases in Hawaii & Philippines.* There were two pictures below it, President Roosevelt's and MacArthur's. The Commander despised FDR, but life continued to throw them together.

The cop blew his whistle again. The traffic stopped and she joined a stream of people cross the street. Another block and she was home: a four-story building without an elevator. She climbed the stairs to the third floor and unlocked her apartment door.

Claro sprawled across the couch, face down.

"You're home! Have you heard the news?" she said.

He lifted his head then buried his face in the sofa again. "That's why I'm here." His voice was muffled. "They let us go home because of the terrible news."

They lived in a one-bedroom apartment furnished with hand-me-down couch, arm chair, and china cabinet from Claro's relatives. The small bathroom and the kitchen with an icebox were far from luxurious, but they sufficed. At least, they didn't live with his parents.

She set down the brown bag and her purse on the side table, but she carried the newspaper. "*Dios mio*, will you sit up, please?"

He wore a long-sleeved shirt and gabardine slacks. His necktie, socks, and shoes littered the floor.

She tugged on his arm. "*Mahal*, talk to me, please." She called him love, Mama's nickname for her and Ben. "Don't you want to read the paper?"

He grumbled but didn't move.

It was like having another brother. Like Ben, Claro was fickle. His indecision, which made him enroll back and forth between welding and auto mechanic without finishing either one, reminded her of his youth. He was twenty-four years old, but he behaved like he was eighteen, somehow making it part of his charm.

She sank into the chair across from him and removed her high heels. "I got your shaving cream. The blades were not on sale, so I didn't buy any."

At last, he sat up. "How am I supposed to shave?"

His cosmic eyes, the color of coal, made his nose and mouth look tiny. He was handsome, though he didn't seem to care.

She rubbed her left sole, then the right. Her stockings itched. "I didn't throw your old blades. They're still good."

He stretched his legs in front of him and rested his bare feet on the coffee table. He stood a head shorter than most American men, but he was compact, not a pound wasted on him. He could throw a punch, which meant he sometimes came home with a busted mouth and bruised fists.

He and his Filipino friends spent hours practicing their jabs and uppercuts at a boxing club, if only to prove their virility to white men. They brawled to stop the taunting and to vanquish the perception that Filipino men were faggots.

He rolled his sleeves up, his toned biceps peeking out, his skin a golden brown. "You're like my mama. *Kuripot*." He flashed a killer smile.

Calling her stingy was bad. Comparing her to his mother was worse. The smile and the muscles, however, pleased her.

"Give me that." He leaned forward to snatch the newspaper from her hand. He reared back in the couch and read it. "I see...your geezer boyfriend is on the front page. Are you going to cut out his picture and paste it in your scrapbook?"

"The Philippines and Hawaii are in ruins, and that's all you can say?"

Men who liked MacArthur called him a hero or a legend. His detractors labeled him an egotist or an ass or a pompous son of a bitch. Only a boy would refer to him as somebody's "geezer boyfriend." Claro, despite his good looks, couldn't hold a candle to the Commander, not even in his insults.

"Don't change the subject." He waved the paper at her. "I know you keep a scrapbook of him."

"What are you talking about?"

He tossed the paper. "The book that you carry around, the one with the pink cover."

"It's a journal. I don't have a scrapbook."

He rose and pushed the coffee table out of the way. "Is that where you hide all your secrets?" He knelt before her, letting his hands run up and down her legs. "Tell me one secret, just one."

Her skin tingled. He had a knack for pushing her buttons. She'd done the same with MacArthur. Now she was the "older" one in the relationship, wrapped around her husband's little finger.

Claro's family didn't mind their age difference because of Isabel's good influence on him. She'd convinced him to go back to school long after his parents had given up on it. Not to mention that she supported him. He worked only part-time as a gas station attendant. To make ends meet, she spent some nights singing in a supper club and other nights as a restaurant hostess. After abandoning her beauty salon in Colorado, she didn't want to work in another beauty shop.

He took her face in his hands and pressed his mouth on hers. Then he slid a hand underneath the hem of her dress and fidgeted with her garter belt.

She cocked her head away from his, swatting his hand. "Stop it. I have to go to work." She glanced at the wooden clock atop the china cabinet. It was almost five o'clock.

He leaned back and sat on the floor, sighing. "I'm going to get drafted in MacArthur's war. I just know it. We talked about the draft in school."

She rose, staring down at his winsome face.

"Can you imagine me fighting in the Philippines under the command of your old boyfriend? I don't want to be in the Army. What am I gonna do?"

His whining reinforced his similarity to Ben. She should stop calling him *mahal* because *that* made her sound like Mama. Did she marry Claro because he reminded her of everything she loved and left behind in Manila? Was it because he was the male version of herself ten years ago?

She crossed her arms over her chest. "It's *not* MacArthur's war. Besides, we don't know yet what the president is going to do. Harry at the drugstore thinks this war is going to be short."

He reached out for her leg and stroked it. A wicked grin materialized on his face.

"I have to go." She bent down and pushed his hand away. She crossed to the bedroom.

He followed her, the door opening like a whisper. "Stay a little while."

She packed her cosmetics and costume jewelry in a case, her back toward him. "I have to practice a new song, so I have to get to the club before it opens."

He stood behind her and parted the curtain of her hair, kissing the hollow at the back of her neck. "Come on, don't be such a bore."

That was how she used to think of the Commander, always working, always bossing everyone around. His image floated into her mind. The dress uniform, the knee-high boots, the riding crop.

She closed her eyes and pushed MacArthur's memory away. She savored her husband's touch. Better to let her body welcome Claro than succumb to hopeless longing for a specter that belonged to the past.

When he unzipped her dress, she didn't resist. She didn't go to work at all.

A day later, Congress declared war against Japan. Isabel and Claro stayed home. She watched sheriff's patrol cars zoom by, their sirens blasting, lights flashing. While her husband passed the time sitting on the stoop downstairs with his friends, she followed the news on the radio. Authorities were out in full force to protect oil storage centers from possible sabotage. Sightings of hostile airplane and ship formations had turned out to be false alarms.

At night, while Isabel and Claro ate a dinner of chicken adobo and rice, the overhead light in the kitchen blinked twice before the apartment plunged into darkness. Claro struck a match, while Isabel grabbed the flashlight from the cupboard.

He opened the window. "Julio! What's happening?"

"Blackout!" Julio's voice boomed from the unit below. He and his pregnant wife, Paz, were fellow Filipinos.

Claro planted both hands on the window sill, his face turned downward. "Blackout? Why?"

"So the Japs won't be able to target us from the air! That's what I heard on the radio."

"All right. Thanks, *amigo*."

A loud crash upstairs, like a piece of furniture toppling, followed by the scream of a child, and someone yelling, "Oh, my God! Are you all right?"

In the distance, dogs barked. A vehicle started.

Isabel stood beside her husband, looking out. A convoy of blaring police cars passed by.

People had gathered on the sidewalk gossiping, the beams of their flashlights puncturing the night. After a while, they all dispersed, leaving a trail of eerie shadows.

Isabel and Claro tidied up the kitchen as best as they could, with only the weak gleam of flashlight, before slipping into bed. It wasn't even nine o clock, but they wanted to conserve the batteries. They left the windows open, the mild breeze lulling them into stupor.

He slithered lower, resting his head on her thigh. "I couldn't sleep last night. I thought the Japanese would be here by morning." He let out a long yawn. "I'll sleep better tonight. At least I know they won't find California with this blackout."

She tousled his hair as she hummed.

"What's that tune?"

"It's from that movie with Fred Astaire and Rita Hayworth, remember? He plays a choreographer who gets drafted?"

"Hmm… I fell asleep halfway, so I don't remember. What's the song called?"

Instead of answering him, she sang. "My dear…I've a feeling you are…so near…and yet so far…" She combed her fingers through his thick hair. "You appear… like a radiant star…first so near…then again so far…"

The melody was dreamy, the air cool. Outside, nothing stirred. She relaxed for the first time since the news about Pearl Harbor had jolted her. By the time she finished the song, they were ready to go to sleep.

In the following weeks, they kept their routines as normal as possible, though everything around them had begun to shift. Like their neighbors, they'd gone to the American Legion Hall to learn what to do during air raids. *Stay wherever you are; don't congest the streets. If you are in an automobile, abandon it and seek shelter or lie prone. Refrain from unnecessary phone calls. Put out small fires. Read the Fire Department's leaflets for handling incendiary bombs.*

They'd followed directions during air-raid drills. There had been more blackouts, sometimes lasting through dawn. The stores had run out of flashlights, but Claro's father had fixed his rusty Justrite, a heavy-duty piece that could have illuminated a coal mine, and gave it to them.

Ever since the bombing of Hawaii and the Philippines, Isabel prayed a daily novena to the Virgin Mary for her family's safety. It was all she could do apart from mailing a letter to Mama and Papa and wait for their response.

Two days before Christmas, Isabel woke up to the odor of cigarette smoke. She knuckled her eyes, shaking off sleep, and glanced at the alarm clock. It was noon. She'd worked at the restaurant until eleven last night. Most of the time, it closed early because people were too jittery about the war to eat out.

She got up and put on a robe. "Claro?"

In the living room, he stood smoking by the window, his back toward her.

"Why aren't you at work?"

School had been on Christmas break since last week, which allowed him to work at the gas station during the day. This year, there would be no Christmas tree or presents. No one knew how long the war would last. She'd embroidered his initials on a dozen white handkerchiefs. That would be her gift.

He turned his face aside, his handsome profile backlit by the sun. "I got my notice of classification today."

Her eyes darted from him to the coffee table, to the form and a copy of the newspaper. She picked up the form. *Fit for active military service. Notify your employer of this classification.*

Her heart dropped, the skin of her neck rising like the bristles of a brush.

"You know what it means, right?" He turned around and took a quick puff at his cigarette. "Next, I'll get my draft order. I'll be sent to war."

She fell onto the couch, her mind racing. When would he leave? Where would he go? As if to answer the latter, the newspaper headline drew her attention. *Manila Declared Open City, MacArthur Retreats to Corregidor.*

She dropped the notice and grabbed the paper, reading as fast as she could.

MacArthur had issued a proclamation declaring Manila an "open city" to spare it from Japanese attack. He'd evacuated the capital and established his headquarters on the island of Corregidor at the mouth of Manila Bay. American and Filipino troops had retreated to Bataan, a peninsula less than fifty miles from the capital. Eighty thousand Japanese troops had conquered Luzon, twice the size of MacArthur's forces on the island.

Knowing the Commander, deserting Manila probably killed him, not to mention shattered his pride. She couldn't imagine his wrath against Japan.

Claro walked toward the side table and poked out his cigarette in the ash tray. "I don't want to fight in MacArthur's war. I'm getting out of here."

"What?" She set the paper aside.

"I'm leaving."

"Where are you going?"

"Mexico, by way of Texas."

"When?"

"Today. Papa and Uncle Tony will drive me to El Paso. Herminia will meet me there and take me to Juarez for the night. From there, we drive on to Ascension, where they live. I have to brush up on my Spanish, but it's better than getting killed in combat."

"You're going to live with Herminia?" His cousin was married to a Mexican immigrant, an older man who had been in search of a young wife. They'd relocated to his hometown last year. "Don't be reckless. Let's talk about this first."

He crossed to the bedroom. She jumped to her feet and followed him. "What about me?"

"You're better off here. My family will take care of you. Give up this apartment and move in with them. My mother will come here tonight to help you pack up."

"What?"

"You heard me." He crouched down and pulled out a suitcase from underneath the bed. He threw it on top of the bed.

"You've been planning this with your family. How come you never mentioned it to me?" Tears burned in her eyes.

"Because you won't approve of my plan." He snatched a handful of clothes hanging in the closet and tossed them across the bed. "You'll think I'm a coward…You'll compare me to your geezer general boyfriend and ridicule me."

"What are you talking about?"

"You love MacArthur!" His eyes flashed with contempt. His fists were clenched. "You'll always love him. How ironic would it be if I end up serving under him? The Mariano brothers are shipping out of San Francisco next week. They're going straight to Corregidor. Not me. I'm not taking a chance."

She clutched her chest. "You're leaving me because of MacArthur?"

"He's everywhere, like a ghost. I can't compete with him, Belle." He resumed packing, opening and closing drawers, and picking up socks and underwear.

In the beginning, he'd been fascinated by her stories about MacArthur. He'd asked about the general's cars and corncob pipes, how much Tagalog he spoke, whether he was kind. What was it like to live in New York and Washington? Eventually he'd stopped asking. He had pointed out when she'd repeated a story. Lately he'd grown quiet when their friends talked about MacArthur's Pacific campaign. She should have known MacArthur's star was too bright for Claro.

She perched on the edge of the bed, watching him. "You wanted me to tell you a secret."

He stopped, his forehead wrinkled, as if trying to recall a past conversation.

"I'll tell you a secret." She locked eyes with him. "I see myself in you…the impulsiveness, the sulking, and whining. You remind me of a cherry blossom in springtime in Washington, beautiful but gone too soon."

She picked up the strewn shirts and folded them.

"So, what's the big secret?" His eyes were trained on her, suspicious.

"*You* are the closest I've ever gotten to happiness." Her voice, thick with emotion, sounded strange, like it belonged to someone else. "Please don't leave me."

"But you don't love me. Not as much as you love *him*."

The room fell into a grievous silence, at once intimate and rancorous. She couldn't refute him. Her heart, once conquered could never regain its freedom. Douglas MacArthur, her country's protector, the love of her life. How would she ever survive him?

She got up and retrieved the embroidered handkerchiefs from her nightstand drawer. "These are for you. I was going to wrap them as a Christmas present, but I guess we don't have time for that."

He accepted the bundle. His expression had softened. "Thank you."

She tucked her hands in her robe's pockets. "I'm going to make you a sandwich. You can eat before you leave or you can take it with you for the trip."

"When this war is over, maybe things will change. Maybe I'll come back."

*Maybe.* That word alone told her she would never see him again.

She nodded before pivoting around, not wanting him to see her tears. She was thirty-one years old, MacArthur's kept woman for four years, twice married, once divorced, and facing the possibility of being alone yet again.

# 33.

# Los Angeles, October 1944

ISABEL SAW the cowboys first and then the studio. They milled outside an arched gate at the intersection of Gower Street and Sunset Boulevard. Many aspiring actors hung around studios.

They were all spiffed up in Western outfits, in fringed or plain leather jackets and riding boots. One wore a velvet suit adorned with rhinestones, which reflected the sunlight, making her squint. They were an older bunch. Most young men fought the war abroad.

She stopped at the gate—unlocked, unmanned, and without a sign. A long, paved driveway led to a couple of buildings.

The cowboys tipped their wide-brimmed hats.

She nodded. "Good morning. I'm looking for the Momentum office."

"You've found it. Welcome to Poverty Row." The man in the glittering suit swept his arm in a theatrical manner. "The red brick building behind the gate is Momentum. If you can't get a job there, try Marquee and Golden Crown. They're both housed in the building across from Momentum."

"Thank you."

"To get to the back lot, go past the buildings and make a right," said a man in a sombrero. "Are you here for an audition?"

"No. I was called in."

An enthusiastic chorus of "good for you" and "congratulations" followed.

She pulled a handkerchief from her purse and patted the sweat on her forehead. The bus stop was farther than she'd expected. She adjusted her hat. "How about you, fellows? Are you auditioning?"

They glanced at each other before one of them said, "Cowboys don't audition. You just show up ready and hope that a studio bus will pick you up and give you work."

She put her hankie back in the purse. "Thanks again. I better get going." She pushed the gate and got in, the metal door clanking behind her.

They all wished her good luck. She needed it, given her uncertainty. Was there room for another desperate soul in show business?

Although the blackouts had ended, life remained bleak during the Second World War. Gasoline, kerosene, and oil were rationed. Isabel saved household items she used to discard, from cooking grease to toothpaste gel tubes. She gave everything she could to the war effort, buying ten pennies of Defense Savings stamps every week and donating blood for injured soldiers once a month.

Her hardship was meager compared to the sacrifices of Filipinos and American troops in the Philippines. After MacArthur had been forced to abandon the Philippines and retreat to Australia, seventy-five thousand of his men had surrendered to the enemy. One newspaper headline told her everything she needed to know. *Bataan Death March: Yanks & Filipinos Starved, Beheaded, Buried Alive.*

Was it any wonder that MacArthur's pledge to save the Filipinos and the troops had echoed throughout the world? *I shall return*. She believed him, body and soul.

She entered the brick building, making a beeline for the ladies' room. She powdered her nose and re-applied crimson lipstick.

Yesterday, a producer named Peter DeMille had called her. She'd been referred by Eddie Palma, of all people. "DeMille?" She'd said it twice before writing it down. The man had replied, yes, just like Cecil B. DeMille, his uncle. That took her breath away. "I'd be honored to audition," she'd said. He'd assured her of a job because he needed lots of Oriental actresses for a movie called *Willy Wu.*

She owed Eddie a thank you. They'd bumped into each other a few weeks ago. He'd just returned from military service. Unlike Claro, Eddie had served with pride as a mess boy on *USS Nautilus*, which was some kind of a submarine. He'd traveled to places she'd never heard of. "Were you scared?" she'd asked.

"Not for myself, but for the Marines who were on the mission with me," he'd said. "Those white boys put their necks on the line. The least I could do was to clean and cook for them."

How mature Eddie had grown. The military had done him a lot of good. They'd talked for an hour over vanilla milk shakes, which he'd missed during his service. Whatever hurt feelings between them had been brushed aside. He was engaged to a Filipina. She didn't have the courage to admit her husband had evaded the draft.

If only Claro had waited instead of fleeing. He might have served in non-combat duty like Eddie. He could have been home by now. He'd written her twice between January 1941 and March 1942. Not another word since then. She'd finally filed for divorce last week.

Eddie had told her about Poverty Row, where small production companies made B movies. Those films were shown with a big-studio movie during a double-feature presentation. "They're shorter and cheaper to make than the main feature. Lots of Western, action, and horror flicks," he'd said. "I just got a job in a thriller." His optimism had been contagious. She would give show business another try. They'd exchanged addresses and phone numbers.

She tightened the belt of her shirtwaist dress, gave her white gloves a tug, and tilted her hat a la Bette Davis in *Now, Voyager*. She had to make the best of this opportunity.

She trotted to the main office, where a secretary led her to a conference room. Two men and another woman, all Asians, were filling out forms. Isabel did the same, attaching her headshot. The other woman's name was Lilith Rose Chan, or was it Chen? Her middle name reminded Isabel of Bruce.

Soon after Claro had left, Bruce had repaid her five thousand dollars. He'd been apologetic for the delay. He'd remarried and business thrived. The money had allowed her to live on her own, instead of depend on Claro's family.

She and Amalia had been sharing an apartment ever since Amalia's divorce from a Filipino factory worker who drank too much. They split the rent and other costs fifty-fifty. Amalia worked as a telephone operator. Isabel had gotten over her failure as a beauty salon owner and went back to cutting hair and giving facials at a shop.

The secretary came back to collect their forms. "Are you ready to start working?"

They traded puzzled looks. "You mean, right now?" squealed Lilith Rose.

The woman flashed a smile worthy of a Colgate advertisement. "Follow me, please."

They lined up like school boys and girls and strutted behind her, all the way to the back lot. She motioned for them to stop.

Isabel gasped. A movie set!

A crew filmed inside a living room with only three walls. An actor dressed as a butler spoke on the phone, his expression changing from surprise to bewilderment.

Isabel took it all in, her skin rippling with excitement. The sets were laid out like a diorama. There was a building with only a façade. A long hallway with doors that didn't open. A stairway that led nowhere. An office interior with the exterior of a warehouse.

The studio was a small-scale version of the Paramount and Warner Bros. complexes, where Isabel and Eddie used to wait around with hundreds of desperate extras in search of jobs. Her head swam in the moment. She hadn't been in front of a camera since 1930, when MacArthur had connived to shut down her movie because of a kissing scene.

"Aannd cut!"

Her pulse rushed at the familiar sound of a clapperboard going down.

The secretary signaled for them to proceed. A woman who introduced herself simply as "wardrobe" met them. She handed Lilith and the two men costumes. Off they went to the dressing rooms.

"Miss Cooper?"

She turned back around. A tall man in a navy blue suit with a matching vest underneath the jacket approached her. "I'm Pete."

"Hello, Mr. DeMille."

"Everyone calls me Pete." He shook hands with her. "Eddie said you're beautiful and he was right. Those dimples are striking."

Her cheeks grew warm. What else did Eddie say about her? How on earth did he come to know a DeMille? Nobody could beat Eddie in hunting down movie roles.

The producer led her to a round table shaded by a red umbrella, the kind you see at an outdoor café. The film crew had moved on to another part of the lot.

She sat opposite him.

There was a tray cart beside him, and he offered her a cup of coffee, complete with a saucer and spoon. He poured the cream for her. "Should I call you Dimples or Isabel? Tell me about yourself." His eyes were cornflower blue, his dark hair slicked back.

"Please call me Belle." She added a cube of sugar in her cup and stirred it. "I'm originally from Manila, like Eddie. I've appeared in motion pictures. The last one was in 1930." Surely even small roles counted.

"Hmm." He glanced at her form, touching her photograph. "Nothing since then?"

"Unfortunately, no."

He poured coffee in another cup. "Do you mind telling me why you stopped acting?" He took a sip without adding cream or sugar.

How could she tell him Douglas MacArthur had forbidden her? Not to mention she was too damn ethnic for Broadway shows?

She cleared her throat. "I tried Broadway several years ago. I was the understudy for the lead part in *Lovesick*."

That drew a blank stare.

"It was a musical produced by Samuel Prentice."

"The New York real estate magnate?"

She nodded.

"I didn't know he was in the theater business."

"Just that one time, but the play wasn't successful."

"I see."

The secretary cut them off, whispering something to him. She handed him a folder.

Perhaps he was in his forties. Few men wore waistcoats because fabric was scarce nowadays, but Pete appeared unaffected by any shortage.

After the woman left, he slid the folder across the table toward Isabel. "Did Eddie tell you about Momentum?"

"He said he got a part in one of your films."

He nodded. "I'm producing a film about a Chinese PI named Willy Wu. It's my answer to Charlie Chan. Don't you think Sidney Toler is looking tired lately? The man is in his sixties. The public wants to see an exciting, young character. And that's Willy Wu."

She'd never liked the Charlie Chan movies, but there was no denying their popularity. "Who's your leading man?"

"I handpicked Frank Storm for the role. Have you seen him with Boris Karloff in *Doomed to Die*?"

"I'm afraid not." The actor was probably a white man who would need special makeup to look like a Chinese.

"I first met Frank when he was an extra in my uncle's movie. You might have heard of it…*The Sign of the Cross*."

She smiled. Of course, everyone knew about Cecil B. DeMille's epic hit about Emperor Nero.

"Hollywood is cutthroat," he continued. "It's tough competing with the big guys. I have to be smart and efficient. My budget is limited to thirty days of shooting per film. We work fast. We don't waste any money. We won't feed you steak and merlot for dinner, but I can guarantee that your paycheck won't bounce."

She held her breath. What exactly did he want from her?

He pointed his chin at the folder. "Take a look at the script."

She opened it. *Willy Wu #1*. So, the movie didn't have a title yet. She thumbed through the pages describing a character named Jade as a beautiful, exotic woman who needed Willy Wu to find her husband's killer. The character had many scenes.

She swallowed. "You want me to audition for the part of Jade?"

"Do you have an agent?"

She shook her head. No talent agency would waste its time on a non-white nobody. She didn't even bother registering with Central Casting. She'd tried years ago. The head of the women's division had given her a perfunctory glance and said, "Why don't you think of something else you can do with your life? Hollywood doesn't need you." She would never go back there.

He sipped his coffee. "Take the script home. It's a fast read. The finished film is going to be seventy minutes long. If you like the part, come back here at nine o'clock tomorrow. It means you will be playing Jade."

"Shouldn't I meet with the director? What if he has another actress in mind?" *Dios mio*, she had stammered. She could hardly breathe.

"Roland is in Burbank shooting *The Double-Crosser*. Frank is also playing Willy Wu in that movie. I think *The Double-Crosser* is going to be a smash, and people would want to see Willy Wu in a movie of his own."

Roland Brockman made action movies, which Claro had enjoyed and she'd skipped. She knew nothing more about the director.

As if reading her mind, Pete said, "You'll like Roland…a funny guy and very easy to work with. He's in great demand. Everybody's raving about his newsreel. You might have seen it? It's a recreation of the Pearl Harbor attack."

"Yes, it's very realistic. I didn't know he directed it."

Pete guzzled his coffee. "We're lucky the government doesn't interfere with the movie business. The auto, manufacturing, and construction industries are used for the war effort, but we here in Hollywood have been spared. The public needs entertainment to forget these hard times." He wiped his lips with a napkin. "Roland would love to do a documentary about General MacArthur. 'I shall return' was brilliant! No screenwriter could have written *that*. The khaki uniform, the corncob pipe, and the sunglasses—MacArthur would look great on screen."

Her ears grew hot, her heart thrashed. The mention of his name never failed to flabbergast her.

"So far, no luck in convincing the Army. Obviously, we don't want to distract the general right now. He and Admiral Nimitz are busy whipping the enemy and retaking Pacific islands."

She'd nodded. Just this morning, she'd heard on the radio that American forces had defeated the Japanese in a series of battles. The names of the places blipped through her mind. New Guinea, Marshalls, Marianas, and some place or another. History happened so fast—impossible to remember which was which and whether MacArthur or Nimitz was responsible.

"How old are you?"

The question jolted her back to the present. "I'll be thirty-four next month."

"Hmm…I would have guessed twenty-seven or twenty-eight." He rubbed his chin. "If you accept the role, let's make you twenty-seven."

"I beg your pardon?"

"I can't have a leading lady in her thirties."

It didn't shock her. Still, she hesitated. She no longer lied about her age ever since her promise to MacArthur.

Pete stared at her, waiting for her reply.

She closed the script. "Whatever you think is best, Mr. DeMille."

He smiled and got up. "I have another meeting. I hope to see you tomorrow."

"Yes, absolutely." They shook hands before she left.

At home, she spent the rest of the day reading the script. The part was hers! She stood before the full-length mirror memorizing lines. After a few pages, she tried calling Eddie, but he wasn't home.

As soon as Amalia stepped inside the living room, Isabel ran to hug her. "I got the part!"

They jumped up and down, giggling. "Here's more good news." Amalia showed her the *Los Angeles Times.*

Isabel plopped on the couch, slack-jawed. MacArthur had landed in Leyte in central Philippines. He had fulfilled his vow. The newspaper quoted his radio address to the Filipinos. *I have returned. By the grace of the almighty God our forces stand again on Philippine soil—soil consecrated in the blood of our two peoples.* At last, he had freed the soldiers who had survived the forced march.

Even at the height of MacArthur's defeat, she never doubted he would return to save her people. God bless the Commander and all the troops.

"The war is going to end soon. I can feel it in my heart." She embraced Amalia again. They celebrated her new job and MacArthur's return to the Philippines with Chinese takeout food.

The following morning, Pete himself greeted Isabel at the Momentum office. His secretary would be coming in late. He introduced her to Roland Brockman, only a few inches taller than Isabel. His head was too large for his narrow shoulders and small build. He wore slacks and a dress shirt with a sweater vest instead of a suit.

"Let me see my Jade." He walked around her like an inspector.

She was melting. She shifted her weight from one foot to another, her old high heels tottering. At least her gray blazers and matching pleated skirt were comfortable. A Filipina seamstress had tailored them for her.

Roland let out a low whistle. "Pete, you're a genius. She's the perfect Jade."

She smiled. "Thank you."

The producer pulled a chair. "Belle, please have a seat."

She acquiesced, her purse on her lap.

Pete took the chair behind the desk, while Roland sat across from Isabel.

"I love the script. I can't thank you enough for giving me a chance." She modulated her tone to contain her excitement. "When do we start filming?"

Pete offered her a Camel, which she declined. He took one and lit it with a lighter. "We'll start as soon as we get your contract drawn up. Perhaps in a day or two? Do you have a lawyer who can review it?" He passed the cigarette packet and lighter to Roland.

"No, but I'm sure Eddie can help. He knows a lot of people."

Pete shot a glance at Roland. The director lit his cigarette. "About Eddie. He told us a most interesting thing about you. It's incredible, really. I couldn't believe it when he said you used to be General MacArthur's mistress."

Her heart leaped, her ears rang. He might as well have shot her in the gut. She gripped the sides of her chair.

Roland, noticing her reaction, looked at her squarely. "You must have heard about MacArthur's dramatic landing yesterday. He's going to liberate your country soon. And when that happens, he's going to be larger than life."

"What's that got to do with me?"

His face brightened. "My dearest girl, your connection is priceless."

How atrocious his toupee looked, plastered flat on his ill-shaped skull. Did he think he was fooling anyone? "That connection was severed a long time ago."

"There are two things you can do." Pete interrupted, gesturing with the hand holding the cigarette. "First, you can talk to General MacArthur on our behalf about Roland's documentary. If the general agrees, Momentum will produce a serious and relevant film. We won't be forever known as a B movie producer."

"You have no idea—"

"Let me finish, Belle." He took a drag before continuing. "If you don't want to talk to him, I can understand. I hate calling my ex!" He chuckled. "The second thing you can do is make this *Willy Wu* movie and just be yourself."

"Be myself?"

"You can be our greatest publicity asset."

"I don't understand."

"You see, we don't even have a publicity department. But with you, publicity is built-in."

Roland stubbed out his cigarette in the ashtray and hunched toward her. "When the press finds out who you are and *what* you are to General MacArthur, Hollywood will explode. Everyone will talk about you and our movie. All you have to do is indulge the gossip columnists and talk about MacArthur…how long you were together, what kind of a lover he was, that sort of thing. And *Willy Wu* will be a hit, and you will be a star!"

Her heart slammed against her chest. Fury steamrolled through her, but she composed herself. "Why don't you film General Marshall or General Eisenhower or Admiral Nimitz? They're all great."

Pete shrugged. "They're *not* MacArthur. They didn't say 'I shall return.'"

"Do you know what Nimitz and Eisenhower look like? Forget about Marshall." Roland smirked. "All three of them combined have the personality of a military clerk. My eyes are wide open, but I'm snoring inside. They're boring! They don't look or act like MacArthur."

She rose, clenching her purse with both hands. "You were never interested in me as an actress. You've always wanted MacArthur." She glanced at Roland, then at Pete. "They say that in Poverty Row, an actress must sacrifice many things—hair and makeup, rest and sleep, and fifty percent of what other studios would pay. But I won't give up my dignity."

Pete blew a smoke, as cool as could be. "Why don't you sleep on it? I can replace you in sixty minutes flat, no sweat. I have a binder full of actress bios. But this may be your only shot at being a Hollywood star."

"No, thank you."

Roland got up and perched his hands on his hips—his expression potent like pure vodka. "You're thirty-four years old and a half-breed to boot. You're a failed actress rejected by a general. What did you expect?"

She spun on her heel and ran out the door. Tears blurred her eyes. Eddie Palma, the traitor! He'd sold her confidences for a measly role in a B movie. She staggered toward the gate, her sobs uncontrollable.

A different set of cowboys were waiting for the bus. They turned their heads toward her. A jangle of remarks ensued. "Did you get rejected?"

"Now, Miss, don't lose faith. There are other studios in town."

"Try Silver Lining Productions…two blocks east of here."

She stopped and wiped her face with her handkerchief.

"Don't give up," said a man fanning himself with a ten-gallon hat. "Like they say, you can't fail if you don't give up."

She nodded, then walked away.

Honking cars with cursing drivers jammed Gower Street. A monstrous cement truck had broken down. A cop directed the traffic to go around it. "Keep moving!"

It was no surprise Hollywood sought the Commander. He'd captivated the world with a fulfilled promise. Pete and Roland were just like the rest of humanity, magnetized by Douglas MacArthur for better or for worse.

She was no different. Was it a display of strength or utter weakness to protect the man who'd eviscerated her? Fourteen years after they'd first met, he remained the dream she liked to have every night, the reverie she looked forward to during the day.

And when he obstructed her life like a stalled behemoth of a machine causing traffic havoc, she would make a detour and go around him. Long ago she'd forgiven him and made peace with who he was and what she'd become. *Keep moving.* Life would go on regardless.

# 34.

# New York, July 1960

MACARTHUR SAT in his study reading a letter from Carlos Garcia, the president of the Philippines. He smiled at the invitation to visit and accept the highest award the Filipino president could bestow on anyone.

He put the letter on top of a pile of correspondence. He rose and looked out the window—a perfect new day. He wore a business suit. At eighty, he was retired from the Army. He'd joined the business world as Sperry Rand's chairman of the board for the past eight years.

From the perch of his apartment at Waldorf-Astoria Towers in New York, the view of the Manhattan skyline was magnificent, the spires of Saint Patrick's Cathedral poking through the landscape. But when he shut his eyes, he saw Manila. Blazing tropical sun, the chaos of *jeepney* traffic, and the clatter of haggling in the marketplace. What was Manila like today?

It had been fifteen years since he'd liberated the Philippines from the Japanese. He'd spent five tours of duty there, more than a quarter of his professional life.

Was it any wonder that President Garcia's invitation filled him with joy? Manila would always be in his heart. It was his spiritual home. But a journey to the Far East would be grueling, especially at his age. His days of riding horses and playing tennis were over, though he still enjoyed walks with Jean in Central Park. How would he fare in a long flight?

There was a quick knock on the door before it swung open, revealing Jean. "General, you have some time before your meeting at Sperry Rand?" She called him General, which he found endearing. "Someone's here to see you."

His wife possessed the quintessential Southern charm and the grace nurtured by her privileged background. Her love had sustained him through the darkest days of World War II. Marrying her was the smartest thing he'd ever done. "Yes, ma'am. Who is it?"

"Hello, Commander." Edward Marsh entered. He was now a brigadier general serving as the army adjutant general.

"Why, Ed! You're early!" MacArthur crossed the room to shake his hand.

"Six hours early to be exact," said Marsh. At sixty, he had less hair and more girth around the waist than MacArthur. "As it turned out, I'm needed back in Washington earlier, so I have to catch a train at noon. I couldn't pass up this opportunity to see you."

"I was looking forward to seeing you, no matter what time." He gave his former aide a hug.

"How about some coffee, gentlemen?" said Jean.

They both said "yes, ma'am." She left the room.

"Please sit down." MacArthur pointed at a chair opposite his mahogany desk.

Marsh eyed the leather chaise lounge next to it.

"I know what you're thinking…What's the world coming to if MacArthur has a chaise lounge in his study? That's for Jean and the Sergeant." He referred to his son as "Sergeant."

Marsh sat down. "How's Arthur?"

"He's spending the summer in Europe with some friends. They're in London right now, but they plan to travel to Paris, then Rome and Florence, then Madrid. What I wouldn't do to be twenty-two years old again like the Sergeant."

"I can understand his choice of Europe after spending so much time in Manila and Tokyo."

"Thirteen years." MacArthur sat down as well. "He lived in the Far East for thirteen years, longer than in America so far."

Jean came back with coffee. They chatted about Arthur's European trip and his studies at Columbia University. A maid summoned Mrs. MacArthur, who was wanted on the telephone, leaving the two men alone.

MacArthur set his cup down on the desk. "How's Margaret? How are the kids?"

Every Christmas, he received a card from Marsh and Margaret, who had been married for twenty-nine years. The last one included a photograph of the couple and their three grown children who all lived in California.

"Margaret's staying here in the city for the rest of the week, so she can spend more time with her relatives. But I have to return to Washington today. This has been a whirlwind of a vacation for us, from California to New York."

Marsh finished his coffee before continuing. "We were visiting the kids and the grandkids in Los Angeles last week. While we were there, I read something in the newspaper, and that's why I wanted to see you this morning." A stitch appeared in his forehead.

"What is it?" MacArthur offered him a humidor and a cigar cutter.

"Thank you." Marsh picked a cigar and cut its tip. MacArthur did the same, and Marsh lit both of their cigars.

"Sir, I hate to be the bearer of bad news...Belle died two weeks ago."

MacArthur was about to put the cigar between his lips, but he stopped. The news hit him like a wallop in the gut. He drew a sharp breath. The hair on the back of his neck rose. "Who told you this?"

"There was a small item in *Variety*."

*"Variety?"*

"It's a newspaper for the movie industry. Belle worked in Hollywood for a while."

MacArthur puffed on his cigar. "What did the article say?"

"It was very brief. She died on June 29—from an overdose of barbiturates. It was a suicide."

MacArthur winced. He set his cigar down in an ashtray. "A suicide."

Isabel's image ripened in his mind. Wide eyes, complexion lighter than honey but just as smooth, dimples showing when she smiled. Her beauty had bewitched him, beclouded his good judgment. She'd been so young he'd mistakenly thought of her as an empty bottle waiting to be filled. She was twenty-three when he'd seen her for the last time.

Marsh crossed his legs. "Sir, I took the liberty of checking what happened. I hope you don't mind."

"No, of course not. She was your friend, too."

"Do you remember Eddie Palma?"

"How can I forget?"

"I spoke to him on the phone. He lives in an area called Little Manila, or Filipinotown as they sometimes call it. He owns a grocery store there."

"Did he marry Belle?" MacArthur brought the tips of his fingers together, apprehensive.

"No, sir. Eddie married another Filipina. Belle married twice, both ended in divorce. First, to a Caucasian man, then a Filipino. Eddie said after Belle left Washington for the second time in 1934, she'd gone back to Los Angeles and just drifted."

"I gave her money."

"She used it to start a beauty salon with her first husband, but her heart was not in it. After two failed marriages, she tried acting again. She had small parts. Things didn't work out."

"Did she have any children?"

"No, sir."

"She should have gone back to Manila."

"Sir, Eddie said Belle's first suicide attempt was in August 1934. We thought she'd gone back to Manila, but she was in L.A. She'd ingested a bottle of insecticide. A friend had found her and taken her to the hospital." Marsh puffed on his cigar.

MacArthur creased his eyebrows and looked away. His eyes were drawn to the brilliance pouring through the window. *A suicide.* Unbelievable. She never even cried in front of him, not until the end when it had been too late.

He'd been shocked when Pearson and Allen's attorney had threatened to produce Isabel as a witness. Blackmail, pure and simple.

And the perpetrator had been a woman he'd loved, someone he'd risked his career for. She'd asked for fifteen thousand dollars—the ultimate betrayal. Pearson, Allen, and the press had not been the real menace.

Isabel had been the enemy whom he'd welcomed into his heart and life. He'd almost married her. She'd asked for a truce at the Washington Monument, of all places. He'd almost fallen for her trap. She must have known a glimpse of her was all it would have taken to finish him.

MacArthur shook his cigar in the ashtray, the ash falling. "You know, after she'd attached herself to Pearson and Allen, I thought of her as *the* enemy. Of course, I had no inkling of the other enemies yet to come. The Japanese, the North Koreans, and Harry Truman."

Marsh chuckled. MacArthur managed a dry smile. Mentioning the name of the son of a bitch who had fired him in 1951 brought an awkward silence in the room.

President Truman was a gaping wound in his soul. He did the man a huge favor by accepting the risky assignment of leading the U.S. and the United Nations forces against the Communist troops of North Korea. MacArthur had won the Battle of Inchon and re-captured Seoul, for Christ's sake! But in a single stroke, Truman had knocked him off his pedestal. He'd been fired by a man who had been a private in the Missouri National Guard. One moment MacArthur had been the exalted hero, the next moment he'd been unemployed. The embarrassment, the indignity of it all! He was well acquainted with losses, but Truman's blow was the worst.

He shook his head. "Why did I ever think of Isabel as the enemy?"

"Sir, it was a bad time." Marsh sounded apologetic. He rubbed the back of his neck, his expression sheepish. "You had FDR breathing down your neck and the press on your back. Pearson and Allen used Isabel. She was caught in the crossfire."

MacArthur drew a thick puff of cigar into his mouth, then opened his lips to blow a smoke ring. Marsh was right. She'd been a victim in MacArthur's war with the press. It was unfortunate, but he himself had been a casualty of Truman's political game. Life was full of casualties. Unlike Truman, MacArthur had wanted to take the Korean War to China, to fight communism as a whole. He'd told a Congressman, America must win. "There is no substitute for victory," he'd said. His words had been splashed across the front pages of newspapers, enough reason for Truman to accuse him of defiance.

He puffed on his cigar. "Sometimes I wonder if Truman fired me because I never saluted him."

Marsh grinned. "Sir, you were simply out of the habit of saluting. After all, you were used to everyone saluting you."

"That was the thing. There was only one man I had to salute—and with Truman, it was easy to forget he was the commander in chief."

They laughed.

"Sir, President Truman had no idea how much the public loved you."

"Ah, yes. I couldn't believe it myself." He turned his face toward the window, enjoying the sight of Jean's potted ferns soaked in sunlight. "I was fired, but wherever I went, I was welcomed like a conquering hero, complete with ticker-tape parades. Remember? A few days after I lost my job, I was speaking before a very grateful Congress."

"I do remember, sir. The press called you America's favorite general. Everyone thought you'd be Senator Robert Taft's vice president."

At the mention of Taft, an ancient envy he'd buried long ago rose to the surface. Ike Eisenhower, not Taft, had ended up the Republican frontrunner and had won all the way to the White House. It was one of life's cruelest jokes—MacArthur had been outshined by his former aide! Eisenhower had never led a charge, for Christ's sake!

MacArthur rolled his neck from left to right, making a crackling sound. It felt good. "Ike Eisenhower was the last person I sent to talk to Isabel. I wonder if she had any inkling she was talking to a future president. Ike had never met her before, so I didn't know how their meeting would turn out."

"Yes, sir, I remember that time."

"Ike was quite taken with Isabel, but who wasn't? Of course, he felt sorry for her. He probably cursed me behind my back for breaking up with her."

MacArthur rose and moved toward the window. He could feel Marsh's eyes on him. He straightened himself to maintain a soldierly posture. Like someone with a five-star rank. *Protector of Australia. Liberator of the Philippines. Conqueror of Japan. Defender of Korea.*

That was the inscription on his Congressional medal. He wanted to be remembered that way forever.

He'd fought and led thousands of men in three major wars, but at the moment, he didn't feel courageous or victorious or even at peace with himself. His heart flailed away. He struggled to contain his emotions.

Without looking at Marsh, he said, "Tell me, is Isabel's suicide my fault?"

"Of course not! General, you can't possibly think that."

He glanced over his shoulder. "I failed her."

"General, you helped her and her family—"

"If I hadn't taken her away from Manila…from her family, she might have gone on to become a bona fide movie star."

"Sir, you brought her here during the Great Depression, something her American father couldn't do. You gave her everything she could only dream of."

"I could have saved her!" MacArthur turned around, raising his hand with the cigar. "I liberated the entire Philippines, but I failed to save the *one* Filipino girl I loved."

He looked away, afraid he'd be reduced to tears. Ah, Isabel—the girl whose dream had been so huge she'd almost conquered MacArthur. He'd thought of her as an intruder in his life—their relationship a distraction that nearly ruined him—but it was *he* who had intruded in her young life and rearranged her destiny. She might have been still alive if he had refrained from sending her a note on that fateful evening at the Olympic Boxing Club.

He sat back in his chair. For a while, they smoked without saying a word.

MacArthur tapped the ashes off his cigar. "Do you remember the day I met Al Jolson?"

"Of course…1950 in Tokyo, when Mr. Jolson was entertaining the troops. He'd begged to meet you."

"I was up to my ears in work. But you know why I agreed?"

Marsh shook his head.

"Because of Isabel." He cast his gaze upward. Sometimes he couldn't remember what he ate for breakfast, and yet his memory of her remained vivid. At Chastleton, he used to sit on the sofa, smoking and reading a report, while she would be sprawled across, her head on his lap. "Swanee" would be playing in the background.

"I met Al Jolson sixteen years after I left Isabel," he continued. "But I was thinking of her the whole time I was having lunch with Mr. Jolson. I told him I knew a girl who was his biggest fan in the world. Of course I couldn't even tell Isabel about it."

"She would have been thrilled to hear it, sir."

"You know, President Garcia wants to award me the Philippine Legion of Honor's highest rank…the rank of chief commander."

"That's wonderful, sir! So, you are traveling to Manila?"

"I was thinking about it. But now, I want to go."

Marsh nodded. "You should go, sir."

MacArthur slid back deeper in his chair, the cigar glowing in his hand. "I'll never be able to see Belle again, but at least I'll see Manila one last time."

There was a knock on the door. Jean peered through the partially opened door. "I'm sorry to interrupt. The chauffeur's here to take you to Sperry Rand."

"Thank you, ma'am." MacArthur stubbed out his cigar in the ashtray.

Jean left and MacArthur stood up.

Marsh's cigar had burned itself out. He dropped it in the ashtray. He rose as well. "Sir, if you want me to travel with you to Manila, I'd be happy to do so."

MacArthur buttoned up his jacket. "Yes, let's plan on it. For old times' sake."

He put an arm across Marsh's shoulders. "Thank you for letting me know about Belle."

"You're welcome, General. It's so good to see you." They shook hands.

Marsh headed for the door. But he stopped and turned back around. "Sir, Isabel was a lovely person."

"Yes, she was." He smiled. "You know, Al Jolson asked me who she was…the girl who was his biggest fan in the world."

"What did you say?"

"I told him it was someone who belonged here." MacArthur placed his right hand on his chest.

"I understand, General." Marsh nodded and then he stepped out.

MacArthur stared at the door. He had to get going or he'd be late for his meeting. But he gave in to his memory of Isabel, just for a moment, savoring the picture in his head. She was gone and memories were all he had left anymore.

He saw the Spanish mansion on Calle Victoria. The doors of the veranda in his bedroom were wide open, the breeze off Manila Bay stirring the curtains, waves splashing in the distance. She danced to her own humming—twirling round and round—her hair flying, her skirt blowing, her laughter ringing.

She was beautiful.

End

# Author's Notes

*My MacArthur* is a fictional account of General Douglas MacArthur's love affair with Isabel Rosario Cooper from 1930 to 1934. While MacArthur's life is well documented, little is known about Isabel. Almost all of the books I've read about MacArthur mentioned his affair with Isabel, and the meager facts about her were usually included in the footnotes. In my mind, Isabel was "the Filipino girl in the MacArthur footnotes."

Who was Isabel Cooper? What was her relationship with MacArthur like? These questions haunted me. I wanted to write about Isabel, but it meant writing about MacArthur, who intimidated me. His larger-than-life image could not be any larger than in my native Philippines.

Eventually I mustered the courage to organize my research about MacArthur and Isabel. I faced two major challenges in writing this novel. First, MacArthur is one of the most famous American military leaders in history, which means his career has been extensively documented by historians. Trying to absorb the abundant information about him and preserving historical accuracy was a daunting task. I tried to stick to the facts about his career and background as much as possible, but I also took the liberty of changing certain things for the sake of storytelling.

The second challenge: The sparse information about Isabel's life and career was riddled with contradictions. There's the matter about her age. A review of her marriage licenses, census data, newspaper articles, and ship manifests showed different ages. Even her name was inconsistent. In primary sources, she was identified as Isabel Rosario Cooper or Elizabeth Cooper or Isabel Rose Cooper or Isabel Cooper Kennamer.

In spite of the conflicting, and often confusing, information about Isabel, there are a few things that are well-established about her relationship with MacArthur. They include the following: He first saw her at a boxing match in Manila and he had sent her a note on the spot; she followed him to Washington, D.C., after he became the chief of staff of the U.S. Army in 1930; and the relationship ended badly in 1934, with MacArthur ultimately paying Isabel fifteen thousand dollars for her silence and for the return of his love letters. It's also public knowledge that in 1960—twenty-six years after MacArthur and Isabel had separated—Isabel died from an overdose of barbiturates in Los Angeles, presumably a suicide.

My novel is not meant to reconcile any contradictions in existing literature or to set the facts straight. As a novelist, my job was to fill the huge gap between 1930—when MacArthur and Isabel first met—and their breakup in 1934.

Then the inevitable question came: What happened to MacArthur and Isabel after 1934? History books and documentaries provide the details of MacArthur's life and career after 1934, all the way to his death in 1964. But I had to fill another gap as far as Isabel was concerned.

I wrote this novel using available facts about MacArthur and Isabel as a framework for their story, but I also took the artistic license to make up events, people, places, and other details to build their story out of a sketchy framework.

MacArthur always fascinated me because of his enduring relationship with Filipinos and the Philippines. Growing up in Manila, I met people and read books that ran the gamut of the love-hate relationship Filipinos have with MacArthur. Some saw him as our liberator and hero and others saw him as an opportunist who used the Philippines to advance his career.

I saw MacArthur's affair with Isabel as the embodiment of the complicated relationship he had with Filipinos in general. They were both reckless and brave for pursuing a relationship that broke so many taboos during their time. MacArthur risked his career to be with Isabel, but it was she who ultimately paid a higher price to be with him.

Isabel Rosario Cooper remains an enigma to me, but I now see her as a woman who, against all odds, was not afraid to live the life she wanted. Her suicide did not make her any less courageous, at least not to me. This novel is my token attempt to shine a light on Isabel, to give her a chance to be more than just "the Filipino girl in the MacArthur footnotes."

**Chapter 1:**

Several history books say that Isabel was sixteen years old when she first met MacArthur, and that she was born in 1914. Some books say she was born in 1910, which would have made her twenty years old when she met MacArthur in 1930. A news clip announcing Isabel's divorce from Frank E. Kennamer described Isabel as a "23-year-old exotic actress." The news clip does not show the date of publication or even the name of the newspaper, but it mentioned that Isabel and Frank separated in 1942. If one assumes that the announcement of her divorce also happened in 1942, when Isabel was allegedly twenty-three, then it would have meant that she was eleven years old when she first met MacArthur.

Bottom line: Isabel was an actress and it can be assumed that she lied about her age. Given the uncertainty of her age, I made her twenty years old, but pretending to be sixteen, when she met MacArthur.

Manila Carnival Queen contestants were sponsored by newspapers and magazines, such as *Graphic Magazine*, *The Tribune*, and *The Herald*. I don't know if *Manila Times* ever sponsored contestants. I made it up in this novel.

History books about MacArthur say that Isabel Cooper's father was Scottish. But in the same 1942 news clip announcing Isabel's divorce from Frank E. Kennamer, she was quoted as saying that her father was an American citizen of Scottish-Irish descent. I've always wondered how she managed to stay in the United States (legally, I assumed) until her death in 1960. This bit of information seemed to explain it, and so in my novel, I made Isabel's father an American citizen.

**Chapter 6:**

In history books, at least two of MacArthur's aides in Manila were identified as Ford Trimble and Thomas J. "TJ" Davis. In my novel, I made up their names and characteristics.

MacArthur used the word "Chinks" to refer to Filipino-Chinese in this chapter. Indeed MacArthur used the derogatory term in one of his letters to Isabel when he referred to Chinese men in gambling clubs in Shanghai during a stop there in one of his trips.

**Chapters 17-18:**

In my novel, Isabel arrived in the States via a ship in December 1930. I made up this scenario based on a letter from MacArthur to Isabel saying that he was going to meet her when she arrived at "3 p.m. docking at Pier 9 in Jersey City." This letter did not specify a date, but another letter of his referred to "December ninth" as the date of her arrival in the U.S.

In my novel, Isabel lived in New York before moving to Washington, though in reality, she most likely lived in Washington the whole time she had a relationship with MacArthur.

Did Isabel really call MacArthur Daddy? I have a copy of a cable MacArthur sent to Isabel, which was indeed signed "Daddy." In another letter, he'd written: "I will radio you in middle Atlantic, signing it Daddy."

**Chapter 28:**

In this chapter, dated May 1934, MacArthur had an argument with President Franklin D. Roosevelt over the military budget. In fact, their disagreement happened in March 1934. I took the liberty of changing it to May 1934, which was when MacArthur sued Drew Pearson and Robert Allen for libel in real life.

**Chapter 30:**

In this chapter and in reality, Isabel received fifteen thousand dollars from MacArthur as a settlement. In letters written by Drew Pearson to his attorney, Morris L. Ernst, he said Isabel was being very reasonable for asking only such amount from MacArthur. Pearson quoted a friend who had said "any Broadway flapper would have gone at him for $500,000."

Also in this chapter, Isabel met Major Dwight "Ike" Eisenhower, who was sent by MacArthur to talk to her. The meeting is fictional. In real life, Eisenhower served as one of MacArthur's aides in the 1930s, including the time of the Bonus March War. When MacArthur returned to the Philippines in 1935 to assume the role of military adviser and field marshal, Eisenhower was one of his aides in Manila. Eisenhower later became president of the United States and served two terms, from 1953-1961.

**Chapters 31-32:**

Census data shows Isabel was married to Frank Kennamer in 1935 and they lived in Oklahoma. Their divorce announcement was published in 1942. I obtained images of two marriage licenses showing Isabel's marriage to Milton Moreno on June 13, 1944, and on Nov. 21, 1946. Judging by his name, I'm assuming Moreno was Filipino. In my novel, Isabel was married twice. I made up the names and characteristics of her former husbands.

**Chapter 34:**

In real life as in my novel, Isabel died of overdose in Los Angeles on June 29, 1960. MacArthur, who died on April 5, 1964, never mentioned Isabel in his autobiography. The wistful MacArthur at the end of my novel is entirely fictional.

Douglas MacArthur's autobiography, *Reminiscences,* is a key source of information for this novel. In addition, there are other books and a documentary film listed below, which served as invaluable resources for me. I also used newspaper articles as references, but there are too many to mention here and some of them didn't carry any attribution. I'm forever indebted to the creators of all those works.

Special thanks to Carol Morris Petillo for her correspondence with me and her very informative book and Austin Hoyt for his seminal MacArthur documentary, *American Experience: MacArthur.*

**Resources** (in order of importance to my research):

Douglas MacArthur. *Reminiscences.* New York: McGraw-Hill, 1964.

Carol Morris Petillo, *Douglas MacArthur: The Philippine Years,* Bloomington, Indiana: 1981.

Austin Hoyt, director, screenwriter, and producer of the PBS documentary, *American Experience: MacArthur* (1999).

Geoffrey Perret, *Old Soldiers Never Die: The Life of Douglas MacArthur.* New York: Random House, 1996.

Stanley Karnow. *In our Image: America's Empire in the Philippines.* New York: Ballantine Books, 1990.

David E. Kyvig, *Daily Life in the United States, 1920-1940,* Chicago: Ivan R. Dee (publisher), 2004.

**More Thanks**

I want to thank the following institutions whose collections were essential resources for me:

• The Harry Ransom Humanities Research Center at the University of Texas at Austin, which owns and keeps the papers of Morris L. Ernst, including Douglas MacArthur's letters to Isabel and other correspondence related to the libel case filed by MacArthur against Drew Pearson and Robert Allen.

• The Lyndon Baines Johnson Library, which maintains the personal papers of Drew Pearson, including Isabel Cooper's letters to Pearson, as well as her photographs.

**Cindy Fazzi**

# Acknowledgments

*My MacArthur* was a long journey for me. I can't let this moment pass without acknowledging the following people:

• My publisher, Tory Hartmann, at Sand Hill Review Press, LLC, for taking a chance on me. I can't thank you enough for this great opportunity.

• The women who believed in me against all odds: my mother-in-law, Angela Fazzi, and my dearest friends, Tammy Best and Susan Sample.

• My critique partner, Elizabeth Fyne, for your insights and patience when this novel was in its earliest stage.

• My late father, Hernando Melliza, whose memory sustains my spirit, and my late father-in-law, Michael Fazzi, whose kindness I will never forget.

# About the Author

Cindy Fazzi is a Filipino-American writer and former Associated Press reporter. She has worked as a journalist in the Philippines, Taiwan, and the United States. *My MacArthur* is her literary debut. She writes romance novels under the pen name Vina Arno. Her first romance book, *In His Corner*, was published by Lyrical Press in 2015. Her second romance novel, *Finder Keeper of My Heart*, was published by Painted Hearts Publishing in 2018. Her short stories have been published in *Snake Nation Review*, *Copperfield Review*, and *SN Review.*

If you enjoyed this book, please review it on Amazon, Indiebound, Goodreads, or your favorite place to find books!

Book club discussion guide available on www.cindyfazzi. com

Made in the USA
San Bernardino, CA
09 August 2018